...but names will never hurt me?

Michael Gasson

Published by Chestnut Publishing.

Chestnut Publishing
9 Harold Heading Close
Chatteris
PE16 6TL

www.chestnutpublishing.co.uk

ISBN: 978-0-9565012-1-9

Any resemblance in this story to any person or specific location is completely unintentional.

Prologue

He traced the tip of the blade around her nipple. A bead of blood quickly became a bright crimson circle. She was too scared to scream, her throat too tight, a stifled sob was her first reaction. Then her bladder muscles gave way and the rough wooden platform she lay naked on was soaked in urine.

He smiled, it was the fear he wanted to see. The thrill of making someone scared.

He slowly ran the knife along her stomach, down towards her belly button first and then returning to pass between her breasts. Not marking her, just letting her watch its progress towards her face.

The blade was about five inches long and an inch wide. Both edges were razor sharp.

The girl's eyes followed the tip of the blade as it moved up her neck to her chin and stopped at her lip. He pressed the side of the blade gently on her lip, gently, so that the sharp edges didn't cut. She couldn't move her head; there was tape wound around it binding it to the platform. Her arms and legs were similarly bound tightly to the rough wood.

For a second tears blurred the image of the blade, she blinked, almost the only movement left to her.

She pleaded, begged, 'Please... please, don't...' another sob caught the words, her breath coming in gulps, '... hurt me again.' She had already felt the damage this blade could do when he had driven it through the palm of her hand.

He laughed, 'Not hurt you? Why shouldn't I hurt you?' He turned the blade so that one of the edges was resting on her lip and without applying any pressure drew it towards him slowly. The weight of the slim blade was enough make a shallow cut in her lip and blood sprung from it trickling into her mouth.

Through her sobs she tried again. 'Please, don't hurt me. I won't resist if... you know... you're going to...'

He knew what she was thinking and was immediately angry. They were all the same, they thought they could get what they wanted just by offering their bodies. He pushed the knife under her chin, 'You stupid little bitch.'

Now he could smell more than fear, more than blood, her bowels had emptied. He looked at the mess seeping from under her lower back.

5

The thrill of the fear she felt made the anger go away. Her chin was bleeding heavily, her eyes were closed with tears running down the side of her face.

'Daddy,' she cried.

That was when he slid the blade underneath her ribs, straight into her sixteen-year old heart. Her body arched against the bonds and she gave a deep groan of pain before flopping back onto the wood.

Damn! He hadn't meant to do that. He wanted to keep her alive for a little while longer.

Chapter One

Thursday

Detective Inspector Davis followed the young constable the short distance along the overgrown path alongside the filthy looking dyke. There had been a light shower earlier this morning and the long, uncut grass had soaked his trousers by the time he reached the cordoned off area.

The constable lifted the tape for Davis to pass underneath, although Davis still grunted as he bent under it, scowling at the constable as if it were his fault Davis was struggling. The body lay some twenty feet further along the bank in a small, dilapidated, disused barn. Although he'd been told by the station radio room that a girl's body had been discovered, seeing it still gave him that jolt of pain that he felt every time he saw the lifeless body of a young female of a certain age. The age his daughter would have been if she'd lived more than a few hours after birth. This girl looked mid-teens, younger than the eighteen Grace would have been.

The pathologist had yet to arrive and one of the scenes of crime officers was taking photos of the body. Davis nodded as he looked up at him. 'Spot anything I need to see yet?' he puffed. At nearly three stones overweight he had found the going hard following the young constable.

'Apart from the body there doesn't appear to be anything. We've made a brief search of the area.' He shrugged. 'Nothing yet.'

Davis nodded again, there would be a thorough search made of the surrounding area as soon as more men arrived. The barn had a beaten-earth floor and several items of broken farm equipment had been dumped haphazardly against the wooden walls. It was full of spider's webs and smelt musty. There were double doors at one end, one of these had been wrenched open, presumably by whoever had left the body here, and the rusty bottom hinge had snapped making the door lean oddly. He knelt down a few feet away from the body not wanting to get too close yet before the ground had been checked for evidence. The disturbing pictures of Grace disappeared from his mind as they always did. She had been hours old when her fragile grip on life had been exhausted. He turned his full attention to someone else's daughter now.

She was lying on her back with her legs slightly parted. She wasn't spread-eagled, but she had been placed on the floor carefully rather than dropped by the look of it, that was Davis's impression as he looked at the body. He was detached now, could see the body as a piece of evidence. Something that might allow him to catch the killer if he was lucky. There were various cuts on her body but there was no sign of blood on the wounds. He could see the puncture wound just under her ribs.

'Get a close-up of that, will you.'

The photographer barely grunted his reply, 'Already have.'

A heavy sadness filled Davis. What kind of place was this for a young girl to lose her life in? This girl, lying naked on the cold ground, had, until brutally murdered, her whole life ahead of her. Relationships to form, a career to follow, a family of her own maybe. Now some bastard had deprived her of that. Davis was going to have to break the news to her parents, was going to blight their lives as his had been blighted.

Focus, he couldn't help her now, but he had a job to do. He could see red marks on her legs, arms and forehead. Not rope marks he could tell, but what had caused them he wasn't sure.

Voices approaching from the way he had come heralded the arrival of the pathologist. Davis looked up as the man entered the barn. 'Hello, Greg, I shall be glad when we're both out of work,' he pointed to the body, 'this never gets any easier.'

The pathologist, Greg Watson, put his bag down beside the girl. 'If it did, Phil, if we didn't hate seeing people treated like this, how long before we couldn't be bothered to catch the scum that kill them?'

Davis just snorted; this was a well-worn discussion between the two men. Their chosen careers meant that they regularly saw the brutal, murderous acts committed by their fellow man. The fact that it sickened them didn't dissuade them from their careers, just made them more determined to catch those responsible.

'Who found her?' the pathologist asked.

'An elderly lady walking her dog. It went in the barn and started barking.'

Watson shook his head, 'I bet that's ruined her day.'

'According to the constable who took her home she's bearing up well, I've got to go and see her when I've finished here.'

Watson went about his job quietly and methodically. Occasionally he spoke into a hand-held voice recorder, making observations about what he saw. He turned the body over. Watson was looking at the girl's back with some interest. 'Look at this.' He pointed to her shoulders.

Davis had to move in closer to see what Watson was showing him. 'What is it?' he asked.

'Probably wood splinters, I'll check later.'

'Are there anymore?'

Watson laid the girl face down and studied her from head to toe. 'Here, look.'

On the back of her ankles the same splinters could be seen and there were a few tangled up in her hair on the back of her head. 'What do you make of it?' Davis asked.

Watson shrugged, 'Nothing, yet.'

He had to ask the inevitable question that he knew Watson wouldn't give a precise answer to. 'How long has she been dead?'

He glanced up at Davis, 'Quite a while, probably yesterday evening.

Davis knew not to pressure the pathologist. Over the years they'd been colleagues Watson had been thorough and totally professional at his job, Davis would get all the answers Watson could give him in his report.

Both men stood up. Watson said, 'I'm finished here. I'll do the pm as soon as the body arrives at the mortuary, we're a bit quiet at the moment.'

Davis nodded. 'I'll be there. For now I'll go and see our dog-walker, and find out if she's been reported missing,' he said pointing to the body.

They walked back to their cars and Watson asked, 'How's the diet going?'

Davis had recently been diagnosed as diabetic and placed on a strict diet by his doctor.

'Bloody torture,' Davis said with passion, getting a laugh from the slim doctor.

He had to drive slowly for the first mile, eager as he was to talk to the lady who had found the body. The narrow fen roads that led to the track rose and fell alarmingly. The constantly shrinking sub-soil meant these little used roads rarely stayed smooth for long after repairs were made. He turned onto the main road and put his foot down. Soon he was up to the speed limit. He'd stick to it, the girl was already dead, there was no emergency.

As he drove along he considered what resources he would have available on this case. His team was already under strength due to the difficulty in recruiting detectives to what was considered a dull, rural area. What they really meant was there was little serious crime, something he was glad of. He had one detective sergeant and three detective constables, one of those only recently out of uniform. What with the strain of the huge demonstrations at the new research animal breeding centre at Wisbech he was unlikely to get many uniformed officers loaned to him after the first couple of days.

He'd better tell Anita that he wouldn't be home much unless they solved the crime quickly. That wouldn't go down too well. After nineteen years of marriage to a policeman she didn't like that, always complaining that he'd rather be out dealing with other people's lives than getting on with theirs. Her grief at the death of their daughter had built a wall between them that he knew he would never penetrate. One year after Grace's death Anita had decided she must have another child. The resumption of their sex life had been solely for that purpose and as soon as her pregnancy had been confirmed she stopped it again.

Davis had eventually accepted it, he had no choice, but he often wished his marriage were a closer one. He and Anita hadn't always been distant from each other, she hadn't always treated him as though he was someone to put up with rather than someone to love.

Davis parked his car outside number 10 Vermuyden's Drove. It was a small two-bedroom bungalow in a close of similar properties.

Mrs Margaret Foyle opened the door. 'Your police constable who is minding me says you are the detective in charge of the investigation into that poor, unfortunate girl's death.'

She had said this as she indicated he should come in. He saw the police constable, who had accompanied Mrs Foyle home, raise her eyebrows slightly at him, a small smile on her face. He could imagine what she meant. Mrs Foyle looked as if she needed no minding. It was going to take more than finding a body to upset her.

'Would you mind if we sat in the kitchen? I don't want you walking all over my carpet and it doesn't seem right asking a police officer to remove his shoes.'

Davis joined Mrs Foyle and the constable in the kitchen. 'Can I make you a cup of coffee, inspector?'

'Yes, thank you.' He waited whilst the coffee was made. Looking through the open kitchen door into the lounge he could see a small Jack

10

Russell terrier sitting on a blanket covered pouffe in front of the window. Undoubtedly the discoverer of the dead girl.

Mrs Foyle offered Davis a biscuit to go with his coffee. Davis hesitated, he always joked that a hot drink was 'too wet' without a biscuit, or preferably several, to go with it. Now he politely turned it down. Mrs Foyle sat on a stool at the small table joining the constable. Both of them helped themselves to biscuits and Davis tried to ignore the crunching they made as they ate them.

'Well, inspector, how can I help you?' Mrs Foyle asked.

'Can you just explain how you came to discover the girl?'

'I always take Twist out early for his walk. We usually drive to Bennett's Lane during the week.'

Davis interrupted, 'Bennett's Lane, is that the name of the track leading to the barn?'

'Yes, it is. We park where the tarmac runs out and walk to the barn and back, that takes us about forty minutes.' She smiled at Davis, 'We are neither of us young anymore, inspector.'

Davis politely inclined his head, it seemed rude to voice an agreement with her.

She continued. 'This morning started off as any other has done. We walked along and, as you will have noticed, the track is very straight. I could see from some distance away that the door had been moved. Twist was off his lead and before I got to the barn he went inside. He'd only been in there moments when he started barking. I called for him to come back, but he ignored me.' She cast a reproving glance towards the dog, who completely ignored her again.

'Did you enter the barn, Mrs Foyle?'

'Yes. I didn't like to, not so much because it was trespassing but because it looks so decrepit I was worried it might fall down. It was a little gloomy but there is plenty of light coming through the broken planking and I could see Twist jumping around in front of something in the middle of the barn.'

She hesitated for the first time. Davis gave her a few seconds then encouraged her to go on. 'Did you approach the girl?' He avoided saying body so as not to put her off.

'I got close enough to make sure she wasn't still alive.' She hesitated again. 'Unfortunately, when you get to my age, you've seen enough of death to know when a body is dead. There was no help to be given to that poor child.'

She got up from her stool and took the three now empty cups to the sink to wash them. Something to distract her from the memory of the dead girl perhaps.

'What did you do then, Mrs Foyle?'

'I always carry a mobile phone with me when I go out, I don't want to be stranded miles from anywhere, and besides, my daughter tries to insist I do. What she thinks we did before mobile phones came along I don't know. Never mind that. I telephoned the emergency services and waited outside the barn for your men to arrive. Much to his annoyance I kept Twist on his lead while we waited.'

Having heard his name several times the dog decided to come into the kitchen to investigate the stranger. He walked slowly up to Davis and sniffed around his lower trouser leg. Seeming satisfied that there was nothing of interest to find there he trotted over to his bowl in the corner of the kitchen and noisily slurped water from it. Happy now, he returned to his pouffe in the lounge where he could watch the world go by outside the window.

Davis looked back to Mrs Foyle after the brief interruption of the dog. 'Did you see anybody or any cars that you didn't recognise?'

'No, inspector. I rarely see anybody during my walks and I didn't this morning.'

'One final question, Mrs Foyle, can you be sure that the door to the barn is usually shut completely?'

'Oh yes, Twist is always sniffing around it. He's as nosey as a terrier can be, if there had been a way into the barn before today he would have found it.'

Davis drove himself and the constable to the recently built police station at Chatteris. The town's rapidly expanding population had outgrown the small station in the middle of the market square and this new one had been situated on the newly built industrial estate on the east of the town. The flat fenland surrounding the town spread out for miles, although Davis had no time for the view today as he walked the few yards to the door.

Once in the building he used his swipe-card to pass from the public enquiry office into the inner areas of the station. As he did so his superior, Detective Chief Superintendent Malloy, came down the stairs.

'Phil, I hear there's been a young girl's body found, what can you tell me so far?'

'Very little, Sir.' As bosses went Malloy wasn't too bad. He'd been a good detective and although his recent promotion meant he had a budget and the politics of the job to contend with he never forgot that their primary task was to catch criminals. 'It's definitely murder, she was stabbed. She's naked and it looks as if she'd been tied down in some way, I'm not sure how yet.' He shook his head as the image of the girl came too vividly to his mind. 'She's little more than a kid, Kevin.'

What he'd told Malloy was almost all he knew at the moment about the girl. 'Look, I've got to see if she's been reported missing before I go to the lab. I'll catch you later.'

With a nod from Malloy, Davis carried on down the corridor to the control room where any missing persons reports would have been logged.

Five minutes later he'd found out that no girls of that age group had been reported missing in their area.

'Check the national database, she may be from out of the area,' Davis said gruffly to the constable at the computer, knowing he would do that anyway. 'She's mid-teens, about five-feet-six, dark-haired and slim.' He waited while the constable finished writing down the description and then said, 'I'll check with you after the pm, see if you've got anything for me.'

With a brief, 'Sir,' the constable turned back to the computer keyboard and Davis left to join Greg Watson as they tried to find any clues the girl's body might give up.

Two hours later Davis knew little more than he had when he first saw the girl on the ground beside the dyke. Watson was reading a brief summary of his findings.

'She was stabbed to death. The wound under her ribs penetrated her heart. The cuts to her hand, breast, chin and lip were done whilst she was alive. Apart from the one that went through her palm they weren't deep, but the knife that made the cuts was very sharp. The wood splinters on her head, shoulders and ankles were from a rough wood, probably plywood.'

He stopped for a minute scanning the list. 'The marks on her legs, arms and forehead were made by adhesive tape, about two and a half inches wide. She was probably bound to the plywood when she was stabbed.'

Davis had listened in silence to the dispassionate listing of the brutality meted out to this young girl. 'Was she raped?' he asked.

Watson looked up, 'No, Phil, she wasn't sexually molested in any way as far as I can tell.'

Davis sighed, at least that was some small crumb of comfort he could offer her parents when he was able to track them down.

'She had been sedated though, probably chloroform, there were small blisters around her nose.'

'Do you have any idea where she was murdered?' he asked.

'All I can tell you is, not where she was found. There was no blood to be found on the ground around her body or anywhere else in the barn, and that puncture wound to her heart would have bled considerably.' Watson wished he had more to offer Davis, both of them had children of the same age as the murdered girl, although in both cases they had sons. 'She died between six and nine o'clock yesterday evening.'

'So she could have been dumped there any time between then and when our walker found her. There was no moon last night, that track must have been pitch black. If she was taken there after dark whoever put her there knew the area well. He didn't come across that barn by chance, he knew it was there.'

'If he put her there in daylight he took one hell of a risk,' Watson said.

'You're right.' Davis pondered on this for a moment and then said, 'Okay, thanks.' With a brief goodbye Davis made his way out into the hospital car park.

Not for the first time Davis was faced with a brutal murder and had little idea of where to start looking for the killer. He turned his face up to the still cloud-laden sky and felt a chill deep inside. 'I'll get you, you bastard', Davis said to himself.

He checked his phone, which he'd had on silent mode. There were no missed calls. He was no nearer finding out who the girl was.

He'd go back to the station. The team would have finished searching the area where the body was found, maybe they had something for him.

Chapter Two

Graham Peterson, Davis's one detective sergeant, was just walking out of the CID office as Davis returned. Like Davis, Peterson was a local man. Unlike Davis, Peterson was tall with a thick head of dark hair, in contrast to Davis's closely cropped, grey hair. Davis had called him after the body had been moved to the laboratory and asked him to take charge of the search of the area where the girl's body had been found.

'Peterson, has the team finished?'

'Yes, sir. There was nothing found of any interest to us. I had uniform check the roadside verges leading along the road towards the track. We've been over the track itself, the barn and continued past the barn until the track meets the road that comes off the A141.'

'Could the person who dumped the body have come from that direction?'

'Unlikely, Phil, the barn was used to store farm machinery years ago. I remember it when I was a lad. When the farm was bought by a much bigger concern at Ramsey they obviously had no use for it and it's been shut up for years. That barn was what the track was for, there was never any need to go beyond there and I don't think anybody had for some time before today.'

'Okay.' In the time Davis had known Peterson he'd come to respect the sergeant's thoroughness, if he'd said there was nothing to help them on the ground that was almost certainly the case. So far they had no idea who their victim was and no idea how she got to where she was found. 'Check with constable Crawford, see if he's come up with anything from missing persons. I want Green and Lewin to do a check on the few residents of the road that leads to the track to see if they saw or heard a car travelling along it from early evening to early this morning.'

Davis stopped in thought for a moment, tapping his pen on the edge of the desk. 'Get Bellamy to go to St Andrews and Fenland Comprehensive schools. Find out if any of their pupils that fit the girl's description have not arrived this morning.'

'What about a radio appeal?'

'I don't know. Even if she only went missing yesterday surely her parents would have reported it by now? The local news lads were on the scene fairly soon, it'll be on the news bulletins that we've found a body whether we run an appeal or not. Let's see if anything comes in today.

15

We need to find her clothes as well.'

Peterson had been jotting down notes as Davis spoke to him. When they had first worked together Davis had thought it was because Peterson had a bad memory, but he'd learned over the last couple of years that Peterson's habit of reading back through these notes as a case progressed had jogged their memory on several occasions about lines of enquiry that had led to a much needed breakthrough.

Peterson put his notebook back in his pocket and said, 'How long before the pm notes will be ready?'

Davis got up from his chair. 'Not long, I reckon, Watson's not too busy. I'm going back to the scene again, I'll see you back here later, ask the others to be here.'

With a brief, 'Sir,' from Peterson they both left the CID office. Peterson always liked to read the pm notes in a murder case. Davis was happy to allow Watson to summarise them, but Peterson wanted to absorb every fact and clue. Find the links, find the killer, was his approach.

Davis set off for the barn, he wanted to know why the killer had dumped the body there. What was it about that barn that made the killer travel to it? Why not any other barn? Perhaps seeing it again might give him an insight.

Vyvyan dialled the number again. He had called the parents of Alice Beresford twice already. Each time they had picked up the phone almost before the first ring was complete. They did so again this time.

'Are you ready to do as I ask?' he said, not giving them a chance to ask the questions he knew they wanted to. Was their daughter unharmed? What had he done to Alice?

The father had answered, just as Vyvyan had instructed. It must always be the father. It was him this was all about. Although Alan Beresford wouldn't remember Vyvyan after all these years, Vyvyan would never forget Alan, or the other three. Four of them and Vyvyan. Why Vyvyan had hung around with them he didn't know. Was it the fear that nobody else would accept him? Was it that the trial of gaining acceptance with new friends was too much to bear? Was he just too weak to break the bonds of what passed for friendship?

The other four had bullied Vyvyan mercilessly because of his name, Vyvyan Wilde. Something he had no control over, but it had blighted his life. Now Vyvyan was going to blight theirs. Each of the

16

four had, amongst all the other petty acts, done one thing that had caused Vyvyan acute distress. Distress that felt as real now as it had when he was a child.

In Alan Beresford's case he had made Vyvyan steal sweets from the shop Vyvyan's mother had worked in. If he'd had been caught Vyvyan would have been in trouble and his mother would have lost her much-needed job. Beresford's constant threats had persuaded Vyvyan to take the risk, but for years he had endured nightmares about the consequences of getting caught.

Now he had a task for Alice's father to complete if he wished to see his daughter again.

Alan Beresford didn't know his daughter was already dead and was lying in a cold store at the general hospital, or that the police were trying to identify her, trying to locate her parents. He was going to do whatever it took to get her back home, alive, in one piece. Not knowing, yet, that nothing he did could help her now.

'Yes, anything, please, is she okay?' Alice's father could barely get the words out as his throat choked with fear. He was reluctant to use her name to this monster who had taken her. This monster who had threatened to mutilate her if his orders were disobeyed. If the police were called. If Mrs Beresford answered the phone. If Mr Beresford didn't do exactly as was asked of him. So many demands that the Beresfords were almost paralysed with fear.

Vyvyan made the father wait before he answered. 'It depends what you mean by 'okay'. She's alive,' he lied, 'but she probably wouldn't say she was okay.'

Beresford could swear he could feel his heart beating wildly. 'Please, please don't hurt her anymore, I beg you.'

'You're begging now, are you?' Vyvyan said that with such sarcasm that Beresford didn't know what to say for a moment. Before he could think of another way of pleading for his daughter's life there were more instructions. 'You will walk to Robinsons the bookmakers in Chatteris High Street and pretend to have a gun in a black plastic bin liner. You will not disguise yourself in any way. You will demand money from the cashier. Whether they give you any money or not you will walk out of the shop and along the High Street. After leaving the shop you will dump the bag into a bin and carry on walking towards the market square. You must not make any attempt to escape if challenged. Do you understand so far?'

'Yes… why am I doing that though?'

Vyvyan's temper flared, 'Because I demand it. Because you'll do whatever I say.' He tried to calm down, he needed to be in control, he must be in control. He mustn't reveal why Alice's father had to do it. That would reveal his own identity.

Alan Beresford was panicking, 'Whatever, I'll do anything. I'm sorry, I didn't mean to annoy you.' The desperation in his voice was unmistakable, the fear that he'd upset the man who held his daughter, who'd made vile threats about what he'd do to her.

Vyvyan waited a moment before continuing, savouring the fear Beresford felt.

'When the police catch you admit the robbery and do not make any excuses. Do not tell them why you have done it. You must make them believe you acted alone, without my threat. Do you understand?'

Alice's father wasn't going to make the same mistake again, he quickly agreed.

'Do it as soon as I put the phone down. After I hear on the news that you have been arrested and charged I will release Alice. You can then tell the police you acted under duress, if you're lucky they'll believe you.'

Alan Beresford could see absolutely no point in what was being asked of him. The man had not asked for any money stolen from the bookies to be passed to him. In fact, he'd not asked for a ransom at all. When Alice was released and he was able to explain why he had carried out the robbery the police would drop the charges. Surely they would. But even if they didn't, what on earth would the lunatic who had taken Alice get from this?

Too scared for his daughter's well being and too intent on carrying out the instructions he had been given to think clearly anymore, he went into the hallway to put on his coat and shoes.

His wife followed him. 'Where are you going, what are you doing, where's Alice, what's he doing to her?' The questions tumbled out in a tear-punctuated stream. Mrs Beresford's normally immaculately made-up face was a testament to the torment she had experienced since the first phone call the man had made. Her eyes were swollen from hours of crying. Her streaked make-up ignored, her hair a mess from her fingers running through it in anguish.

The first phone call had scared Alice's parents more than they had ever been scared before. Coming just as they were beginning to wonder why she was late home from school, they had expected it to be their daughter. Maybe she had stopped of at a friend's house, or in town.

But it wasn't.

It was a man who threatened that he would deliberately harm Alice. That he would use a knife on her. That he would make sure she never wanted anyone to look at her face again. He would cut her so badly she would wish he had killed her. He held the phone to her and instructed her to say just one word. 'Daddy.' It was enough that her father knew it was Alice. The second she had uttered the word there had been a piercing scream as a blade was driven through the palm of her hand. They were left in no doubt this man meant what he said.

Alan Beresford wasn't used to taking orders. At forty-one he had spent six years managing a busy builder's supplies yard. He had eight staff and made it clear that when he said jump, staff jumped. But he considered himself a fair boss. He could do any of the tasks he expected his staff to do, and he wanted them done the way he would have done them. He was usually respected but rarely liked by those who knew him. Head office sent initiatives and guidelines. He dished out orders. Now he had to follow them, without any understanding of why he had to do what had been ordered. Other than saving Alice's life.

He was a good husband and father, if a slightly strict one. His wife, Clare, worked part-time in Nicolson's department store in the town's High Street now Alice was older. They had a reasonably good standard of living and their lives ran along quite smoothly, or had done until yesterday.

The first phone call had shattered their peaceful lives, and although the Beresfords didn't know it yet their lives would never be whole again. Alan Beresford could hear the brutal proof in the background that this monster had their daughter and that he would do as he said and harm her. His daughter's pained sobs continued as the man spoke to him. He must sit by the phone and wait for further calls. It must be him that answered. Above all they must not call the police if they wanted Alice to live.

Of course they wanted Alice to live. They wanted her back with them, safe and well. They had sat downstairs by the phone all night. The second call had been just after midnight, after Alice had been murdered and her body dumped, although they didn't know that.

Had they gone to bed? Had they given up waiting for the call? Didn't they care what was happening to their daughter?

Alan Beresford had tried to deny all the hurtful accusations but hadn't been allowed to. 'Shut up,' the man had shouted. 'You sit there and wait for me to call again.'

With that completely unnecessary instruction he had hung up. They had sat and waited for over twelve hours. Twelve hours during which they had been unable to sleep, unable to eat, although they had managed several cups of coffee. Twelve hours during which they argued with each other about calling the police. Each in turn wanting to and being persuaded by the other not to, for fear of what would happen to Alice. In the end they had done the only thing they felt was possible, wait for the man who held their daughter to call again.

Now, bizarre as they were, he had instructions to follow. A task to complete after which Alice would be released. He had to believe she would be, must be.

There had been tears from Clare Beresford, she didn't want to be left alone. She didn't want Alan to do what he had been ordered to do, but she knew he would, must. Her task was going to be almost as hard. To sit at home alone. To wait, for hours possibly, for news of her husband's arrest for attempted robbery. Then to wait for Alice to come home, please, God, she would.

Alan Beresford walked through the High Street. He came to the mobile phone shop that was next door to Robinsons and stopped. He took from his pocket the black plastic bag and wrapped it around his hand. It wasn't that warm today but he began to perspire heavily. His mouth felt dry and he dreaded that when he walked into the betting shop he would be unable to say anything. He looked down at the bag on his hand, it didn't look anything like there was a gun in there, but it was what he'd been ordered to do, so he did it.

He carried on the few steps to Robinsons and pushed the door open. It was darker in here, most of the light coming from the banks of screens attached to the walls. He waited a few moments to allow his eyes to adjust and used the time to try to wet his mouth enough to talk.

One or two faces turned his way and looked away again. Men who were looking to see if their mates had arrived, the ones they gambled away the odd pound here, the odd fiver there with every day of the week. His face wasn't known in here, they weren't interested in him, yet.

There were three people behind the screen taking the punter's money. The two women were doing just that now, the man wasn't. He walked hesitantly towards the counter, sure that with every step he took some one would know what he was going to do.

Alan Beresford stopped as he reached the counter and put his face close to the screen. He started off hesitantly. 'Give me... I want...' Then he remembered why he was doing this, what was at stake. More firmly now he barked out, 'Give me money, now.' He shook the black plastic bag towards the cashier. 'Do it quickly.'

The cashier, a thin, hard-bitten looking man in his late fifties, just stared back at him blankly and then said, 'Fuck off. If that's a gun in there prove it.'

Everything else in the bookies had stopped. The screens showed their action from various racecourses unwatched. The dozen or so customers were all watching the mini-drama unfolding. One of them slipped slowly out of the door. The others remained rooted where they were.

The words of the man holding Alice came back to him. 'Whether they give you any money or not, walk out of the shop.'

He wasn't going to waste any more time in here. He turned to the door and ran. Pushing back into the bright sunlight he looked around for a bin to throw the bag in.

Just as he did so a stern voice shouted out, 'You, there, stand still.'

He looked up to see a police officer approaching him with the customer who had slipped out of the shop pointing straight at him. 'That's him, said he had a gun he did.' The nervous looking man was trying to edge his way to the corner of an alley that ran alongside Robinsons. Looking for somewhere to hide in case there was a gun and it got turned on him.

The policeman had his canister of pepper spray in his hand. 'Just stand still, sir.'

Beresford did as he was told, getting caught was part of the plan. He held his arms out, palms up to show they were empty, ready to be handcuffed. 'I won't resist, officer.'

The policeman handcuffed him and then talked into his radio, asking for back-up, asking for transport for a man under arrest. Setting in motion a process that only a few hours ago Alan Beresford could not

21

have imagined in his wildest nightmares being caught up in.

Alan Beresford had never been in a police station before, much less a custody suite. The constable who arrested him was busy filling in reams of paperwork. Beresford had been fingerprinted, photographed and had a swab run around the inside of his mouth to obtain a DNA sample. Now he was being led to a cell to wait for a Detective Constable Gillian Lewin to interview him. Couldn't they hurry this up? Alice needed help, he didn't know what that man had done to her, but she was sure to need medical help.

Lewin had led Beresford from the cell to an interview room and asked him to sit on a chair at the table in the middle of the room. A uniformed police constable was stationed near the door. Beresford had seen this enough times on the television to know what was going to happen. This detective would shout at him, harangue him, until he confessed to every crime they had not solved at the moment.

Chapter Three

He was surprised when Lewin sat down opposite him and asked if he was okay.

Beresford was so stunned at the question, the polite tone of voice, that he couldn't answer for a moment. Then he found his voice. 'I want to admit what I did. I tried to rob the bookmaker's shop. It wasn't their fault I didn't get any money, I ran outside too quickly. I pretended to have a gun.'

Lewin held up a hand to stop the torrent of words. 'Sir, shall we start from the beginning? You've been read your rights, did you understand them?'

'Yes,' Beresford confirmed.

'Do you wish to have a solicitor present?'

'No, I just want to get this over and done with.'

Lewin looked at the man carefully, he didn't seem drunk or appear to be on drugs, she would proceed as normal. 'Why did you want to commit an armed robbery at Robinsons?' she asked.

Beresford hesitated, did they know about Alice? Did they know she was being held? They couldn't, he had to stick to the plan. 'I wanted money. I... needed money.'

Lewin just looked at him blankly for a moment and then just as Beresford was about to speak she asked him, 'So, when you want money you hold up a shop? You don't do what everybody else does and use a cash machine?'

This wasn't going the way Beresford wanted it to. He needed to be charged, for the police to release the information to the local press and radio. He needed the man holding Alice to hear it so he would let her go. That's what he'd promised; he'd let her go when he heard it on the radio.

Lewin was calmly looking at the paperwork on the table. 'Shall we keep this simple? Because I think I'm missing something here. We'll start with the basics, shall we?

'You are Alan Beresford according to the driver's licence in your wallet. You've never been in trouble with the law before. The address on your licence is a fairly pleasant part of Chatteris,' Lewin lifted her head to look at Beresford with a smile on her face, 'not somewhere we'd expect to find an armed robber living. So what's going on?'

Beresford had no choice, he had to be charged, he had to be. 'I needed that money, I… had nothing in the bank.'

'Why did you need it so urgently, Alan?'

The use of his Christian name unnerved him, suggested they didn't regard him as a criminal. They were almost being friendly to him. Or was it a trick? Was she just getting him to relax before she tore into him with aggressive questions? He couldn't think clearly. Every time he tried to concentrate on what Lewin was asking him pictures of Alice flooded through his mind.

Alice as a small child, always happy, always smiling. Alice at her birthday parties with her little cousins. Alice dressing up and pretending she was a princess. He could see all the images in his mind clearer than any photograph. Would he see her alive again?

Yes! Yes! Yes! He would if he could hold it together long enough. If he could get this policewoman to take him seriously, to charge him with armed robbery.

He shouted an answer to Lewin. 'I wanted the money, I told them I had a gun, I admit it all and I'm not saying anything else until you've charged me.'

'You're not helping yourself, Mr Beresford. I'm going to suspend this interview now. I think we'd better pay a visit to Mrs Beresford, maybe she can shed some light on you're activities.'

Beresford jumped up out of the chair. 'No. No. You can't go to my house. You mustn't.' He was almost incoherent, Lewin couldn't make out if it was anger or fear, but Beresford was loosing control. There were tears springing from his eyes. He looked desperate. 'Please, please, don't go to my house.'

Lewin turned to the constable, 'Take Mr Beresford to the cell.' She left the interview room to the sound of Beresford screaming, 'No, no,' over and over.

As she walked along the corridor towards the exit Inspector Davis was just coming in. 'Lewin, how did that house to house go?'

Lewin shook her head making her shoulder length blonde hair swing from side to side. 'Nobody heard or saw anything, sir. There are only three houses on that road. It is just a back road link between Warboys and the Forty Foot Bank road. The track the barn is on is nearly half a mile from the nearest house.'

Davis hadn't expected much from the enquiries but he was disappointed never the less. They kept asking questions and not getting any answers.

Lewin said, 'Before I can get back to that I've got a strange one, sir.' She outlined the Beresford hold up and his interview. 'He was desperate for us not to go to his house.'

'And you say this chap's never been in trouble before and won't offer a rational explanation for what he's done?

'No, sir.'

Davis looked at his watch. 'I'm not getting anywhere with this girl at the moment, I'll come with you to Beresford's house.'

They left the station and drove to Beresford's house. The town had expanded considerably in recent years; it wasn't the town Davis remembered from his childhood. Most of the new housing had provided homes for those who worked elsewhere. The employment opportunities had lagged far behind the residential growth. The result of that was that the police were far less likely to know people they were coming into contact with now. When Davis had started as a policeman just over twenty-five years ago he and his colleagues would have been able to put a name to most of the faces walking along the high street. It had been a long time since he could say that was true.

As they drove along the bypass that separated the industrial estate the police station was on, from the town itself, Davis asked Lewin the question that had been bugging him all day.

'If your daughter hadn't come home, if she hadn't phoned or been in touch, wouldn't you have reported it?'

'It depends, Sir.' Gillian Lewin wasn't sure how she'd feel, at thirty-nine she was single and had no children. 'Maybe she had planned to stay with a friend, the parents wouldn't expect her home then.'

'No, that's not it. The friend would have expected her. When she didn't turn up they'd have phoned her home. Anyway, it's the middle of the week, she should be at school. That reminds me, has Bellamy been in touch about his enquiries at the schools?'

'Not as far as I know, sir.'

They were turning into Hardcastle Road. Named, Davis knew, after a popular English teacher at the local school, it was a road of smart detached houses. Number sixteen was half way along on the right. They pulled up outside and got out. As they walked to the door Davis was sure he saw one of the net curtains twitch slightly.

Davis knocked on the door and waited a few moments. Sure that someone was in he knocked harder. Nobody came to the door.

'Wait here, Gillian, I'm going to check round the back.'

Davis made his way round to the back of the house, through a small gate and along the path. He came to the kitchen window first and looked through. There were several cups in the sink but otherwise the room was immaculately clean. There was nobody in the kitchen.

He moved along to the patio doors, unlike the front of the house the back didn't have net curtains. As he looked through into the living room he saw a woman on the settee. He was shocked; he'd never seen a woman looking so distressed before, so terrified.

He tried the door, it was locked, he indicated to her to open it but she ignored him. She just sat there, tears running down a face that was marked with streaks of make up and countless earlier tears. He quickly returned to the kitchen door, it was unlocked and he opened it. He called to Lewin to join him and entered the Beresford's home.

He quickly walked through to the living room and was about to speak to the woman sitting on the settee when he saw a picture on the wall. A picture of a family of three. The smiling daughter between her doting parents had a face he recognised. He'd last seen it on a post mortem table just a few short hours ago.

The torture the Beresfords had been living with soon came flooding out. As Davis had stood looking at the picture Mrs Beresford had leapt up from the settee and rushed at him, pounding clenched fists against his chest.

'Where's my daughter. Where's my Alice. Tell... tell me she's safe.' She was almost incapable of standing unaided and Davis guided her back to the settee, which she slumped on, sobbing.

'Get an ambulance.' Davis instructed Lewin.

Davis turned back to Mrs Beresford and sat beside her on the settee. 'I have some very difficult news for you.'

Before he could say anymore a howl of anguish, the likes of which Davis had never heard before, escaped from Clare Beresford, eventually subsiding into a repeated 'No, no, no,' just as her husband had done. She was rocking back and forth and had her head down with her hands clamped together at the back of her head.

Davis knew he had to tell this mother that her daughter was dead, although he could see she knew already. He dreaded this moment as much as the doctor who had told him of Grace's death must have dreaded it.

'Mrs Beresford, a girl was found dead this morning who I have reason to believe is your daughter.' He knew as he said the words that their formal structure could never take away the brutality of the message, that he couldn't soften the blow. That no words could change what he had told Clare Beresford. Her only child was dead.

As Davis looked with pity at the distraught woman he knew he would find no peace in himself until he had the killer in custody. Although Davis wished with all his heart that there would never be another murder on his patch, he knew he enjoyed hunting down the bastards who took someone else's life.

The battle had started again and Davis was determined to win it.

Now he knew that Alan Beresford was the father of the murdered girl, and seeing the state his wife was in, Davis was even more confused by Beresford's attempted robbery at Robinsons. They had waited with Clare Beresford until an ambulance crew had taken her to Hinchingbrooke hospital at nearby Huntingdon. She had been too upset for Davis to ask her any questions.

Now Davis and Lewin were headed back to the police station at Chatteris to interview Alan Beresford again.

Davis took a tray with three cups of coffee with him to the interview room. Just after he arrived there Lewin brought Beresford in.

'Please, Mr Beresford, sit down.' Davis indicated a chair. They had yet to tell him of his daughter's death and had the duty doctor on standby in case the strain within Beresford was released in the same hysterical way it had been in his wife.

All three of them sat down and Davis pushed a cup of coffee towards Beresford who stared at it for a moment and them lifted the cup to his lips and drank the lukewarm liquid in one draft. He took a handkerchief from his pocket and wiped his lips. He was ready to get this over with. Have the statement taken, be charged. They'd let him go on bail. Then he'd see his daughter again. God knows why that psycho had taken her, but he had promised he would release her if he, Beresford, carried out the orders he'd been given. He had to keep reminding himself of that. He had to believe it. He had to see his Alice again.

'Mr Beresford,' Davis began. 'I have some very unpleasant news for you.'

Beresford was worried, were they not going to give him bail, would they keep him in jail. They couldn't, he had to get out, he had to see Alice.

The policeman was still talking, Beresford forced himself to listen.

'... unfortunately we now know it is your daughter, it is Alice.'

Beresford was confused; he hadn't heard the first part of what the policeman had said. What did they know about Alice, had they rescued her, was she safe?

'Where's my daughter? Is she okay? I want to see her. I did this for her, he made me...' His words ran out as he saw the look on the policemen's faces. He knew then. He knew Alice was dead.

Over the next couple of hours the whole story came out. The phone calls the Beresford's had received from a man claiming to have kidnapped their daughter. Her pain filled scream in the first call. The bizarre instructions they had received, and were to follow if they wanted to see their precious daughter alive again.

Now Davis was with Chief Superintendent Malloy.

'You can't find any reason for this man to have kidnapped this particular girl?'

'No, sir. Any parent trying to protect their daughter could have carried out the demands made, and they were pointless anyway. Harsh as it sounds, I think the Beresfords were just unlucky that it was them. At the moment it looks random.'

'You've still no idea how he got the girl?'

Even though he knew Malloy intended no criticism Davis felt irked at the questions. 'Not at the moment, sir. I've got Lewin and Green at the school interviewing the girl's friends to see if anyone saw her taken or go willingly with someone. Bellamy is trawling through the records to see if we can find anybody with this kind of form.' He tried not to sound defensive as he listed the team's tasks.

He ran a hand over his face, tired, as well as sick at heart. Although during many years in the police service he had seen much of man's inhumanity to his fellow man he never understood it, never got used to it.

Malloy, knowing the feeling Davis had, having shared it more times than he wanted to remember, said without pressure, 'What are you going to do now?'

'Peterson and I are going to talk to the father again.'

28

'Has the doctor seen him and cleared it.'

'Yes, sir,' Davis replied. 'He's distressed, but under the circumstances we need to interview him.'

'Well, go easy on him.' Malloy instructed unnecessarily.

When Alan Beresford had realised Alice was dead he had thrown up the coffee he had just drunk. He had slumped, head on his arms, on the table sobbing. Huge, pent up sobs of grief, of loss, eventually of anger. Had the police gone charging in and panicked the man into killing his daughter? If they'd let the man's plan play out would she now be alive?

When he had been told that Alice had been dead before the kidnapper had given him his instructions Alan Beresford had looked straight at Davis and with a chilling determination had said, 'If I ever get my hands on that bastard, I'll kill him.'

Davis had heard many threats from many types of people before, but he had never before believed that the threat had been made with so much intent to carry it out.

Beresford had been taken back to the cell, although there was no intention now of charging him for the attempted robbery. The doctor had seen him and declared that apart from strain and grief there was nothing else wrong with Alan Beresford. He would be allowed to go home when he'd been picked clean of any information he might have, however unwittingly, that might lead the police to his daughter's killer.

Vyvyan Wilde sat at his kitchen table enjoying a light snack. He'd watched Alan Beresford's attempt at robbery, and his subsequent arrest, from the newsagents across the road, the same one he had been forced to steal from whilst his mother worked there. So many years of fear and worry swirled around in his mind. As each of his tormentors was punished the fear would go, he would find his peace as theirs was lost.

Chapter Four

Detective constables Lewin and Green were surrounded by sixteen-year-old boys and girls. Green was surprised how many of the boys were taller than him; he was six feet three inches tall. A couple of the girls weren't far behind. Their headmistress had explained to a stunned group of about one hundred and thirty year-eleven pupils that Alice Beresford had been found murdered. She had told them that the best way they could help was to tell the police if they had any knowledge of Alice's movements when she had left school yesterday.

Through the buzz of so many voices the detectives had learnt that Alice had been seen to get in a black car, almost certainly a three series BMW, just yards from the school gate.

Now they had just one girl in the headmistress's study. The girl sat next to Mrs Major with Lewin and Green the other side of a large desk. The desk was empty apart from a computer monitor and Lewin's notebook.

'Now then, Rachel, you take your time. We just need to find out as much as we can about the man that took Alice. Even if you can only remember one thing it will help.'

Lewin hoped she'd remember a lot more than one thing, but wasn't going to expect too much. She expected that if she asked too much this girl would collapse into tears and they'd get nothing from her. Rachel Wallace was level-headed, though upset at the death of a girl she knew slightly, she was not distraught.

'I don't know anything about the car other than it was black, Dean Harris said it was a Beemer, but I've never heard of that make.'

Lewin didn't think it was worth pointing out that that was a BMW, the car that several pupils had mentioned.

'I did hear the man though. I was standing just a few feet away as he wound down the window. He called to her.'

'Did you hear exactly what he said?' Lewin asked eagerly.

'Yes. He asked if she was Alice Beresford. Alice said she was. Then the man said, "I've been asked to collect you. Your mum's had a fall at the shop and they've taken her to the hospital, she asked me to fetch you." And Alice got in the car.'

'What kind of accent did the man have?' Green asked.

Rachel thought for a minute before replying and then said, 'He must have been local, because I can't remember an accent at all. That probably means he spoke just like we all do around here.'

'Did you see the man?' Green asked hopefully.

'No, the windows were quite dark and I was standing slightly back from the open window.' Rachel looked confused, worried. 'I didn't know Alice very well, the only class we shared was English, but I was upset for her that her mother had been hurt.' She hesitated. 'I… I wish now I'd said something to her, maybe offered to go with her.'

Mrs Major put a hand on Rachel's. 'I'm sure you have nothing to reproach yourself for.' She looked up at Lewin. 'Do you need to ask Rachel anymore questions?'

Lewin had none in mind but asked, 'Is there anything else you can remember at all that might help?'

Now Rachel did look distressed. 'No, I wish there was. I want to help you, I really do.'

Lewin stood up. 'You've helped us a lot already. I'm sorry to have upset you.' She glanced at Mrs Major and couldn't make out if her look of disapproval was meant for Rachel because she was now crying or Lewin for causing the tears. 'If we need to speak to you again we'll come to see you at your home, your parents can be with you.' She was just about to end the interview when she thought of one last thing. 'Alice was wearing uniform,' she pointed to Rachel's, 'like yours?'

Rachel looked down at her grey skirt and white blouse. 'Yes, we all do.'

With that Lewin and Green took their leave of St Andrew's Comprehensive School.

Lewin had just finished briefing Davis with the details they had obtained from the interview with Rachel Wallace.

'So the Beresfords were targeted.' Davis said. 'It wasn't just some random snatch.'

He sat thinking for a moment. The five of them that made up the Chatteris CID unit were sitting around a table, coffee and sandwiches finished they were trying to make sense of what they knew so far about Alice Beresford's brutal murder. It was just after six o'clock and it had been a long day. None of the detectives wanted to give up for the day though. There was a madman out there. A man who had sadistically tortured a young girl and, no less, tortured her parents.

Davis had rung Anita and given her the briefest details of the case. She knew he would not come home until he was ready to drop for the

31

day and she had been as indifferent as ever. 'Your dinner will be in the fridge, I'm going out.' With that she'd hung up.

Bellamy kept looking at his watch. He had recently married and his heavily pregnant wife wasn't too keen on the long hours he worked. It would be a pity if it got in the way of his career; Bellamy was shaping up to be a good detective.

Lewin, Peterson and Green weren't worried about what time they got home. Lewin and Peterson were single, Peterson after a recent divorce. Green's partner, Martin Stone, was a fireman and he was on the late shift this week, there'd be nobody at home for Green to be in any hurry for.

'You're sure it was her, he didn't just strike lucky?' Bellamy asked.

Green replied, 'He said her mum had a fall at the shop. Not at work, the shop. It was her he wanted.'

Peterson was doodling on a notepad. 'What we need to work out is, was it her he was interested in or the parents.'

Davis said testily, 'That would be easier to determine if we had any bloody idea of who he is.'

They were all silent for a few moments, all turning the case over in their minds, all wanting to see the one thing that might give them a lead. All of them aware that so far they had very little to go on.

There was a large wipe clean board on one wall. It currently held a picture of Alice, one each of the interior and exterior of the barn and various notes written down the right-hand side of the board. Davis got up and walked to the board, picking up a marker pen as he did so.

'We need to concentrate on three lines of enquiry at the moment. The car she got into, a black BMW by all accounts.'

Peterson interrupted, 'It's not likely the killer used his own car, it would be too risky. We should check it against reported thefts.'

Davis wrote: Black BMW, on the left of the board and drew a large box around it. 'Let's find out what we can for this. Item two, the murderer phoned the Beresfords, the number was withheld but the telephone company can give us the number. The phone is almost certainly an untraceable mobile, but we'll check.'

'If it was a mobile the phone company can give us a general idea of where it was used.' Lewin said.

'Which brings us to item three,' said Davis. Where did he kill the girl? He took her at just after three o'clock. She was dead by nine at the latest and in the barn before seven the following morning.'

32

'That could give him a fair amount of time to travel.' Peterson said.

'But he had to do what he did to Alice, not just travel,' Green pointed out.

'I think he was local.' Bellamy then counted off on his fingers his reasons. 'We think he targeted the family, he knew the mother worked in a shop, I'd say he knew it was Nicolsons, he knew where Alice went to school, what she looked like and he knew where the barn was.'

Davis said, 'I agree, Paul. I think this character is local, but accepting that doesn't get us much further forward.'

Davis had added items two and three to the board and given each of them a box which he hoped they would soon be able to fill with information.

'Tomorrow I want another word with Alan Beresford to see what he can tell us about the man, for example; his accent, possibly an age range, now he's had some time to think about it, did he recognise the voice at all. I also want a list of names for the employees at both Mr and Mrs Beresfords places of work.

'Peterson, you and I will interview both parents. Green, you concentrate on the car and the colleagues. Lewin, you get on to the phone company, we want the number and where it was used. Bellamy, get a map, I'm going to stick my neck out here, mark a ten-mile circle with Chatteris at the middle. Alice screamed loudly, that suggests the murder was carried out in a fairly isolated location or we would probably have had reports about the noise. I want all such houses, barns and disused industrial units marked.'

Davis looked around his small team and demanded, 'Suggestions, anything?'

'What about the Beresfords families, the parents I mean, you know, brothers, uncles. We shouldn't ignore a possible family link,' Peterson said.

Davis thought for a moment. 'We'll get a list tomorrow, carefully though, I don't want to upset the parents. If we turn nothing else up we'll make discreet enquiries about them.' He looked at his watch, it was now well past seven. 'Let's call it a day now.'

Bellamy was out the door quickly. Peterson called to Green, 'You fancy picking up a pizza?'

Since Peterson's divorce he had often joined Green after work for a fast-food dinner if Green's boyfriend was working the late shift, neither man being too inclined to cook properly for himself.

Green agreed readily. 'What about you?' he asked Lewin.

'Why not,' she said, 'I'll only sit in front of the telly and fall asleep if I go home.'

The three of them left knowing there was no point asking Davis if he wanted to join them, he would go home in the vain hope that his wife might enjoy his company.

Phil Davis pulled up on the drive of his modest detached home. He had bought one of the new houses on the Poppyfields estate. Their previous home had been a semi-detached and he was glad of the extra privacy of the new home. As he turned off the ignition he hoped, vainly he knew, that just once Anita would be pleased to see him arrive home.

The light over the door came on as he approached but he didn't need to put his key in the lock, his son opened the door for him.

'Hello, Dad, I saw you pull onto the drive.'

Adam Davis was as slim as his father was fat and although only sixteen was the same height at six feet one inch.

'Mum's in the kitchen, she held dinner off until you got here.'

'I bet you're starving,' Davis joked with his son. 'I thought she said she was going out?'

Adam frowned, 'She was, but she got a call and then said she wasn't.' He looked concerned, he was beginning to notice the tension in his parent's marriage. 'I don't know where she was going, she was dressed up smart, she's changed now though. She's not in a good mood.'

Davis didn't like his son worrying. 'I wouldn't take too much notice,' his stomach rumbled and he rubbed it, 'I hope your mother's cooked a lot, I'm famished.' He knew, however, that Anita was controlling his diet as carefully as she could. It was something she did willingly, partly, he thought, because she knew how much he enjoyed his food.

Davis took off his jacket and hung it in the cupboard. He walked through to the kitchen followed by Adam.

Anita was just dishing up. 'You managed to get home then?' she said without looking up from the food she was preparing, the tone of her voice suggesting that she was surprised he'd bothered. Davis felt an irrational twinge of annoyance, after so many years of her indifference to him he should have been immune to it. The hope never died though, not quite. Davis knew not to rise to the bait; he would only invite a pointless argument.

He gave his wife a brief outline of what he was working on. He hoped telling her of the seriousness of the case might soften her attitude to his lateness a little.

'It's a bad case. A young girl kidnapped and murdered.' Suddenly he felt the pressures of the days weighing on him and rubbed his hands over his face. 'The man's a damned sadist and we haven't got a clue where to start looking for him.'

Anita said nothing and asked Adam to take his plate into the dining room and brought hers and her husband's. Tuna and a salad again, what Davis would give for a fry-up. He'd been told of the future consequences of failing to control his weight and supposed it was worth the effort, but he was sick and tired of being hungry all the time.

They began eating and after a few minutes Adam said, 'It's Alice Beresford's murder you're working on, isn't it?'

'Yes,' his father said, 'did you know her?'

'Not particularly well. She was in my year but we didn't share any classes.' He continued eating. 'She was a quiet girl, she didn't have too many friends. I think her father could be a bit strict, you know, who she could bring home, where she went.' Adam blushed slightly, thinking that his parents were careful about both those things, although he wouldn't have called them strict. 'I think her dad was a bit too controlling,' he said trying to explain himself.

Davis considered what his son had said for a few moments. 'It still doesn't explain why she was taken, does it?'

Adam looked at his father and, with a maturity that surprised Davis, said, 'No, but it might explain why she was willing to get in a car with someone she didn't know. He said he'd been sent by her mother, and she was used to obeying her parents without question.'

Davis stopped eating and put his knife and fork down. If Adam was right that might mean that someone close to the family, someone who knew that Alice would do as she was told, could be responsible for her death.

Chapter Five

Friday

Davis was at work before the rest of the team. Anita had not said where she had intended going yesterday evening and had hardly said anything before bedtime. As they were on their way to bed Davis had mentioned that she'd said she would be out in the hopes she'd talk about it. 'I didn't go, did I?' was all she'd said. She had stayed in bed as he got up for work and although Davis was sure she was awake she had feigned sleep to avoid conversation.

He had allocated tasks for each of the team members yesterday before they went home and today he wrote each of their names against the tasks on the wipe clean board. As each team member uncovered information it would be added to the board in the hope of finding a link between the various pieces, a trail that led to a suspect. By eight o'clock when Peterson arrived he was ready to get going on their task, interviewing the parents.

They went in Peterson's car, which meant listening to his choice of music. Peterson was a huge fan of early seventies heavy rock. At the moment Deep Purple were playing 'Strange Kind Of Woman' loudly enough to annoy Davis but not quite loud enough for him to reasonably ask for it to be turned down. Davis was glad the journey was a short one. They were half way through a guitar riff and Peterson would like to have sat in the car and finished listening to it, but he knew not to try his boss's patience too much.

Alan Beresford answered the door as soon as Davis had knocked. He looked as if he'd barely slept. He stood aside to let them in, as if he expected them to have arrived now, although no appointment had been made.

They went through to the living room; the picture on the wall still portrayed a loving family, although after what Adam had said he wondered if that pose had been genuine. Had the smiles been natural or conjured out of their imaginations for the world to see?

At Beresford's invitation they sat down. 'I'm sorry,' Beresford started, '…my wife's…' he stopped.

Davis could tell Beresford was having trouble controlling himself, tears were close to the surface.

'Take your time, Mr Beresford. We need to ask you and your wife a few questions, but we'll take it at your pace.'

Davis had a great deal of sympathy for the man. Even if he'd been strict with his daughter there was no suggestion that he'd been other than a devoted father. Davis considered what state he would be in if Adam had been brutally murdered and had to suppress a shudder of fear that rose at the mere thought of it.

Beresford continued, 'My wife's still in bed, the doctor has given her something to take.' He stopped, fighting the tears under control again. 'She couldn't sleep, she couldn't sit down, she's... she's.' Thinking about his wife's distress was too much for Beresford and he couldn't control the tears this time.

Embarrassed he got up from the armchair he'd been sitting in. 'Excuse me... one moment.' With that he went into the kitchen.

Peterson said, 'I don't think we're going to get much out of him this morning, and it certainly sounds like we won't get to talk to the mother.'

Davis shrugged, at the moment he didn't think there was too much to be got from the mother anyway. But he was determined that, upset or not, Alan Beresford was going to answer at least a few questions. They still had the charges relating to the robbery to hold over him, although Davis knew they were not going to proceed with them.

Beresford returned from the kitchen. 'I'm sorry,' he said, 'it's been difficult.'

'I can quite understand that, Mr Beresford, and I'm sorry, but we do need to get some help from you.'

Beresford looked puzzled. 'How can I help? What could there be that I know that I wouldn't already have told you?'

'What you might be able to help with at the moment are small things in themselves, but sometimes those small things, when added together, provide the solution we're looking for.'

Beresford made a shrug of acceptance and said, 'Where do you want to start?'

Davis had prepared a mental list of questions, he didn't want to be reading them from a notepad, but he did see Peterson slip his notebook from his pocket ready to write down anything Beresford might be able to tell them.

'When the man first called was it you or your wife who answered?'

'It was me, after that he insisted I pick the phone up every time.'

'Did you at any time think you recognised the voice?'

'No,' Beresford said indignantly. 'Are you trying to suggest it was a friend or worse a relative who's done this?'

Davis held up a placatory hand. 'Not at all. At the moment I'm not trying to suggest anything. But we know that Alice got in the car with the man willingly, we also think we know why.' They hadn't told the Beresfords yet about the lie the man used to get Alice in the car. 'Given that we at least need to consider that the man was known to your family.'

Beresford sat for a moment thinking, remembering. 'Although it was a local voice there was nothing familiar about it, I didn't recognise it at all.'

'How did he address you the first time he spoke?'

Beresford didn't hesitate this time. 'He asked if I was Alice's father.' He looked strained again. 'As soon as he said that I thought something had happened to her, you know, an accident.'

Davis and Peterson both knew what he meant. As parents they, like every other parent, would have had the same thought if their child was late home and those were the words that started a phone conversation.

'But it wasn't an accident he told you about, was it?' Davis asked.

Beresford's head dropped, and in a quiet voice, almost too quiet to hear, he said, 'No.'

'I'm sorry, Mr Beresford, I can't begin to imagine how distressing this is, but we need to find this man.'

Beresford looked up at Davis now, eyes ablaze with anger. 'You've got to find him now, now it's too late for Alice. Even though you can do nothing for us we've got to answer your questions.' He jumped up from the settee. 'How the hell do you think this makes me feel, going over it all again.'

Davis was trying to think of something to say to calm the man. Aware that Beresford was right, none of his answers would bring back his daughter, no matter how painful it was to give them.

Before he could say anything a quiet voice, a voice that was flat and lifeless said to Beresford, 'Tell them Al, tell them what they need to know.' Clare Beresford had come downstairs. She was still wearing her dressing gown and her stained face told of a night of torment. It was clear she was still feeling sedated to some extent by the pills the doctor had given her.

Beresford moved to her side. 'Come on, darling, are you sure you should be up?'

She gently held up a hand to stop him. 'I heard the police arrive, I want to help them, I want to stop him... I want to stop him doing this to any other mother.' Silent tears ran down her face although she took no notice of them, not even wiping them away. She moved to the armchair her husband had been sitting in and, having sat down, wrapped the folds of her dressing gown around her.

She turned to Davis, 'You're in charge of this investigation, aren't you?'

'Yes, I am.'

'Do you have children?' she asked him.

He didn't tell her he'd lost a daughter, it might have shown them he understood their grief but he wanted to keep the focus on Alice and her abductor. 'I have a son,' Davis said, adding, 'the same age as Alice, in fact he knew her slightly.'

This information seemed to provide her with some comfort; there was a slight relaxation of the muscles in her face. 'Then you will understand what a nightmare the last two days have been for us.'

Davis nodded an agreement.

'I know there is nothing you can do for us, my husband is right. But I couldn't bear it if any other mother has to go through this because we didn't tell you something that might help catch the bastard.' She spoke the last word with so much venom that it silenced the three men for a moment. She scrunched her hands tightly together in her lap and for a few seconds her face screwed up as if she were going to cry. Still none of the others said anything.

Clare Beresford opened her eyes again. 'What can we tell you, inspector?'

Clare Beresford was probably a very attractive woman, Davis thought. When he had first seen her yesterday she was dressed in good quality, well chosen clothes that showed she had a trim figure. Her hair had then retained some of its lustre from a recent trip to a good salon. Although she had been distressed, it was still possible to see that her face was unlined and she could have passed for someone of thirty rather than forty. Now, however, she looked strained, aged and close to collapse. Her hair was uncombed and straggly, her face had streaks of old makeup rubbed under her eyes and those eyes were dull and told Davis that she was in despair.

'I know this is unpleasant for you both, but we need to go over everything that happened from the minute you realised Alice was late home.'

Alan Beresford moved to his wife's side and sat on the arm of the chair, he spoke first. 'It was when I got home that we started to worry. Alice sometimes went to a friend's house after school, Kay, her name is. She lives over on Meadow Drove. When she did that she walked to the yard where I work just before I finish, it's only a five-minute walk from Kay's. I'd bring her home with me.'

Clare sat, listening to her husband but not reacting at all.

He continued, 'When I got home the first thing Clare asked was "Where's Alice". We rang Kay but she had been off school unwell that day. We were just thinking of ringing the school when we got the first call.' He stopped, remembering the moment of short-lived relief that must have been. 'It was him,' he closed his eyes for a few seconds, 'that man.'

Davis asked softly, 'Can you remember what time he rang?'

'It would have been no later than twenty minutes past five,' Clare Beresford said.

'That's right,' her husband confirmed. 'I leave work at five and it takes me ten to fifteen minutes to get home, depending on the traffic in town. He rang about five minutes after I got here.'

Davis was trying to work out the time the man would have had Alice for before he rang her parents. She had been taken from outside the school just after three o'clock. Davis assumed that the man had stripped her and used the tape to secure her before phoning the parents. That would leave up to two hours that the man could have been driving Alice to where she was murdered. Davis didn't believe that was the case though, he still had this down as something local.

'Can you tell me exactly what he said?' Davis asked Alan Beresford.

Beresford looked crushed, beaten. The anger he'd shown earlier had been replaced by a defeated feeling. They were talking about his daughter's last moments. Moments when he had been unable to do what every father wants to do, is driven to do, protect his child. Without meeting Davis's eye he said, 'He asked if I was Alice's father. I told him I was. I thought it was someone from the school or one of her friend's fathers. But he said, "Alice hasn't come home yet, has she?".'

Now Beresford did meet Davis's eye, the anguish he saw in Alice's

40

father almost made Davis flinch. 'I asked who he was,' Beresford continued. 'He said he was the man who knew why she hadn't come home.' Beresford stopped talking and swallowed quickly. Davis knew he was reliving the conversation, reliving the moment he knew his daughter was in the hands of a maniac.

'What did he say then?'

'He asked me if I wanted Alice to be able to see me again. I wondered what he meant by that, it was a strange question, and I was shocked. Before I could think of anything he said, "If you don't do as I tell you I'll cut her eyes out.".'

Clare Beresford was crying again, silent tears that fell down her face unheeded.

'How did you react to that?' Davis asked, although he could imagine the horror he would have felt as a parent to have someone threaten his son like that.

'I … I shouted… I couldn't think straight. I thought it might be someone playing tricks. But he kept on. He said if I didn't do as he said he'd cut her face so badly she'd wish he had killed her.' Beresford's hands were bunched in fists and his voice was thick with suppressed anger and fear. 'He said if we wanted to see her again we had to obey him. He said if we called the police he'd kill her and we'd never find the body. I asked him how we were to know he did have her. He said, "I'll let her talk to you". I was going to tell her we'd get her back, we'd do whatever it took. But he didn't give me the chance. She just said, "Daddy," and then there was a terrible scream.' Beresford started to sob now, huge gulps of breath in and out, his eyes awash with tears. His wife looked at him but didn't react, didn't make a move to touch him, comfort him.

Davis gave him time to recover, to at least hold the emotions in check, then asked, 'Did he say anything else?'

'He said he'd give us time to think about it and put the phone down.'

Davis couldn't imagine the panic that call would have induced in a parent. It was making him feel sick just thinking about the call being made to him about Adam. For the caller to hang up like that must have caused total misery.

'How long before he called again?'

Beresford looked at his wife, but she gave no reaction. He appeared confused, as if the time between the calls was too difficult to remember.

'I don't know, we were worried … my wife wanted to call the police.' His head hung slightly, he wasn't looking at his wife or the policemen. 'But I'd heard the man's voice, I knew he meant what he said, we'd never find her again.' The last few words were almost a plea, as if he were defending his decision not to call the police, to his wife, to Davis, to himself.

Davis said nothing, could think of no comfort to give this fellow father. After a few seconds of silence Beresford said, 'It was hours. It was gone midnight.'

Davis thought they must have been the longest hours of the Beresford's lives. After the threats made against their daughter they must have wanted to hear the man's voice, just some reassurance that he hadn't killed her yet, that there was some glimmer of hope, that they could do something that might get her back. Unaware that she was beyond help by then.

'I know I've asked you before, but I must ask again, did you at any time recognise the voice at all?'

This time Beresford didn't get angry, didn't fly off the handle. He just shook his head back and forth, once each way.

The silence in the house was absolute. There was no ticking clock, no sound of a refrigerator running in the kitchen, no music in the house, nothing. In the brief second Davis was aware of the silence he was almost afraid to break it, almost afraid to speak. For just a couple of seconds it was almost as if there was peace in the house. But then the spell was broken by a small sniff from Clare Beresford and Davis realised there would never be peace in the Beresford's lives again. Whatever they did there would always be the turmoil of their daughter's death in their minds, in their lives, impossible to forget, impossible to hide from, impossible to silence the scream of despair.

Davis spoke quietly but his voice seemed to be loud when he asked, 'When the man called the second time, what did he say?'

'He said that my asking him to prove he had Alice had caused her pain. That it was my fault. He said I was a bad father.' Beresford jumped up from the chair to pace across the room, anguish prompting more tears. 'How was I to know he'd hurt her? I wouldn't have asked if I'd known.' He sat back on the arm of the chair and put his head in his hands. Davis heard a muffled groan, 'I didn't know he'd hurt her.'

Beresford had identified his daughter's body. He'd been driven from the police station to the hospital on the way home. He's seen the wound on her hand, realised from what the police had told him that this was probably the wound that had been inflicted by the murderer after Alice had called, "Daddy".

He lifted his head and looked at his own hand then looked at Davis. 'I would have done anything to save her, anything. He asked if we'd gone to bed. Christ! As if we would.'

This was the worst aspect of Davis's job as far as he was concerned, interviewing the relatives of someone who'd died. Trying to tease information out of them. Making them relive the last memories of their loved ones in the hope of getting vital clues to trap a killer. More than once he'd had relatives collapse into grief, unable to answer questions, unable to function. Looking at Clare Beresford he was worried she might be close to that stage. But he had so little to go on at the moment he needed whatever answers Alice's parents could give him.

Gently he said, 'Was there anything else he said?'

'He said that I was going to have to carry out a task to save my daughter. He said that was fair.' Beresford banged his fist down on his knee. 'Fair... fair.' He was crying again, he used the palms of his hands to rub away the tears. 'Why should it be fair that I had to save my daughter? What right did he have to use her like that? He said he wanted to know how far I would go to save my child.'

Davis felt a chill run through him; this man had been playing with Alan Beresford, a cold, cruel game.

'What did he want you to do?'

'He hung up again. He just said, "You'll have to wait, wait until I call you again.".'

Davis looked across at Peterson; they both knew that the Beresfords were now aware that their daughter had been dead by the time of the second call. Peterson looked as if he was ready to call it a day, to end the current nightmare for the grieving parents, to leave them to find whatever comfort they could in each other's company. But Davis knew that nothing he'd been told yet was going to help him find Alice's killer. He had to prolong the agony, pry deeper, hurt more in the hope that one piece of information the Beresfords had would lead them to the murderer.

Although Davis knew the answer he asked them when the next call had come.

Alan Beresford was answering bleakly now; he had the same dead look in his eyes as his wife had. 'Just after twelve.'

Davis waited for him to say more, then when it was obvious he wasn't going to asked, 'What did he want you to do?'

Beresford said, 'You know what, I told you at the police station, you caught me.' Again, a flat monotone response.

'I'm sorry. Maybe if you go through it again there might just be one thing we can make sense of.'

Beresford repeated what he remembered of the instructions, his question to the man and the angry retort. Every word seemed etched on his mind and the telling of it this time seemed to Davis to be almost word for word what he had heard yesterday. There was nothing new, nothing helpful. The Beresfords had told Davis everything they could and he was no nearer finding the man who had murdered their daughter.

He got up and Peterson followed. 'I'm sorry Mr and Mrs Beresford that we've had to put you through this. If you remember anything else please get in touch.'

There was no reaction from either of them and the two policemen left.

Chapter Six

They sat in the car for a minute without starting the engine. Both detectives felt drained by the emotions of the Beresfords. Peterson turned to Davis and asked, 'What now?'

Davis took some seconds to reply, then he said, 'We need to see what the others have come up with, but first I want to go back to the barn, something's been bugging me.'

'What, we checked everything thoroughly.'

Davis didn't want Peterson to think he was questioning his efficiency, but he had a nagging feeling in the back of his mind that he had seen something that had not been mentioned in the report.

'I don't know yet, Graham, it might be nothing.'

They drove to Bennett's Lane. As Peterson turned the car onto the lane Davis was looking at the wind turbines that had been installed a few hundred yards from the road. The Fens flat landscape made it a good location for these devices, but Davis was in two minds as to whether they spoilt the view or not. Sometimes watching the blades whirring round was quite relaxing.

The change of road surface was immediately apparent, Peterson had slowed down but the bumpy road was still making the car rock on its suspension. As they passed the houses on the road Davis realised that it would have been possible for at least two of them to have seen any lights that might have been showing at the barn. If a car had used its lights or the murderer had used a torch it would have been visible. Davis was well aware just how far a light could be seen over these flat fields, he would have to check the reports to make sure the householders had been asked the right questions.

They reached the track and Peterson carried on past the end of the tarmac, driving slowly along the rutted dirt track until he pulled the car onto the verge where Davis had parked yesterday. The track followed the path of the dyke until it came to the barn. The barn stood some fifteen feet from the bank of the dyke and as they approached the barn Davis moved towards the bank. Picking his route carefully he indicated that Peterson should keep back.

When he got close to the edge he called to Peterson, 'This is it. Move round that way.' He indicated a circular approach that brought Peterson to stand some ten feet further along the bank from where Davis was. 'Look, the grass has been flattened. Somebody's landed here.' He knelt down and moved his hand through the grass towards a dull, black piece of metal. 'See, it's a hook buried in the ground, it's for tying up a boat. He pointed towards the barn, 'Somebody's definitely climbed this bank.'

He stood up. 'Maybe that's why the house owners didn't hear a car, he could have used a boat.'

Peterson was not the type to start making excuses for not having spotted this when he searched the area, or to pour cold water on his boss's suggestion to minimise the importance of the discovery. He said, 'We'll need to check out the dyke in both directions, see where a boat could be put in the water.' He looked along the length of the dyke, 'You know, this dyke feeds into the Forty Foot Drain, for most of the way there the banks are too steep to get a boat in the water and there's a weir at the junction.'

Davis turned to look in the other direction. 'What about that way?'

'It peters out near Warboys, it's meant to drain the fields between Warboys and the Forty Foot.'

'You know it well?' Davis asked.

'I know when I was a lad at school some of the boys who lived on these farms used to put little boats on the dykes, you know, just mucking about.' Peterson looked into the dull water. 'It might have been a bit of fishing or just larking around.

'It's rare that people use a boat on these dykes, they aren't like the main drains. You can get almost anything on those, up to the big narrow boats, but these little waterways are often too shallow or blocked with vegetation to make it practical to travel on them. Not only that, they often don't go anywhere as such, they're meant to drain the water away, nothing else. It was just the lads mucking about really,' he repeated.

'So you think it's unlikely our man came this way?' Davis asked, wanting to get on.

Peterson thought about it for a minute. 'Unlikely, yes, impossible, no.

Davis looked both ways along the dyke, it was probably around five miles in length and most of it was bordered by fields with crops in. It would take hours to walk the entire five miles. 'I think we'd better check it out anyway. I'll call air support, get the helicopter to take a look.'

They had driven back to the police station and Davis arranged for help from the air support unit. Now he and Peterson returned to the CID office. Green was sitting at one of the desks and had just put the phone down. He got up as Davis walked in and switched the kettle on. 'We've had a call from traffic, sir. They found a BMW burnt out at Carter's Farm early this morning.'

'Carter's Farm,' Davis said questioningly, 'that's on the road to Somersham, isn't it?'

'Yes,' Green said, 'the car was found just on the edge of a field, about a mile outside town. It had been reported stolen a few days ago.'

'So whoever set fire to the car wouldn't have had far to walk home if he lived in Chatteris.' Davis knew he'd been right about the murderer being a local man. They still had to find out where the girl had been killed though.

'Have you got the staff lists from both parents' places of work?'

'From the father's so far, sir. Alan Beresford works for Total Builder's Supplies. They've got branches spread over most of East Anglia. He manages the branch he works at and has eight men there.' He stopped talking for a minute as he poured the boiling water into three cups. 'I went down to the yard first thing.'

Green took the coffees to Davis and Peterson and collected his own before sitting back at his desk. 'He made a brief call yesterday to say he wouldn't be in, no explanations according to his deputy.'

'Were all the staff on the premises yesterday?' Peterson asked.

'Yes, and today, they arrive at eight and I had a quick word with all of them.'

'What sort of reaction did you get?' Davis asked.

'Complete shock. They had no idea that the murdered girl was Alice Beresford.'

The local and national news bulletins had carried the story of a girl being found dead. So far her name had been withheld. Beresford's forced hold up at the bookmakers had not made the news yet, partly due to him not being charged. Davis had gone to the shop and had a word with the manager explaining why Beresford had acted as he had and Robinsons had agreed to drop the matter as no money had been taken and nobody hurt.

'The timing of each of the incidents means that some of them could have been done outside working hours,' Peterson pointed out.

'What are you suggesting?' Davis asked him.

Peterson sat with his coffee cup in one hand whilst the other hand

47

was being slowly rubbed through his thick, dark hair. 'Just that we shouldn't rule any of them out because they were at work.'

'Alice being collected from school was in working hours, as was the call to her parents to order her father to rob the bookmakers,' Davis pointed out.

Davis thought about Peterson's suggestion for a few moments. He'd better check everything. Finishing his coffee he said to Green, 'Patrick, go to each of them at home tonight. Ask each of them if they can remember any of their colleagues being absent for any period of time. See if they're edgy, if they're trying to hide something.'

Green acknowledged his boss's request and made sure he put a note of the addresses in his pocketbook.

'Did you get the list of Clare Beresford's colleagues?' Davis asked.

'It's on the way. I rang the store but the manager wouldn't give me the information without head office authority, company policy she said. I rang the personnel department myself and they're emailing me a list of all full and part-time staff.'

Davis was used to these frustrating delays. 'I don't really think that our killer is one of Clare Beresford's colleagues, but make sure we get that list today. Have you run Beresford's staff through the criminal records files?'

Green picked up a small notebook. 'I started, it's what I'm working on at the moment.'

Davis nodded a response just as Lewin entered the office. She turned towards Davis, 'Sir, the phone calls to the Beresford house were made on an unlisted mobile phone. The phone company are trying to locate all the records for that handset so that we can find out where it was used.'

Davis wasn't too sure that this would turn out to be worth much. If the murderer had got any sense he would have moved about. In any case the phone company would only be able to indicate an area to look at, not pinpoint an address. 'I want to know if the timings match what the Beresfords have told us. How's Bellamy getting on with his map?'

Green answered, 'He's got one, it's over there,' he said pointing to a large roll of paper.

'Where is he?' Davis asked.

Green looked uncomfortable but knew better than to tell a lie to his boss, even a white one for a friend. 'He got a call from his wife, she's had some rather big twinges.'

Davis was not amused, whilst he accepted that Bellamy would want to be with his wife when she gave birth to their child, he didn't want him running off every five minutes in the middle of a murder investigation. He had almost missed the birth of Adam, arriving just as the boy was being delivered. A detective constable then, just as Bellamy was now, he'd been working on a fraud case, but his inspector had expected him to pull his weight on the investigation rather than running back and forth to his wife. Not that Anita had made many calls to him at work, well, not until she actually was in hospital getting ready to go to the delivery suite. Even then she considered him as little more than a father for her child and a breadwinner, she wasn't fussed either way whether he was at the birth or not.

Times had changed, he knew that, Bellamy would probably ask for paternity leave, and Davis knew that he would have to grant it. Hmm, Davis snorted to himself, when Adam was born he was back at work an hour later and that was it, Anita stayed with her mother for two weeks and he visited for a few hours at a time when he could.

He had to get on. 'Patrick, get scenes of crime to take a look at the car, see if there's a chance of any forensic evidence. If I remember there aren't many houses along that stretch of road, get out there later and see if anybody saw anything.'

'Sir.' Green acknowledged and left the CID office just as Bellamy arrived. As they passed just outside the office Green gave Bellamy a grin and drew his finger across his throat.

'Oh God! He's not back is he?'

'Yes, I am, Bellamy,' said Davis who had just been about to go to see the Chief Superintendent. 'Try to give us as much of your time as possible,' Davis said sarcastically to Bellamy.

He walked along the corridor to Kevin Malloy's office. His boss had asked Davis to bring him up to date at around midday.

'Come,' was the response to Davis's knock at the boss's door. 'Sit down, Phil.' Kevin Malloy closed the folder he had been reading and put his pen down. One of the things Davis liked about Malloy was that when he was discussing a case with you, he gave you his full attention.

'How far have you got?' Malloy asked.

'So far we've got a lot of negatives. The car that was probably used has been found burnt out, I've asked scenes of crime to see if there was any part of the car that escaped the flames and might have something for us.' Davis shrugged, 'It's unlikely, but I don't want to miss something that's sitting there.'

Malloy gave a nod of agreement and waited for Davis to move on to the next point. He wasn't going to lead the questions, when he was an inspector he'd felt that suggested the senior officer didn't quite trust the junior one to do a thorough job.

'We're getting lists of colleagues and family...'

'Do you really think it could be family?' Malloy asked, surprised.

'No, I don't, but I'm going to check their records, if we don't and one of them has a record for violence we'll look stupid.'

'You're right, just keep it low key unless you turn up anything concrete.'

Davis nodded an agreement and then ran through the other lines of enquiry he had instigated.

Malloy knew Davis was a good detective and had no intention of interfering. 'Let me know if I can help, although uniformed officers are in short supply whilst we have those protesters at Millslade Laboratory.'

The meeting over, Davis went back to the CID office. Bellamy had got his map on the wall and was marking known empty properties with a bright pink marker pen.

Realising there was nothing he could do on this case for the moment he decided to prepare some of the paperwork for a previous case that was going to court next week.

Vyvyan was cleaning up. He'd got rid of the car, now he made sure that there was nothing left to suggest Alice had been here. Her clothes were burnt in the multi-fuel heater along with her school books and bag.

Now he had to make preparations for the next one.

It was just after four o'clock when Lewin interrupted Davis just as he was finalising his notes for the upcoming court appearance. 'Sir, one of Beresford's staff has form for violence and threats.'

Davis looked up quickly. 'That's taken some time to find out, hasn't it?'

Lewin wasn't put out by this. 'He has changed his name; it took a bit of digging to find his history.'

'Who is this chap?'

'His name now is Roy Keane,' Lewin laughed, 'Ten to one it's a tribute to a particular ex-footballer.'

'What was his previous name?' Davis asked.

'David Griffin.'

Davis's mood changed, 'I know him, or I did. Twenty years ago we used to nick him regularly for fighting and being a general nuisance. Then he did time for locking a thirteen-year old boy in the back of a van until the lad's older brother had paid a drugs debt. He threatened to cut the kid and tell the parents the older boy had done nothing to save his brother from coming to harm.'

Lewin looked hopeful, 'Do you think he could be our man?'

'He's kept out of trouble since he came out as far as I know, but it's too close to form to ignore.' Davis was wondering why Keane might have targeted the Beresfords.

Lewin glanced over the sheet she'd printed from the computer. 'He's not even been done for speeding since he came out of Littlehey fifteen years ago. Shall we go and see him?'

Davis got up and put his jacket on. 'Oh yes, he's the best option we've got so far.'

Chapter Seven

Davis and Lewin drove to the Total Builders' Supplies yard, which was situated at the far end of the old industrial estate. Davis parked his Volvo in the empty space reserved for the manager; obviously none of the staff were prepared to risk being in Beresford's space, even if it was unlikely that he would return yet.

They entered the main building at the front of the yard and asked the man at the desk to speak to Roy Keane. 'Timber shed,' the man said barely looking at Davis, 'bottom of the yard.'

Davis and Lewin walked down to the timber shed and found two men loading a lorry with fencing panels. 'I'm looking for Mr Keane.' Davis announced.

One of the men had a surly look on his face as he said, 'I've been waiting for this.' He turned away from the lorry and spat on the ground. He was just short of six-feet tall and very heavily built, with a close-cropped haircut and an array of faded tattoos. Just the sort of man you wouldn't want to meet when he was in a bad mood.

Davis wasn't easily intimidated and stood close up to Keane. 'Why have you been waiting for us, Roy? What have you done that you think might warrant a visit from us?' he asked.

Keane faced Davis and with an aggressive jab of his finger just inches from Davis's face said, 'I ain't done nuffing, I've stayed out of trouble since ... well I ain't done nuffing wrong for years.' He looked more closely at Davis. 'And I remember you, you can't touch me this time, I ain't guilty of nuffing.'

'If that's true you won't mind telling us what you were doing on Wednesday evening.' Davis said with a rough edge to his voice.

Keane was in no mood to cooperate. 'I don't have to tell you nuffing. I've got work to do.' With that he swung away to carry on loading the lorry.

Davis used his bulk to block the way. 'We want some answers from you, you can satisfy our curiosity now or you can come to the station with us, it's up to you.'

'You can't arrest me, I've done nuffing wrong.'

'So you keep saying,' said Lewin, 'but if that was the case why not tell us what you were doing?'

Frustrated, Keane kicked a pallet loaded with fence posts. 'Because you want someone to nail for this girl's killing and you'd rather it was an old con like me instead of having to do any real work finding the bastard who did it.'

'If you've done nothing wrong we won't want to put you away, we'll want the real killer,' Davis responded.

'Right, so I tell you what I was doing and you'll go away. Well I ain't falling for it this time, so you can fuck off,' he said trying to push past Davis.

Davis had run out of patience now. 'Right, you're under arrest on suspicion of being involved in the murder of Alice Beresford.' Davis cautioned him as Lewin handcuffed the angry Keane.

Davis delivered Keane to a custody sergeant at the station and asked that he be put in a cell whilst a search warrant was obtained for Keane's house. He thought he'd better let Malloy know of the arrest.

'Well done. What chance is there that he's our murderer?'

'I'm not convinced yet, if at all. He's got form and he wouldn't tell us where he was on Wednesday, but that might just be anti-police bravado.' Davis laughed, 'after all it was me that had him put away.'

'Okay, keep me posted.' Davis left to find out if Lewin had the warrant yet.

Keane's terraced house was dirtier than any house Davis and Lewin had searched before. When they arrived a woman considerably younger looking than Keane's late thirties answered the door. Her streaky blonde hair was dirty and her makeup was smudged. As she held the door to try to stop the policemen looking inside the house Davis noticed a thick layer of grime under her unpainted nails. Lewin showed her the search warrant. 'You can't just barge in here,' she screamed at her.

'This says we can, now be a good girl and keep out of the way or we'll take you in as well.'

'You bastards used to persecute my dad, now you're trying to screw my Roy.'

Davis looked carefully at the girl. 'I thought I'd seen you before, you're Kelly Collins, aren't you?'

'I ain't telling you nuffink,' she said, sulkily.

Davis turned to Lewin, 'Her dad had a problem with his fingers, they were sticky. You know, other people's money, other people's bank cards, other people's cheque books.'

'I get the picture,' Lewin laughed, 'anything that wasn't his to take.'

'You two fink you're so fucking funny, my old man was an easy nick for you lazy sods,' the girl said as she moved away from the door to let the detectives in.

Davis said, 'Your old man was an easy nick because he was too stupid and couldn't keep his hands in his own pockets.'

Kelly flounced off into the kitchen and Davis nodded to Lewin to follow her. He quickly scanned the untidy sitting room and decided to look upstairs.

A quick look round the main bedroom, a cramped and dark room with the curtains still drawn and the bed unmade, told him there was nothing to find here. He moved into the spare bedroom, it was piled high with junk in one corner, there was no bed in the room, and nothing of interest here. There was another door on the landing and Davis opened it to reveal the airing cupboard. He was just about to close it when he noticed an electrical cable had been pushed through a roughly cut hole in the ceiling into the loft.

The loft hatch was directly over the banisters and he debated trying to climb up there. Realising that he was kidding himself, he called down to Lewin. She came upstairs with Kelly following her.

Davis pointed to the hatch, 'We need to look in there.'

Kelly Collins shouted at Lewin, 'You've got no business going up there, you bastard, that's private.'

'Nothing's private when we have a warrant,' Lewin responded as she used the airing cupboard door to lever herself up onto the banister post and push the loft hatch open.

Lewin grabbed hold of the side of the opening and said to Davis, 'Give me a boost up.'

Once in, the dim light from the open hatch allowed her to see a switch cord hanging a foot or so in front of her. She moved forward to pull it and heard her feet move over something smooth that made a scrunchy noise. She turned the light on and saw that the entire loft area was boarded out and the boards were covered in plastic sheeting. Over against one wall was a rough wooden platform about six feet long and two wide. Underneath the platform were two buckets with a scrubbing brush in one of them.

She walked back to the open hatch and looked down to Kelly. 'What's all this for then Kelly, you been spring cleaning?'

Kelly just said, 'bastards,' under her breath.

Lewin looked around the loft. She noticed little puddles of water on

54

the plastic. 'What have you been doing up here, Kelly? We'll find out, you know.'

Kelly said nothing. Lewin took one more look around and climbed down from the loft. 'I think we'd better get forensics up there.' She nodded towards Kelly, 'You're coming with us.'

Davis had booked Kelly in with the custody sergeant and decided it was time to question her boyfriend. He asked Peterson to collect him from the cells. As Keane sat down Davis inserted the discs into the machine and went through the formalities.

He turned to Keane. 'You are aware that you are still under caution and that you can have a solicitor present if you wish?'

Keane nodded a yes to both questions. Davis said as he sat down, 'Mr Keane has just nodded that he understands.' Turning to Keane he said, 'Try and speak your answers, this is just like radio, not television.'

Keane scowled in response.

'Now, Roy, we've been to your house and found something of interest in the loft. What do you want to tell us about that?'

Keane looked shocked, 'You had no right to search my house.'

Davis was in no mood for any nonsense. 'We had every right, this is a murder inquiry.' Davis didn't give Keane time to respond and asked sharply, 'Why was your loft floor covered in plastic? What was the bench doing there? Why had you washed the floor?'

Keane sat quietly for a few seconds, as if Davis's quick-fire questions needed time to sink in. Like his girlfriend's, his nails were grimy. As Davis looked him up and down while he waited for an answer he noticed a plaster on Keane's arm just above the elbow.

'What's that, Roy? It's not a shaving cut, is it?'

Keane took his time answering. Eventually he said, 'I cut meself.'

'I can see that, how?' Davis's voice had a harder edge to it now and Keane heard it.

'It was in the garden, I was tidying up a bit.'

'Don't lie to me,' Davis snapped, 'your garden is a mess, you haven't tidied it up for years.'

Keane almost whined his answer, 'I started to... honest.'

'You wouldn't know what honest was if it moved in with you, now you answer my first question, what's been going on in your loft.'

'We've got forensics there now, Roy, they'll find out,' Peterson said.

Keane was clearly rattled but still said, 'I'm not sayin' nuffin to you, you'll only twist anything I say and bang me up anyway.'

'If you've done nothing wrong, if you didn't have anything to do with the murder of your boss's daughter, then why not tell us what we want to know?'

Keane maintained a sulky, injured air but said nothing. Davis changed tack. 'Did you leave work early on Wednesday?'

Keane looked mystified. 'No, why should I 'ave?'

'Were you working in the timber shed on Wednesday?' Peterson asked.

'I always work in there, you ask Beresford, he'll tell you.'

'Did anybody see you in there that afternoon? Customers, delivery men, your colleagues?'

'How do I know? Wednesdays are quiet.' Keane looked as if he had been caught doing something he shouldn't have. 'I usually take a nap on top of one of the wood piles if nobody's about.'

'And Beresford doesn't mind?' Davis asked.

'Don't be stupid, he'd 'ave a bloody fit if he knew. There's a beam across the door so I know if anybody comes in. We don't want 'em nicking wood, do we? It wakes me up if anybody comes in the timber shed and I climb down from the wood pile, I just say I was checking the stock.' He looked proud of his little scheme, the knowledge that he was getting one over on a strict boss.

'Why is your loft covered in plastic?' Davis shot at him again.

Keane lowered his head and said nothing. 'We'll find out, Roy, and then we're going to be annoyed with you if you've not told us something you should have.' Davis had lifted himself from his seat and was inches from Keane's face, he spoke quietly so his words wouldn't be clear on the recording. 'If we find you've had anything to do with this murder we'll make sure the word gets round in prison while you're on remand. It might save us the cost of a trial.'

Keane leaned back, trying to edge away from Davis, panic on his face. 'You're fucking mad. I never done nuffin' to that girl, I wouldn't.'

'Well tell us where you were on Wednesday night and why your loft has plastic sheets in it,' Davis thundered.

Keane shook his head, 'I can't, I can't.'

Davis stood up and Keane flinched. Davis ignored him. 'Interview suspended at nineteen forty-three.' He turned to the uniformed constable standing beside the door, 'Put him back in the cell,' and walked away.

Davis had told the others to go home and had arrived home himself just after eight-thirty. He'd been promised that the air support team would check out the dyke tomorrow and he'd continue to question Keane and his girlfriend. The list of Clare Beresford's colleagues had come through as promised and the only two male members of staff were not likely suspects due to their ages. One was seventeen and didn't drive the other was a security guard who couldn't have chased a one-legged shoplifter. He was sixty-eight and, according to Green's notes that had been attached to the printout, weighed nearly twenty stones. Neither man was likely to be Alice's killer and Davis wasn't going to waste any time on them.

Anita had a dinner ready for him and was not in a good mood when he got home. Almost as soon as he'd hung his jacket up she relayed to him what she'd obviously been bottling up for some time.

'We've had a letter from the school about Adam again,' she said with a tear in her eye.

Davis's heart sank. Two years ago their otherwise well behaved son had been involved in bullying younger boys. A stern lecture from Davis and being made to go to the boy's homes and apologise in person to them had stopped it then. What had made him start again?

'What's he done this time?' Davis asked.

'It's that Jardine boy he's mixed up with again. They've been making the younger lads run around the playground until they can't run any more and when they collapse, exhausted, they turn a hose on them.'

Davis almost laughed, as bullying went it was fairly harmless, not that the younger boys would agree to that. At least he, Adam, and his friend weren't assaulting the boys or stealing from them. But it was unacceptable; Davis had always tried to teach Adam to treat people fairly.

'Where is he?'

'I've told him to stay in his room until you come home.' She looked bitterly at him, 'Maybe if you were home more often he wouldn't do things like that.'

Davis had no answer to that. He didn't think it was true, but Anita was obviously looking for someone to blame for Adam's behaviour.

Davis climbed the stairs wondering what he could say to his son to make him understand how wrong it was to bully people. He had to admit that when he was Adam's age he'd thrown his weight around a bit. He didn't think it was wrong then and he was going to have a job convincing Adam it was now. The realisation that you had the ability to make others do as you wanted was a new one to children as they grew up and they wanted to use it. Add in the encouragement of peers and bullying was almost inevitable. Davis also knew how easily the relatively harmless bullying Adam was guilty of could escalate into something worse.

Whether the victims of the bullying felt it was harmless at all he didn't know.

Adam was lying on his bed listening to music when his father entered his bedroom. Sitting up he switched off the stereo.

Davis sat on the chair in the corner of the room and asked the question his own father had asked him on more than one occasion. 'What have you got to say for yourself?'

Adam knew his father was a fair and usually easy-going father. But he also knew that he would not tolerate being lied to. 'It just seemed a lark, we didn't do any real harm.'

'So if we go and see these boys they'll agree it's all just a bit of fun and you can do it whenever you like?' Davis said with a hint of anger in his voice.

Adam was silent for a moment, he knew he'd started off on the wrong tack if he was to avoid trouble. 'We were... we...' He decided honesty would be best. 'We knew we could make them do it, I suppose we got fed up with everyone telling us what to do, so we had a go at them.'

'How did you make them do it? What threat did you use?'

Adam smiled and tried to hide it. 'We said if they didn't we'd soak them with the hose.'

'Which you did anyway.'

'We said they looked hot so we'd help them cool down.' He at least had the decency to look embarrassed now.

Pointless, humiliating for the victim, what did the perpetrators get from it? The root of all bullying, the exercise of power.

'Did you stop to think how those boys would feel? Whether they would feel humiliated in front of their friends? How they would explain their wet clothes when they got home? Did you consider how you would feel if someone did it to you?'

Adam shook his head in silence, knowing there wasn't an answer he could give that might mitigate his bullying.

Davis thought for a minute about how to deal with it. He agreed that little harm had been done and restitution to the lads bullied would be difficult and probably counter-productive. If Adam and his friends felt humiliated in front of their victims they would find subtler ways to extract revenge.

Davis knew the father of the other bully and knew he wouldn't approve of what his son had been doing and would probably agree with his solution. 'You had so much fun with a hose, I think I can find you some more.'

Adam looked worried, what was his father going to suggest? Whatever it was he'd have to go along with it.

'Next Saturday some of the uniformed constables are washing cars for the public to help the National Benevolent Fund. You and your mate can get down there by eight o'clock and help out. I'll have a word with the constable organising it and make sure you're kept busy.'

Adam wasn't happy, the police station was out of the town centre now but there was still a chance that some of his friend's parents might take their cars to be washed. He'd have to pretend he had volunteered for the job, at least he'd preserve some dignity. To his father he said, 'Fair enough, I'll have a word with Alex.'

Davis nodded agreement and went downstairs to get his dinner.

Chapter Eight

Saturday

Davis was in the office by eight o'clock again even though it was Saturday. The air support team had flown along the dyke between Warboys and the Forty Foot drain. They reported that there were several places along the five miles where a small boat could be put in the water. What caught Davis's eye was that two houses backing onto the dyke had small boats in the garden. Davis made a note of the addresses just as Peterson walked in.

'We've got the report from the helicopter crew. They found two boats on the bank of the dyke, let's go and see the owners.'

They drove out of Chatteris south towards Warboys and turned off onto one of the small roads that crisscrossed the fens. This one led to the road that ran from the forty foot drain to Warboys, parallel to the A141 about one and a half miles across the fields. Close as it was in distance it was miles away in other respects. It was the road that led to the track the barn was on. The barn where two days ago Alice Beresford's naked, tortured body had been found. Unlike the A141 this road was narrow and bumpy. Davis hesitated at the junction; one of the houses with a boat in the garden was towards Warboys the other towards the Forty Foot. Davis decided on the one to the south, nearer Warboys, first as that was closer to the barn.

After a couple of miles they came to Morten's Farm. A large farmhouse standing off the road by forty or so feet looked neat and well maintained. Several barns of different ages stood around the house boxing in a farmyard area. A wooden gate kept the outside world away from the yard. Davis parked the car just off the road and walked to the front door. He wasn't sure if he'd find anybody at home, most farmers were busy people working long hours.

To his surprise a knock at the door soon brought a response. An elderly man came to the door and greeted Davis with a friendly, 'Hello.'

Davis showed his warrant card and introduced himself and Peterson. 'We're investigating a suspicious death and want to talk to anyone who is able to put a boat on the water, we've noticed you have a boat at the water's edge.'

The man didn't ask how they had seen the boat from here, although it was at the bottom of a very long garden whose furthest boundary was the dyke.

'The boat - that'll be young John's, he's my grandson. He paddles up and down, just a bit of fun,' said the man looking worried. He was shuffling about, finding it difficult to stand.

Davis asked how old Jonny was.

'He's almost fourteen, he's out at the moment, gone into town with his mum and his sisters. What do you want him for - has he done anything wrong?'

Davis tried to reassure the man, 'John's far too young to be the man we're looking for, is there any other adult male living here?'

'Well, of course, my son, Charles.' Now the man seemed to be agitated. 'Look, Charles works hard, he doesn't go in the boat, it's for the kids.'

Davis tried again to reassure the man. 'We really are just trying to get a picture of who could have been on the water, where can we find your son now?'

'I can't stand up any longer, my hip hurts too much. Charles is out on the tractor, out on the farm.' He pointed to a field further down the road and with that the old man closed the door and hobbled back down the hallway.

Davis and Peterson returned to the car. Peterson asked, 'What do you think?'

Davis took his time answering, scanning the fields looking for the farmer on his tractor. 'It doesn't sound promising to me. We're looking for someone who killed Alice. She screamed loudly, the killer was able to spend some time alone with her and finally dispose of the body.' He turned and looked at the farmhouse, 'I can't see anybody living in that busy house being able to do that.'

Peterson pointed towards a tractor moving slowly across a field almost a quarter of a mile away. 'That's him.' They got in the car and drove further along the road, stopping briefly at the top of a single-track dirt road that led alongside the field the tractor was on. Davis decided he had better go to the farmer rather than hope the farmer came to him.

Davis drove down the track slowly and pulled up at a spot where he expected the tractor to arrive in a few minutes. It was working its way first one way then the other spraying something on the field. It had just turned round at the opposite side of the field and was now making its way back to where the policemen were waiting.

As the tractor got to the edge of the field the farmer turned it off and climbed out of the cab and jumped down. Davis identified himself.

'I know who you are, Dad's just been on the radio saying you're looking for a murderer who used the dyke.' Charles Morten was a big man with broad shoulders and a smile on his face.

'Well, I suppose that's just about what we're asking at the moment. Your father tells us your son John uses the boat, is he the only one to do so?'

'What you really want to ask is, did I kill that poor girl who was on the news and move her in a boat.' His smile was replaced with a grim look, 'I can tell you I didn't, nor did my lad, but I want you to find the bastard that did. I've got two girls of my own and one's the same age as the one you've found.'

Davis looked at the farmer, he'd said to Peterson that the murderer was not likely to be found here and now, having met the only person that otherwise fitted the profile at the farm, he was even more convinced of that.

'Do people use boats on these dykes?' Davis asked him.

'No, they don't really go anywhere you might want to go. Most of them are too choked up with vegetation as well or too narrow to start with. My boy goes on the one at the back of the house sometimes, he tries to fish from it, but there's not much in the water this far along. He mostly punts up and down for the fun of it with his mates. Kids mucking about,' he said, echoing Peterson's words.

There was nothing more to be found out here and Davis thanked the farmer for his time.

Morten was climbing back to his cab and stopped and turned to Davis, 'You catch the bastard and bring him here, I'll spend some of my time on him. He won't do it again, I promise you.' With that he slammed the door of his cab shut and started up the powerful tractor.

A father worried about his daughters, would he take the law into his own hands? Just how far would a parent go to protect their child, Davis knew he would do whatever it took to protect his son. He'd better find this murderer before anybody else did.

They got back in the car and made their way to the other house that the helicopter crew had spotted owned a boat. As they got nearer to the address Peterson said, 'I don't believe it. This is where that lad lived when I was at school, it's where they used to get in the dyke from.'

'Was he a friend of yours?'

'No, not really, he and his friends were a bit younger than me.'

Davis parked the car on the gravel just in front of a rickety gate. None of the care that had been lavished on Morten's farm had been given to this rundown cottage. The wooden windows had paint peeling from the frames and the windows had grubby net curtains keeping prying eyes out. A rusty, battered pickup van was parked just inside the open gate. Davis knocked on the front door. Getting no answer both men walked round the back. They could hear someone working in one of the ramshackle barns across a concrete yard. Peterson pointed to the far corner of the yard; the remains of a dying bonfire smouldered slightly.

They walked over to the barn where the noise was coming from. As they approached the open door a man came out. He was in his early forties and dressed in greasy, muddy overalls. He looked warily at the policemen and said gruffly, 'Who are you?'

Both men held out their warrant cards. Davis said the same to this man as he had the old man at Morten's farm, 'We're investigating a suspicious death and want to speak to anybody who has a boat that can be put on the dyke.'

'What's that got to do with me?' asked the man.

'Our air support unit has identified this property as having a small boat on the bank of the dyke, Mr...?'

The man looked at Davis long enough for Davis to suspect he wasn't going to give his name. Eventually he said, 'Ramsden, George Ramsden.'

'The boat,' Davis said, 'when did it last go on the water?'

Ramsden picked up a metal bracket he'd been hammering at and walked out into the yard towards a tractor. 'I don't see as that's your business,' he said.

'I'm investigating a murder, it's my business if I say it is,' Davis said roughly.

Ramsden dropped the bracket behind the tractor and turned to look at him. Davis couldn't work out if the look was insolent or stupid, but again Ramsden took his time before answering. 'It goes on the water when I can be bothered, sometimes it's a couple of times a month, sometimes it's more.'

'When did you last go on the water and for what purpose?' Davis was getting impatient with Ramsden now and was beginning to suspect the man was hiding something.

'I haven't been on it for days and when I do go on it, I fish, there's always something to catch.'

'That's not what Mr Morten says, his lad reckons there's not much in it.'

Ramsden wouldn't look at Davis as he gave his reply. 'Depends what you're after I suppose.'

'Mr Ramsden, I don't think you're being straight with me and it's straight answers I want.'

Ramsden kicked the tyre of the tractor savagely and said, 'Well I'll give you a straight bloody answer, I didn't kill no girl and I ain't answering no more of your busybody questions. Now I've got work to do so if you're finished I'll get on with it.'

Peterson pointed to the bonfire, 'What are you burning there?'

'Rubbish from that barn,' he said pointing over his shoulder, 'if it's any of your business.'

Davis didn't know what to make of the man, he was definitely uncomfortable answering Davis's questions, but they had no evidence against the man other than access to a boat. They weren't even sure that Alice had been moved to the barn in a boat, it was just a theory at the moment. 'Do you mind if we look at the boat?' he asked Ramsden.

'Do as you like,' Ramsden said with a shrug of his shoulders before going back into the barn.

Davis and Peterson started to walk towards the dyke but Davis made a detour to the bonfire. There was little of anything left but Peterson kicked over the few solid bits of wood still to be found. He bent down and pointed to something under the wood.

'Look,' he said pointing to some scraps of material, 'that looks like a bit of grey fabric, just like Alice's uniform.'

'Right, get these bits away from the heat. Get on your mobile, I want forensics and a search team over here as soon as we can organise a warrant. I'm going to look at that boat.'

Davis quickly walked to the bank of the dyke. The boat was turned upside down and Davis lifted it from one side and easily flipped it onto its almost flat bottom. It was just over six feet long and no more than three feet wide, big enough for two people to sit one behind the other. There were two planks stretching across it, one near the back and one just more than halfway along. Lying on the grass next to the boat was a pole about eight feet long, which Davis assumed was used to punt the boat along, the dykes being too narrow to row using oars. The inside of the boat was still damp so it had probably been used in the last couple of days. Davis gave the boat a careful study and soon found what he'd half expected. Several threads of grey material were caught in various places in the front of the boat.

That was good enough for Davis. He left the boat and returned to the yard, Ramsden was coming out of the barn again with another metal bracket in his hand. As Davis approached he called out, 'Ramsden, I want a word with you.'

Ramsden carried on walking and said over his shoulder, 'I've got nothing to say to you.'

Davis was in no mood to be messed about. He had suspicions that Alice might have been moved on a boat, there were strands of fabric of a type similar to her uniform on the fire and in the boat and this taciturn character was being difficult. He grabbed at Ramsden's collar and said, 'You're under arrest on suspicion of involvement in the death of …'

Before he could say anymore Ramsden had swung the bracket round at Davis's hand trying to knock it away. Davis had seen what was happening and pushed Ramsden hard in the back knocking him off balance. The bracket caught Davis a glancing blow but as Ramsden fell to the floor Davis jumped on him and pinned him down, Ramsden cursing with Davis's full weight on him. He heard Peterson running over.

'Cuff him, quickly.'

Peterson got the cuffs on the struggling, swearing Ramsden. 'You've got nothing on me, you bastards. I ain't done nothing to no school girl.'

Davis had processed the arrest of George Ramsden with the custody sergeant who had jokingly asked if he, Davis, wanted the custody suite extending. 'If I have to arrest everybody in Chatteris to catch the sadist who killed the Beresford girl, I will,' Davis said without rancour, he knew the sergeant had seen his share of violence and was only indulging in the black humour used by those who have to deal with the worst people can do to each other.

He walked up to the CID office to see if any information had come in whilst he was out. He'd let Ramsden stew in a cell for a while. Green was at his desk. 'Morning, sir. The forensic team think that Keane's loft had been used for growing cannabis. There were several waterproof electrical sockets up there. Various markings on the roof trusses suggest equipment had been fixed there, probably heat lamps. They also found some traces of peat, and one small piece of leaf, which is being analysed.'

'So no evidence of any blood, no evidence that a murder could have been committed there?'

'No, sir, although the official report won't be here until Monday.'

Davis didn't need to wait for the official report. Keane wasn't the killer, he'd had his doubts from the beginning. The reason he didn't want to answer questions wasn't because he had something to hide about Alice; he didn't want to have to confess to growing cannabis. If it could be proved that he'd been growing it he'd be prosecuted for that, but they'd let him go for now. To Green he said, 'we've finished with him, give the drugs squad a call, let them have him.'

Davis sat at the computer and checked to see if they had a record on Ramsden. Nothing, he'd never come to the attention of the police before. Peterson had remained at the farm cottage to oversee the search there. Although they only had twenty-four hours to question Ramsden, Davis wanted to read all the case notes before he interviewed the man. It was often the little, easily forgotten details that tripped up a murderer.

He'd just finished going over the notes when Green came back in. 'Sir, we've just had a call from uniform.' Green looked shaken. 'They're at the Beresford's house. The next-door neighbour called them. They're dead, sir.'

66

Chapter Nine

Davis and Green had driven straight to the Beresford's house. The uniformed constable showed them the note he'd found when he entered the house. 'There were two notes, sir. The neighbour came round to see if they needed any shopping doing. There was a note taped to the back door telling whoever saw it not to come in but to call the police.' He pointed to a note on the kitchen table, 'That was there when I opened the door, which wasn't locked. The bodies are upstairs... I... I left them as I found them.'

Davis walked up the stairs. Alan and Clare Beresford were both dressed in pyjamas and were hanging from a rope going up through the loft hatch. Each had a noose around their neck. They had swung one rope over a rafter in the loft and tied a noose at each end. They had climbed onto a stool to place the nooses around their necks and tighten them before kicking the stool away. The drop had been less than a foot, but it was enough. Davis was shocked by the determination it had taken to kill themselves, this was no split second attempt, this had been planned. The drop wasn't enough to break their necks, they had suffocated. They hadn't tied their hands; if they'd had second thoughts as the rope cut off their life's breath they could have grabbed the edge of the loft hatch and hauled themselves up enough to release the rope. As far as Davis could tell neither of them had tried to. 'Has Dr Watson been called yet?' he asked the constable from the top of the stairs.

'Yes, sir, he said he's on his way.'

Davis had picked the note up from the table and read it now.

"We are sorry for causing any of our family and friends added distress. Our darling Alice was our whole reason for living and we cannot continue without her. She was the most beautiful daughter any parents could want and we can only hope that we will meet her again in death. Please do not condemn us for what we have done, every day would be as bleak as today no matter how long we lived."

No mention of the man who had killed Alice, no direct blame attributed to him. In their despair they couldn't link him to Alice's memory, couldn't mention him in their note recalling their beautiful daughter.

Davis looked again at the bodies still hanging from the rope. The constable had left them there, they were dead, of that there was no doubt. Davis wondered if the brutal murder of his only son would drive him to take his own life. Maybe not, but he could understand the depth of their loss, the sense that there was nothing left for them to live for. When they got Alice's murderer in court, as Davis was convinced they would, he would stand trial for one killing, but Davis had no doubt he had caused three deaths.

Greg Watson arrived and Davis heard him clumping up the stairs. He stopped as he saw the bodies. He was a man whose daily job involved dealing with those who had died violently, but what he saw couldn't fail to shock. 'Poor people,' he said as he reached the top of the stairs. He made the usual checks to confirm what was obvious; the Beresford's had ended their lives.

He called to the constable for help, 'Let's get them down from here.' The constable took the weight of Alan Beresford and Davis lifted Clare Beresford slightly, Watson used a sharp knife to cut the rope hanging from the loft hatch, preserving the nooses as they were. Although they all accepted it was a joint suicide nothing would be overlooked.

'They tell me you've got someone for the girl's death, Phil.'

Davis hesitated for a moment longer than he would have done if he were sure he had the right man, sure he had the man responsible for three deaths locked away.

'You're not convinced?' the pathologist asked.

Again Davis hesitated, then he said, 'I've had two men in and I'm not convinced either of them is the right man. I've let one go, he's just a fool, not a murderer.' Davis hesitated again, looked at the bodies then at Watson. 'The other one, I don't know, Greg, you get a feel for people after so long in this job. He's got questions to answer, that's for sure, but our man? I don't think so.'

'So, he's still out there.' Watson turned to the bodies and then back to Davis. 'Do you think we'll have anymore? Bodies I mean.'

'Christ knows!' An explosion of doubt from Davis. Thoughtful for a moment, then, 'Not if I can help it.'

'Don't take it all on yourself, Phil,' Watson said, as he examined the marks around the Beresfords' necks, 'he's left you precious little to go on at the moment. Terrible as it is you need him to be active, to make a mistake, leave us something.' He'd been working as he talked and now closed his bag with a snap. 'It's a bastard, isn't it?'

A rhetorical question, Davis knew that and didn't answer. Watson patted him on the shoulder and said, 'I'll see you later.'

Davis left the Beresfords' house to return to the police station. As he started the car he thought he'd use the journey time, short as it was, to frame a few questions to ask Ramsden. In the ten minutes it took all he could think of was the despair of the Beresfords that was so deep, it made life unbearable. If Ramsden was their man he'd better not muck Davis about.

Davis's first action when he arrived at the station was to ask the sergeant at the desk if Peterson was back yet. 'No, sir,' was the brief reply.

Davis dialled Peterson's mobile and after just two rings Peterson answered. Davis brought him up to date on the Beresfords.

'My God! Have you questioned Ramsden yet, Phil?'

'No, I'm just about to. I'm hoping you've got something for me to go on.'

'There's not a lot to offer. He lives alone, we've got that from his boss. The main house is far enough away that if he'd had Alice in the barn nobody would have heard her.'

'Anything to suggest he did?'

'No. I'm sorry, but at the moment there's nothing. The only thing out of the ordinary is the amount of porn he's got here. Magazines, I've looked for videos and discs but there don't seem to be any. No computer either.'

'What sort of porn, fetishist style?' He had a sudden thought, 'Not kids?'

'No, straightforward boobs and bits. It goes back years and it's the only reading material in the house.'

'I don't think he bought it to read,' Davis said and both men laughed. 'Have forensics finished?'

'Yes, they've taken samples of the fabric in the boat and from the fire. They found some bits of wood in the barn that look like the wood on the bonfire, they've taken a piece of that to see if it matches the splinters on Alice.'

'What do you think?' Davis asked. After years working together Davis trusted Peterson's instincts. Most of the work that led an offender to court was based on solid evidence, but all too often what led a policeman to that evidence was the instinct to know where to look for it in the first place.

'I don't know, the man's clearly obsessed with the naked female, but if that was enough to make a man a murderer then half the men in the world would be killers. He seemed to be on edge. I think he's hiding something, but Alice's murder, probably not.'

'Okay,' Davis said, 'I'll see you later.' He disconnected and decided it was time to question Ramsden.

He arranged for him to be brought to the interview room and made his way there. The room was about fifteen feet square. Being a new built station it had the latest type of recording machines that used discs rather than tape. Davis took two of these from the stock but wouldn't open them until Ramsden was in the room. There would be a constable sitting on a chair near the door, although he would take no part in the questioning. This battle would be between Davis and Ramsden; two men. One trying to hide something, one trying to discover it.

Ramsden was brought in and Davis asked him to sit at the desk. Davis opened the sealed discs and inserted them into the machine. Once they had started he went through the formalities of saying who was in the room and the time and date.

As soon as he had done that he sat down opposite Ramsden and without any preamble asked, 'Did you murder Alice Beresford?'

Ramsden shook his head and looked even more mulish than he had at the farm. 'No, I told you. I never done nothing to anyone.' He leaned back in the chair and wouldn't meet Davis's eyes.

'What were you burning on your bonfire?'

Ramsden shrugged his shoulders, 'Rubbish, bits of wood. I've been clearing out one of the barns.'

'Why, to get rid of the blood?'

'Don't be stupid,' Ramsden said aggressively, 'it was just rubbish.'

Davis didn't react at all to Ramsden outburst. 'What was the fabric on the fire and on the boat?'

'Fabric, what bloody fabric?'

'There were traces of a grey fabric on your bonfire and on your boat. Where did they come from?'

Ramsden was silent for a moment, brooding, wondering. Davis pushed on. 'It looks awfully like the material Alice Beresford's uniform was made from. Did you know that the forensic laboratory can test it

70

and say if it was exactly the same? They'll tell us if you had Alice on your boat.'

Ramsden jumped up from the chair. 'I didn't have her on my boat, I didn't kill her. Why won't you listen?'

'Sit down,' Davis barked. After glaring at Davis, Ramsden did as he was told. 'I'll listen when you start telling me what you've been doing since Tuesday and answering my questions.'

Ramsden sat head in hands groaning. Without looking up he said, 'I never hurt that girl. I don't even know who she was. I was at home all week, I never left the farm. I don't much, I go to the pub on Friday nights. Sometimes I go into town on a Saturday. Mrs Boyle gets me my shopping.'

It was the most Ramsden had said in one go. He was trying to get Davis to believe him and despite Davis's dislike of the man, he was succeeding. 'Who's Mrs Boyle?' Davis asked.

'She's my boss's wife. I don't like shopping. I tell her what I want, she gets it and takes it off my wages.'

'When does she bring it to you?'

'When she's done it.' He stopped again and Davis thought that was all he was going to say. Then, 'Fridays. After lunch time. I stop work at three o'clock on a Friday, she brings it then.'

Davis wanted to get him talking, relaxed as much as that was possible, maybe then a quick question slipped in suddenly might tell him more than badgering Ramsden would.

'What does she do then?'

Ramsden was on the defensive again. 'What do you mean? Why should she do anything else?' His face was puce and his fists were bunched. Had Davis hit a nerve? He remembered the large amounts of porn in the house.

'Is your shopping the only thing your boss's wife does for you? Does she clean for you, or cook, or is it something else? We've found your magazine collection, George, don't tell me you're not interested.'

'I ain't saying anything else. You're fucking twisting what I'm saying,' Ramsden shouted furiously.

Davis thought giving Ramsden some time to consider the benefits of telling the truth might be in order. 'Interview suspended at seventeen-thirteen.' With that Davis left the interview room.

Davis returned to the CID office. Lewin was working at one of the desks and glanced up as Davis walked in. 'Afternoon, sir. I hear you have a suspect in custody.'

Davis slumped down on a chair. 'I don't think so, Gillian.' He rubbed his hands over his face, trying to rub away the tiredness he felt. 'I'm not ruling him out yet, but I don't think it's him.' This admission sent a chill down Davis's spine, it meant, as Watson had said, that the killer was still out there. They had nothing to catch him with yet, no clues, no evidence, no ideas. They needed him to kill again to find him.

Davis had left just after six o'clock. Peterson's search of Ramsden home had produced nothing that implicated him in Alice's murder. Tests would be made on the fabric and the wood but they wouldn't be done over the weekend. The burnt-out BMW had been re-examined and there was nothing there for Davis. It was the first few days after a murder that were important, clues were discovered, people's memories triggered. If too many days passed the murderer could destroy evidence, people would have read about the case and would 'remember' whatever they thought the police wanted them to have seen. But Davis felt now as he had done in other murder cases, rudderless, drifting, waiting for the next break to come along rather than finding it himself. The same old fears set in that he would never catch the man. In all Davis's years as a detective he only had one unsolved murder, yet each time he had the same doubts.

He wondered what Anita had prepared for dinner, since his diagnosis as diabetic Anita had tried to cook more healthily, but all three of them liked a full roast and a sweet on a Sunday. To compensate Saturday night's dinner was usually salad based.

He was right, peppers stuffed with rice and herbs with a leaf salad. If it helped shift some of the weight he was carrying he would put up with it. The dinner was eaten around the table as a family, but none of them had much to say to each other tonight.

After dinner Davis liked to settle down and watch television with his wife and son, although recently Adam had been going out with his friends more and more. Davis worried, as any parent would, what his son might do on these nights out. He was still young and Davis had warned him not to try to get into any of the pubs in town. As he told Adam, the local beat bobbies know your face, know you're my son. It would soon get back to Davis if Adam tried to buy alcohol whilst he was still underage or got up to any other teenage mischief.

Davis flicked through the Sky television guide. As usual he couldn't see much they'd want to watch. He wanted to watch the football but Anita wouldn't put up with that. She'd watch a game show if there was one on. A compromise was needed, they'd watch a Morse, he liked to see how his job was made to look easy on the box. If he spent as much time in the pub as Morse did no crime would be solved in Chatteris.

Anita sat on the sofa as Davis made them both a cup of tea. Saturday night used to mean a beer in front of the telly until he had to control his calorie intake. It also used to mean cuddling up together as they watched when they were first married, but not for more years than he could remember now. Davis sat down beside his wife and they waited for Morse to start.

'Have you got anywhere yet with that girl's death?'

Davis had yet to tell her about the parents killing themselves, he tried not to discuss work over dinner. He told her now and she was as shocked as he'd expected her to be. 'Phil, you've got to catch this man, he's evil.' For once there wasn't a note of censure in her voice, just concern.

'I'm doing what I can. It's so difficult when there's no link between the killer and his victim, well none that we can find. He's left no forensic evidence either.' He pointed to the television, 'That's the problem with all these detective programmes, they've made the crooks aware of how much we can find out about them from microscopic traces they leave behind.'

'And he didn't leave any?'

'No. It's not quite as easy as the telly makes out, but we usually find something. Not this time, not yet.'

'And now the parents are victims too. How awful.'

Davis thought for a moment and said, 'The parents were victims right from the start, he put them through hell.'

There was little more to be said about Davis's case and they watched Morse neatly solve his in the allotted two hours. Davis was just glad that he got more support from his Chief Superintendent than Morse did from his.

Chapter Ten

Sunday

Sunday morning found Davis at his desk by seven o'clock. He had almost eight hours left to question Ramsden; then he had to be charged or released. He had nothing more to use against Ramsden than he did yesterday but Ramsden didn't know that. He'd go in confident, as if he did know something new. If that didn't work he'd have to let the man go.

He asked the custody sergeant to bring Ramsden to the interview room. He said nothing as he inserted fresh discs into the recorder then went through the formalities quickly, reminding Ramsden that he was still under caution.

As soon as that was done he said aggressively, 'The strands of fabric on your fire and your boat match the fabric on Alice Beresford's uniform. How did they get there?'

This wasn't quite true, the tests hadn't come back yet, but Davis hoped if there was anything for Ramsden to confess he might think he'd be better served by coming clean early on.

Ramsden looked confused, 'I never done nothing to that girl. I wouldn't know what she looked like if she walked in here now.'

'Well she's not going to, some bastard killed her,' Davis shouted inches from Ramsden's face. 'Where did those strands of fabric come from, do you keep a girl's uniform at home?'

'No! I don't know what they was from.' Ramsden had his head in his hands. His red eyes and dishevelled appearance suggested he hadn't got much sleep last night. Was it the fear of knowing he'd been caught having committed a dreadful crime or that he might be charged with a crime he had no knowledge of? 'It was in the barn, it was just a pile of rubbish. I was clearing the barn out.'

'So how did some get on the boat?'

Ramsden shrugged, 'I may have used it to wipe my hands when I'd taken a hook out of a fish.'

'And it just happens to be the same material as Alice Beresford's school uniform. A bit of a coincidence isn't it?'

Ramsden wouldn't meet his eyes. 'I don't know. There's all sorts of rags in them barns.'

'When did you last use the boat on the dyke?'

Ramsden didn't answer for a few moments, just sat there thinking. Then reluctantly, 'Wednesday.' The day Alice was murdered. Ramsden knew that, Davis could tell.

'What were you doing, where did you go?'

'I was on the farm all day. In the evening I decided to catch a fish for supper.' The last admission was made quietly, as if whispering it might prevent Davis from hearing it.

Davis was stunned, so Ramsden had been on the dyke after Alice had been murdered. 'And what? You expect I'll believe that you were in a boat, on the dyke on the night a girl is murdered and dumped yards from the water and it was nothing to do with you?'

Ramsden jumped up from his chair wide-eyed and angry, 'I never hurt that child. I didn't touch her, we just got out of there.'

There was a momentary silence in the room, Davis was aware of the faint hum of the recording machine. Ramsden, realising what he'd just said, slumped back down on his chair and rubbed his hands over his face in despair. Davis heard him utter a sound, almost a sob, and then, 'I'm sorry.'

Davis sat down opposite Ramsden and said, quietly this time, almost sympathetically, 'Isn't it time you told me the truth.' He believed more than ever now that Ramsden wasn't the murderer, but he was definitely hiding something, maybe shielding someone. 'Would you like a cup of tea?' he asked.

Ramsden nodded his head but said nothing. Davis looked at the constable at the door who slipped out of the room. Turning back to Ramsden he said, 'Come on, George, it'll be best if you tell me what happened. At the moment I've got enough to hold you on a charge, is it worth it? What have you got to hide that's worth being held on remand in prison? The other prisoners will know who you are, they'll know all about Alice.' It was a threat he had no qualms about using. Those who had harmed children were always at risk in prison, there was no denying it, and the fear of what might happen once in prison, especially if a man wasn't guilty of the crime he was being charged with, could persuade even the most reluctant detainee to talk.

Ramsden looked up for the first time since his outburst. 'It's all gone wrong, I said it would.' He ran his hands through his hair roughly with frustration. 'She was always demanding, always telling me nobody would know. God! I must have been stupid.'

Davis waited; Ramsden was going to tell all now, once he started he wouldn't be able to stop. He would want to make Davis believe he hadn't killed the girl. The constable came back with three cups of tea from a vending machine. It was just about the worst tea Davis had tasted, but he drank it gratefully, the tension he felt had dried his mouth completely.

Ramsden took a sip of his and put the cup down. 'It's my boss's wife.' He stopped almost immediately and looked Davis in the eyes. 'I know you're going to have to check out what I'm telling you. If my boss finds out I'll lose my job and my house.'

Davis said, 'I can't make you any promises, but if I can check your story without your boss finding out, I will.'

Ramsden seemed satisfied with that, he had to be. 'We've been having it off for months now.' He stopped, as if that crude way of describing what was going on might be inappropriate. After a few seconds he carried on, his voice had lost all the bravado he'd had the first time Davis had spoken to him. 'She comes with my shopping and we do it in the house, but as the weather got warmer she wanted to do it outside, sort of, everywhere.' Ramsden's face mirrored some of the fear that this must have caused him. 'She must have been mad and so must I to have agreed. We put the boat in the water and punted along to that barn.' He was rubbing his grubby hands up and down on his knees, agitated, worried.

'Why use the barn?'

'Because nobody never goes there, it's been empty for years. We usually tie up on an old hook that's in the bank, it's a bit steep getting up there but you can't get up it anywhere else. If you're careful you can get the barn door open enough without disturbing nothing too much. We put a blanket on the floor.'

He stopped and took another sip of his tea. Davis took the opportunity to ask a question. 'We found the door with one of the hinges broken, was it already like that?'

Ramsden put his now empty cup down. 'No, it was rusty, but you could move it a bit, you know, enough to get in. That's what worried me that night. The door was leaning a bit, the hinge had been snapped. I said to Sally, that's Mrs Boyle, I said we shouldn't go in there, someone had discovered our place. She wouldn't have it, said nobody was there. I think it added to the fun for her, but it scared me.'

To Davis's surprise Ramsden whispered the next words so quietly he could hardly hear them. 'Sally went in first and as I squeezed in the door I heard her gasp. Well, I'll tell you, for a split second I thought her husband was waiting for us.' He was forcing the words out, reliving the moment of fear. He smashed his fist down hard on the table making Davis jump and the constable at the door, who was still holding his half full tea cup, cursed as he spilt his drink over his shirt. 'I wish to god he had been, least that young girl would have been alive.'

'Alice was there?'

'She was there all right. Dead, with nothing on, poor cow.' He stopped again and looked between the two policemen, Davis sitting just an arm's reach across the table and the constable at the door. 'If she'd been alive I'd have called for help, I would.' A small choke of a sob escaped him, 'Dead... she was dead. I'm not an evil man, Mr Davis. I know I was cheating with another man's wife, and I might not have been everything I should have, but I saw her dead and I've hardly slept a minute since then. She was just a bloody child,' he shouted out and almost immediately looked deflated.

Silence returned to the room for a few brief seconds, then Ramsden carried on, his voice dull. His secret was out now and he was glad. 'I wanted to help her. Sally said, "what help can we give her, she's dead. We've got to get out of here." so we pushed the door back as much as it would go and got back in the boat.

'I haven't seen her since we got back to my house. She didn't come with my shopping this week.'

That triggered a thought in Davis's mind, something had been niggling him for the last few minutes. 'You said you have these illicit meetings with your boss's wife on Fridays after she brings your shopping, how come you were with her Wednesday?'

'The boss was going out to a meeting with the farm owners at Ramsey, he's only the manager. Sally came to the house just after he'd gone and... pestered me until I agreed to go to the barn with her.'

Davis wondered for a moment if somebody had known of Ramsden's little trips to the barn on a Friday night and had planned that the body wouldn't be discovered for a couple of days more than it had. Maybe if they had been able to keep news of the death quiet the murderer might have returned to the barn.

'George, think as carefully as you can, is there anybody who could possibly know about you using that barn?'

Ramsden looked shocked, 'No, no way. Mr Boyle would kill me if he found out. We made sure no one knew.'

Maybe the killer had just been unlucky Davis thought, maybe he had no idea that the barn was used for clandestine meetings.

'One final question George, have you ever seen anyone else using a boat on the dyke?'

'Only Morten's boy, he punts up and down fishing with his mates sometimes, kid's stuff, that's it though.'

Davis got up, 'I've got to check what you've told me. You sit with the constable and he'll write up what you've just told me as a statement. If Mrs Boyle corroborates your story you'll be released.'

Ramsden said nothing, just nodded twice.

Davis went back to the CID office to find Peterson had come in. 'Hello, Phil. I was just looking at Bellamy's map. He's identified most of the unoccupied buildings, we'll have to check them all out I suppose.'

'How many are there?'

'About fifteen so far, but these are the ones we know aren't used at all, mostly industrial plots that are unrented, some isolated barns. There must be dozens of places that get used rarely, if ever, we'll never find them all.'

Davis said, 'That's something to look at during the week. I've just about finished with Ramsden.' Davis brought Peterson up to date on the results from his interview.

'So what are you doing?' Peterson asked.

'I'm going to see Mrs Boyle.' Davis thought for a moment, 'Come with me, you might be able to distract her husband if he's there.'

Davis and Peterson returned to the farm where Ramsden worked. The entrance to the Boyle's home was just yards past the gate to Ramsden's own house. A tarmac track led to a much larger house. The contrast between the two houses was startling. Where Ramsden's house was in need of paint and much care this house was spotlessly clean and well maintained. There was a sign on the gate telling visitors that this was Balecroft Farm, part of the Wright's of Ramsey group.

The journey in Peterson's car had been enlivened by Led Zepplin's 'Dazed and Confused'. Davis wondered if it should apply to him as this case stagnated. If Mrs Boyle backed Ramsden's claims Davis was all out of leads.

Peterson parked the car just behind a large green tractor outside the Boyle's house. Just as they pulled up both the Boyles came from the

78

back of the house, Mr Boyle heading towards the tractor and Mrs Boyle towards an almost new Mazda sports car.

Davis said to Peterson quietly so the Boyles wouldn't hear him, 'You tackle him, find out what you can about Ramsden, anything, just keep him talking.'

As they got out of the car and identified themselves Peterson said to Mr Boyle, 'You're George Ramsden's boss, aren't you?'

Boyle, a tall, thin man of about fifty gave Peterson a friendly look. 'Yes, what's he been up to? Nothing too much I hope, I need him working hard.' He laughed as if to suggest it wouldn't take much to stop his employee working hard.

'It is just routine, because his house backs onto the dyke.'

As Boyle started talking to Peterson Davis moved over to Sally Boyle, 'Mrs Boyle, I need a word with you about George Ramsden.' He could see by the flushed look on her face that she could guess what this word entailed. She was a good-looking woman in her late forties. Her natural blond hair was neatly styled and her clothes showed an attractive figure. Davis was surprised that she should risk her marriage for a rough, slightly grubby character like Ramsden.

They walked towards her car, further away from Peterson and Mr Boyle who were now the other side of the tractor.

'Mrs Boyle, George Ramsden is under arrest in connection with the murder of a young girl. That's mainly due to his using the dyke on the night the girl was killed. He tells me that you and he were together, will you confirm this.'

'No, no I won't,' she said hotly. 'Inspector, I'm not in the habit of meeting my husband's employees, either on or off the dyke.'

Davis could tell she was lying, there was a look of panic in her eyes.

'Mrs Boyle, George Ramsden tells me that you have been meeting him for sex when you bring his shopping for him, you've recently added the barn at Bennett's Lane to the locations for this affair.' Davis thought that harsh reality might produce more results with Sally Boyle than pussyfooting around. 'On Wednesday night he says that you used his boat to go to that barn and discovered a girl's body there. If you can't confirm this I'll have to ask your husband if he did go to a meeting in Ramsey, as George suggests.'

'You bastard,' she swore quietly. 'My husband did go out on Wednesday.'

'Did you go with George Ramsden that night?'

'Yes, all right,' she said angrily, eyes flashing with temper, 'we went to the barn and the girl was dead. I said we should get out as quickly as possible, there was clearly nothing we could do for the girl.'

'You didn't think to call the police?'

'What, and have to tell them what I was doing there? I don't think so,' she said scornfully.

'Well I'm going to have to ask you to come to the station to make a statement.'

'No way, how am I going to hide that from my husband?'

'You were just on your way out, come to the station before you go anywhere else.' Davis could see she was going to refuse. 'If you don't agree to that I'll arrest you now and I'll tell your husband why.'

She moved towards the car giving Davis a look that told him she thought his blackmail despicable. 'I'll be waiting there, it's better than following you out of the yard,' she said looking at him as if he were the last person she'd want to be seen with.

As she drove off Peterson walked back to his car. 'Did you get what you want?' he asked Davis.

'She's confirmed Ramsden's story; she's on her way to the station to make a statement to that effect.' Davis didn't mention how he got her cooperation.

Good as her word, Sally Boyle was waiting in the car park when the detectives returned to the police station. Davis decided to take her statement himself, he still had a couple of questions he wanted to ask her. He led her through the security doors to an interview room.

'Mrs Boyle, I need you to make a statement confirming what you've already told me. Mr Ramsden has made it clear that he doesn't want your husband to find out about your affair and I'm sure you feel the same.'

'Of course I don't want him knowing,' she said, alarmed, 'he'd throw me out.' She fixed her eyes on Davis for a moment, assessing, coming to a decision. 'My husband has virtually no interest in sex,' she laughed, a hollow, humourless laugh, 'he is, however, interested in appearances. If he knew I had a lover and there was a chance that information would get out he'd act quickly to minimise the damage to his reputation.'

'So George fulfilled that need?'

'I could tell he fancied me. I get his shopping for him, it's no trouble and he hates doing it. We agreed that when he first got the job and I used to take it to him as I drove past his door. His eyes would be all over me as I brought the bags in.'

Her eyes had a gleam in them and Davis could tell she was pleased that Ramsden had found her attractive, God alone knew why, Ramsden wasn't exactly hunk material and to be honest Davis had found him to be smelly and grubby.

She continued, 'One day as I put the bags on the table they knocked a box on the floor. Dirty magazines spilt everywhere, George was mortified, he was on the floor scrabbling about trying to pick them up grovelling apologies as he did. I picked one up and flicked through it, there was a picture of a woman 'committing a sex act on a man' as the papers put it.' She laughed and blushed slightly. 'Before I knew I was saying it I said to George, I bet you'd like me to do that to you? He was stunned.'

Davis thought that was probably an understatement. Ramsden's affair with his boss's wife wasn't really his concern, if it provided Ramsden with an alibi that was the end of it as far as Davis was concerned, but Sally Boyle seemed to need to justify herself.

'Do you have any idea how demoralising it is when your spouse shows no interest in you? How deeply it affects your sense of self-esteem? When you make an effort and they'd rather watch television? When you find them attractive but they return nothing, not a scrap of attention?'

They'd both been standing and she sat down on one of the plastic chairs. 'I know George is a bit of a wreck, but do you know what he has that my husband could never match?' Davis shook his head. 'He wanted me. I could see it, almost feel the lust in him, and I wanted that. My husband makes me feel like a wife, inspector, George Ramsden makes me feel like a woman.' The glow on her face, the triumph in her voice said to Davis that her affair with Ramsden would survive this worrying interruption.

He pulled a statement form towards him and said, 'Let's get this done.' Now he had no use for these people he just wanted this diversion out of the way.

Chapter Eleven

He'd let Ramsden go just before twelve, two suspects, two men eliminated. He'd gone back to the CID office and spent some time looking over the information they had gathered so far. He must make the search for the place where Alice was killed the priority on Monday. That was where they were likely to find a link to the killer.

He also needed to find out if there was any link between the killer and the Beresfords. That would be hard as he had no idea who the first was and the latter were dead. It was such an unusual crime; if the murderer had a thing about young girls why subject the parents to the ordeal he had? If the parents had been the intended victims, if the crime was aimed at them, why kill the girl?

Davis knew the answers were out there; it was up to him to find them. He left the station just after three o'clock to go home.

As he opened the front door Adam greeted him, 'Hello, Dad, Peterborough won again.' Both father and son were enthusiastic supporters of the football team from the nearby city. 'If they win next week and City don't they'll be guaranteed promotion.'

'I'll see if I can get tickets for the game, all being well we'll go.' He remembered he'd set his son a punishment for the bullying. 'After you've helped out at the station,' he added.

Adam wasn't sure whether to be pleased about the football or disgruntled about the punishment, instead he settled for, 'And as long as you don't get a case you can't leave.'

Davis wasn't sure if that was Adam hoping his father would be available or getting a dig in because he'd been let down before. He went through to the kitchen where he could smell roast pork being cooked. His favourite. He had rung before he'd left the station to say he was on his way and as he went into the kitchen Anita said without any greeting, 'Half an hour should see it finished. I've boiled the kettle, do you want a cup of tea?'

Davis sat at the little corner table and gratefully accepted his wife's offer. He sat thinking gloomily about the murder, Alice had been dead four days now and he still knew nothing about the man who had done it.

Anita put a cup of tea on the table. 'I take it you aren't getting anywhere?' she asked brusquely.

'Obvious is it?'

'You wouldn't have come home yet if you'd anything to go on.'

'It was bad enough that the girl was killed, but to have the parents…' his voice trailed off as he thought of the torments Alan and Clare Beresford must have suffered.

'Remember their deaths aren't your fault,' Anita said, surprising him, 'they would probably still have killed themselves even if you'd caught the man red-handed.'

'But if he kills again I'll have that worry on my mind, I'll want to wrap the parents in cotton-wool.'

'You're assuming he'll kill a child?'

'Murderers usually stick to a pattern. It wasn't a spur of the moment crime, you know, a sudden killing. He'd planned this. He knew where to take her from, he had the parent's phone number, he knew where to dump the body.' He took a long gulp of the still hot tea. 'This one's probably got his next victim selected, we've just got to wait until he does it and hope to learn something from it.'

'You might get lucky, maybe he'll be seen trying to take her, or she'll fight back.'

'Luck, huh, I'll take as much of that as I can get,' Davis said as his wife put the plates in the bottom of the oven to warm.

Davis had fallen into a welcome sleep soon after going to bed. The three of them had spent the evening watching 'Who Wants To Be A Millionaire?' with each of them trying to guess the answer before the four options appeared on screen. Much to Davis's chagrin his wife had finished a clear winner. He and Adam had urged her to apply to go on the show.

'No way am I making a fool of myself in front of an audience of millions,' she had responded tartly.

Elsewhere in Chatteris a father sat waiting for a phone call.

His seventeen-year-old daughter Abigail had gone out with her new work colleagues for a Sunday evening's entertainment in nearby March. Mr James had agreed to collect her when she called. The group of friends were meant to finish their pizza meal in time for Abigail to be collected at the bus stop by her father, before the others got on the last bus that did the rounds of the town.

Bob James and his wife, Heather, were trying to give their daughter more freedom now she was at work. She was their eldest of three daughters. As a child she had given them many moments of worry as she struggled from one illness to another, before the doctors discovered what should have been an easily diagnosed hole in the heart. At eight she'd had an operation to close the hole and caught a 'superbug'.

Heather had feared for her daughter's life many times but this time she truly thought she would lose her. She had slept by Abigail's bed at the hospital and everyday she had washed with an antiseptic cleaner the bed frame, the bedside locker and anything else her daughter might touch.

At long last her daughter had come home, weak but growing stronger every day. Her sisters were doing things she wanted to, spaced at two year intervals the girls were now seven and five and Abigail's ninth birthday had been a bumper celebration. To Abigail the bouncy castle and McDonald's party made this the best birthday she'd ever had.

She was into her teens before she seemed free of her problems, but they had left her small for her age and particularly close to her mum. Her youngest sister, Poppy, was as tall as Abigail although she was four years younger.

Abigail had left school last summer and had wanted to work with children. A few months later she'd found the job too demanding, too stressful. Her new job had proved ideal, her new colleagues had taken a shine to her straight away and she had begun to blossom into the beautiful young woman her mother always knew her to be.

Tonight was the first time she had gone out with the group from work. These monthly outings, on the first weekend after their monthly pay went into their accounts, had been going on for some time. All the other girls lived in March and used the bus. Abigail had been dropped off by her dad with the exhortation to enjoy herself.

A couple of drinks in 'Trendies' the brightly lit wine bar had been followed by a pizza. Later they rushed from Tony's Pizza restaurant, knowing they had cut it fine. Abigail rummaged in her handbag for her mobile phone as the bus pulled in.

'Go, go, my dad won't want to run you all home. I'll be okay.' Abigail looked down at her phone, 'Damn, no signal, I'll go round the corner. I'll see you all tomorrow.'

The four other girls giggling and happy got on the bus. Sue Hargreaves looked concerned, the eldest of the girls at twenty-four she was also their supervisor at the fashion accessories counter in the department store they worked in. She wasn't happy leaving Abigail alone but knew it would only take Mr James ten minutes to get here.

The bus started off as Abigail walked round the corner waving, a broad smile on her friendly face. She brushed her long blond hair away from her face and glanced down at her phone again to see if the signal had returned but looked back at the road again as a pair of headlights came into view. The car slowed down, oh dear, it was her dad, she must have been a lot later than she thought and he'd come to get her rather than wait for the call. He wouldn't be in a good mood.

The car pulled up and as the interior light came on she realised it wasn't her father. The car was the same model, a Vectra, and the same colour, but the man inside was smaller, neater looking. He got out. 'Are you Abigail James?' Vyvyan asked her.

Relief, he knew her, she couldn't quite place him, although she thought she might have seen him before.

'I work with your dad, his car's broken down, he asked me to collect you. Are you ready?'

She felt uneasy; dad would surely have rung her to tell her about the change of plan. The signal, she remembered the signal was too weak to receive calls. She was shivering with cold. She had worn a new dress tonight and hadn't wanted to spoil its look by wearing a jacket over it.

Vyvyan could see she was unsure, 'Get in the car and phone your dad,' he said.

Abigail hesitated for the merest second and then thought, what the heck, he must be okay, he knew I'd be here and he knew my dad was meant to collect me.

She got in the car and was grateful for the warmth. The man drove off straight away. She checked her phone and noticed the signal strength was good enough to make the call. Just as she started to flick through her contacts for her home number the car stopped. Expecting it to be at the traffic lights she only glanced up. What was this, they were in a little side street, almost totally dark and certainly deserted at this time of night. She looked over at the man to ask what was going on and noticed him taking a white pad from a plastic bag. He was wearing gloves, she hadn't noticed that before. He lunged at her, one hand going behind her head and the other clamping the pad to her face.

The phone eventually rang at the James's house. 'Abigail,' her father said as he noticed her name on the caller id.

'Have you been worried about her?' a voice asked.

Bob James quickly looked at the phone again but a counter showing how long the call was lasting had replaced the caller's name. 'Who is this?' he asked.

'I'm the man who is going to bring you so much grief you'll wish you were dead,' Vyvyan said. The voice was harsh, loud and it scared Bob badly. 'How have you got Abigail's phone? Where is she?'

'Oh, I've got her.' He laughed, 'Your daughter, but I had to collect her from her night out. What kind of father are you?'

Angry now as well as scared Bob shouted down the phone, 'Who the bloody hell are you? I'm going to call the police.'

'You can if you want, but wouldn't you rather see your daughter alive again?' The coldness in the voice scared Bob more than what was said. His daughter's life had been in many hands other than his over the years, but all of those people had wanted her to do well. All of them had wanted nothing but good for her. Bob James knew already that this man was different, there was no compassion at all in the man's voice.

'What do you want?'

'Wouldn't you like to hear from her? Just to make sure she's okay.' Vyvyan was taunting Abigail's father.

'Please, please let me talk to her.' Bob couldn't hide the catch in his voice, couldn't mask the terror he felt.

Abigail was taped, naked, to the same bench Alice had been. Vyvyan held the knife he had used on Alice out of sight as he held the phone to her face. 'Daddy, help...' whatever else she was going to say was cut off by a piercing scream as the knife was driven through her palm.

'Oh no, Bob, I think she's hurt.' Vyvyan's laughter came across to Abigail's father as more torture.

'What are you doing to her, you bastard?' Bob James was panicking, he thought his heart would burst out of his chest, 'She's only a kid, please, please let her go. Don't hurt her, tell me you won't hurt her again.'

'That's entirely up to you, Bob. Will you do as I ask?'

'Anything, tell me, please, I'll do it.' Bob James was begging. He knew it, but he'd grovel if that were what it took to get his precious Abigail back.

He had no idea that what he was going to have to do was the result of his bullying a fellow pupil over twenty years ago. He and his friends had gone skinny-dipping in the dyke. Bob had taken a pink skirt and blouse from his sister's wardrobe and while Vyvyan was swimming Bob had taken Vyvyan's clothes and replaced them with his sister's. When Vyvyan had got out of the water Bob and his friends had refused to give him back his own clothes. Vyvyan wouldn't put on the blouse, but he'd had to walk home in the skirt, it was that or naked. Vyvyan had been laughed at by just about everybody they'd passed. Now it was Vyvyan's turn to laugh.

'We're going to play a little game. I want you to walk through the streets of Peterborough dressed in your wife's clothes.'

Bob wasn't sure he'd heard the man correctly. 'You want me to do what?'

'Are you too stupid to understand?' Vyvyan shouted. 'Or don't you want to do it?' He balanced the knife on the fleshly tip of Abigail's chin and just pushed slightly. She squealed as the blade dug in. 'Do you hear that, Bob? I think little Abbie wants you to do it.'

'I'll do it,' Bob said in a panic, 'I'll do it.' He tried to get his breathing under control. 'When do you want me to do it?'

'Tomorrow, between nine and ten. Is your wife with you?'

'She went to bed earlier, why?'

'Well let's make this more interesting, shall we? You mustn't tell her about me having Abigail. Tell her Abigail phoned and she's staying with a friend. When you get to Peterborough go to Cathedral Square walk around there for a bit, then down one side of Bridge Street and back up the other. Then go to the Queensgate Centre and walk all round that. I'll be watching, Bob, somewhere, I'll be there.'

He laughed enjoying himself. 'Make it good, Bob, a nice dress, high heels. Make sure you take your mobile with you, I might want to have a word with you.'

Vyvyan was enjoying this, the sense of power, making someone do what they ordinarily wouldn't dream of doing. 'I'll tell you what, Bob, you've got a beard, haven't you?'

'Yes,' Bob answered.

'Well, don't you go shaving it off, I want to see it tomorrow.'

Bob said nothing, all Vyvyan could hear was his ragged, frightened breathing. 'Bob, if I don't see you walking around, head held high, I'm going to send you a little package in the post. What would you like? An ear, a toe, one of those tiny little breasts or maybe an eye?'

Bob tried to scream a protesting, 'No', but the phone was dead.

Bob James collapsed onto the settee. Thoughts were racing through his mind so furiously that he didn't know what to do first. Abigail kidnapped? Who the hell would want to do that? He would normally talk over anything, good or bad, with Heather but the man had forbidden that. How the man would know whether he had or not Bob wasn't sure, but he couldn't take the risk.

He decided to go to bed, he'd never sleep, his guts were churning with fear for his daughter, but if Heather woke up he needed her to believe everything was all right. God alone knew how he was going to tell her about his trip to Peterborough, she'd want to go with him. An idea came to him, the washing was in the utility room waiting to be ironed. He slipped a dress from the pile of clothes and selected a pair of open-toed sandals from the rack of shoes. Heather was a little bit overweight so the dress would fit, but she only had size six shoes and he was a ten.

He took the items out to the car and hid them in the boot. How to get away without alerting Heather he'd work out in the morning.

Chapter Twelve

Vyvyan turned to the girl on his bench; he was determined not to rush this one. Careful planning, that was what made him sure he would see his scheme through to the end.

Tonight was an example, he'd been watching the James house on and off and tonight he had seen Bob take his daughter to March. He hadn't wanted to get too close to the girls so hadn't gone into the nightclub. He'd seen them go into Tony's though and followed them in. He'd ordered a pizza to take out and while he waited overheard one of the girls ask Abigail what time her dad was collecting her. After that it was just luck that they'd had to leave her on her own. If they hadn't, there'd have been another night.

He looked up and down her naked body. She didn't turn him on, that wasn't why he had kidnapped her, stripped her. It was to make her feel vulnerable. He wanted her to be scared of him. Power. That's what he wanted, she was scared of him, her father was scared of what he'd do to her. God! It was better than sex. But, he had to keep reminding himself that it was the father, not his daughter, who was to suffer the most. That was the whole point of this little game.

He'd just prepare the next part of Bob's torture and then he'd get some sleep.

He had already checked Abigail's phone. It would record a video, with sound, and he could then send that to Bob's phone. Abigail had told him that her father's phone would play it.

He had a device that was meant to hold a mobile on a car dashboard. Secured to a strap around his chest it was would show whatever he did without any risk of identifying himself.

He moved to the bench Abigail was taped to. There was blood beginning to dry out where he had pierced her hand. Her chin had trails of blood running down it and her face was tear stained. Her eyes though, terrified. Brilliant, he loved this. He started the video on the phone and turned first to Abigail's face capturing the terror it revealed. He grabbed her hand and forced his thumb through the hole the blade had made. The scream she let out almost hurt Vyvyan's ears.

He pulled his thumb back and dropped the hand, the scream subsided to a pained whimper. He picked up the knife with one hand and grabbed a handful of blond hair with the other. Hacking away he reduced her lovely, well-maintained locks to an uneven stubble. Abigail kept her eyes tightly shut throughout the ordeal.

He slowly trailed the tip of the knife up and down her thin body, down her face, between her small breasts, across her bellybutton and down to her groin. 'Where next?' he asked as she trembled. He brought the knife back along her front and down her arm to the uninjured hand.

'Please, please, my dad will do anything you want... please don't do any more...' her terrified, childlike voice rose to a scream as he slowly pushed the knife into the middle of her palm.

Monday

Bob James had drifted off. He woke in a panic, remembering immediately that his beautiful, precious daughter was in danger. How could he have gone to sleep? He quickly looked at the clock, six-fifty-three. Heather, always a heavy sleeper, was lying silently beside him. He slipped out of bed and picked his clothes from the chair he had put them on last night. He checked Abigail's bedroom in case he'd had some dreadful nightmare and she was tucked up fast asleep. The bed was empty, no dream could have been as devastating as last night's phone call. Abigail's life depended on him, humiliating or not he would have to do what that sick bastard had ordered.

Down stairs he wrote a brief note to Heather, telling her that Abigail had stayed with a friend and he'd had to go to work very early. He got in the car and drove steadily to Peterborough, it wouldn't do to get stopped for speeding or worse, crash the car and not be able to fulfil his task.

By the time he had parked the car in the Queensgate car park it was just gone eight o'clock. He had an hour to kill. Bloody hell! Even thinking that word made him feel sick. Please, God, let Abigail be okay.

Not wanting to risk his neighbours seeing him dressed in women's clothes he had wrapped Heather's dress and sandals in a bag and he carried them in that now. He wasn't sure where he could change. McDonald's were open; he'd use their toilets. Realising that, despite all the turmoil he felt, he was hungry he decided to go there now and have breakfast first.

Even at this early hour there was a queue of customers, early starters who'd skipped breakfast at home for the convenience of McDonald's fast food. When it was his turn he ordered a breakfast roll and coffee. Sitting near the window he slowly ate the roll and drank the coffee. As he did so he wondered how this was happening to his family. He'd done no wrong to anybody. He worked hard as a transport manager for a large haulage company in Ely. He and Heather had a small circle of friends and his daughters were all decent children. Okay, he'd been a bit of a lad at school, but not got into any real trouble. That was well over twenty years ago now. What could he, or any other member of his family, have done to drive some nutter to kidnap and hurt his daughter? Why, oh why was somebody tormenting him?

He had no answer to that question. He considered again calling the police, but without any clues to follow he'd just be putting Abigail's life at risk. If that man kept his word and let her go after humiliating him Bob considered walking round Peterborough dressed as a woman a small price to pay for his daughter's return.

He looked at his watch again, ten minutes to nine, if he was going to be walking around in Heather's dress by nine he'd better get moving. With a thudding sense of impending doom he picked up the carrier bag from the floor and carried it to the toilet.

As he walked up the stairs to the toilet his insides were twisting with dread. As he entered the toilets he rushed for a cubicle and, without time to shut the door, threw up in the toilet pan. He went to one of the sinks and washed his face.

Get a grip! He had to get a grip. Fix an image of Abigail in his mind. That's what he must do. He would have walked over hot coals for her. Jumped off the town bridge. How hard could it be to walk through town dressed as a woman? It wasn't going to kill him. He groaned, not that word again.

He returned to the cubicle and locked the door. There wasn't much room but he was able to slip his shoes, jumper, shirt and trousers off. He folded them and put them on the closed toilet lid. He took the dress from the bag and pulled it on over his head. It was a struggle to get it pulled down smoothly. The back was tight and it was a good job it was a sleeveless dress. Although Heather obviously had a much rounder figure than he did, his shoulders were broader. He put his own clothes in the carrier bag and opened the cubicle door. A smart looking man in his early thirties was just coming in the door, he took one look at Bob and stopped. His eyes raked up and down Bob and without turning round he slowly backed out of the door. Bob couldn't afford to let it stop him; he looked at himself in the mirror over the sink.

He looked ridiculous. There was no way he could fill the dress the way it was meant to be filled. Heather had a large bust and the front of the dress looked like a deflated balloon. Then there was the beard, it wasn't a long one, but it was undisputedly a beard. There was nothing he could do about it, he glanced at his watch. Shit, it was one minute past nine. He quickly put the sandals on and walked out of the toilets and down the stairs.

Nobody paid him any attention to start with but as he got to the door two teenage girls were coming in. They looked at him and stopped talking, their mouths hanging open. They quickly looked away and as he walked out into the open air he could hear their laughter ringing out.

He turned left and walked towards the Cathedral. Almost everyone who passed stared at him, but nobody said a word. He remembered what the man had said: "I want to see your head held up high." He thought of Abigail, lifted his head high and strode on.

He had reached the top of Bridge Street, as he turned right to walk down it he passed a burger stall with several tables arranged in the open air. Sitting at one of the tables were two men who looked like they lived on the streets. One almost choked on his chips as Bob walked past. Nudging his mate he pointed at Bob and shouted, 'Oy, look at that fuckin' weirdo.' To Bob he called out, 'I 'ope you're not chargin', you're fuckin' ugly.' Both men laughed loudly.

He carried on. He had never felt so humiliated in his life. This was worse than any nightmare. What if any of his friends, or worse, family, were to see him? His feet hurt in Heather's sandals because his toes were sticking out the front and the dress was tight round his legs making walking an uncomfortable experience.

Passing a coffee shop he caught sight of his reflection in the mirrored windows. He could almost have cried in shame, he looked worse than any grotesque parody of a transvestite would have done. A woman sitting at a table the other side of the glass stared at him, her coffee cup half way to her lips. A look of revulsion spread over her face and she glared at Bob. He turned his head to the front and determined to complete his task as quickly as possible.

As he passed the bookshop on the way back towards the Queensgate centre a small group of school age boys were walking along. He tried not to catch up with them but they stopped to look at a window display, one of them saw his reflection. Swinging round to get a better look he said to his friends, 'What the bloody hell is that?'

Suddenly they were all jeering, laughing, pointing. Bob was

desperate to run away, to escape down some side street, but what if the sadistic bastard who had his daughter was watching? He concentrated on images of Abigail laughing, happy, and carried on walking, trying to block out the raucous taunting of the boys.

He had been walking for some fifteen minutes and was now about to enter the Queensgate Centre. He had been looking for anybody who might have been watching him especially, but seen nothing suggesting anybody was, nobody whose face he recognised, just the mocking stares of passers by.

As he pushed the door open to go into Queensgate his phone rang. He had it in his hand as there were no pockets on the dress. He saw it was Abigail's name on the display and knew it would be his tormentor.

'Hello, Bob, how are you?'

'Is Abigail all right?' Bob asked immediately.

'She didn't sleep too well last night, she's cut up about something.' Vyvyan laughed loudly at his own joke.

'You bastard,' Bob swore.

'Tut, tut, tut, Bobby. That's not a very nice thing to call the man who's trying his best to look after your daughter.'

Bob was angry with himself, 'I'm sorry, I apologise. I've done what you told me to.'

'I know, you look delectable.' Vyvyan laughed again, this was such a thrill, he gloried in his power to make this man do as he told him.

Bob was tucked into a corner just inside the doorway facing the wall hoping that nobody would notice him.

'You do seem to be a bit shy at the moment though.'

Bob swung round, the man could see him. He scanned the faces around him. Some of them looked startled as the bearded man in a dress looked wildly from left to right. But he couldn't see anybody using a phone.

'You can't see me, Bob, can you. You wouldn't recognise me if you did, would you?'

The question tantalised Bob, did he know this sick bastard. He kept scanning the faces around him and looked through the glass doors to see if he recognised anybody outside.

'I've got a good idea, Bob, I can see you looking around, I'll send you something to watch, a little video. Hang up now and wait for it.' The phone went dead.

He held the phone staring at the screen as if it were already showing him something. The minute or so wait dragged on for an eternity, the seconds counted down by the thudding pulse of the blood pumping through his heart as if it were trying to burst out. He jumped when the phone beeped to say it had received a message. He pressed to open it. After a few seconds as the video loaded he saw his darling daughter, naked, scared and bloodied. He slumped to the floor as her screams echoed from the phone.

A small crowd had gathered around him when Bob finally looked up, their startled and angry faces just a blur to Bob. Some of the legs were moving apart and he saw a pair of shiny black shoes approach him. A policeman! He mustn't tell them about Abigail.

He climbed to his feet and picked up the bag holding his clothes. Get away, he must get away, outside, continue his walk, let his tormentor see that he wasn't reporting him.

'Just a moment, sir, I'd like a word with you.' The police officer gently held his arm. 'Can I see that phone?' Before Bob could respond the officer had taken it gently from his hand and pressed play.

Bob hung his head as he heard the sounds from the phone. Abigail's screams once again echoed around the shopping centre. Suddenly the sound stopped, he looked up at the policeman whose face had paled. He held Bob's arm more firmly, 'I think you'd better come with me.'

'No, you don't understand.'

'Then you can explain at the station.' Anything else Bob said was ignored as the policeman talked into his radio.

People had moved in and out of the crowd, as the policeman steered Bob towards the door one voice shouted out, 'Pervert.' Others joined in the jeering, a gob of spit landed on the front of the dress he was wearing and the policeman called out, 'Enough, go about your business.'

Unsure of just how guilty of anything Bob might or might not have been the crowd reluctantly dispersed. Bob was led past the Guild Hall towards the road. Just as they reached the roadside a police Transit van roared up.

Chapter Thirteen

Vyvyan had watched Bob being taken away. That was the end of the fun with this one, or maybe not. He took Abigail's phone from his pocket and rang her home number. After several rings her mother answered. 'Abs, where are you?'

Vyvyan said quietly, 'I know where she is, and where Bobby is.'

A silence of a few seconds was broken by Heather's shocked voice, 'Who is this, where's my daughter?'

'You're not interested in Bobby then?'

'Who are you?'

Vyvyan could hear the mounting panic in her voice. 'I'm the man who's going to ruin the rest of your life, and it's all Bobby's fault.' he said as he hung up. He'd said that on the spur of the moment but he was pleased, it would add to Bob James's nightmare having to try to explain that.

As Vyvyan walked back to his car he took the back off the phone and wiped it before dropping in a bin as he passed. He did the same with the battery a little bit further on. He took the sim card out and snapped it in half before dropping it down a drain cover in the road. The rest of the phone went in another bin.

Davis had started early again. He was looking at Bellamy's map showing the unoccupied properties around Chatteris. The first thing he'd done was fill the kettle up and switch it on. Just as it boiled Green and Lewin came in together.

'Three cups of Columbian magic?' Green asked.

Davis and Lewin both nodded a thanks. Just as Green had made the drinks Peterson arrived. 'Excellent timing, thanks, Pat,' he said to Green who pulled another cup from the shelf.

'Sir,' he said as a greeting to Davis. Peterson and Davis had known each other many years and often used each other's first names in the office. But first thing in the morning Peterson always called him Sir as a mark of respect for his rank.

'Had a call from Bellamy, Phil, his wife's gone into labour, he won't be in.'

'Damn,' Davis swore, 'I want all the bodies we can get today.' He put his cup down and spoke to the three officers he had at his disposal. 'As you know we've released both the men we were holding. One was trying to hide a cannabis farm rather than a murder, the other has what appears to be a good alibi.

'Today I want all these premises checked out.' He indicated the map behind him. 'We'll work in pairs, Green, you come with me. We're looking for any signs that Alice Beresford was murdered in one of these premises. Particularly a rough wooden bench or, obviously, signs of blood.'

'I thought we were going to cover all isolated properties?' Green asked.

'I would like to but our resources won't run to that at the moment,' Davis replied.

He turned to Lewin and said, 'Make up two lists splitting those places between us, I'm going to have a word with the chief.'

Fifteen minutes later Davis was back. 'I ought to climb those stairs more often, I'm sure the exercise does me good.'

His three subordinates looked at his still overweight frame and said nothing.

'Right, Lewin, have you got our lists?'

'Yes, sir.' She handed one to Davis.

Davis looked at the clock, almost eight, 'Let's go then, Patrick. Keep in touch, if you think you find what we're looking for ring me straight away,' he said somewhat unnecessarily to Peterson.

Davis and Green headed out in Davis's car. Davis had his choice of music on, a fan of classical music, he had Richard Edlinger's 'Best of Baroque music' in his cd player at the moment. He could tell Green thought little of it.

Green held their list and had marked the buildings off in order of closeness. Davis was painfully aware that there must be plenty more unused buildings spread over the fenland farming area, but they had to start somewhere unless some other line of enquiry came in.

The first place to visit was little more than a mile outside Chatteris, as they approached it Green pointed to a dilapidated brick built barn. Davis parked the car just off the road and they both got out. The doors were on the other side of the barn. A four-foot high fence ran around the large field the barn was on. The gate was some distance away and Davis decided to follow Green's example and climb over the fence. He lifted one leg up to the first crossbar and hoisted himself up. He swung the other leg up and over the fence. Just as he was about to bring the first leg over Green came round from the far side of the barn.

'He's not been here, sir, there's a ruddy great lock on the door and it's all rusted up. It's not been opened in years.'

Davis hesitated, should he continue getting over the fence just to prove he could or should he let Green feel smug for being younger and fitter than his boss. Common sense won the day and he clambered back over to the road side.

As they sat back in the car Green said, 'This barn is on Tenderings Farm, the next one is Abbot and Sons at Sutton.'

Davis started the car and they drove on.

Two barns and three unoccupied industrial units later, and nothing to show for it, they had two more on their list. The sun had been trying its best today and they were both getting hot despite Davis turning on the air-conditioning. Green had stepped in a cowpat and no amount of rubbing his shoe on the grass could remove the overpowering smell in the car. Being a detective inspector was feeling distinctly unglamorous at the moment, Davis thought.

Davis looked at the digital display on the dashboard, nearly ten o'clock. Their list had taken them through Haddenham after Sutton, then Witchford and they were now on the A10 heading for Welney. Just before they were to turn off on to the A1101 there was a lay-by with a snack bar in it. Davis steered the car to a halt behind a lorry and switched off the engine. He fished a couple of pound coins out of his pocket and said to Green, 'A coffee to keep us going, you get them, I'll see how the others are doing.'

Green returned to the car. 'Have they had any luck, sir?'

'No, same as us, although Lewin got chased by a bull.' Both men laughed at the thought of that. As they sipped their coffee Green said, 'It's the pointlessness of what Beresford was told to do that I can't understand. What the hell did the murderer get out of it?'

'Who knows, power maybe, you know, he's made Beresford do something ridiculous just because he's been told to.' As Davis said that a thought niggled at the back of his mind but before he could work out what it was his mobile rang.

He answered it and all Green heard was Davis saying, 'When?' then, 'where?' ending with, 'we're on our way, get in touch with Peterson, tell him to meet us there.'

He put the phone back in its place and started the engine. 'Blast it, we need to be in Peterborough in a hurry and there's no quick route.' He quickly worked out in his mind the fastest way to the city, these fen roads were cursed with being narrow as well as uneven, he'd better stick to the A roads. Up to Denver and then via Wisbech, a long route but probably the fastest. He got a blue light from the glove box and plugged it into the cigarette lighter. He wound down the window and put it on the roof of the car, powerful magnets in the base would ensure it stayed there.

As they started off Davis said to Green, 'We've had a report that a man has been found dressed as a woman walking through the city. He had a phone with a video on it of a girl being tortured as she was taped to a bench. They've taken him to the city centre police station.'

'Alice?' Green asked.

'That's what we don't know. Hopefully, we'll be able to find that out when we get to Peterborough.' Grimly he added, 'I hope it is, if not there's another girl in trouble.'

Davis pulled into the police station car park fifty minutes after the call. Peterson's car was already there; they had been working to the west of Chatteris and had not had so far to drive. He asked for Inspector Bridges at reception and was pointed in the right direction.

Davis knew Bridges, close to retirement, Detective Inspector Bridges was a thorough, decent officer whose many years service had not diminished his humanity, despite the horrors he'd seen.

As they walked through to the CID offices Bridges came to the door to meet them. He was a big man, taller than Peterson's six foot-four and broad shouldered. He held out a huge hand, 'Phil, how are you.'

'I've been happier, Bill. This is DC Green; you've met my sergeant and DC Lewin already I see.'

'Yes, come and see this video. The techie boys have put it on the computer while you were on your way here.' He led them to an unusually tidy desk and sat down. Clicking an icon on the monitor he started the video.

It lasted little more than two minutes. The four detectives watched it in total silence. When it had finished Davis said, 'My God.'

'If you have one,' Bridges said, 'you'd better appeal to him now.' He shook his head, 'That poor lass needs divine intervention if anybody ever did.'

Davis said, 'That's not Alice Beresford.' He turned to Peterson,

'Get on to Chatteris, we'll assume he's local still, see if anybody's reported her missing.'

He turned to Bridges, 'Do we know who the man you have is?'

'One Robert James, The Brambles, London Road, Chatteris.'

'We need to have a word with him as quickly as possible,' Davis said, 'if Alice's case is anything to go by that poor chap is the girl's father.'

Bridges got off his seat, 'Come on then, the man's downstairs.' Bridges led them to the custody suite. 'He's not under arrest, we just had no where else suitable for him.'

Davis's phone rang before he could get up. He listened to the caller and hung up.

'That was Crawford, Mrs James has had a call from a man claiming he's holding her daughter, I think he called just to taunt her. They've got a constable going there now, she's hysterical with worry. Peterson, you and Lewin head back now, go straight to the James's. We'll have a word with him and bring him home.'

Davis waited whilst Bridges unlocked the door and saw that Bob James had at least been able to change into his own clothes. He was clearly distressed and Davis decided that straight talking would produce the quickest results.

'I'm Detective Inspector Davis. I'm investigating the death of Alice Beresford, I believe the man who killed her has your daughter. It was your daughter in the video, wasn't it?'

James's haggard face lifted up to look at Davis. 'He's going to chop her up. You stopped me, he told me what to do, he said he'd let her go…he promised…' Bob James could say no more as he fought back tears.

'Mr James, I don't think he intends to let her go. We need to find him as soon as possible. Is there anything you can think of that might tell us who this man is?'

'I've no bloody idea,' he said desperately, 'do you think if I knew who he was I'd have walked round Peterborough dressed like that? If I'd known who the hell he was I'd have gone round there and killed the bastard.'

'Do you have any connection with Mr or Mrs Beresford?'

'No, I've never heard of them.'

Davis could see James thought these questions were a waste of precious time, but at the moment he was no nearer discovering who the murderer was than he had been when Alice's body had been discovered.

'Do you know if your daughter knew Alice Beresford?'

'I have no bloody idea. Can't we get out there and look for her, for Christ's sake,' James shouted.

'Where, Mr James, where,' Davis asked, a little defensively. 'If I knew where to look for your daughter, believe me, I'd be there. But we don't know who this man is.'

James held his head in his hands, 'I don't know, I don't know,' he whispered.

'I think we'd better take you home, Mr James.'

Bob James let out a groan, 'She doesn't know yet. Heather doesn't know. Oh God, how am I going to tell her.'

'I'm sorry, she does. She's had a call from the man holding your daughter.'

'What did he say,' Bob asked with a surge of hope.

'I'm sorry, Mr James,' Davis said gently, 'he only called to taunt her.'

'It'll kill her, she worships our Abigail,' Bob said wretchedly.

'Let's go,' Davis said as he guided Bob out of the office to the car.

Vyvyan considered whether he should let Abigail live. His campaign wasn't really against the children; they were just the most effective weapons he could use. He had let her see him though, she'd have to die. Let her parents suffer, like he'd suffered for years. Like the Beresfords would he thought, not knowing they were beyond suffering.

As he drove back home he thought he might be able to make use of her death. If he recorded it he might use that to good effect with one of his next victims. He'd have to think about it, after all, nobody could stop him, he had all the power.

Davis had struggled to make any sense from the killing of Alice and the kidnapping of Abigail. In each case the object seemed to have been to cause the parents as much anguish as possible before revealing their child had been murdered. They hadn't found Abigail yet, dead or alive, and Davis had finally been given a few extra men drafted in from other local areas.

These men had been checking out every family member of both the Beresford's and the James's to see if there was any connection. Davis had considered checking every barn and shed on every farm in the area, but he would have needed ten times the resources he had for that, and they weren't positive the crimes had been committed in that kind of place. It just needed to be somewhere remote, Abigail's screams had been horrifically loud. The problem was the fens were dotted with remote farms, houses, barns and sheds.

He had driven to March after reuniting the James's so that he could interview Abigail's friends. He parked in Hereward Department store's car park and entered the store. Just inside the door was the customer service desk.

The staff here already knew something had happened to Abigail. When she hadn't arrived for work this morning a worried Sue Hargreaves had called her home. The telephone had been answered by a police constable, who, having found out why she was calling, had told her a detective inspector would come to see her.

Davis identified himself and asked to speak to Miss Hargreaves. He was shown to a small staff room where a distraught Sue was waiting for him in tears.

'I knew we shouldn't have left her. What's happened? Has she been hurt?'

'Miss Hargreaves, I need to know what happened last night. I understand you and some friends went out in March town centre.'

Sue nodded. 'Yes, her dad dropped her off outside Trendies and we stayed there for a while. Then we had a pizza at Tony's. We didn't notice the time until too late. We were all catching the bus home, everybody except Abigail, she lives in Chatteris and the bus doesn't go there that late on a Sunday. Her dad was going to pick her up.' She was gabbling and started crying again. 'If we'd remembered earlier we could have waited for her dad to arrive.'

'But you didn't?' Davis asked. 'Had she called her dad before you left?'

'No, she couldn't get a signal on her phone, she was just walking round the corner into Darwin Road as we got on the bus.'

'Did you see anybody else there at all?'

Sue Hargreaves was screwing up a now damp hankie in her hands, she used it to dab her eyes again. 'No. She waved as she went round the corner, she was smiling, she looked really happy.' More loud tears followed and Davis had trouble making out what she said next.

'I'm sorry, I didn't hear that.'

Sue looked up at him, her red eyes brimming with more tears,

'Please tell me, she's not dead is she?'

Davis couldn't give her an answer to that. All he said was, 'Not if we can help it.'

A brief word with the other girls who had been out with Abigail left Davis with the disappointment of learning nothing new. None of the girls had seen anybody or noticed anything unusual.

Chapter Fourteen

Davis faced Malloy over the latter's desk. 'We need those bodies on the ground, we might still find the girl alive.'

Malloy tried not to get riled as Davis's voice rose. 'I'm sorry Phil. My orders are crystal clear, those protesters must be contained.'

'Because of some bloody politician?'

'It's no good you getting high and mighty with me,' Malloy said, wishing he didn't have to defend himself to Davis. 'The Home Secretary has staked his reputation on getting that place opened and he wants to be there without some rent-a-mob protesters getting all his air time.'

'We've got one bloody girl dead and another one missing. I couldn't give a damn about the Home Secretary.'

'The Chief Constable does,' Malloy shouted and instantly wished he hadn't. Davis was a good cop and a good friend. He was as angry at the demands of the Chief Constable as Davis was. But it would be his own job on the line, not Davis's, if those protesters ruined the opening ceremony.

'Look, I'm sorry,' Malloy said. 'I'll see the Chief tomorrow and try to reason with him, but you know as well as I do that he's looking for a Knighthood, and the bastard won't let some real police work get in the way of that.'

Davis knew it wasn't Malloy's fault, he'd seen the internal memo that the Chief Constable had sent out to his senior staff. Little short of an order from the Queen would get Davis his extra men until the Home Secretary had visited the research animal breeding plant.

Back at the office the team were quietly sifting through the information that they had amassed during the investigation into Alice's murder looking for any link between Alice's family and that of Abigail's.

Lewin said, 'They didn't even go to the same school. Alice went to St Andrews School and Abigail went to Fenland Comprehensive.'

'It's going to be difficult proving there was a link between them because the Beresfords are dead. We can't check anything with them,' Green said.

'Well how about we check the things we can verify with other people?' Peterson suggested.

The CID office was much larger than the one they'd had in the old police station. Each of the three constables and Peterson had a desk of their own. In one corner there was a small kitchen sink and a worktop that gave enough room to hold tea and coffee making facilities. Davis had an office to himself next door but preferred to use the main team office when possible. He had been sitting at Bellamy's desk in his absence.

He got up and walked to the wall that held the wipe clean boards. He drew a line down the middle of the only clean one and headed each side of the line with the families' names. He said, 'I want a list of similarities, parents or children, by the end of today. I want checks made on job history, church attendance, schools, clubs, you name it, I want to know about it.'

'It could still be random, no link between the families,' Green said.

'I don't think so,' Davis replied. 'There was a certain amount of planning. He knew Alice's mum worked at a shop, probably knew which one. He knew her name. He knew where to find Abigail it would seem.' He sat thinking for a moment. 'I want a list of all known sex offenders, and any kidnappers in our area.'

He looked across the white boards. Every piece of information they had gathered since Thursday was written up there. Still frustrated from his meeting with Malloy he brought his fist down on the desk. 'We're meant to be bloody detectives. The postman could have told us almost all of that.'

To the others he said, 'Let's get going, this time tomorrow I want to know everything about the Beresford and James's lives. Just remember one thing, although I'm certain he'll kill Abigail, she may not be dead yet, we might save her if we can find this bastard.'

Vyvyan had some shopping to do on the way home, ordinary stuff, food, beer and a newspaper. He thought he might as well enjoy the late spring sun and stopped at the Drove Inn at Whittlesey for lunch. As he ate his ploughman's lunch at a wooden table in the pretty garden he tried to work out what to do about Abigail. At the moment she was still alive and he was trying to decide whether to persecute her parents a little bit more or use her death to help him with one of his next victims.

By the time he'd finished his lunch he'd made his mind up. Victim number four was to be the big one. Oh yes, he had plans for two more young ladies. Funnily, he hadn't intended it to be all girls when he'd first had the idea. It just so happened that each of the four target families had daughters of the right age.

He drove back to the remote house he was renting about a mile outside Chatteris. It had been two labourers' cottages when farms had labourers. Now they had been knocked into one. There was a brick built barn behind the house that had housed livestock at some time. Vyvyan had laid a sheet of thick plywood over two wooden bay dividers to form a sturdy bench about three feet high.

He had been planning this campaign for some time. Over twenty years really. Well, not planning it all that time, just thinking about it. It was only in the last year that he'd really been working out how to achieve what he wanted.

Since Andrew died. His only real love. It had taken him until his mid-twenties to accept he was gay. The bullying he had endured at school because of his name had made him fight hard to deny what he now knew couldn't be denied.

He had dated only one man prior to Andrew and he'd known all along he didn't love Stuart. He'd been finding his feet, so to speak, finding out about being gay. He hadn't had a girlfriend, ever. He'd never wanted one.

With Stuart he'd gone for candle-lit dinners, long weekend breaks and, once, taken him home to his mother.

She had taken the news that her only child was gay very badly. Throughout Stuart's visit she had insisted on steering the conversation away from any talk of their friendship. When, after a meal eaten almost in silence, Stuart had gone home Mrs Wilde had said to her son, 'I think it's time you found yourself a place of your own.'

She'd never referred to Vyvyan's private life again and never visited when he had found a small flat to rent.

Vyvyan's relationship with Stuart had ended soon after that visit. Within a year Vyvyan had met Andrew and fallen in love.

Vyvyan had read a lot about love, seen it portrayed on television, but he'd never felt it before, not like this.

Andrew was a year younger than him but so much more experienced in life. He had a joy about him, a happiness that was infectious. And Vyvyan was happy with him. For the first time in his life he was happy.

They had bought a small cottage together and furnished it as they could afford to. Andrew's mother was just as upset as Vyvyan's about her son's choice of partner. "That queer" she called Vyvyan, forgetting her own son was gay.

For sixteen years they had enjoyed each other's company and had been content. And then Andrew had a heart attack, not a fatal one, not the first one.

They had driven from their cottage in Ilfracombe to Clovelly, that time-warp village set on a steep hill. Andrew was slightly overweight but considered himself fit. After a leisurely lunch in The Red Lion restaurant on the harbour side they had started the walk uphill. Half way up, when you have a clear sight of the next hundred yards or so of cobbled hill that you have to climb, Andrew stumbled forward.

Vyvyan thought he had tripped and went to help him up, but Andrew was barely conscious. Local first-aiders carried him on a stretcher to a Land Rover and he was driven to the visitor centre. An ambulance took him to Barnstaple hospital.

Despite Andrew's mother's antipathy towards him Vyvyan thought it only right to call her and tell her about her son's hospitalisation. Within the hour she was at the hospital.

Mrs Blackstaff was a heavily built woman in her late sixties. She considered that she took no nonsense from anybody. Other people considered her rude and overbearing.

She saw Vyvyan sitting in the waiting area at the emergency department but ignored him and went straight to the reception desk. With a sigh of dread knowing she wasn't going to be pleasant he got up to join her.

'My son has been admitted with a heart attack.' He heard her say.

'Hello Mrs Blackstaff,' he said, worrying what kind of response he would get.

She turned to Vyvyan, and with a smile he'd never seen on her face before said, 'Thank you for coming with him, I'm sure he'd appreciate it. If you want to get off home now we'll be all right.'

Before Vyvyan could respond Mrs Blackstaff turned to the receptionist and said, 'My son's lodger.' She smiled, a guileless smile, 'A nice boy, but a bit of a nuisance, if you know what I mean.'

Vyvyan tried to protest. 'I'm his partner, we live together.'

Mrs Blackstaff ignored the confused look on the receptionist face and said to Vyvyan, 'You lodge with my son. How could you be his partner, you silly man?' She put a hand on his arm. 'I'm sure you mean well, but I think you should leave this to me now dear, go home.'

Vyvyan tried to appeal to the receptionist. 'We own our home together, we have done for years. We are a couple.'

Mrs Blackstaff was ignoring him and asking when she could see her son. Vyvyan would have to concede, later, that he had got a little bit angry.

'He's my bloody partner,' he shouted. Pointing to Mrs Blackstaff he shouted, 'She won't even talk to her son because he lives with me. I want to see Andrew now.'

The receptionist pressed a buzzer on her desk and within seconds a security guard appeared from an office behind her. After a quick few words from the woman the guard approached Vyvyan.

'I'm sorry, sir, you'll have to leave.'

'I damn well won't. That's my partner in there and I want to see him.'

The guard remained impassive. 'If you don't leave, sir, I'll call the police.'

Vyvyan looked around at the three faces all staring at him. Mrs Blackstaff had a sly grin on her face. 'When he wakes up I'll tell him you asked after him,' she said sweetly.

Vyvyan yelled 'Bitch!' at her and stormed out of the door.

With tears in his eyes he made his way back to his car where he'd left it after following the ambulance. Dreading what was going to happen in the next few days, how he was going to visit Andrew, whether Andrew was going to survive, he sat in the car for a while to calm down.

Eventually he drove home alone.

He waited until six o'clock. He noticed the visiting times were between two and four o'clock and between seven and eight o'clock. That meant it was unlikely Andrew's mother would be on the ward at six.

He rang the number that would put him straight through to the ward. A nurse answered and he asked about Andrew.

'Can I ask who you are?' the nurse said.

'I'm his partner, Vyvyan Wilde.'

'I'm sorry, we have instructions to release information to his family only.' The bitch. His mother was determined to keep Vyvyan away.

'I'm his partner, we live together.'

There was no moving the nurse. 'I'm sorry, sir, I can't help you.'

Vyvyan didn't bother arguing, he just put the phone down.

Vyvyan spent a miserable night. Scared he might never see Andrew again. Scared that the life he loved might be over. More frightening than he could ever imagine it might have been was the thought that his lover might die.

At eight o'clock the next morning the phone rang. Dreading what he might hear he picked it up.

'Hello, stranger, I thought I might wake up to find you here.'

It was Andrew! His spirits soared, tears of relief pricked at his eyes. All he could say was, 'Thank God!'

Andrew was serious for a moment. 'You worried about me?'

'Of course, I thought you were going to …' He couldn't say it, but Andrew knew what he meant.

'Of course I won't. I hear mother has been her usual objectionable self.'

'Yes, she wouldn't let me see you. She told the staff I was only your lodger.'

'I'm sorry. I want you here. How long will it take you?'

Vyvyan was overjoyed. 'I'll be there in less than half an hour.'

Andrew laughed, 'Don't you have an accident, we'll both be in here then.'

Vyvyan had a sudden thought. 'What if they won't let me in?'

'Don't worry,' chuckled Andrew, 'I've give the nurse that picture of you I had in my wallet. I've told her you are the only person allowed to say who visits and who doesn't.'

Eager to get going Vyvyan said, 'Love you,' and put the phone down.

Later, on the ward, Vyvyan was telling Andrew how scared he'd been. 'I thought I'd lost you,' he said.

Andrew looked into Vyvyan's eyes. 'This makes me even more determined to do something I've been thinking about for a while.'

'What's that,' Vyvyan laughed, 'start a fitness regime?'

'Don't be silly,' Andrew said, feigning injured feelings. 'I want us to get married. You know, a Civil Ceremony.'

Vyvyan could say nothing for a moment. He had wanted this since the law had allowed it but thought Andrew wasn't interested. He had always maintained they were as committed as any married couple so a piece of paper wouldn't make any difference.

'You do want to, don't you?' Andrew asked.

Vyvyan held his hand, 'Yes, yes, of course I do. It's just a surprise.'

'You start organising it; it'll keep you busy whilst I'm in here. Keep it low-key. After what's happened I don't want my mother there for a start.'

A nurse came over to check Andrew's blood pressure. 'What are you two so happy about?'

Vyvyan told her.

'Oh, lovely, can I come?' she asked with a big smile on her face.

'You mean you're not gutted, nurse Collins, that you can't have me?'

'Well, I had thought about it,' she teased, 'but I think you two make a wonderful couple, so I'll stand aside.'

'Will I be able to get out of here soon?' Andrew asked.

'Yes, I'm taking as much care of you as I can, I'd like to see you enjoying your big day.'

Vyvyan left the hospital far happier than he'd been when he arrived. He couldn't believe that yesterday he'd felt so worried and now he was planning his and Andrew's future.

He parked the car and as he put the key in the lock he could hear the telephone ringing. He rushed into the living room to answer it.

'Hello.'

'Mr Wilde? It's nurse Collins.'

What could she want so soon after he'd left the hospital?

'I'm sorry, I've got some awful news for you.'

Vyvyan couldn't quite make out the tone of her voice, was something wrong or was she merely going to change her mind about coming to their ceremony?

'I'm sorry, Mr Blackstaff had another heart attack just after you left.'

'My God! How is he? Is he still conscious?'

The nurse hesitated. 'I'm sorry Mr Wilde, he didn't recover.'

Vyvyan wasn't quite sure he'd heard that properly. 'What do you mean, didn't recover?'

'Mr Blackstaff has died. I'm sorry.'

She kept apologising, why was she saying sorry? How would that help? Would that change what she'd just said?

The nurse was still talking. 'Mr Blackstaff had insisted you should be his next of kin.'

Some time ago Vyvyan and Andrew had discovered that living together, sharing each other's lives, didn't make you each other's next of kin. But you could nominate somebody, anybody, to fill that function. It had little real significance, unless you were in hospital.

Suddenly Vyvyan needed to see Andrew, to see for himself that he was dead. 'I'm coming down now,' he said and put the phone down.

Chapter Fifteen

How he got safely to the hospital he didn't know. If he'd been asked to describe any part of his journey he would have been unable to. He parked the car and ran the length of the car park to the hospital entrance. It was all he could do not to run down the crowded corridors to the ward Andrew was on.

He finally turned the corner onto Elm ward. Nurse Collins was at the desk and saw him coming. 'Mr Wilde, I'm so sorry. We've moved Mr Blackstaff into a side room for privacy's sake.'

She guided him into a single bedded room just off the main ward. Andrew lay on the bed looking as if he were asleep. As he looked closer he realised that wasn't true, he could tell the spark of life had gone from Andrew. The utter stillness of his body, the change in his colour without the flow of blood through his veins. Andrew was dead.

'I'll leave you with him for a while,' the nurse said. 'Oh, I'm not sure if I should have but I've phoned Mrs Blackstaff, I thought she should know.'

At least, Vyvyan thought, I won't have to tell that cow.

He wasn't sure how long he spent looking at Andrew. Talking to him. Telling how much he was going to miss him. Eventually nurse Collins came back and said they needed to get on with things.

He drove home. The indignity of life carrying on around him stung. People were going about their business, the sun was shining, he could see couples walking arm in arm. But his world had crashed to a halt.

Again the journey seemed to pass without him being aware of driving.

As he pulled up in front of the cottage he could see movement through the window. He ran up the path, the front door was unlocked with Andrew's keys hanging in the lock, he threw it open and rushed in.

Mrs Blackstaff.

'What the bloody hell are you doing in my house,' he thundered.

'It's not your house. My son owned it,' she said petulantly.

'We owned it. We bought it together.' He felt tears pricking at his eyes. He wanted to be alone and this wretch of a woman had stolen Andrew's keys at the hospital and was violating their personal sanctuary.

'I'm his mother, what he's left is mine.'

'I'm his partner whether you like it or not,' Vyvyan said through tears. 'We both made wills leaving everything we own to each other, so get out of my house now.'

'That's an evil lie. You're nothing but a filthy little pervert.'

As they had been arguing they had moved about the room. Mrs Blackstaff was standing near the open door, although she had no intention of leaving.

Vyvyan rushed at her. 'Get out, you fucking bitch.' He pushed at her heavy body. She was caught unawares and couldn't resist. As she staggered over the threshold she slipped and fell.

'Help,' she screamed, 'he's trying to kill me, help.'

It was so ludicrous Vyvyan would have laughed if he wasn't so distraught.

A neighbour came out from her house. She saw the elderly woman on the ground and looked accusingly at Vyvyan. 'What are you doing? Leave her alone.'

Vyvyan went back into the house and slammed the door shut. He needed to be alone.

It wasn't to be. Within a short while the police arrived. By the time they left over an hour later Vyvyan felt like he'd gone ten rounds with a boxer, even though he won the argument, if it could be considered a victory.

The police had initially believed Mrs Blackstaff's claim of assault. But the more she ranted, the more she abused Vyvyan, the more she showed what an unpleasant individual she was, the more the police were inclined to take Vyvyan's side.

Eventually she was persuaded not to make an allegation of assault and they wouldn't find a way of charging her for entering the cottage without permission. She was warned not to come to the cottage again and Vyvyan was warned that if she did he was to call the police rather than manhandle her.

As he sat down on the settee he remembered what he had said to the policeman; 'I'm sick and tired of being bullied.'

Mrs Blackstaff wasn't the first person to bully him. He'd put up with it all his life. As he thought about how easily people had bullied him he felt a surge of anger. Maybe it was time to deal with this.

Vyvyan parked the little Fiesta at the front of the house. He'd registered the car in a made-up name. He made sure he didn't break any driving laws whilst he was in it. He wanted to be able to drive around when needed without coming to the attention of the police. The stolen Vectra was in the barn. He'd use it one more time, then set it on fire. There'd be no evidence linking him to the crime. He meant to ensure that if he were ever arrested in the future they'd never be able to link him to these crimes. He wanted to finish this campaign, exorcise his demons, and then get on with living his life quietly. He had got an emergency plan ready to put into action if somebody did recognise him.

He walked round to the barn and unlocked the heavy padlock on the doors. As he walked past the Vectra he could see Abigail on the bench. He knew she was aware that he had come back but the tape binding her head to the bench meant she couldn't turn her head to see him.

He stood beside her and enjoyed the look of terror he saw on her face. He couldn't be bothered to waste anymore time on her; he picked up the roll of tape he had used to bind her and tore off two strips, each about eight inches long. He put one over her mouth and smoothed it down over her cheeks.

She tried to fight against it but couldn't. He heard the muted whimpers and unvoiced pleadings she was trying to make.

He put the second strip of tape lengthways down her face, pressing it in around her nose. He deliberately left her eyes uncovered; he wanted to see the fear, the knowledge in her that she was going to die. They darted from side to side, as if by their struggle she could prolong her life. After thirty seconds the muscles in her chest stopped trying to drag air into her lungs. Her eyes sought out his, begging, terrified, begging. Then they dulled, stopped moving about. Then they were lifeless, she was lifeless.

He removed the strips of tape from her face and those binding her to the bench. Her lifted her and put her in the boot of the car, not caring that that the frail naked body had been a much loved daughter and sister. Not caring at all for Abigail.

He returned to the bench and swept up, clearing every trace of Abigail he could. He knew he wouldn't get all the hairs, all the bits of skin. It just needed to be enough so that a cursory look wouldn't find anything. He was going to burn the barn down when he had finished, a little accident.

It was nearly half-past eight. Davis, Peterson and Lewin were just going home after a long shift.

The board listing possible links between the two families didn't have much on it. The team had gone through work history and found no links. Alan Beresford worked for a builder's merchant in Chatteris; Bob James worked for a haulage company in Ely. Neither family attended church. Their children had gone to different schools, had been born in different hospitals. They shared membership of no club, group, society or association. None of their extended families had ever married into the others as far as enquiries had found. The only common link Davis and his team had found was that both fathers had attended the same school as Alice, St Andrews Comprehensive School. As that was almost twenty-five years ago Davis couldn't see that being a factor, but as he had no other lead tomorrow he would visit the school.

Tuesday

The muted ringing of the bedside phone woke him. As he picked it up he looked at the clock, three-twenty-two, he knew with a dread that there was only one reason for a phone call at this time of night.

It was the duty sergeant at the station. 'Sir, we've got a body.'

Davis felt a chill creep through his body. He'd said he'd need another killing before he could find the murderer but he'd hoped there wouldn't be one. He asked the sergeant where the body was.

'The barn!' He was stunned. 'The barn where Alice Beresford was found?'

'Yes, sir,' the sergeant confirmed.

Davis was fully alert and sitting on the edge of the bed trying to open the draw on his bedside table to get some clean underwear out. Anita turned her bedside lamp on.

'Sorry,' he mouthed to her. She slipped out of bed and went to the wardrobe, getting out the clothes that Davis would need. Many years as a detective's wife had given her a tolerance to these disturbances and she knew the best way of ensuring she could get back to bed was to help her husband get out as quickly as possible.

'Get Peterson, Lewin and Green out. Has Watson been called?'

The sergeant confirmed Watson was on his way and that he would alert Davis's team. Once off the phone Davis dressed in minutes and was on his way.

He drove through the orange-lit streets of Chatteris. At the

114

roundabout he joined the A141 and speeded up. The late April air was cold but he didn't put the heater on, he'd soon be in the open air anyway. As he drove along he could see the stars in a clear sky. As he passed through the bend and the road stretched ahead in a straight line for the next three miles his gaze drifted in the direction of the barn. Still some distance away the flat land meant he could pick out the lights that wouldn't normally be there, the headlights of the patrol car that had been called out. Davis had learned in the brief telephone call that Mr Morten had called the station to say he'd seen a car leaving the track the barn was on and due to the murder thought he'd better alert the police immediately. A patrol car had been diverted from its nightly drive through a handful of fen villages to this back road. The young constable had probably thought he was wasting his time as he'd left the car on the track and walked to the barn. What his torch had picked out when he got there soon changed his mind.

Davis parked beside the police car that was facing up the track, its headlights offering some guidance along the way. He walked the short distance to the barn; he was the first to arrive of those called out. Called from their slumber to deal with the brutal murder of another young girl.

Davis held his hand out for the constable's torch. The constable was still looking shaken and had been waiting outside the barn for his superiors to arrive.

The door was open but not quite enough for Davis to get his bulk through. He pulled at the door from as high up as possible, there was a chance the killer had touched the door and left fibres from whatever he was wearing.

She was laying on the floor in exactly the same way that Alice had done. He felt the same jolt of pain at the sight of the body. The same, fleeting thought of his daughter. But this wasn't his daughter; somebody else was going to suffer now. Davis slowly turned his torch to look around the barn, nothing else had changed. He looked back at Abigail, this man was playing games with the police. He'd taken the risk that the barn wasn't being watched. He was like a cat, catching its prey and leaving it for its master to find. Wanting to be admired. Or was he taunting them, showing them that he could murder at will. Come and go at will. That he was cleverer than the police.

Davis heard cars arriving. He left the barn to see who it was. Lewin and Watson. Watson's neat appearance was in contrast to Lewin.

Watson had on his customary suit with a smart shirt and silk tie. Lewin had clearly been asleep when the call had come. She wore jeans, which she normally avoided for work, and her usually neat, shoulder length hair was uncombed. Davis imagined that he looked almost as bad as Lewin did. There was nothing either could do about it, their priority had been to get to the scene as quickly as possible.

Lewin went into the barn, she would come back in daylight, but this first look whilst Abigail's body was there, might be important. Maybe something would stick in her mind, not useful yet, but later maybe.

Davis moved to the bank of the dyke. He called to the constable to shine his torch on the bankside.

The metal hook on the bank was still there but the grass didn't look as if it had recently been disturbed. Given that the farmer had reported a car leaving the track he would have to abandon his theory that the murderer used the water to transport the body. Ramsden was definitely in the clear.

He turned back to the barn. Watson was still examining the body and saw Davis come through the door. 'You don't need me to tell you it's the same person. The wounds are similar, especially the hands.' He pointed to Abigail's palms. 'There's no blood now but these were done while she was alive.'

Davis was disgusted, 'He's a sadistic bastard. He filmed this and sent the pictures to her father.'

'He also taped her down, just like Alice Beresford,' Watson continued. He pointed to her nose. 'She's had tape stuck over her face but you can just make out blisters around her nose. She was chloroformed I would imagine.'

'Just like Alice. Damn,' Davis swore, 'this man's running rings round us.'

Davis looked down at the pathetically small body on the ground. At seventeen she would have considered herself a woman, but she appeared childlike to Davis. The unevenly and savagely cut remains of her blond hair made Abigail look mutilated. Her eyes were open and Davis could no longer stand the accusation he imagined she might make if she could. If he had done his job better, quicker, she would be alive.

Chapter Sixteen

He walked out into the chilly open air to find Mr Morten, the farmer, had arrived at the barn. Lewin was asking him if he would recognise the driver of the car he'd seen.

'No, I haven't been sleeping too well and I'd come down stairs to make a cup of tea. I heard a car engine in the distance, the sound travels over these fields, but when I looked out of the window the car was turning out from the track away from me. It's much too far away to recognise anyone in daylight, never mind the dark.' He was trying to defend himself, feeling guilty that he hadn't seen what was impossible to see.

Davis wanted to confirm which way the car had gone. 'Where would that be heading, Mr Morten?'

'Well, it could be towards the bridge over the Forty Foot or towards Chatteris if he turned off up the road a bit.'

'You didn't notice whether he did or not?' Davis asked.

'No,' Morten said, 'I couldn't see that far down the road from my window.'

'Did you notice what type of car it was?'

'It was too far away, I'm sorry.'

Any further questions were put off by the arrival of the mortuary staff. Watson came out from the barn and said they could take the body. He walked over to Davis.

'I'll start the pm at eight, I'll see you then.'

Davis nodded a reply and was about to ask Lewin a question when they all heard an explosion. The sound had come from some distance and they all scanned around for any sign of fire.

'There,' Lewin said pointing across the fields.

'That's where we found the BMW burnt out, I'm sure.' Davis said. 'It's the road out of Chatteris. The bastard's torched the car he's used tonight exactly where he did the last one.' He called to the constable, 'Get on the radio, I want the helicopter up immediately. I want to know about anything moving out that way.'

The police helicopter was stationed at the RAF base at Wyton. It would take about three minutes from the call to get airborne and a further two minutes to reach the area the car was in. Assuming the car had been alight for a few minutes before the tank had exploded, the culprit could be at least a mile away before the helicopter was overhead, but it was worth a try.

Davis shouted to Lewin, 'Let's get over there now. You go through Pidley and Somersham, I'll go back through Chatteris. We've got to assume he's working alone, that means he's probably on foot.'

Both detectives drove off quickly leaving the constable to guard the barn.

Davis braked heavily to negotiate the roundabout that would take him into Chatteris. He drove as fast as he dared along the road which was lined both sides with parked cars. It was just after half-past four and the streets were empty. He stamped on the brakes as he reached the end of the road and with one brief look swung right onto London Road. This was the road that led out of town towards Somersham, the road the car had been set alight on. He accelerated up to eighty miles an hour and prayed that no early riser would pull out in front of him. As he got to the outskirts of town he slowed down. He had seen nothing moving so far.

Now as the houses spread out and gardens gave way to fields he was trying to see through hedges and across fields. The bastard had to be out here somewhere. He saw a powerful beam of light sweep across the ground towards him, the helicopter. He didn't want it wasting time looking at him. He quickly got the blue lamp from the glove box. He plugged it into the cigarette lighter and held it out of the window.

The beam from the helicopter was switched off for a few seconds and them back on again in acknowledgement, then it moved along the road towards Chatteris.

Davies braked heavily as he approached a sharp left-handed bend. As he swept through it he accelerated again. Down one of the few hills in the fens he kept scanning the fields for any sign of movement, the car rocking heavily on its suspension as he drove along the bumpy road. The truth was if anybody was hiding in the hedgerows he wouldn't see them at this speed, he just wanted to cover the ground as quickly as possible. The helicopter would use its heat-seeking camera to search for the person who set the car on fire. Assuming he was still in the area.

Davis negotiated another bend and could see the blazing car now. A moment later he was pulling up at what he considered a safe distance. He knew looking at the car that there would be no hope of recovering forensic evidence from it.

Davis used the police radio to get in touch with the control centre at the station. 'Have the helicopter crew spotted anybody yet?' he asked.

'No, sir,' responded the radio operator, 'nothing suspicious.'

Davis was furious, with himself, the helicopter crew, the world, but most furious with the bastard doing this. He was running rings around the police, around Davis. And whilst he was doing that Davis was convinced more young girls would die.

He'd been there a several minutes when Lewin arrived. She'd had a longer route to travel than Davis, and on slower roads. She came to a halt next to Davis's car and got out.

'Nothing, sir, what about you?'

Davis shook his head.

Fifteen minutes later the helicopter crew called off the search, whoever set fire to the car was long gone.

By the time Davis got home it wasn't worth going to bed. He had a hot shower and ignoring his diet made a plateful of bacon sandwiches for his breakfast. As Davis ate them he knew he was going to have a hard time explaining this to Malloy. The Chief Superintendent was the one who had to face the media. Two girls murdered and dumped in the same place and the murderer using the same spot to torch his cars both times wouldn't be ignored by a critical press. Davis was going to have to get results soon or even Malloy's patience would run out.

At the station by seven-thirty Davis checked the white boards to see if any information had been added. None had. The only possible link they could find so far was that both fathers had gone to the same school, St Andrews Comprehensive. Davis decided to go there this morning. If he got there by eight most of the teachers would be there but they wouldn't yet have gone to their classes. Lewin came through the door as Davis was preparing to leave.

'Morning, sir.'

'Morning, Gillian. Have you heard from the others yet?'

Peterson and Green had stayed at the barn whilst Davis and Lewin had gone to see the James after Abigail's body had been found.

'The sarge' is going to the pm,' she looked at her watch, 'should be on his way now, and Patrick's back at the barn now it's properly light.'

'Right, you go to the council at March and find out what cctv coverage they have of the area where Abigail was on Sunday night. I'm off to school.'

Davis himself had gone to St Andrews, as his son did now. The front entrance had changed little in almost thirty years but he knew there were several new buildings to accommodate the growth in pupils over the years. The biggest of these was the IT block. When he was at school computers had been a thing of the future as far as the pupils had been concerned. Now computer studies were compulsory and most of the kids could tell the teachers a thing or two about them.

He pushed the door open and was reminded of one change he'd seen on his last parent's evening visit. The reception area was now secure. Visitors could no longer walk through the doors and access the school without someone inside opening the heavy security doors. He approached the reception desk and showed his warrant card through the grill.

'I'd like to speak to the head teacher, please,' he said to the woman sitting at the desk. She looked old enough to have been there when Davis was at school but he didn't recognise her.

'Do you have an appointment?' she asked in the tone of voice that said without one he wouldn't be seen.

'No, but all the same I want to see her.' He held the woman's gaze and said no more and after a few seconds the woman picked the phone up and spoke briefly.

Putting the phone down she looked up at Davis and said, 'She has a few minutes to spare, she'll see you now.'

Davis pushed at the security door as the lock buzzed and was shown to Mrs Major's office. Davis was invited to sit down and Mrs Major said straight away, 'We've told your officers all we can about Alice Beresford, I can't think what else we can say.' She was in her early fifties and was smartly dressed in a knee length skirt and matching jacket. Her dark hair was cut short, but not too severely. The overall impression Davis gained was of a woman who took care of appearance but wasn't fussy about it.

As Abigail James had left school and had never attended St Andrews Comprehensive anyway the police hadn't informed them of her disappearance. Davis quickly outlined the latest murder to a shocked headmistress.

'What I'm really interested in is the past,' Davis said. 'Both the girl's fathers attended this school and as the murderer seems to have been targeting the fathers as much as the girls we are looking for any possible links. I realise they left school almost twenty-five years ago but

I was wondering if any of your teachers may have been here that long and remember them.'

Mrs Major was quiet for a minute then said, 'Do you know, I think I do. Let me explain. I started here as a student teacher. I was here for three years. I moved about a bit and then when the headship became vacant last year I applied for it as I'd enjoyed my time here.'

'And you remember both the men?'

'I remember Alan Beresford vaguely, I'd have to check the records, but when poor Alice died I remembered the name from the past, that was her father.'

'Can you remember anything about him, particularly if he was friends with Mr James?'

Mrs Major looked strained. 'I can't say he stands out in my memory in anyway. I probably taught him at some time, as a student I would have covered many classes, but I can't even remember what he looked like.'

'And Mr James?'

'I have no recollection of him at all. If you say he was a pupil here then he was, but it's such a long time ago. The only reason I remember Beresford is because I had a school friend of the same name.'

'Are there any other teachers here now from that time?'

'No, I'm sorry, but this isn't a very attractive school for some teachers. It sits in the middle of the league tables. That means the high-flyers won't come here and those who think it's their duty to work with difficult pupils in run-down areas don't come here either. Add in the fact that it's in a very rural area and those teachers who do start their careers here soon want to move on.'

Davis was surprised that the school he and his son had attended was so poorly thought of. 'But you came back.'

'I'm a local girl, my family have lived in Ely for years, I like the Fens. My husband took a post at Cambridge just weeks before this position came up. I'd been at Kings Lynn school for a while and thought it was time for a change.'

Davis realised that he was going to find nothing more of interest to him here.

Davis got back to the station before nine o'clock to find Peterson at his desk. 'Morning, sir.'

'Morning, Graham. Any news from the pm?'

Peterson looked tired, but then none of them had got much sleep.

'Nothing to help. He tortured this one pretty much the same as he did Alice. The only difference was the way he killed her.' Peterson hesitated for a moment. 'Phil, this man's going to get worse if we don't stop him.'

'How did she die?'

'The doc told you she'd had tape on her face?'

'Yes, but Alice was taped down as well.'

'Abigail had tape over her mouth and nose, he suffocated her.'

Davis swore silently, he knew this man was a sadist and that Peterson was right, if they didn't catch him the next girl would suffer more than Abigail had done. This killer was getting a taste for it, and thought he was too clever for the police.

Green came into the office. 'Morning, sir, sarge.'

'Was there anything new at the barn, Patrick?' Davis asked him.

'No, sir. But I did get this just after I got back.' He held up a file. 'Bellamy was checking on known sex offenders before his wife went into hospital.'

Peterson interrupted, 'I'm sorry, I forgot what with finding the body. Bellamy's wife had a boy in the early hours, he rang me earlier.'

Davis groaned, 'I suppose he'll be off for days.'

Peterson said, 'You're right, he's taking his paternity leave and he's asked for two weeks leave he's owed.'

Davis was not amused, 'You are joking I hope?'

'No, he's said he mentioned to you that he was holding back some leave for when the baby was born.'

'But I didn't expect it to be born in the middle of a major murder enquiry,' he said savagely, knowing as he did that it wasn't Peterson's fault.

Peterson shrugged, 'Nor did he, I suppose.' He was used to Davis's flying off the handle and took no notice.

Davis gave up, he knew there was nothing he could do about it, they'd just have to cope without Bellamy. Green had been quiet whilst Davis had ranted about his colleague. Davis looked at the file Green was still holding. 'What is that then?'

'Bellamy had checked out the known sex offenders on our patch. There were five serious ones, those who have used violence or threats. Two are still inside. One has died. One is living in Thailand now.' Green looked up, 'One is living in Chatteris as we speak.'

Chapter Seventeen

Davis felt a small surge of hope. Would this be their man? 'Who is he?' he asked Green.

'One Mark Sibley. Fifty four years of age. Numerous previous. Minor assault when he was a teenager, sexual assault and battery leading to six months jail a bit later.' Green skipped down the list. 'This is the bit that interests us. Four years for kidnap, battery and rape just over ten years ago, released after three years. Six years for rape, sexual assault and battery, released eighteen months ago.'

Green put the file on the desk. 'He lives in Fern Street.'

Davis looked at Peterson, 'I think it's time we paid Sibley a visit.' To Green he said, 'See what you can dig up on this Sibley. Previous addresses, jobs, any family. When Lewin gets back get her to locate his previous victims, we'll want a word with them.'

Vyvyan was making preparations for his next victim. Tania Symonds. He was worried about this one. She was a much bigger girl than the others, fitter looking as well. He would have to make sure he subdued her quickly. He would think carefully about how to get close enough to use the chloroform pad. It was an old-fashioned way of rendering somebody unconscious, but it worked well.

Davis pulled up outside nineteen Fern Street. One of five similar streets at this end of town, they were what was euphemistically called social housing. They were a dumping ground really. Shoddily built and poorly maintained they housed the kind of misfits who couldn't afford to live anywhere better.

Peterson looked around the area. Battered cars, some obviously still in use, littered the communal parking area. Piles of rubbish bags were thrown against the fence at the end of the road. From an open window of one of Sibley's neighbours came a noise that somebody called music.

'If he held the girls here nobody would have taken any notice of their screams,' Peterson said.

Davis nodded to him, 'I think you might be right. Let's find out.'

They made their way up the concrete path, as they approached the front door they passed the kitchen window. Peterson cupped his hands around his face and looked through the window. After a few seconds he swore violently.

'What is it?' Davis asked.

'Look, through the doorway into the living room.'

Davis did as instructed. There was a man sitting at a desk looking at a computer monitor. On the screen was a picture of a pre-teenage girl in a pose that would make any decent person sick and Sibley was clearly masturbating whilst he watched it.

'That's it, come on.' Davis swiftly moved to the door and rushed it, throwing his bulk hard at the wooden door. The door flew open and Davis almost fell to the floor. Sibley jumped up in fright and tripped over an extension cable trailing from the wall to the computer.

As Davis shouted, 'Police,' Sibley tried to lunge for the switch on the wall and turn the computer off.

Peterson rushed past Davis and kicked Sibley's hand away, 'Oh no you don't.' He took a pair of handcuffs from his pocket and locked Sibley's hands behind his back. Pushing him roughly onto the settee he said, 'We've got some questions for you and you'd better have some bloody good answers.'

Davis was opening all the windows he could, the house smelt appallingly of sweat and old cigarettes. The kitchen was filthy and Davis was finding it nauseating.

Sibley himself was just as grubby as his surroundings. It was unlikely his clothes had been washed in weeks and he had several days' stubble on his face. Davis pointed to the monitor. 'You know that's going to put you back inside, don't you?'

Sibley sneered, 'That's nothing to do with me, someone sent it to me by mistake, I was going to delete it.'

Davis wanted to smash the man's face in but just held himself back. 'So that's why you were tossing yourself off to it is it? God! You make me sick.'

Peterson sat down at the computer. 'There's no internet connection open, this image is stored on your hard drive.' He got his phone from his pocket, 'Let's get the techies in, they'll make sure we've got enough to give you a long break in one of our roughest hotels for paedophiles.'

The scenes of crime officers would make sure there was no chance of Sibley creeping out of this. The computer would be photographed with its sick picture on the monitor. A record would be made of all the connections to and from the computer before it was taken to the labs to have the hard drive analysed.

'You've got no right, you can't just burst in here without a warrant.'

'Shut up. You're coming with us as well, you were found committing an arrestable offence. We've got a lot of questions for you and I can't stay in this shit hole much longer.'

Peterson said, 'Phil.' He pointed to a roll of grey tape on the floor of the type that had been used on both girls.

'Check upstairs, I'll have a quick scout round outside,' Davis said. Turning to Sibley he said, 'On your feet.' Davis pushed him to the stairs and used a second pair of cuffs to secure him to the thick newel post. 'We don't want you getting near that computer, do we?'

Davis opened the back door and with a grimace realised this garden was even more uncared for than Roy Keane's had been. The grass and weeds were waist high. There were old bikes and bits of car bodies scattered everywhere. Two old engines were on the ground outside a brick built shed. Davis noticed there was a heavy padlock holding the door shut. He picked up a garden spade and slammed the blade down on the lock. The hasp twisted and came away from the wooden door slightly. Davis wedged the spade in the gap and twisted, the screws gave way and Davis opened the door. The shed was about six feet by nine. All the houses on these streets had one. It was meant to keep bikes, lawnmowers and other possessions safe from the thieving gaze of the tenant's neighbours.

Sibley's shed had various tools and bits of car engines lying on the floor but what immediately caught Davis's attention was a home made wooden bench. Running the width of the far wall, it was made up of old kitchen units topped with a rough sheet of plywood. One thing stood out glaringly, amongst all the mess the bench top was empty. Its surface was completely free of the general clutter and filth the house, garden and shed shared.

Davis pushed the shed door shut and used the spade to wedge it as best he could. He went back to the house to see if Peterson had found anything interesting.

As he walked in the back door Peterson was coming down the stairs. He had a bag in one hand. 'Can you explain these,' he asked Sibley. He tipped the contents of the bag onto the settee. Mobile phones, almost a dozen.

Sibley shrugged, 'I've got to make a living, I buy and sell them.'

Davis snorted, 'You mean you steal and sell them.'

Sibley said nothing. Davis asked Peterson, 'Anything else?'

'Not really, though I pity the poor sods who have to search this place, it's filthy and I've smelt cesspits that were sweeter than this.'

Sibley glared at him and muttered, 'Bastard,' under his breath.

Davis ignored him and waved a hand in front of his face, 'How anybody can live like this I don't know.' He told Peterson about the bench.

'We'd better get him down the station,' Peterson said.

'I'm not having him in my car,' Davis said, 'I'll phone for a van.'

While they waited for the van Davis made a cursory search of the house. He was careful not to touch anything he didn't have to. Just about everything was greasy or stained. There were piles of magazines on the floor and on the armchairs. When Davis looked they covered two subjects, computers and porn. Davis picked up a handful of the porn mags and flicked through them. Some of them were standard top-shelf fare, some of them weren't. Bondage, sadomasochistic and underage girls featured in some of the others.

Davis turned to Sibley, 'If I had my way you and your scum friends would never be let out on the streets.'

Sibley sneered again, 'That's only because you don't know what you're missing. You can't beat some young flesh, mind you, I like beating it...'

Anything else he was going to say was cut off by a yelp of fear as Davis rushed at him. 'You fucking bastard,' he yelled.

It was all Peterson could do to hold him back, 'Phil, Phil, for fucks sake. He's not worth it.' He was face to face with Davis trying to hold him in a bear hug.

Red-faced with fury Davis shouted, 'Okay.' Peterson let him go. Davis avoided looking at Sibley. 'I'll wait outside, I can't stay in here with him.'

Davis was angry with himself for losing his temper, it wasn't the first time a villain had tried to wind him up. He had to admit that this case was getting to him. The two young girls had looked so vulnerable. Although his Grace had been only hours old when she died, and Alice and Abigail were teenagers, their deaths had reawakened the pain he'd felt at her loss, as did every case like this. He'd have to get a hold of his emotions because once Sibley was at the station Davis was going to have to question him. If he was their man, and Davis was convinced he was, then the interview must be totally above board. One hint of over the top questioning by Davis would allow a good barrister to destroy the police case against Sibley.

After a ten minute wait the police van arrived to take Sibley to the station. Davis watched the van drive away and turned to Peterson. 'I want you to stay here until the SOCOs arrive.' He cast a glance around the neighbourhood. 'If these people know why he's been in jail and about the dead girls they might not wait for us to make a case. I don't want his house torched before we get the evidence we need.'

'You think he is our man?'

Davis thought for a few moments. 'If he is we're going to have to work hard to find all the links. We'll need to show some connection between him and both families, we know the murders weren't random.'

'You can see from his choice of reading material that he's sadistic enough to have done it,' Peterson said.

'At the moment all we can prove is he's a foul-smelling pervert. We need positive evidence linking him to the girls. Anyway, I'm off. Have a poke around, see what you can find.'

Vyvyan had been watching Tania for a couple of days now. After school each day she cycled to a riding stables a mile outside Chatteris. The road she used was the one that led to the farm track where he had torched both of the stolen cars he had used. It saw very little traffic, in fact on the two days he'd parked further down the road at the time she was on it nothing had passed him. He had decided that he would have to knock her off her bicycle. Then he could play the concerned motorist and offer her a lift home. As soon as she got in the car he'd put the pad of chloroform to her nose.

Tomorrow would be the day, Wednesday; it was on a Wednesday that Tania Symonds father, Geoff, had made Vyvyan pierce his ears with a needle and thread. Symonds had said that Vyvyan was a girls name and that as girls had pierced ears so would Vyvyan.

Geoff Symonds had brought a sewing needle and thread from home and used a cigarette lighter to sterilise the needle. Then he had threatened to kick Vyvyan's balls to mush if Vyvyan didn't push the needle through his ears. He had refused at first and Geoff had swung hard at Vyvyan's groin. He had collapsed in agony and it had been several minutes before Alan Beresford and Wart had been able to haul him to his feet. He had tears running down his face.

'Oh, look. He cries just like a girl,' Symonds had mocked. 'If you don't get on with this Vyvyan Wilde we'll make you put lipstick on as well.'

127

Vyvyan held the needle to his earlobe. He just couldn't do it, he couldn't. The tears started again. Symonds said, 'I'll give you a count down from five, if you haven't done the first one then your balls pay the price.'

'Just do it,' Alan Beresford shouted.

Symonds started his count. 'Five, four.'

Vyvyan pleaded, 'Please...'

'Three.'

'It'll hurt too much.'

'So will a kick in the bollocks,' Bob James said. 'Get on with it.'

'Two.'

Vyvyan did it. One hard push. He screamed with the pain. His ear was on fire. Blood ran over his hand.

'Pull the needle through,' Symonds ordered.

Vyvyan was still holding his ear, the pain was throbbing.

'Pull it through or I'll kick your balls so hard they'll turn into earrings,' Symonds threatened.

The other three laughed raucously.

Vyvyan gripped the sharp end of the needle and gave it a quick tug. The fire in his ear flared again. The needle was dangling on the end of the thread that was now running through the hole in his ear.

'Hold the needle away from your ear,' Symonds said. Vyvyan did as he was told and Symonds used his lighter to burn the thread from the needle. He handed the needle to Bob James, 'Thread it again.'

James did and handed it back to Vyvyan. 'Please, I've done one, please don't...'

'If you don't do it your balls are history,' Symonds said. He was actually surprised Vyvyan had done it. He had been prepared to kick Vyvyan a couple more times then give in. Seeing the needle go through Vyvyan's ear had made him feel a little sick, but seeing as how they were saying that Vyvyan was a big girl he could hardly wimp out now.

Vyvyan was holding the needle to his ear and was crying again. Symonds was getting angry. He took a step back. 'No count down this time, do it or else.'

Vyvyan did it and let out a yelp of pain. More blood ran out, now both sides of his shirt were stained bright red. It was his turn to be livid, 'You bastard,' he swore at Symonds swinging a punch at him. 'My dad's going to go mad when he sees this.'

Symonds easily dodged the ineffectual punch and hit Vyvyan hard on the nose. 'He should have thought of that before he gave you a girl's name, you poof.'

The four bullies walked off laughing.

Tomorrow it would be Vyvyan's turn to laugh. That would be three of the four people he wanted revenge on. The fourth would be the big one.

Chapter Eighteen

Davis was having a coffee in the CID office before he questioned Sibley. The search team was going through Sibley's house and would miss nothing in their attempt to find any evidence that either of the murdered girls had been in the house.

There was an air of relief about the place. The team were convinced they'd got their man. Whilst Davis and Peterson had been arresting Sibley, Green had trawled through the records to get as much information as he could about the man. Now he read some out to the others.

'At fifteen he was arrested for sexual assault of a thirteen year old girl. No charges were brought. At seventeen there was the assault he went to jail for, but that wasn't sexual.' Green looked up at Davis, 'This one's interesting, age twenty two he was arrested for sexual assault on a woman. She refused to testify. The case notes suggest Sibley threatened her enough to stop her.'

'Why wasn't he done for that,' Peterson said, outraged.

Green held the notes up and waved them about, 'It doesn't say, but there's more.' He searched out the bit he wanted. 'He only had a few minor charges after that until just over ten years ago, he beat up a woman he had been out with. They had gone for a drink and when they got home Sibley wanted sex and she didn't. Sibley battered her enough to break two ribs, black her eyes, fracture her wrist and cause numerous bruises and cuts. He then raped her repeatedly throughout the night before warning her that if she reported him he'd kill her.'

'What did he get for that?' Davis asked.

'Four years, although he only did three,' Green said.

Lewin, who had so far been quietly listening to Green said, 'I bet if she'd stabbed him to get away she'd have got done more than three years.'

None of the men said anything; they all thought she was probably right.

Green carried on reading the notes, 'He hadn't been out long when he took a woman home, beat her almost to death and raped her. He also used a knife on her, cutting her all over her body.' He looked up at the others, 'in the words of the judge, "a sadistic, gratuitous use of violence purely for his own pleasure." He got six years and did four and a half. He's not been caught at anything since then, until today.'

'Yes, we caught the shit looking at the picture of a young girl. A bit younger than Alice and Abigail,' Davis said.

'That bothers me, sir,' Lewin said.

'What does?' Davis asked.

'His form is mainly sexually motivated. You caught him looking at a pornographic picture of a young girl.'

'And it looks like he's killed two young girls,' Davis said.

'But according to the lab reports neither girl was sexually molested in anyway,' Lewin responded.

'They were found naked,' Davis said. 'I've seen him, I'm convinced he's our man. I'm going to interview him now, Gill, you come in with me, see what you think then.' He turned to Peterson, 'I want to cover all angles on this. Whilst we're with him I want you to dig up any crimes that are similar to our case now. Then any like Sibley's record. Then see if any of them were committed whilst he was inside. We'll find out if there're two of the bastards out there.'

Lewin had her doubts, maybe there was someone else out there, maybe he'd only just started up and there would be no overlap of Sibley's crimes and this new man's.

Davis and Lewin went down stairs to the interview room to start interrogating Sibley.

Vyvyan hadn't used this car park before. It was for the local nature reserve and at three o'clock in the afternoon it was almost empty. There were just four cars in it. Two of them were too new; he wouldn't get past their immobilisers. With both the previous cars he'd stolen he'd got them with the keys in the ignition. Stupid owners. The BMW had been left with the engine running outside a newsagent's shop in Wisbech. Vyvyan had gone there because it was unlikely that anybody would recognise his face. As he walked past the car he'd opened the door, slipped the car in gear and driven away before the owner even realised his car had gone. The Vectra had come from Wisbech as well. He noticed on a previous visit that drivers who were posting letters in the main post office letterbox often left their cars at the kerb with the engine running. The box was across a twenty feet grass verge. Most of the cars were left just nudging into the bus stop, so Vyvyan sat on the bench at the stop and waited until a lone driver left his engine running. Both cars had ended up burnt out.

Now he was making sure that nobody was around. The Ford Escort was old and rusty but what was important to Vyvyan was that it wouldn't have an immobiliser. In his early twenties he had worked in a breaker's yard for a few months. He knew how to snap the steering lock off and hotwire a car in less than a minute. He was carrying a thin strip of metal that had a notch cut in one end. He slipped that between the glass and its seal and with one quick movement had unlocked the door. As he got in the car he jerked the steering wheel savagely and the lock gave way. Reaching under the dashboard he pulled at a handful of wires and quickly joined two of them together. Brushing a third one over them engaged the starter motor and the engine roared into life. Twenty eight seconds after walking up to the car he was driving it away.

Sibley sat across the table from Davis. Davis had the interview room windows open and had positioned a floor standing fan behind his back blowing the air away from him and towards Sibley. Sibley's personal hygiene was so bad that Davis didn't think he'd have been able to sit too close to him for long without the precautions he'd taken.

Sibley had requested the duty solicitor be present. Luckily for Davis it was the inept and lazy Colin Brown on call today. Brown, in his fifties and lacking all ambition, had the opinion that most of the people he came to represent were probably guilty of whatever crime the police accused them of. His attendance merely provided a source of income for the practice that employed him.

Davis had inserted two new disks into the recorder and as soon as they were ready went through the usual preliminaries; the time, date, location and who was in the room.

Now he sat on the chair facing Sibley. 'Mr Sibley, my colleague and I saw you looking at a computer monitor with a picture of a young girl on it. The picture can best be described as pornographic, or by any reasonable, decent person, evil filth. What do say about that?'

Sibley stared at him for a few seconds. He had a perpetual sneer on his face and Davis had to resist the almost constant urge to hit him. Sibley was, according to his records, just over six feet tall and around fourteen stones. He didn't look as if he took any exercise, he wasn't what Davis would have called 'in shape' but he was physically imposing. Davis had no doubt believing that he was capable of abducting both girls and moving their bodies around.

Sibley hesitated for a few moments, then said, 'I've already told you, I opened my emails and that was one of them, I don't know who it was that sent it to me and I wasn't expecting it.'

'My sergeant checked, there was no internet connection open.'

'I closed it down as soon as the picture opened, I panicked.' As Sibley said that he had a grin on his face that said he knew Davis wasn't going to believe that.

'Is that why you were masturbating over it then?' Davis asked angrily.

Brown stirred into life looking worried and leaned over to whisper in Sibley's ear. He recoiled for a moment wrinkling his nose then carried on. After a hurried few seconds of conversation masked by Brown's hand in front of his face, to prevent Davis hearing him rather than to block Sibley's smell, Brown said, 'My client denies er... masturbating.'

Lewin asked Brown, 'What was he doing then? I wasn't there, perhaps he can tell me?'

Sibley leered at Lewin and said, 'I bet you'd like to know if I was wanking.'

Lewin, who had faced too many perverts and rapists across the interview table to be disconcerted by Sibley, said 'The only thing I'm interested in is why you think it's acceptable to be looking at pictures of young, naked girls? Aren't you capable of getting it on with a real woman?'

Sibley's leer was replaced with a snarl, showing his yellowed teeth. 'I could show you what a real man could do, you'd soon be begging for mercy.'

'Is that what you like, to see a woman beg, to be in control?' Lewin's asked, keep her voice neutral.

Sibley shrugged his heavy shoulders, 'It's what they want, sometimes they know it, others, they need encouragement.'

'And you provide that encouragement, whether they want it or not?'

Sibley was relaxing slightly. As far as he could tell they'd moved off the subject of the picture on his computer and this copper was trying it on with him.

'They all want it, and I just give them what they want.'

'Is that what you did to Alice Beresford and Abigail James, gave them what they wanted?' Davis asked angrily.

'What the fuck are you on about?' Sibley asked defensively. Davis was sure he detected a hint of guilt in Sibley's face.

'Why was the bench in your shed the only clean surface in totally filthy shit hole you call a home?'

Sibley looked mystified, he turned to his solicitor. 'What the hell are they on about?'

Brown looked uncomfortable. 'Inspector, my client was brought here because of a misunderstanding, he ...'

'He was brought here because he's a bloody pervert who can't keep his hands off women who want nothing to do with him,' Davis thundered.

Brown seemed to shrink, his mouth moved to make a protest but no words came from him. Davis said, 'If we can continue,' he turned back to Sibley, 'why was that bench the only tidy area in that shit hole you call a home?' Davis was hoping the repeated insult might rile Sibley.

Sibley's face was set like stone. 'I don't have to answer any of your questions. There's nothing you've got on me.'

'By the time forensics have finished with your computer we'll have enough to put you back inside for another stretch.' Davis sat back in his chair and tried to appear relaxed. 'Of course, if you help us, we might be able to help you.'

Sibley hesitated for a few seconds, wondering what it was Davis wanted. He decided to go along with Davis, hoping this copper was man enough to know that despite their differences he, Sibley, was right with what he said about women. After all he'd cut that stupid female cop out of the questioning, she was probably a dyke given the way she was glaring at him and that she didn't have a wedding ring on.

He sat up straight. 'What's this about them girls?'

'Alice Beresford and Abigail James,' Davis said quietly. 'Two decent young girls who were taken away and restrained on a wooden bench, just like the one in your shed. There somebody tortured them and subjected them to a terrifying ordeal before killing them.'

Brown blinked hard and looked from Sibley to Davis several times but said nothing.

'You think that was me, I don't need to tie anyone down if I want them,' Sibley said.

'You usually beat them up first, don't you?' Lewin asked. 'Is that your idea of foreplay?'

Sibley sneered at her and turned to Davis. 'I haven't touched no girls. I've never heard of them two. What would I want with young girls?'

'You had a picture of one on you computer when we called round,' Davis said.

'That was just a picture,' he spread his hands out as if to portray openness, 'we all need something to get us going, you know,' he leered, 'get us ready for the pull.'

Davis swore he would never know how he kept from launching himself at Sibley. 'That picture was of some poor child whose life filthy fucking perverts like you ruin,' Davis shouted. 'What were you getting ready for, to kill another girl?'

Brown tried to interrupt, 'Really, inspector, you can't …'

'Yes, I can,' Davis said, slamming his hand down on the desk. 'Come on Sibley, you reckon you're a man, be man enough to tell me what you were going to do? Who's next?'

Davis saw the first trace of fear in Sibley's eyes. 'I haven't done nothing with those girls.' He turned to the solicitor, 'You tell them, they can't prove I had them because I didn't.'

Before Brown could say anything Davis cut in. 'Then what was the bench for? Who's next? Why did you attack the other two?' Davis punctuated his questions with his hand pounding on the desk.

Sibley jumped up knocking his chair over. The constable at the door moved to restrain him. Davis held a hand up to stall the constable as Sibley shouted, 'I never touched any girls, I've never heard of them.'

Brown was looking startled and afraid of Sibley. Davis was beginning to worry, Sibley's constant denial of any involvement with the two dead girls had the ring of truth about it. He'd better cover some basic questions.

'Sit down, Sibley.'

Sibley looked mutinously at Davis as if he was going to refuse to do as Davis had ordered. He glanced over at the constable who had moved back to the door. It was the same constable who had discovered Abigail's body and the look on his face said he would just like an excuse to have a go at Sibley. Sibley sat down.

'Right,' said Davis, 'now, let's go back a bit. Where were you on Sunday night?'

'I was at home,' Sibley said with an air of resentment.

'What about Monday night?' Davis asked.

Sibley sighed, 'At home.'

'You don't go out much do you?'

'I can't afford to. The social don't pay much and I can't get a job.'

'Have you got a car?'

Sibley looked at Davis and then at the constable. 'Yes, but it's not on the road at the moment.'

'Why not?' Davis asked.

'Because I can't afford the road tax.'

'So there's nothing stopping you taking it out apart from you being a law-abiding citizen?' Sibley didn't answer.

'Where did you go to school?' Davis asked.

The change in direction of the questions seemed to throw him. 'St Andrew's, why?'

Davis remembered that Green had said Sibley was fifty-four, he would have left school before the girls father started at St Andrew's, but it was a link.

'Did you know anybody called Beresford or James when you were there?'

Sibley shrugged, 'I can't remember, it was nearly forty years ago.'

'Do you get on with your neighbours?' Davis asked him.

Sibley looked surprised by the question. 'What's that got to do with anything? They're always complaining about something.'

'What do they have to complain about, girls screaming, maybe?'

Sibley was angry again. 'I've fucking told you, I never touched any girls.'

Davis had gone as far as he could for now, he needed something more, some evidence that put the girls at Sibley's house. He'd have to hope forensics came up with something pretty quickly.

He stood up. 'I'm charging you with possession of a picture of an underage child. Further charges may follow. You'll be bailed for now but we will be seeing you again.'

With that Davis walked out of the room followed by Lewin.

Vyvyan parked the stolen car in the shed. Luckily the car had half a tank of petrol. He'd had to use a can to put some in the Vectra. That had almost been empty when he'd stolen it and he couldn't risk going to a filling station in it, they all had forecourt cameras now.

He went into the house and made himself some tea. As he ate it he looked again at the photos of Andrew. It was the way he'd been bullied by Andrew's mother when he was dying that had triggered off this campaign of his, but it was the actions of four schoolboys that had made him afraid of people all his life. These attacks were going to remove that fear. He was going to get the upper hand.

He had often wondered why he had hung around with those boys when they had tormented him. The fact was he'd had no friends, at least when the four weren't tormenting him they let him tag along with them. His craven desire to be liked, to have the appearance of having friends had meant he'd put up with whatever they had meted out.

He'd learnt his lesson. He had made no friends over the years. Andrew had been his one true love and now he was gone. He looked at the last photo he'd taken of him before he died. 'Don't worry, Love, I'll be careful.'

He'd stay at home until it was time to catch Tania tomorrow. He needed to stay calm; he needed some time to get in the right frame of mind. He had to believe that Tania's life was completely unimportant.

Chapter Nineteen

Gillian Lewin was angry. As she followed Davis down the corridor she had trouble keeping that anger out of her voice. 'Why have we let that disgusting weirdo out on bail?'

'Gillian, we have nothing linking him to those girls unless we get some forensic evidence. That's not going to come in for a day or so. The picture's not enough to hold him and I'm not wasting all the time we are allowed to keep him in the cells with no prospect of charging him for murder.'

'But the man's got pervert written all over him,' Lewin protested hotly.

Davis pushed open the door to the CID office and they both went in. 'Before we interviewed him you were trying to convince me he wasn't the right man and I was sure he was.'

'And now it's the other way round. I know, sir.' She was frustrated and sat down heavily on a chair. 'It's just that he gave me the creeps, he's sick enough to have done it.'

Davis didn't want to make it look like he was simply disregarding Lewin's point of view. He valued her experience highly, in fact he was sure that she'd make sergeant at the next board. 'I haven't ruled him out, but I do have to say that although I accept he's a pervert, and I'd rather he never saw daylight again, I don't think he killed our girls.'

Green came back from the toilet. 'Sir, Mr Malloy wants to see you as soon as you finished Sibley's interview.'

Davis groaned, 'Oh God. That's all I need. Where's Graham?'

'He's gone down to the canteen to have a word with sergeant Reynolds.' Reynolds was a uniformed sergeant who had been on the Chatteris force longer than anybody else. 'He thinks there might have been a girl kidnapped years ago but can't find it on the computer.'

'What are you working on?' Davis asked Green.

'The sarge had me looking for crimes that have any similarities to the girl's murders.'

'Any luck?'

Green shook his head, 'No, sir. We've got rapes, we've got murders, but we haven't got anything like this.'

Davis said, 'Keep searching. Gillian, get on to the SOCOs, see if there was anything obvious we missed at Sibley's.' He looked grim, 'I'll go and face the boss.'

Davis climbed the steps to Malloy's office and knocked on the door. Malloy called him in and waved him to a chair. 'I hear you've got our man,' he said with relief evident in his voice.

Davis wasn't sure how to start and Malloy picked up his hesitation. 'Not a third man in custody only to be released?'

'Well at least this one's going to be charged with something.' Davis told him about finding Sibley with the image on his computer. 'But I just don't think he's our murderer.'

'Christ sake, Phil, if he's not you'd better get your act together. This man's kept ahead of us all the way. He's not going to stop unless we stop him. Do you not have anything positive I can give the press, and more importantly, the Chief Constable?'

Davis felt stung by the implied criticism, 'If I had do you think I'd be sitting here getting blasted by you? I'd be grilling the bastard.'

Malloy held up a hand, 'I'm not having a go at you, yet. I do remember how hard it can be, but we can't afford anymore dead girls.'

'I know, I'm sorry.' Davis got up. 'I'll have more for you when forensics get back to me, but at least Sibley will go to jail for the pictures.'

'Get me the killer, Phil.'

Davis nodded to Malloy as he went out the door.

Wednesday

Davis was looking through the notes relating to the interview with Sibley that he had written up before going home last night. Although he accepted that Sibley was a pervert and a threat to women of all ages he was still sure he wasn't the man they were looking for in relation to the girl's deaths.

Davis could barely believe it was just a week ago that he'd been called to Alice's body. Now they had two dead girls and still no idea who had killed them.

As usual he was in the office early and had skipped breakfast at home. Since the diagnosis of his diabetes he had been told he should make sure he ate a sensible breakfast, preferably a high-fibre cereal. That was not Davis's idea of a good breakfast and he often left home without eating the rubbish Anita insisted on buying.

Just as he was thinking about food Lewin walked in. 'Hello, Gillian, have you had breakfast yet?'

He knew that she was unlikely to have eaten before she left home.

Living alone she tended to eat either at work or in cafes if she could during the week. 'No,' she replied, 'I couldn't be bothered.'

'Well, let's go down to the canteen. We could both do with something to eat.'

As they settled down at a table with their trays Davis looked enviously at Lewin's plate. She had a large fry up on it and was just squeezing her second sachet of brown sauce over it. He had decided he'd better not flout his restrictions too much. He had two slices of toast with a low-fat spread and an apple.

Lewin looked at Davis's plate and said, 'Mmm, that looks so good I wish I could swap with you.'

'That'll do, constable,' Davis said grimly, to much laughter.

After a few minutes of steady eating Davis said, 'I've been giving the focus of our investigation some thought.'

Through a mouthful of bacon Lewin said, 'Me too.'

Davis took another bite and was silent for a few seconds as he chewed. 'We've looked at what the girls have in common and what their parents have in common. We've got nowhere doing that. Three arrests and three dead-ends.'

'You're ruling Sibley out then?' Lewin asked.

'Unless forensics turn up something we didn't find, yes. We need to look at what the murderer is getting out of this.'

'I thought we had tried that, all we came up with was he's a sadistic bastard.' Lewin mopped up the last of the sauce and egg yolk on her plate with a slice of bread.

'Taking that point as if it were serious, if he were just a sadistic bastard I think he'd have hurt the girls more than he did.'

'If he were a sadist there probably wouldn't be a link between the girls or their families, and so far all we've been able to find is that their fathers went to the same school over twenty years ago,' Lewin said.

'I want that followed up some more today. Go with Graham to the school and see if you can find the records for pupil attendance covering the years both men were at that school. Then, long job as it will be, I want to trace all the other boys.'

'That could be thousands!'

Davis shook his head, 'I don't think so. If this is linked to his school days I think there will be a fairly limited number of people to consider.' He held his hand up to count off points as he made them. 'Firstly, kids tend to stick to their own year groups, so we only concentrate on boys of the same age as the fathers. Secondly, we have to assume he's stayed in the area, so he's probably on the electoral roll. Thirdly, he almost certainly lives alone. If we get a list of names from the school we check them against the electoral roll, those on it we visit, if they live with anybody else we put them to the bottom of the list and move on.'

'It's still going to be a hell of a task.' She stopped for a moment then looked back at Davis. 'Do we even know if the school keeps records that far back?'

'It was remembering something the headmistress said that set me thinking along these lines. She said she'd have to look back in the records to be sure. In other words they have them.'

'Okay, as soon as Graham comes in we'll go.'

'I want to go over the statements from the Beresfords and James and pick out anything relating to the killer. What he said, how he referred to them. In fact, I'll go and see Mr James again. This time we're not interested in what he said about Abigail, we want to know about the man and his attitude to Mr James.'

Having finished their breakfasts both of them went back to the CID office. Peterson and Green were both there and Green had just made coffees for himself and the sergeant. 'I don't believe that, every time I put the kettle on somebody else turns up.'

Davis flashed him a wide smile, 'It's why you're so popular, Patrick, you make a perfect cup.'

Green muttered something Davis didn't hear as he made the two extra cups of coffee.

Davis said to Green, 'I want you to find out as much as you can about the owners, users and tenants of any houses near the barn and the farm where both cars were burnt out. There must be a reason why he's gone back there twice to each place.' He looked over to Peterson, 'Graham, you go with Gillian, she'll explain on the way.'

It was only slightly later than Davis's visit but at half-past eight the school was packed with children. The noise level was alarming with kids calling greetings to each other, catching up on what happened in the hours they'd been apart, footballs were being kicked around the playground in several directions and other children were just running around. Peterson and Lewin were watching this through the six-feet high fence that enclosed the school. Peterson pointed towards the reception office and they made their way there.

141

The same secretary was on duty and she looked at Peterson briefly. 'Can I help you?' she asked in the same tone of voice as she'd used to Davis that suggested she had done as much as she was going to do by acknowledging he was there.

'I'd like to see Mrs Major, please.'

The secretary peered over her glasses and said, 'Really, officer, I'm sure you understand the importance of making an appointment. We are busy, you understand?'

Peterson was amazed, 'And I'm investigating the deaths of two girls, one of them a pupil at this school. If Mrs Major is on the premises I'd like to speak to her as soon as possible.'

Peterson thought for a moment she was still going to insist on him making an appointment when the issue was made irrelevant by Mrs Major walking through the secure door.

Lewin recognised her and said, 'We need a word urgently.'

Mrs Major replied, 'Of course,' and led the two detectives through the security doors to her own domain.

As they all sat down Mrs Major asked, 'What can I do for you this time?'

'When our inspector spoke with you yesterday he got the impression that the school keeps records of its pupils going back at least as far as the time both Mr Beresford and Mr James were here.'

Mrs Major was surprised, 'Well, yes, we do. You have to understand of course that the records from that era aren't on computer, they're on paper in a storeroom. Usually schools don't keep them but our previous headmaster had some fascination about their historical value. They're not in the way so they're still on the premises.'

'Would we be able to see them without too much bother?'

'That depends on what you mean by too much bother.'

Peterson wasn't sure what she meant.

'The files that are on paper are stored in what was the B-block boiler room.'

Peterson remembered the boiler room. B-block was the science and geography section of the school. It had been built in the late thirties and had a large coal fired boiler that was housed in an annexe off to one side. Peterson's favourite memory was that in his final year at school he and some of his friends had found a way into the boiler room and had spent many a break time over the winter warmer than they could have ever hoped for.

142

'So they finally got rid of the old boiler?'

'Yes, in the early nineties. The room was too small to use as a classroom but it has proved ideal as a storeroom. It has floor to ceiling shelving now. We've tried to keep some kind of order but, as you can imagine, things don't always work that way.'

'If we want to find a particular year would that be too hard?'

'Until we go over there I have no idea.'

'Can we go now, please?'

The three of them made their way to B-block. Peterson was in turn surprised how some parts of the school had changed since his day and at how much of it was still the same. As they walked through a link corridor that joined the earlier A-block to the B-block Peterson saw a completely new building through the windows.

He pointed it out to Mrs Major and asked what it was. 'That's the IT department, I'd be surprised if there was a computer in the office when you were at school, let alone in use for teaching.'

Peterson wasn't sure if she was being cheeky but had to admit she was probably right.

The headmistress led them through B-block and at the end of a long corridor with classes of both sides was a plain wooden door. Mrs Major took from her pocket the key she had taken out of her desk draw and opened the door. As she turned the light on Peterson's heart sank, the room was stacked from floor to ceiling along three sides with large cardboard boxes.

Mrs Major saw his look of despair. 'It's not as bad as it looks. Each box has on the front the year it relates to and the year the pupils were in. So for example 1975/Y3.' She pointed to a box. 'Then in the nineties the pupils' year count started when they started schooling rather than at each level of school, so it might be 1993/Y10.'

Peterson turned to the first stack to the left of the door. On the bottom box was written 1955, on the one on top of it was written 1979.

He asked, 'Are they not in order?'

'I'm afraid pupils were roped in to help move the boxes from the main reception store cupboard when we decided to convert this room and they just put them down as they brought them over. We've never had any need to sort them in to date order, in fact I think this is the first time we've needed to look at them since the move.' She moved into the centre of the small room and asked what year they wanted.

Davis had given that much consideration. If his theory was right he doubted the boys were too young when the problem started. It was best to start from the year Beresford and James had left school, 1983.

Peterson told Mrs Major which year he wanted.

'So they were sixteen, that would be1983/Y5.'

All three of them searched up and down the stacks of boxes and Peterson called out, 'Here it is.' The boxes were stacked three to a shelf with four levels of shelves on each wall. The box Peterson had indicated was the bottom one on the second shelf from the floor.

Peterson and Lewin each removed a box from the stack, both complaining about the weight of the boxes and the amount of dust on them. Peterson pulled out the one they wanted, there were no tables in the room so he put it on the floor.

Mrs Major said, 'Each box should contain the records for each pupil in that year and on top of the box a list of the names of all the pupils in that year.'

Peterson lifted the lid of the box and drew out a folder. From it he brought out three sheets of paper. He looked at the bottom of the last sheet. 'There were one hundred and ninety three pupils in that year group.'

He glanced at Lewin, 'If you take it that it's roughly split between the sexes that means almost a hundred boys that year.'

'We can't even be sure it was their final year they knew each other.'

'Exactly what are you looking for?' Mrs Major asked.

Peterson put the papers on the floor beside the box. 'We think whoever is killing these girls might have gone to school with the fathers, if we have to we'll find every boy of the same age who was a fellow pupil of theirs.'

'That's a tall order, sergeant, it will take hours just to get the names.'

'What I'd like to do is take the lists from the last three years of their schooling; we'll compare that to names on the electoral roll. Whoever is doing this is still local, I'm sure of it.'

'I'd prefer you not to take the records away, we can photocopy them for you.'

Peterson nodded agreement and they began looking for the other two boxes.

By the time they had found the boxes and got their copies it was gone eleven o'clock when they returned to the station.

144

Chapter Twenty

Davis had read the statements made by Alan and Clare Beresford. It was difficult to get any sense of how the killer had spoken from the words written down and it was now impossible to ask them. But he remembered Alan Beresford had been adamant that he didn't recognise the man's voice. Maybe the shock of what was being said had distracted him from the voice itself.

He decided to go and see Mr and Mrs James.

Parking outside their neat house he saw the curtains were drawn. For a moment he dreaded finding them dead just like the Beresfords. In this case though he had insisted on a family liaison officer staying with them, he used the excuse that the killer might try to get in touch.

He knocked on the door and a young, female constable opened the door. She showed Davis into the living room where both parents were sitting in separate armchairs just staring into space.

'I'm sorry to have to bother you at the moment, but we think the killer might have links to your school days Mr James. We need to ask if you've remembered anything about what the man said, or how he spoke, that might trigger any memories from the past.'

Mr James sat up in the chair and said angrily, 'My daughter's been murdered by some sick bastard and you think I've forgotten anything the man who did it said to me? I've played it over and over in my mind and I'm sure I've never heard him before.'

'It's been a long time, his voice might have changed, matured.'

Bob James slumped back in the armchair, 'Who the fuck would want to do that to a beautiful young girl like my Abigail? There was nobody that sick at school with me.'

'They may have been perfectly normal at school, often these crimes are the result of many years of brooding over a real or imagined wrong done to a person. Over the years they magnify what may have been ordinary events into a major personal grievance.'

James gave a humourless laugh, 'About the most we did was take the mickey out a poor lad whose parents had landed him with a girl's name...'

Bob James stopped talking and looked stunned, tears sprung to his eyes and looking at Davis and his wife he began to babble, 'No, no, please tell me no. It can't be...'

Davis was shocked. 'Do you know who it is?' he asked.

James could hardly get the words out. 'I… I should have guessed when he told me to…'

He stopped for a few seconds. Davis didn't dare say anything; he knew this could be the moment that broke the case wide open.

James got himself under enough control to carry on. 'I should have guessed when he told me to walk through Peterborough dressed as a woman.' He looked at Davis and said, 'He was getting revenge, he killed my beautiful Abigail in revenge.'

James was in tears now, his wife looked stunned. 'Do you mean you know this man?'

'Not now. He was at school with us. Damn!' James slammed his fist down on the arm of the chair. 'Now I remember that name.'

Davis expected him to say who he thought was behind the killings.

'Beresford,' James said.

'Beresford?' Davis repeated. 'He was dead before your daughter was killed, Mr James, he couldn't be the man we're looking for.'

James waved a hand at him impatiently. 'No, not the killer, I was at school with Alan Beresford, we were friends.'

Davis knew that, although he hadn't yet mentioned it to James. He told him now.

'Yes, but he was one of us, the group that used to take the mickey out of Vyvyan.'

Now Davis was confused. 'Who's Vyvyan, both you and Mr Beresford said you were phoned by a man.'

'Yes,' James exploded, 'Vyvyan Wilde. Vyvyan a boy!' He wiped a hand over his face, thinking, trying to bring back the memories. 'Vyvyan Wilde. Can you imagine how cruel his parents must have been?' he paused, 'or thoughtless, just like us.'

He sat forward in his chair and put his hands behind his head trying to ease the tension he must have felt.

'I can't imagine how difficult it would have been for a teenage boy to have the name Vyvyan; it must have been awful, simply awful.'

Davis said, 'I've never heard of a man being called Vivian.'

'It's spelt differently for men, v-y-v-y-a-n,' he spelt out. 'You can have Lesley for a girl or Leslie for a boy, the spellings are different. But when we were kids it was very unusual to hear a man called Vyvyan, there were some famous people, posh people with the name.' He gave a funny laugh, 'His parents were fans of Oscar Wilde and, sharing his surname, they decided to name their son after one of Wilde's two sons.'

James shook his head. 'If they'd called him Cyril, the other son's name, it would have been considered old-fashioned but he'd have been saved a lot of anguish.'

Heather James had listened silently to her husband now she said quietly, 'And my daughter would have been alive.' The look on her face told Davis that she was going to lay the blame for Abigail's death on her husband's shoulders.

There was a silence that Davis was reluctant to break. At last he asked, 'Have you heard from this man since you left school?'

James shook his head, 'No, I moved away briefly, a couple of years, almost as soon as I left school. My uncle had a farm in Yorkshire, he needed a labourer, so I did that until I'd had enough of mucking out cows and pigs. By the time I came back everybody had moved on.'

Davis realised he'd have to get this information to the team as quickly as possible. 'I'm going to have to go, I want you to tell constable Smith everything you can remember about this Vyvyan Wilde. Where he lived, who his parents were, and, if you can remember, a description.'

Davis got in the car and considered what he'd just been told. Peterson and Lewin would be checking the school records by now trying to put together a group of names, those who might be in danger and the one who was causing it. Davis had just found one piece of the jigsaw.

Davis arrived back at the station to find Peterson and Lewin going through the school records. They had compiled a list of names of those boys who had been at school with both fathers and were on the local electoral roll.

Davis said to Peterson, 'Have you got Vyvyan Wilde's name on there?'

'We're looking for a boy, not a girl,' he looked up at Davis, 'unless you know differently?'

'That is a boy.' He explained his conversation with Bob James.

Peterson was stunned, 'So it is linked to their school days. I was worried we were on a wild goose chase really.'

He scanned the records he had on the desk at the moment. 'Yes, look,' he said excitedly, 'Vyvyan Wilde.' He checked the name on the computerised electoral roll. 'He's not on here.'

'That doesn't mean much these days,' Lewin said, 'it's all too easy to keep your name off that if you want to.'

'Right,' Davis said, 'get searching. I want to know if he's registered anywhere else. I want an address and a full history of him by the end of the day.'

Vyvyan was getting ready to go out in the Escort. He had his pad of chloroform sealed in a bag. He'd have the knife with him just in case anybody tried to interfere. With Alice and Abigail they'd got in the car willingly and without any suspicion being raised. If by some mischance he were interrupted he would not allow himself to be captured. Although he didn't see himself as a violent man, if he had to he would kill to remain free.

He'd had a light lunch, he didn't like to go out hungry. Then he'd spent the next couple of hours tidying the cottage. Although he only rented the cottage, and would soon be leaving it for good, he liked it to be immaculate.

He had an hour left, it was no good getting to the road where he would abduct Tania too early, somebody might remember seeing the waiting car.

He settled down to go over his photo albums again, to remind himself of the good times he had with Andrew, to give him the courage to do it. That was something Andrew had been good at, giving him the courage to be himself.

Although Andrew was his second relationship with a man, he still felt uncomfortable considering himself gay. Andrew had shown him that there was no need to feel that way. They were living the life they wanted, and in doing so were not hurting anybody else.

Now they had a name to work with the team were galvanised into action. Davis had been checking all the local records he had access to and could find no record of anybody called Wilde currently living in the area. Davis did what Peterson had done yesterday, went to see sergeant Reynolds.

'Hello, Phil. Your team seem to be picking my brains a bit at the moment.'

'Well let's hope you've still got some left for me to pick,' Davis joked.

Reynolds laughed. 'Okay, what is it you want to know?'

'I'm after a chap called Vyvyan Wilde. Does the name ring any bells?'

148

Reynolds thought for a few moments. 'There was a family called Wilde, but not in Chatteris.'

Davis was eager for more information. 'Where did they live?'

'On the Warboys fen. The old man died over twenty years ago.'

Something was niggling at the back of Davis's mind. 'That's where the barn the girl's bodies have been found in is located. I remember Graham told me that the farm was sold to a bigger outfit at Ramsey when the old farmer died.' Davis swore, 'Damn it, he's putting the bodies there because he knew it as a kid. I bet the old owner was called Wilde.'

'That's right, that's what I'm telling you. The lad was too young to run the farm after the old man died, his wife took her and her son back to Devon where she'd got family.'

'How old would the boy have been then?' Davis asked.

'Well,' Reynolds said rubbing his chin in thought, 'he probably wasn't a boy then so much as a young man. He'd left school, but not by much.'

'Is there anything else you can remember? Did he ever come into contact with us?'

'Not that I can remember. Well, he got a ticking off from the sergeant we had then. Some kids stuff, you know, nothing official was done.'

'Can you remember what for?'

Reynolds shook his head, 'I was a constable then and tended to concentrate on Chatteris itself. Young Wilde was one of a group of lads who always hung around together. He was a bit of an oddball, but nothing you could put your finger on.' He looked at Davis in surprise, 'I've just got it, those two whose daughters were killed were part of that group.'

'Can you remember the others? It's almost certain their children will be at risk.'

'No, I didn't know the families, maybe Mr James can help.'

Davis thanked Reynolds for his help and went back to the team office.

'Right,' he said as he walked back into the room, 'we need to check with the Devon force, Vyvyan Wilde moved to Devon around twenty years ago. Prior to that he lived on the farm the Boyle's now manage.'

'If he's come back he must have some kind of presence here,

registered with a doctor, the phone company, letting agency, something, anything' Green said.

'Check that out then,' Davis said. He turned to Peterson, 'Get cracking on that list, I want a cross-check with the electoral roll, any boy at school with the two fathers and Wilde who is on the voters list we'll go and see. We've got to find out who else is likely to be a target.'

He picked up the notes on the Beresford family, 'Gillian, go through that again, identify any of his relatives of a similar age to himself and go and see them. We want to know who he was friends with at school.'

He looked at the three of them, 'There's almost certainly other people on his target list; I don't want any more dead children. Let's get moving. I'm going to see the James again.'

Davis looked at his watch as he went down the stairs, it was ten to three, where had the time gone today?

He stopped in at the canteen and wondered what to get for lunch. There was a selection of sandwiches on offer but he preferred the look of the lasagne. The trouble was if he had that he'd have to sit in the canteen and eat it, the sandwich could be eaten on the go. He bought a tuna in wholemeal bread sandwich and ripped the wrapper open as he left the canteen. By the time he'd walked to the car the first of the two sections of sandwich had gone.

He needed to be careful with the James, they were under a lot of pressure. He needed information from them but he must make sure they had enough time and space to grieve for their daughter properly.

He felt he had never been given the time to grieve properly for Grace. She had been born prematurely and despite the doctor's best efforts, she had not survived. The nurses had tried to comfort Anita. As the distressed mother she had been given much attention. Davis felt that he had been expected to be the strong one, to be there to comfort his wife. To take the burden of organising the proper funeral they both wanted for their beautiful baby girl.

That he might be distressed, that he was grieving the loss of a much wanted daughter, had barely been considered. He was expected to put on a brave face and get on with it. His only solace had been to absorb himself in work. Busy himself in other people's lives. Looking back now he realised it had been to the detriment of his own. His relationship with Anita had never recovered.

150

Chapter Twentyone

Davis parked his car outside the James's house and before he got to the door Constable Smith had opened it. 'They've done what they can with the list. Mr James thinks this Wilde character lived out near the barn, sir.'

Davis nodded, they were standing in the hallway with the door shut. 'Yes, that's right; his father owned the farm the barn was on. How are they coping?'

'Badly, they were obviously very upset anyway, but now Mr James knows his daughter has been murdered because of something he did he's distraught.'

'What about Mrs James?'

'She left it to her husband to tell me what he knew about Wilde, she pottered about in the kitchen and kept their other daughters company.' Constable Smith hesitated, 'I think, sir, it's caused a bit of a rift between them. Before he remembered this Wilde they were constantly holding hands and helping each other. Since you left they've hardly spoken to each other.'

Davis hoped that they wouldn't let this come between them, he'd seen other couples who had lost a child isolate each other, unable to share their grief, just like him and Anita. When one of the parents thought that the other had, however unintentionally, had a hand in the child's death, it could put a barrier between the two of them that was never overcome. He'd investigated a vehicle crash in which a stolen car had crashed into a passing motorist. The nine-year-old son of the innocent motorist had died in the crash. His mother had been powerless to avoid the crash but her husband had been convinced that she should have braked earlier, could have used another road, might have stayed at home. Anything that wouldn't have ended in the death of his son. He had stopped talking to his wife and then left her, unable to live with someone he thought, however wrongly, should have done something to save their child.

If Mrs James took the same attitude Davis didn't give their marriage much of a chance of surviving their daughter's death.

The kitchen door opened and Mrs James came out. 'Not again, inspector, we've had enough, what can we tell you that we didn't tell you this morning.' Her voice was weary, exhausted, her haggard looking face told of the torment she felt.

151

'I am sorry, Mrs James. I wouldn't disturb you if I could avoid it. From what you husband has told us we think there could be other families at risk.'

'My husband has given your constable as much information as possible, including a description of the man, what more can we do?'

Heather James was in tears as she spoke and her voice was rising. The front room door opened and Bob James came out followed by his youngest daughter. Davis was shocked, the girl, Poppy, looked so much like her older sister.

She glared at Davis and moved to her mother's side. 'Come on, Mum, let's go in the kitchen.' Mother and daughter retreated to the kitchen closing the door behind them.

'What do you want now? My wife has already decided Abigail's death is my fault, are you going to give her more reason to hate me?'

Davis felt sorry for the man. Who could ever expect that schoolboy bullying would tear a family apart a quarter of a century later.

'Mr James, you could never have known the boy you were at school with would become a psychopath.' Davis suspected that Heather and Poppy were listening on the other side of the door. 'It could have been anything that triggered this campaign of violence. Your actions towards this character might not pass the test of acceptable behaviour as an adult, but I suspect it goes on in every group of children.'

He could tell Bob James wanted to believe Vyvyan Wilde's actions weren't an inevitable consequence of his own at school.

'If every bullied child turned into a murderer my job would be impossible.'

Bob James shrugged his shoulders, he could probably accept the truth of what Davis said but he desperately needed his wife to accept it as well.

Davis needed to get the conversation back on track. 'Can we go in there and sit down?' Davis pointed towards the living room.

James didn't say anything but led the way into the room and sat down.

Davis sat down and said, 'We need to know who the rest of your group was. Can you remember them all?'

'There were only the five of us, that includes him.' There was no need to say who the him was. 'Myself, Alan Beresford, Geoff Symonds and Wart.'

'Wart,' Davis said, astonished.

152

Bob James said, 'Obviously not the name given to him by his parents.' He looked grim for a moment. 'You know you're right about not all bullied kids turning out bad. Wart was what we called our fourth group member all the time. His real name was William Robert Taylor. When we saw his initials the first time, when we were eleven, we couldn't resist calling him Wart, and it stuck.'

'And he didn't mind?'

James thought about it for a second, 'I don't suppose he was over the moon about it, but he never objected. Geoff was our ringleader, he was the biggest for a start, and once he'd decided on a nickname for you, it stuck.

'It's funny really how the different personalities got along. Alan was the action man, he'd do anything for a dare.' He smiled at a memory. 'I remembered dyke vaulting was popular then.'

Davis had heard about it when he was younger. The competitor had a pole similar to a pole-vaulter's and ran at the dyke, planting the pole as far across the dyke as he could. His momentum would, he hoped, propel him to the other side of the dyke. To help make the other bank the vaulter would attempt to climb up the pole as it swung to the far bank. All too often he would get a soaking.

James carried on. 'We dared Alan to have a go at the dyke near Vyvyan's house.' He almost laughed but the heaviness of his grief was too much. 'He needed a pole to vault with. All we could find was Vyvyan's mum's washing line support, it was way too thin and short really. He ran as fast as he could and as he pushed the pole into the dyke it sank in the mud.' He did laugh now, just a lightening of his mood for a moment. 'He hit the opposite bank with a thud and slid into the water, it was only then we found out he couldn't swim. Geoff pushed Vyvyan in and told him to get Alan out.'

He looked up at Davis, 'Vyvyan's mum worked in a shop, Alan used to make Vyvyan steal sweets from there.'

Davis knew now why Beresford had been made to rob a shop, this revenge was tailored to each boy's own actions.

'What was you're contribution to the group, Bob?' Davis asked.

'I was the comedian I suppose. It would be my idea to play 'knock down ginger', you know, knocking on doors and running away. I'd be the one to put a drawing pin on someone's chair before they sat down.'

A dark shadow passed over his face. 'It was my idea to hide his clothes when we'd been skinny-dipping; we made him walk home in a skirt.' He choked a sob back, 'That's why he made me walk round Peterborough in women's clothes.'

Davis was aware of the time passing too quickly; he needed to be out looking for Vyvyan Wilde. Bob James was talking not so much to tell Davis anything but to stop his mind dwelling on his daughter's death. Sympathetic as he was Davis had to get moving. 'I don't suppose you're in touch with any of the others still?'

James shook his head, 'I told you this morning, I moved away for a couple of years and when I came back, well, I'd grown up.'

He stopped, lost in reflection, then looked at Davis. 'You know what it's like? That gap of two years let me see that we had been kids, what we had in common were the past-times of children. I was only two years older but very much more grown up when I came back here. I got a job and made new friends.'

'I don't suppose you've seen them about town over the years, particularly Mr Wilde? We have no idea what he looks like.'

'Can't help you.' He shrugged, 'It's a small town and yet, without trying to avoid them, I haven't seen them.'

Davis realised he hadn't learnt much more than James had already told his constable, but at least he had a little more insight into the group's personalities. He also had two more fathers he had to get in touch with. Maybe he could stop their daughters falling into Wilde's clutches.

Davis got in the car and headed back to the station. The first thing he would do was find out where Wilde had moved to in Devon and get in touch with the local force. If Wilde had kept out of trouble they wouldn't be much help but it was somewhere to start.

Davis settled down at the desk in his own little office, there was too much noise in the office to make the call out there. He had stopped and made himself a coffee as he'd passed the kettle.

Davis accessed the electoral roll details for Devon and eventually found that Vyvyan Wilde had settled in Ilfracombe. Within minutes he was on the phone to the town's police station and had been connected to the local beat officer.

'Yes, I know your Mr Wilde.'

'Does he have a record then? I couldn't find anything.'

'No, he only really came to our attention after his partner died. There was a bit of difficulty with the relatives, we had to …' Constable

Reed hesitated, 'we had to calm him down.'

Davis was intrigued. 'Why did he need calming down?'

Davis heard Reed sigh, 'I actually felt sorry for him. He and this chap had been living together for over ten years.'

'Another man you say.'

'Yes, why?'

'That might explain why although the girls were found naked they hadn't been sexually molested.'

'Girls?'

Davis had explained that he was interested in Wilde in relation to a murder enquiry but had not yet given him any details, he told Reed the whole story now.

Reed was shocked, 'He didn't come across as the violent type. In fact, as I said, I felt sorry for him. His partner had a heart attack and was rushed to hospital. The chap's mother, as next of kin, asked that Wilde should be kept away. When the partner came round he obviously changed that, in fact it was decided that they would undertake a Civil Partnership ceremony as soon as he got out of hospital. Before that could be organised the chap had another heart attack and died.'

'So what was your involvement?'

'The pair lived in a small cottage in the Torrs Park area, the mother was under the impression her son owned it outright, or so she said, and went round there to clear it out. It turned out they'd owned it between them and your man Wilde used force to get her out of the house. Pushed her out the door so hard she fell and bruised herself.'

'You said he didn't seem violent.'

'You had to meet the mother. All Wilde did was push her, she was so objectionable most people would have strangled her. She wanted him arrested for assault, we persuaded her to drop the complaint. Wilde said it was out of character, he had just got tired of people trying to bully him.'

Davis was stunned, 'He said that, used the word bullying?'

'Yes, I suppose that ties in with your case really, he's decided to have a go at the bullies.'

'So it would seem. That was the last you had to do with him, was it?'

'Yes, the will proved Wilde had inherited everything from his partner and the mother had to lump it.'

'Would you mind paying the house a visit? See if our Mr Wilde

155

goes home between crimes.'

Reed laughed, 'I'll do that, do you have enough for me to arrest him if he's there?'

'Oh yes, if you get him let me know, I'll get down there as soon as I can.'

With a promise to be in touch Reed hung up.

Davis went back into the CID office and told the rest of the team what he had discovered.

'So I might be wasting my time,' Green said. 'He's not likely to be registered up here with anybody.'

Davis agreed it was unlikely. 'But he is probably living somewhere. Check out all the rental agencies. We can rule out hotels and the like for now, he needs his own space for what he's doing.'

'We need to get hold of the two remaining friends,' Lewin said.

Davis said to her and Peterson, 'Take one of them each and find them. Warn them about Wilde. We don't even know yet if they have children. Warn them to keep their children under watch at all times until we find him.'

Tania Symonds was looking forward to tonight's riding. The weather was perfect. She was thinking about taking her horse over the fields towards Somersham after mucking out. She didn't like mucking out but agreeing to help out around the stables after school kept the bill down for having her own horse stabled.

She swung her long dark hair behind her. She was wondering whether she would get away with wearing just her shorts and t-shirt on her ride. Mrs Webb was a stickler for safety and, although Tania wasn't having lessons or anything, she mostly had to wear jodhpurs and a protective waist jacket.

As she was thinking of the best way of getting on the right side of Mrs Webb an overtaking car cut in before it had finished passing her. The rear bumper of the car clipped her front wheel and she was pitched off the bike onto the grass verge. Years of falling off horses had taught her to roll as she hit the ground. Although she was shaken she picked herself up quickly. She looked up the road. At least the driver had had the decency to stop.

He got out of the car and came towards her full of apologies. 'I'm so sorry, the sun got in my eyes and I misjudged the distance. Are you okay?'

156

Tania looked up and down herself, she had grass stains on her knees and her t-shirt, apart from that she was unharmed. She was just about to say to the driver that no harm had been done when she noticed her bike, the front wheel was badly buckled and she certainly wasn't going anywhere on it now.

'Oh, I'm so sorry. Obviously I'll pay for it to be repaired. Can I give you a lift anywhere?' the man asked her.

'Well I am going to the stables, it's about half a mile along here.'

'I know it, let me put your bike in the boot and I'll run you up there.' The man stowed the bike in the boot. He shut the boot lid and they both went to get in the car. 'Sorry,' the man said as she tried the door, it was locked. He reached over and flicked the catch open.

Tania got in and reached behind her for the seatbelt. As she turned back the man's hand was coming towards her with a white pad in it. She wondered what the hell it was, for the few brief seconds she was conscious.

Chapter Twentytwo

Vyvyan pulled up in front of the barn doors and got out of the car. The tension he felt when standing at the side of the road with Tania had begun to drain away. If anybody had driven past he might have had to abort his plan. Once he had her safely out of sight there wasn't much left to go wrong.

Before he closed the doors he looked down the farm track. The cottage was about two hundred yards from the road, there was nobody in sight. He went to the passenger side of the car and opened the door. Tania was still out cold. He lifted her carefully from the car and carried her to the bench, laying her down.

He had to strip her now. This was the bit that he disliked. Although he had tortured the two previous girls and would do the same to Tania, although he would eventually kill her, he wasn't a paedophile; he wasn't even interested in the female body, he still felt guilty that he was undressing these young girls.

He cut her clothes off rather than pull them off and taped her to the bench as he had Alice and Abigail. She was beginning to come round. He moved out of her range of vision. He liked to see what they made of their circumstances as they came out of their drug-induced sleep.

She mumbled a few times and tried to lift her leg. He saw it jerk, once, then twice. She tried to lift her head and when she couldn't she tried to move her arms. Her eyes were wide open now and she was clearly panicking.

'What's happening? Why can't I move? Where am I?' she called out.

Vyvyan moved beside her where she could see him. 'What's happening, my young friend, is that you are going to help me put right a longstanding injustice.'

She didn't understand him, what could he possibly mean? 'Where's my Dad?' she asked.

'I don't know, but you should start to worry about him.'

'Why, what's happened to my dad? Is he okay?' She started crying silently.

Vyvyan laughed, 'He is at the moment, but he might not be for much longer.'

Tania realised that she was naked. 'What are going to do to me? Please don't rape me, I haven't done it before,' she pleaded.

Vyvyan's temper flared, 'Why do you girls always think of sex first? You disgust me. You're naked because I can do what I want to you and it will make your dad so much more afraid for you.'

'What are you going to do to my dad?' she pleaded.

Vyvyan picked up the rucksack Tania had been wearing on her back and tipped the contents out on the bench beside her. It was the phone he was looking for; he would use it to send a video to her father. Vyvyan asked Tania if her dad's phone would show them.

'Yes,' she replied tearfully, mystified, scared.

'Well let's give him something to look at. Firstly we need to make sure he doesn't do anything silly like call the police. Where is he likely to be?'

Tania hesitated for a moment, she didn't want to tell this man anything about her family but she knew she was in trouble.

'He's at work, he's a director at Foxton's accountants.'

'A director is he? Does he have his own office?'

'He works from home, he converted the garage into an office, why?'

Vyvyan scrolled through Tania's contacts list until he reached her father's number and dialled it. 'He might value the privacy, that's all.'

After four rings it was answered. 'Hello, Babe. What's up?'

Vyvyan wasted no time, he wanted Geoff Symonds to be scared straight away. 'Your daughter's life is in your hands, do as I say and she might live to thank you.'

'Who the fuck is this?'

Vyvyan smiled, they never got it straight away, they didn't accept immediately that he was in control. Perhaps it was only natural, not wanting to lose control, or have it taken away. Especially when it concerned your children.

'I'm the man who will kill your daughter if you tell anybody I've got her and if you don't do exactly as I tell you to.' As he'd been talking Vyvyan had moved over to the other side of the room where he had picked up the sharpened knife. Concealing it behind his back he returned to the bench and stood beside Tania. 'I take it you'd like me to prove that I have her and haven't just stolen her phone?'

'Let me talk to her,' Symonds demanded.

'Certainly.' Vyvyan moved the phone behind his back for a few seconds and said to Tania, 'You can say hello, daddy, if you try to say anything else I'll smash the phone. Do you understand?'

Tania mouthed, 'Yes,' quietly. Vyvyan brought the phone towards her mouth and nodded.

'Hello, Daddy,' she sobbed, the chance to talk to her father moving her to even more tears. She didn't notice the quick movement at her side or the glint of light on the blade as it swung down before it was forced into her hand.

She did feel it though. Her scream pierced the air. Vyvyan pulled the knife from Tania's hand and moved away from the bench. He put the phone to his ear to hear Symonds desperately calling his daughter's name.

'She's not able to come to the phone right now. I bet you believe I have her though, don't you?'

'Who the hell are you? What do you want with my daughter? What have you done to her?'

'It's not your daughter I'm interested in, it's you.'

Symonds was stunned, 'What do you want with me? Why have you hurt Tania? What have you done to her?'

'She might not be riding a horse for a while. I'm going to send you a little video, hang up and wait for it to come through. I'll ring you again afterwards.'

Vyvyan hung up and went through the phone options until he'd found the one to record a video. He pressed the button and said to Tania, 'Smile, this is going to daddy.'

Tania hadn't stopped crying since Vyvyan had stabbed her hand, now she screamed at him, 'When my dad catches you he's going to kill you.'

'That's lovely, put more pressure on him. Do you hear that? Your daughter expects you to rescue her. You aren't going to try though, are you? Because if you do, you know I'll kill her.'

While Vyvyan had been talking he'd been holding the camera so that it showed Tania's face. Now he slowly moved it down along her naked body.

'You see how vulnerable your little girl is? I can do anything I want to her and there's nothing you can do about it. You are totally powerless, you can't stop me.'

Vyvyan pressed stop on the phone and went through the process of sending the message. 'Let's see what he makes of that,' he said to Tania. Once the message had been sent Vyvyan turned the phone off. He

160

couldn't guarantee that Symonds wouldn't call the police in and the phone signal might be used to trace him. It wouldn't lead in itself to this cottage, but the police would obviously link this kidnapping to the earlier ones. They would mount a house-by-house search which would probably start with the more remote houses in the area covered by the mast that the signal was being transmitted on.

He had decided that this one would die in a different way to the others. Alice had been a spur of the moment thing, she'd made him angry, but he had to admit that he'd enjoyed the sadistic nature of Abigail's death. Her certain knowledge that she was dying and his knowledge that she was powerless to defy his wish that she'd die had given him a greater thrill than he had expected. Now he had to think of an enjoyable way of dispatching Tania when she was of no more use to him.

Vyvyan left the garage and went back to the house. He'd give Symonds a few minutes to sweat before phoning back. He made himself a cup of tea and took it back to the garage. As he approached the bench he saw Tania's muscles relax. He put his tea down on one of the low walls and went over to her. She had been struggling against the tape holding her down. The bench didn't quite touch the wall; there was a gap of about three inches. That meant that he'd been able to wrap the tape around her and the wooden surface, binding her tightly around the waist and forehead. He'd also cut small holes beside each leg and arm and taped these to the surface. She was stronger than the last two girls though, maybe her riding had kept her fitter, she had managed to slacken the tape at her waist and legs. He got a roll of the tape he used and wound it around her and the bench top just above her knees and again at her shoulders, crossing where it restrained her upper arms but just above her breasts. She wouldn't break free now, that was for sure.

Vyvyan turned the phone back on and dialled Symonds's number. Symonds answered immediately. 'Well, I bet you can't wait to do as I want, can you?' Vyvyan asked.

Just like the other fathers, Geoff Symonds defiance had collapsed. 'What do you want of me?'

'That's better. I have a task for you to carry out.'

Symonds was desperate. 'Anything, I'll do anything. Please don't hurt my daughter, she's all I've got.'

Vyvyan wondered what he meant by that. Putting his hand over the phone he asked Tania, 'Are your mum and dad divorced?'

She looked distressed, 'My mum died two years ago.'

'Don't you have any brothers or sisters?'

She shook her head.

This was even better, Symonds would be more vulnerable, more willing to go along with Vyvyan's demands.

'Whether your daughter gets hurt is entirely up to you, do you understand that?'

'Yes, yes, just tell me, I'll pay whatever you want.' Symonds was frantic with worry.

Vyvyan was enjoying this, it had always been Symonds whose bullying had been physical. He had wanted to inflict pain, the worst example of course was forcing Vyvyan to pierce his own ears. Trust him to think he could buy Vyvyan off.

When Vyvyan had arrived home with his ears bleeding and his shirt stained his father had been as livid as Vyvyan had expected. After much shouting and a few belts Vyvyan had eventually told his father that he'd been forced to do it.

Having got the name of the boy who'd made him do it Vyvyan's father had driven him round to Geoff Symonds's house to confront the boy.

Symonds had immediately claimed that it had been a bet, that both boys had dared each other to do it. Vyvyan had gone through with it but Geoff had chickened out.

He had then pulled a five pound note from his pocket and said, 'I'm sorry I didn't have it with me earlier, but here, you won it fair and square.'

Vyvyan's father had believed Symonds and called Vyvyan a lying little coward. The next day Symonds had demanded the money back and a pound interest, much to the amusement of his friends.

'I don't want you to pay me, Geoff, I want to know how far you'll go to protect your daughter.'

'I've told you, I'll do anything.' Symonds sounded distraught now, not far from total panic.

'Good, I want you to cut your left ear off, all of it...'

'You want what?' Symonds interrupted. 'Are you some kind of maniac?'

162

'Well, I wouldn't say so, but you can, if you want to think of the man holding Tania as a maniac. If I was her father, I wouldn't like that idea one little bit.'

'No, no, I'm sorry, I apologise, I didn't mean that.' Symonds was gabbling, saying anything, anything to stop the man hurting his precious Tania again. 'Do you really want me to cut my ear off? You want me to do it?'

'Yes, and you must film it on your phone using the video function, Tania tells me your phone can do that.' There was silence from the other end of the phone. 'Do you understand what I've told you?' Vyvyan asked.

'Yes.'

'I'm going to hang up now. If you haven't sent the video to Tania's phone in five minutes I'll cut both her ears off and send you the video of that, okay? Just a little bit of encouragement.'

'I'll do it,' Symonds said, but Vyvyan had already hung up.

Davis had left for home while Lewin and Peterson had still been looking for Symonds and Taylor.

Davis had offered to do some of the legwork but Peterson had said, 'You get off home, it'll save us ending up at the pizza take-away again.' Gillian laughed and Davis caught a look pass between the two detectives. He began to wonder how much of their spare time they were spending together. Still, that wasn't his concern as long as it didn't interfere with their work.

Lewin had taken Symonds's details and Peterson was trying to find Taylor. In less than thirty minutes she found three G. Symonds on the electoral roll and had rung the first two. After establishing that neither of these two was Geoff Symonds, one time pupil at St Andrews school, she had tried to contact the third one listed. He wasn't answering his phone so she decided to pay the house a visit.

Davis had arrived home just before six-thirty. Anita greeted him without affection and said, 'It's just as well we're having a lot more salads, I never know what time you'll be home these days.'

Davis was in no mood for a row. 'I'm sorry,' he said wearily, 'we know who we're after but we're no closer to catching him. If the past week is anything to go by he'll be looking for his next victim if he hasn't already got her.'

'How did you find out his name if you haven't caught him?' Anita asked, as interested in this case as any parent would be.

'The father of the girl murdered on Monday night came up with it. He had been part of a group of friends, although the murderer seems to have been there for the others to pick on.'

Davis was quiet for a minute, reflecting on his own family. 'Do know, what those boys did all those years ago wasn't much different from what Adam and his mate have been doing.' He sighed in frustration. 'None of us can have any idea how long someone can brood about these things.'

Anita was shocked, 'Phil, don't tell Adam about it, I don't want him having that hanging over his head as he grows up.'

Davis thought about it for a few moments. He agreed with Anita, but it might have done the boy some good to learn what damage bullying could do.

Chapter Twentythree

The three of them had just sat down to dinner when Davis's mobile phone rang. It was Bellamy.

Davis left the table and went into the kitchen. 'Bellamy, congratulations, I understand you have a son.'

'Yes, sir. Thank you. That's not what I called about though.'

Davis dreaded Bellamy wanted more time off. They were under pressure to find Wilde now they had a name, Bellamy would be useful if he was back on the team.

'What is it then, Paul?'

'Since I've been visiting my wife at the hospital I've found an old mate of mine works here as a porter. Well, I knew that he was due to finish his shift just as I was leaving so I decided to see if he wanted to pop out for a drink.'

Davis wasn't impressed but said nothing. Bellamy was off work to look after his wife, if she was still in hospital and Bellamy had time to go to the pub with his mate then he had time to come to work.

'Anyway,' Bellamy continued, 'I had to wait for five minutes for Gerry to finish.'

Davis was wondering if there was a point to this conversation. It was a good job his dinner was a salad, at least it wasn't going cold.

'As I was waiting a chap came in with a bandage round his head, it seems he'd cut his own ear off.'

Now Davis was paying attention.

'The funny thing was, sir, he wouldn't explain why he'd done it. He was just insistent that they stop the bleeding and let him out as soon as possible. They wanted to keep him in, but he wasn't having any of it.'

Davis knew that Patrick Green had been keeping Bellamy up-to-date on the case. 'You think this is linked to our man?'

'Yes, sir. He's done something unlikely to himself and he can't wait to get back out.' Bellamy hesitated, wondering if he was making too much of what he'd seen, but decided to push on. 'I think he's got a child that might be in danger.'

'I think you could be right, the timing is spot on.' Davis had to think fast, he wanted this child found alive. 'Find out where this chap is now. Identify yourself to the person in charge and ask them to do what it takes to keep this man there until I get there. I want to know his name, ring me as soon as you find out what it is. My bet is it's Symonds or Taylor.'

165

Bellamy almost shouted, 'It's Symonds, sir, he gave a different name, but he just started to say Sym... before he said Haigh. He said his name was Simon Haigh, I just thought he was having trouble speaking clearly because of the pain.'

'Shit,' Davis swore. There was no doubt, Vyvyan Wilde had struck again. 'I'm on my way now.'

Davis put his head around the dining room door and said to Anita, 'Sorry, he's done it again, I've got to go.'

Anita put her hand to her mouth and looked at her son, Davis could imagine that Adam was going to be getting a far tougher lecture about the evils of bullying from his mother than he, Davis, had administered.

As Davis picked up his keys and opened the door he was on the phone to Peterson. He quickly told him of Bellamy's news and said that Peterson should gather the team at the office and wait for news.

It was an impressive house, large and detached, the extensive gardens, maybe when they were this big they should be called grounds, obviously had professional attention lavished on them. Lewin pushed the button on the doorframe and heard a bell peal somewhere in the house.

After a short wait it was clear nobody was at home. She decided to take a look around the property, that was how they'd found Clare Beresford.

She looked in all the windows as she passed them. There was plenty of evidence of extravagant spending in the house but nobody was at home. As she got to the far side of the house she saw the detached garage. It had been converted into an office. She tried to see through the windows but Venetian blinds were pulled down on each of them. Just as she was about to give up she saw that the one nearest the door had snagged on something and allowed her a restricted view into the office.

She bent down and put her hands around her face to cut out stray light. As her eyes focussed on the dim interior she couldn't believe what she saw, there was a puddle of what she was sure was blood on the carpet and a Stanley knife lay in the middle of it.

She pulled her phone from her pocket just as it started ringing. She looked at the screen, Peterson.

'Graham, I'm at Symonds's house, there's blood all over the office.'

'I'm not surprised. That's why I rang. He's at the hospital, he's cut

166

off his own ear.'

'Damn!' Lewin swore.

'He's done it again, he's beaten us to it.' Peterson said. 'The boss has been on the phone, get to the office and I'll bring you up to speed.'

Vyvyan had begun to wonder if Symonds would do it. Just as the five minute time limit was approaching Tania's phone had beep-beeped to tell him there was a message.

He opened the message and waited the few seconds for the video to load. He held the phone so that Tania could watch it with him.

Geoff Symonds was kneeling on the ground, he had presumably propped the phone up on his desk. Vyvyan saw him hold a Stanley knife up to show it to the camera. Then, without any hesitation, he took hold of his left ear with his left hand and sliced right through it with the knife. Blood spurted everywhere and Symonds let out a long yelp of pain.

Vyvyan laughed as Symonds jumped up from the floor and clamped his hand to his head, cursing loudly. Then Symonds turned to the camera again. 'I've done what you told me.' He was speaking through gritted teeth, clearly in a lot of pain. 'Now, please, let Tania go. Please don't hurt her, please.'

The video stopped and Vyvyan turned to Tania. 'See how much daddy loves you? I wonder what else he'll do?'

Tania was distraught. 'What have you done to my dad?' She was crying loudly and calling Vyvyan every unpleasant name she could think of.

'Oh no, I think I'd better make your dad wish he'd taught his daughter some manners,' Vyvyan said.

Tania's expression changed immediately. 'Please, no. I'm sorry, I'm sorry, I'm sorry,' she pleaded. 'Please, don't hurt my dad any more. You've got me, do anything you want to me, but please, leave my dad alone.'

'How touching. I might do both,' he said, relishing the fear he could see in her eyes.

Tania looked terrified, 'What, what are you going to do?'

Vyvyan's response was interrupted by Tania's phone ringing. It was her father.

Vyvyan answered the call. 'That was very brave, but will you be so brave when it's Tania being cut?'

Symonds was clearly still in agony and had trouble speaking clearly. 'You... you promised you'd let her go.' His breath was coming in jerky spasms. 'I've done... I've done it... I've cut my fucking ear off.' Vyvyan heard him groaning between words. 'Let her go.'

Vyvyan said quietly but menacingly, 'I'll keep your daughter for as long as I want to, and if I want you to you'll cut off anything I demand, won't you?'

'Yes,' Symonds replied dreading what this lunatic was going to demand next.

Vyvyan surprised him. 'What I want you to do now is go to the hospital and get yourself patched up. You mustn't tell them...'

'No, please, I want Tania back first. I'll go later when I know she's safe.'

'I think we've established that I'm giving the orders now,' Vyvyan said coldly. There was no response from Symonds so Vyvyan carried on. 'You mustn't tell them why you've cut you ear off, or that I have your daughter. Don't let them keep you too long either, I want to have some more fun.'

Vyvyan hung up and switched the phone off. He was going to enjoy thinking about Geoff Symonds going to the hospital. Not only was he forbidden to tell them why he'd mutilated himself he had the extra agony of worrying about Tania until he could get away from the doctors. That was the real reason he'd ordered Symonds to seek medical help.

Davis was half way between Chatteris and Warboys when his mobile rang. The hands-free kit answered it automatically. It was Bellamy.

'Sir, bad news. I went to the emergency department again but in the ten minutes between him arriving and me getting back there they'd put a temporary bandage on his ear and he'd done a runner.'

'Get back to the office then, you can tell us what you know,' Davis ordered. Bellamy could forget paternity leave for now if he knew what was good for him.

Davis braked to a stop and turned the car round, there was no point in going to the hospital now, they needed to find Symonds and Wilde quickly. He headed back to the station.

Davis said to the team, 'I think we have another girl kidnapped, we still have no idea where this Wilde character is carrying out these crimes and now we have a father running around who has already had to mutilate himself.' Davis wiped a hand over a weary face. 'If the past two girls are anything to go by we have less than twenty-four hours between first contact with the father and the girl being killed.'

Peterson said, 'You have a point there, Phil. This killer is a creature of habit. How about we put a watch on the barn and the track where the cars have been burnt out?'

Davis gave the idea some thought. 'I'm sure I could get some resources now, this case hasn't really hit the headlines yet but I know the Chief Constable is getting worried.'

'The barn would be easy, we could hide out at Morten's farm. The track might be more difficult, there's not much near there,' Peterson said.

'I'll see how many uniform staff the chief will let me have and make my mind up then.' Davis turned to Green, 'Patrick, you take over looking for Taylor. We don't know anything about him yet. I want him found as a matter of priority. When Bellamy gets here he can coordinate a watch on the barn, the track and Symonds's house, assuming I get the bodies we need for that.'

He said to Lewin, 'Gillian, you get to the hospital, I want to know everything that happened from the minute Symonds walked in there. Then get in touch with Foxtons, there's an office in Peterborough, get hold of one of the directors. I want to know if Symonds has been behaving out of character. I also want to know if he has access to any other property.

'Graham,' he said, 'you go to Symonds's house. I don't care how, but get in there. We have reason to suspect a violent crime has been committed there, that'll cover us breaking in. Find anything that might give us a lead, maybe Symonds wrote something down when Wilde called him.'

He looked around the team, 'I'm going to see Malloy at home, I think I'll get the help we need.'

He knew the rest of the team were as tired as he was, a murder case like this meant everybody was working flat out. 'I realise this is going to be an all-nighter, we haven't managed to save a girl yet, let's see if we can keep this one alive.'

The team went about their allotted tasks.

Geoff Symonds had taken two of the painkillers he'd bought at the Tesco store on the outskirts of Huntingdon. He was wearing a woolly hat to cover the bandage. Last year Tania had persuaded him to take her to see the Christmas lights switched on at Peterborough. The weather had been bitter and he realised he'd forgotten to bring his traditional Yorkshire flat cap. Although he was a bit young for the image of a flat cap he liked wearing them. Just to keep his head warm as they'd wandered around Peterborough he'd bought this woolly hat. Now he was glad to have it, it pulled down over the bandage neatly.

He was now driving back to Chatteris. The nurse had wrapped a bandage around his head after applying a sterile pad over the raw wound. This was meant to be a temporary measure until a plastic surgeon had inspected the damage. Geoff couldn't wait for that, Tania needed him to be out there looking for her.

He'd heard about Alice Beresford on the news. There were also reports of another body being found, although a name hadn't been released yet. He'd remembered the name Beresford as soon as he'd heard it and wondered if it was his old school mate.

None of the group had stayed in touch. He had gone to university and gone into accountancy, he had no idea what the others had done, nor was he interested really. But when that bastard had phoned he'd wondered immediately if the kidnapping of his beautiful daughter was linked to the death of Alice Beresford. Then, while he had been waiting for the nurse to patch him up, he'd put a name to the voice. The voice on the telephone. The voice telling him to cut his ear off or Tania would suffer. Vyvyan Wilde.

170

Chapter Twentyfour

He knew then. This was some warped lust for revenge. He and his schoolboy friends had bullied Vyvyan day in and day out. As his ear throbbed he remembered what he had thought was the funniest occasion, when he had made Vyvyan pierce his own ears. It didn't seem quite so funny now.

Geoff kept the BMW's speed to the sixty mile an hour limit, he didn't think the police would be looking for him, but the last thing he needed was to be pulled for speeding.

He wasn't sure what he was going to do; he didn't know how long it would be before Wilde phoned him again. He had the mobile charging up from the car charger so the phone wouldn't let him down.

As he followed the bend before the long straight towards Chatteris he remembered that Vyvyan Wilde's father had run a farm a couple of miles up the road. He had no idea if he was still there but if he was it was a remote enough spot for holding some one against their will.

Three minutes later he made the turn onto the bumpy side road. A mile later he turned onto the narrow road that the farm was on.

He pulled up just off the road. He wasn't sure if this was the house. He remembered it being set further back from the road. He got out of the car and approached the house. He could see no movement so went to one of the windows and peered in. He was looking into the kitchen, the room was a total mess. Just as he was about to move away a man came into the room and immediately saw Geoff looking through the window.

He knew straight away that it wasn't Vyvyan Wilde, but he had a problem, the man was enraged and was making for the door.

Geoff quickly stepped back onto the path to give him a bit more distance between the man and himself when the door opened.

'What the bloody hell do you want?' George Ramsden yelled at Geoff.

Geoff held his hands up in a gesture of submission and made up a quick lie, 'I'm sorry, I'm looking for a friend, I knocked on the door but nobody came.'

'So you thought you'd snoop then, did you?' Ramsden asked roughly.

'I thought I heard a noise and was trying to attract some attention.' Geoff wondered if this man might know of Wilde's whereabouts. 'I'm looking for Vyvyan Wilde.'

Ramsden was suspicious, 'What makes you think you'll find her here?'

'No, no, it's a man.' For a moment Geoff was reminded that the confusion caused by Vyvyan Wilde's name was the cause of his problems at the moment. A boy called Vyvyan didn't seem so funny right now.

Ramsden looked doubtful, 'Well there's nobody else here. Maybe you'd better try up at the manager's house.' He pointed up a lane that ran beside the house.

That was it, this was the labourer's cottage, Vyvyan lived in the bigger house. 'What's their name?' Geoff asked.

He wasn't sure he was going to get an answer, Ramsden studied him for a moment and then asked, 'Who did you say you were?'

'My name's Symonds, Geoff Symonds. I'm trying to find Vyvyan Wilde, I used to go to school with him. Is that the name of the manager?'

'No,' Ramsden said reluctantly. He turned away to go then turned back. 'Old man Wilde died before I came here. You won't find any of his people round here, they left.'

Geoff was devastated, he needed to find Wilde. 'Left, where did they go?'

Ramsden shrugged his shoulders as he turned away to go back in doors but said nothing.

Geoff Symonds returned to his car. Where the hell was he going to look now? Before he could come up with an answer his phone rang.

'Hello, Geoff, how's the ear? Have you got it patched up yet?'

'It's Vyvyan, isn't it?' Geoff asked, trying to keep his voice calm. Perhaps he could talk this perverted lunatic into letting Tania go if he established some kind of connection with him.

Damn! Vyvyan was livid. His whole plan relied on none of his victims recognising him. The girls were easy, he would kill them, but how was he going to deal with Geoff? He needed to stay calm; he would think more clearly if he stayed calm.

'Geoff, how nice that you remember me, it's been such a long time.'

'Vyvyan, please let Tania go, I know things could have been better at school. We...' No, he had to make his own link with Vyvyan, he needed to focus on getting Tania free. That meant trying to form a bond

172

with Vyvyan. 'I could have behaved better. I've often thought about what I did to you over the years, I regret it. I'm sorry.'

Vyvyan's efforts to remain calm disappeared. 'You've regretted it so much it's taken over twenty years and me kidnapping your daughter before you apologise. I'm supposed to believe this remorse is genuine, am I?'

Geoff felt sickened, he'd got off on the wrong foot. What should he do, being aggressive wasn't going to work, Vyvyan had Tania; he had the upper hand. Being contrite had failed. Perhaps meeting him would work, face to face he might be able to persuade him. If they met where he was holding Tania he might be able to overpower Vyvyan and rescue her. After all, Vyvyan was a weedy little shit.

'Look, how about we meet, talk things over. I'm sure it would help.'

Vyvyan was just about to ask how it would help him when he had an idea. He would agree to meet Geoff and kill him. Simple.

'Why would you agree to meet me, Geoff? Are we going to have a drink? Maybe a laugh over old times? Or are you going to try to rescue Tania?' Vyvyan wasn't going to make it look as if he was going to agree to a meet to easily.

'No, no, I promise, I know that would be risky.' The riskiest thing was leaving Tania with this maniac; he had to try something.

'Okay, Geoff. I'll meet you in twenty minutes one hundred yards down the Sutton Gault road on the outskirts of Chatteris. If you bring the police, or anybody follows us, you'll never find Tania alive.'

'I understand, I'll come alone, you have my word.'

'When you get there stay in your car, I want to check you aren't carrying a tracking device before you get in my car.' Vyvyan hung up as soon as he'd said that. He had no intention of checking Geoff out, he wasn't even sure that he'd know what a tracking device looked like. It would be far easier to kill Geoff in his own car and leave him there.

Geoff looked at the clock on the dashboard, did he have time to go home and get a weapon? The worry was that if he attacked Vyvyan and somehow didn't manage to subdue him the weapon might be turned on himself, or worse still Tania. He'd have to go unarmed.

He started the car and reversed in the farmhouse drive way. The journey, Geoff guessed, was a little over five miles. If he drove cautiously it would take about ten minutes to get to the rendezvous.

It took Vyvyan less than a minute to prepare another chloroform pad, this one a bit stronger than he'd used for the girls. With that done, and a small bottle put in his pocket he got going, he wanted to be there waiting for Geoff. What Geoff didn't know was that the meeting place was only a five-minute walk across the fields for Vyvyan. He wasn't going to risk using either the Escort or his own car to deal with Geoff.

Geoff turned onto Horseley Fen Middle Drove. Such a long name for a small road. It linked Chatteris and Sutton but was only used by the farms that were stretched along its winding miles. The main A142 was the road all the traffic used to drive between the two places. There was a small level area in front of a five-bar gate just about where Vyvyan wanted him to stop. He pulled onto it and turned off his engine. He looked around, the light was fading. He opened the driver's window all the way, the car was stuffy and he needed some air. He would like to get out and walk around, try to ease some of the tension he felt, but Vyvyan had said to wait in the car and he wasn't going to risk upsetting the man.

As he waited images of Tania flashed trough his mind. Happier images than he had at the moment. When she was a little girl and first started toddling. When she had her first rocking horse and her love of everything to do with horses since. Her strength since Sonia had died. She had been devastated at the loss of her mother but she had been strong enough to stop Geoff falling too far into a deep depression.

When he'd got her out of this he'd do as she'd asked on several occasions and have stables built behind the garage at home. She used the local stables at the moment but she really wanted her horse at home. She'd need something to help her get over this ordeal.

He heard a slight rustle behind the car, probably a rabbit, as he turned to look a strong hand grabbed at his head pulling it outwards and another hand clamped something over his face. He tried to wrench the pad away from his face but even more pressure was applied. Suddenly everything was going black.

Geoff slumped back in the seat. He was totally unaware as Vyvyan opened the bottle he'd put in his pocket and sloshed petrol around the car. A lighted match was thrown in and Geoff would never order that stable for Tania.

Peterson parked his car on Symonds's drive. The house looked as

174

empty as he assumed it was. There were no lights on even though it was beginning to get dark. He knocked on the front door first, somebody might have been there, or Symonds might have come home. Nobody answered so he walked around the house, checking if there was a door unlocked or a window open. No such luck.

He returned to his car and got an old fashioned wooden truncheon from the boot. He'd noticed that the back door had the key on the inside. He went to it and took a swing at the glass panel. The door was double glazed and the first strike cracked the outer pane from top to bottom. He swung again and the cracked pane shattered and fell to the ground. The inner pane was cracked and a third swing from the truncheon knocked that out.

Peterson put his arm through the hole and turned the key. As he opened the door he called out 'police, is there anybody home.'

If anybody was at home he didn't want them attacking him thinking he was an intruder. Nobody replied. Peterson went from room to room, quickly but thoroughly searching the house.

As he came back down stairs he reflected that Symonds's obvious wealth wasn't doing him much good. His daughter was at the mercy of a pitiless killer.

It put his minor problems into perspective. Although his wife had divorced him he couldn't honestly say he was that upset by it. They had married young, with little in common other than impending parenthood.

He also had to think about Gillian, they had been seeing a lot of each other after work. It had started because they both preferred to get a quick dinner out rather than each cook alone at home. Now they were going out to be together. Peterson wasn't sure if he needed the complication of a new partner, in either his home or work life. But that problem would have to wait until later, he had somebody else's life to think about at the moment.

Peterson left the house and went outside to Symonds's office. In the middle of the floor was the puddle of blood and the knife that Lewin had seen. There was no key on the inside of the door this time. Peterson smashed the window and, after brushing away the shards of glass, climbed through the hole.

The blood on the carpet had dried but still looked appalling. Peterson wondered if he would have had the courage to cut off his own ear to save his child from hurt. He supposed he would have. Most parents would, that was the weapon Wilde was using, a parent's overwhelming desire to prevent harm coming to their child.

There was a picture of a young girl on a horse framed and standing in pride of place on the bookcase. The daughter obviously. There were one or two trophy cups as well. For gymkhanas several years ago, awarded to Tania Symonds. Well at least they knew the girl's name now.

Peterson had a quick look at the paperwork on the desk. He was hoping that Symonds might have written something down about his conversation with Wilde. The desk was neat and all there was on it were a few sheets of paper and a laptop computer.

It was obvious that Symonds had left as soon as he'd cut his ear off. Would he return to his office? That was the question. Peterson decided to leave Symonds a brief note. They couldn't afford to leave an officer here but it might help if Symonds was aware the police were looking for Wilde.

Lewin parked in the hospital car park. The authorities could be difficult about giving out information about patients. If she were face to face with a nurse she might be able to get more from them, especially if she mentioned Symonds's daughter.

She walked through to accident and emergency reception and showed her warrant card. 'I'd like to speak to the doctor or nurse who treated a Mr Symonds, he gave a false name, Haigh.'

The receptionist looked down a list at the side of her keyboard. 'We haven't had a Mr Symonds in.' She turned back to her computer screen as if that was the end of the conversation.

Lewin tried to keep calm, this woman must be busy she told herself. 'This is important, can you check the name Haigh, he came in with a severed ear.'

The receptionist looked at her list again. 'That might explain why we couldn't find him, why would he give a false name at a hospital?'

'I'm sorry, what do you mean, couldn't find him?'

'Every patient has an NHS record,' she explained. 'Normally when a patient comes in we take their details before they sit down, that is unless their injuries are severe.'

'And his were?'

'Well, they looked it to start with. We don't take risks with head injuries and he came in with a towel over the side of his head and there was blood everywhere. Doctor Patel was just coming into the reception area to get a new patient. He took your man straight away.'

'So when did you get his details?'

'We need to access their records so one of the staff went through and had a word with him as he was being treated. He gave a name and address but they didn't check out properly. When my colleague went back he'd gone.'

'I take it he'd been patched up by then?' Lewin asked.

According to Doctor Patel his wound was a very clean severing of the outer ear, self-inflicted the doctor said. A nurse applied a sterile dressing and a bandage to keep the wound clean. The doctor was just checking whether there was a bed available. When he went back to the cubicle the patient had gone.'

The receptionist sounded affronted. Probably because her records were now incomplete.

'Did he not give any indication of where he was going?'

'Not to me he didn't. He rushed out without saying a word.' Lewin got the impression that the woman considered that the paperwork was more important than the medical side of things.

'Can I talk to the doctor who treated him?'

'I'm sure he's busy.'

Lewin said nothing and after a few seconds the receptionist sighed and picked up the phone. After a brief conversation she said, 'Dr Patel will be out in a few moments when he has finished with his patient.'

Lewin nodded a curt thanks to the woman and went into the waiting area and sat down. It was just as well the doctor only kept her waiting a few minutes, she almost dozed off.

Dr Patel was in his late twenties, slim and very harassed looking.

'How can I help you?' he asked Lewin.

She repeated her request for information about the patient who had cut off his own ear.

'There is not a lot I can tell you. He was in a lot of pain but I think he was far more agitated than was caused by the pain.'

'What do you mean? Did he say anything?'

'I asked him how he had been injured and he said, "I had to do it". But when I asked him why he wouldn't say. But he was in a great hurry, he wanted to go as quickly as possible.' Dr Patel was fiddling with the stethoscope hanging around his neck. Lewin could tell that the self-inflicted injury to Symonds was very low on the doctor's list of priorities.

'I thought you were going to see if there was a bed for him?'

'I was. He had brought the severed ear with him; I thought our plastic surgeon might be able to reattach it. I had the wound dressed to keep it clean.' Dr Patel looked at his watch for the second time in their brief conversation.

'One last thing, Doctor, did he give any hint of where he was in such a hurry to go?'

Dr Patel was already on his feet and moving back towards the emergency area. 'No, he said very little, but he shouldn't have left, we could have saved his ear.'

She wasn't going to learn anything useful here. They were desperate to track down Symonds before Vyvyan Wilde could kill his daughter. Whether he would be able to lead them to the killer, or not, they didn't know, but at the moment they had no other opening.

Saying a brief goodbye to the receptionist Lewin left the hospital. She was feeling very frustrated, this case had started with them having few clues as to the identity of the killer. Now they knew who it was they were no nearer finding him.

Chapter Twentyfive

Vyvyan had been back in the house five minutes after killing Symonds. He felt an elation that the killing of the girls hadn't given him. Symonds was one of his four tormenters; to dispatch him to his death had been vengeance indeed. He wondered if he should have gone straight for the four men, killed them instead of their children. He might still do that, after he had finished tormenting them. He wasn't yet aware that Alan Beresford had deprived him of that satisfaction.

This feeling of power was new to him. After Andrew died and he'd had to deal with that bitch of a mother of his, he had needed this. Exorcising demons, that's what he called it. If he could get away with it and move on from his life in Devon he'd settle down and put the past behind him.

He went out to the barn. He'd told Tania that he was going to meet her father. She'd hoped that he would bring him back here. That they would resolve this problem. That she could go free.

He opened the door, he knew she couldn't turn her head to see him. For a moment he said nothing, let her wonder, worry. Then she called, 'Daddy?' in a very shaky voice. A scared, little girl voice. Close to tears, close to losing it altogether.

'Sorry,' Vyvyan said, 'but daddy couldn't make it, things got a bit hot for him.' He laughed loudly at his own joke, he was getting more confident now that his plan would succeed. Nobody had any idea that he was behind the killings, of that he was sure. Geoff Symonds had been the only one to guess he thought. And he wouldn't be telling anybody now.

There was little point in keeping Tania alive now. As with the other girls his only interest in her had been to torment her father. No father, no use for the girl. But he found he enjoyed seeing the pain of others. Enjoyed the inflicting of that pain. He would torment her then he would kill her. But he would make sure she knew it was coming, he wanted her to know she was going to die.

Tania hadn't said anything since he laughed but he could see the fear on her face. He could have played the video of Abigail to Tania but that had gone when he destroyed her phone. There was one way to hurt her though.

'Shall I tell you what's happened to daddy?' he asked her.

'Please, tell me, you haven't hurt him have you?'

'Well,' Vyvyan said playfully, 'he's not in any pain.' Vyvyan saw Tania relax slightly and added, 'now.'

Tania screamed, and then through sobs she asked, 'What have you done to him?'

Vyvyan got up close to her, leaning over her so that his face was inches from hers. 'Daddy's gone to see mummy.'

To his surprise and horror she spat in his face. He jumped back in shock. In fury he grabbed the knife from the ledge beside the bench and in one powerful lunge drove the blade through her throat.

Her eyes opened wide in fear and pain. A rasping whistle of breath forced blood from the wound. Her mouth opened and closed with neither breath nor sound coming from it.

Vyvyan looked at Tania's naked body as it fought a battle it couldn't win, to stay alive. He felt arousal, a stiffening in his trousers. For a moment he felt disconcerted, he knew he didn't find women attractive. Then he realised what it was, he found murder arousing. The power, the command of death, he had the upper hand. It felt good.

After seconds that he didn't count, her body stopped jerking, trying to draw breath in. Her eyes stayed open and he saw how death took the humanity from them. They were no longer the windows to her soul.

Now he had to get rid of the body. He wondered if the police had discovered Symonds's car yet. If not he might simply drive the Escort up to it and set fire to that as well. Appropriate really, father and daughter together again.

He went out to the garden behind the cottage where he could see across the fields to the still burning car. He couldn't see any blue lights from emergency vehicles. As he stood looking though he heard the distant wail of a siren. Somebody had called the fire brigade.

He would have to wait to dispose of Tania.

The control room phoned Davis. He knew that the last two burnt out cars were connected to his case. He had left instructions that he be called to any suspicious car fire.

He pulled up behind one of the fire engines and made his way to the fire crew manager. 'Kenny, what can you tell me?'

'Hello, Phil.' The fireman took off one of his gloves and wiped his hand over his face. A smear of soot and sweat told how close he had been to the flames. 'I'm afraid there's a body in this one.'

'Any chance of identifying it?' Davis asked.

'Not the body, but you could still read the plate when we arrived; I've got it noted down.'

Davis retrieved the number and called the police station. 'I need a trace on this number,' he told the radio operator.

As the name of the registered owner was read out to him he swore.

The fire chief asked, 'Known to you?'

'Not yet, not ever now, Kenny.'

'But it sounds like you wanted to find him alive.'

'Very much so,' Davis said although he was distracted, thinking about this new angle.

'Who is he?'

Davis told the fireman about the case. 'And he's the latest man being targeted by this character.' Davis looked thoughtful for a minute. 'It's a new turn though for him to be attacked himself. The usual scenario is to mentally torture the father.'

The fireman said nothing, until one of his men walked over. It was Martin Stone, Green's partner. He greeted Davis and said, 'It was definitely arson, accelerants were used.' He smiled, 'Petrol to you.'

'Is there any way it could have been suicide?' Davis asked.

The fireman looked grim. 'It could have been.' He shook his head. 'A hell of a way to top yourself though.' He pointed to the car. 'The driver's window was down. If you were going to set fire to yourself you'd probably have the windows shut. But if the window was open somebody could easily throw a flammable fluid and a light into the car.'

Davis was troubled. What had caused Wilde to kill Geoff Symonds? Had he decided to change tack, target the fathers now? Was Bob James now at risk?

Had Geoff realised that his tormentor was Vyvyan Wilde? If so why had that made Wilde kill him? And how had Wilde lured Symonds to this quiet road?

There were so many questions to which Davis didn't have an answer.

Vyvyan was angry with himself. He had intended to take his time killing Tania; he was going to enjoy it. Yet for the second time his anger had got the better of him. Alice had made him angry and died before he wanted her to and now Tania had.

There was little to be gained by worrying about it. He would just have to move onto the next one.

Davis arrived back at the station to find the other team members had met there. Lewin reported her fruitless attempts to discover anything of value at the hospital. 'He was clearly in a lot of pain, but all he was interested in was getting back out.'

'Did he say anything about meeting anybody?' Davis asked.

'Not that the staff mentioned. In fact he said very little, he gave a false name and address, and left as soon as the nurse had put a bandage on him.'

Peterson said, 'Judging by the amount of blood in his office he must have cut his whole ear off.'

'According to the doctor, he did,' Lewin replied. 'The cut was flush to the side of his head.'

'To my mind there could only have been one motive,' Davis said. 'Wilde has got his daughter and he wanted to do whatever it took to gain her freedom.'

'Wilde hasn't let the other girls go, has he?' Green said.

'But Symonds wouldn't necessarily know that unless he's been following the news carefully,' Davis pointed out.

'Whatever, it's cost him his life if that was his body in his car,' Peterson said.

Davis looked grim, 'I think we have to accept it was. I don't know how yet, but Symonds got close to Wilde, too close. He must have worked out that it was Vyvyan Wilde who had his daughter and I'd bet that it was that knowledge that cost him his life.'

'How did Wilde lure Symonds to a meeting in order to kill him?' Green asked.

'What do you mean? How did he get in touch with him or what bait did he use?' Lewin asked.

Davis answered that. 'We saw with Abigail James that he uses the victim's mobile phone to get in touch with the father. It's a fairly safe bet that he offered Symonds some hope of helping his daughter, whose name we need to find out…'

'It's Tania,' Peterson interrupted, 'I saw it on a trophy she'd won for her horse riding.'

'Hopefully Tania is still alive, and if she is I want to keep her that way.' Davis turned to Green, 'Patrick, have you had any luck yet tracing Taylor?'

'No, Sir. I've done a PNC check on him, I've checked the electoral roll, looked in the phone book and Googled him. No William Robert Taylor as yet.'

'Keep trying. He may have moved away, it may be that Wilde can't find him, in which case his family will be safe.' Davis was feeling frustrated. 'I just can't believe that he's one step ahead of us all the time. We know why he's doing this now. We know the names of the victims. We know a bit about him now. Yet we can't find him.'

'He may still live in Devon, sir,' Lewin said. 'Maybe he's going home between crimes.'

'No, I don't think so. It's at least a five hour each way journey to Ilfracombe, these murders, the communication between him and the fathers; it's all too close together for him to be commuting. But where the bloody hell is he doing it, where's he staying.'

Davis had been on the way to see Malloy when the call about the car fire had reached him. He had detoured there immediately. The first thing he had done when getting back to the office was to ring Malloy at home. His wife had told Davis he was taking a shower. She would get him to ring as soon as he was out. The call came now.

'Thanks for getting back to me, sir.'

'That's okay, what do you have for me?'

Davis explained what had happened over the last couple of hours, finishing with the idea that Wilde might be a man of habit and he wanted to watch the barn and the track.

'I can spare two uniformed men and that's it.'

'We can't watch both sites with just two men.'

'I'm sorry, Phil, that demonstration at the new lab has got more heated and the Chief Constable has been leaned on by the Home Office. They want the place tied down tight for the official opening next week.'

'We've got two dead girls and now one of the fathers. I'm convinced there'll be another child in danger almost immediately.' Davis was almost shouting such was his frustration.

'Phil,' Malloy said calmly, 'it's no good having a go at me. I'd like to give you more men, but there just aren't any.' He sighed, 'The Chief Constable is in line for the top job next year, he won't risk upsetting the Home Secretary.'

'I'm sorry, Kev. I know it's not your fault.' Davis wiped his hand over his face. 'None of us are getting enough sleep at the moment, and we don't seem to be getting anywhere for our troubles.'

Malloy laughed, 'I think you need a day by the sea.'

Davis wasn't sure what Malloy meant. 'I don't think I'll be getting away for a while.'

'What I meant was, I think you should go to Ilfracombe and see what you can find out at Wilde's house. I'll get in touch with the locals and arrange a warrant.'

'Do your really think it's worth the time it will take?'

'You've already said you don't seem to be getting anywhere at the moment. We'll look pretty silly if he has a blueprint for these crimes sitting on his dining room table. I'll arrange a car and driver, that'll get you down there quickly.'

Davis wasn't so sure it was a good idea but he didn't have a better one at the moment. 'Okay, Kev, I'll take Green with me, you never know he might be able to provide some sort of insight into Wilde's life.'

Malloy laughed, 'Maybe, maybe not. We're all different, straight or gay.'

Davis promised to keep Malloy up to date with any new developments and, after hanging up, went to find Green.

'Patrick, enough for tonight for you. I want you to come to Ilfracombe with me tomorrow. Pack an overnight bag, just in case.'

'We're going to Wilde's home?'

'Super's orders. He's worried Wilde might have left information there that we could use.' Davis shrugged, 'I'm not so sure, but as I've run out of bright ideas, we're going.'

Davis turned to Peterson, 'Take over the search for Taylor, that needs to be a priority. Gillian, I'm more convinced than ever that our man is operating locally. Get in touch with all the area's rental agencies; I want a list of every property where the rental started within the last six weeks. I don't think our man's been here any longer than that.'

'Are we going to visit every property on the list?' Gillian asked.

'If we don't find anything significant on our trip to Ilfracombe we'll have to,' Davis said. He looked at the clock. 'I think we'd all better call it a day. If the SOCOs turn up anything really interesting from the car they'll ring me at home.'

184

Chapter Twentysix

Thursday

Peterson got up from his desk. His search for Taylor had been as unproductive as Green's the previous day. The problem was if the man had stayed out of trouble he wouldn't be on any of the police computers. He should be on the electoral roll, but he might have moved away. The next check was to check the vehicle licensing centre.

An hour later, and starting on his fifth coffee in just over two hours, Peterson was beginning to wonder if William Robert Taylor had ever existed.

Vyvyan had gone for a walk. If anybody had passed him they would have seen a man dressed for a stroll along a back road on the Fens in late Spring. A warm jacket and a hat kept the wind out. If they'd stopped to talk to him he would have told them that he was off to get his paper. What Vyvyan was really doing was seeing if the police had finished their activity of the previous night.

This time, unlike last night, he was walking along the road rather than across the fields. It would take him nearer twenty minutes this way instead of the five minutes using the short cut, but if the police were still there he didn't want to go putting ideas in their heads.

He rounded the bend at the top of Ferry Hill, just about the only hill around for miles. Another five minutes saw him walking past the junction with Horseley Fen Middle Drove. He tried to be as casual as possible as he looked along the road. There were no vehicles there, no police. He changed direction and walked down the road. The damage the fire had caused to the road surface was apparent, it was blackened and the tarmac was blistered. There was a pile of glass and other debris that had been brushed into the verge.

Vyvyan had been careful to stay indoors the previous evening after killing Geoff and Tania. He wasn't sure if the police would send the helicopter up again as they had when he had killed Abigail. He was sure that the police were so desperate for leads that they might pay a visit to anybody they found in the vicinity.

Today there wasn't that kind of problem. The small area that Geoff Symonds had parked in was the access to a field. Vyvyan leaned against the gate that protected the opening and looked across the fields to the cottage he was renting. It appeared to be further away than it actually was.

Tania's body was still in his barn. He had wanted to ensure the police had left before he moved it. He wanted to put Tania in the barn that he'd left the other two girls in; it was his way of thumbing his nose at authority. Nobody had protected him when he was being persecuted; he was going to show how useless these faceless people in positions of power were.

He thought about the next victim. He had been surprised when he discovered that all four men had daughters of the age group he'd wanted to kidnap. They needed to be almost adult, at least fifteen, preferably sixteen, but still children in their parents eyes. Still very vulnerable.

Wart Taylor's daughter, Laura, was the next victim. Wart wasn't his real name. William Robert Taylor. He'd never seemed to mind his nick-name. All of the group, including himself, had called William, Wart. The initials of his names suggested it to Geoff Symonds and it had stuck. Vyvyan thought now that maybe he should have defended William. But he knew really that he would never have found the courage as a schoolboy to stand up to Geoff. Well that was one problem that was in the past. Geoff Symonds wouldn't be bullying anybody again.

He'd had a stroke of luck tracking down William. He had been unable to find him by searching the electoral roll, the way he'd found the others. Just after he had rented the cottage he'd been reading the local paper and seen a mention of the funeral of William's Father. He had known it was William's father because the man's name was Travers Taylor. An unusual enough name that there was unlikely to be two of them locally.

Vyvyan had gone to the funeral and sat at the back of the church. He had got William's address more easily than he'd expected. An overheard remark that there was a small gathering 'at the oldest son's house, you know, William,' had led to Vyvyan following one of the guest's car until they reached William's house. He still lived in Chatteris, in one of the ex-council houses on the Adventurer's estate, named after the merchants who had paid for the Fens to be drained.

The estate roads were busy enough with cars coming and going that Vyvyan had been able to spend several hours, spread over a week, watching the Taylor family. The eldest daughter, he now knew she was called Laura, worked in the town's largest supermarket. She walked home, a journey that took her about fifteen minutes. He had walked the route a few times himself and knew just where he could take her. Sometimes she called in on her elderly, housebound grandmother for a cup of tea and a chat.

But there were other things to finish first. Tania's body had to be disposed of. Much as he had no qualms about killing these girls he wasn't too keen on having the corpses around for too long.

Davis looked at his watch; they were just driving through the Torrs Park area of Ilfracombe. As he gazed at the house he wondered whether this was going to be a wasted trip. Constable Reed had reported that when he visited the house nobody had been at home. The neighbours reported that since the death of his partner he had rarely been seen there.

The driver pulled up and pointed to one of the houses, 'That's it, sir.'

Davis was surprised, it was a very narrow house in a terrace of six similar houses. Wilde's, number four, was well maintained and appeared clean. The nets that hung at the two windows upstairs and the one downstairs were bright white and the painted window sills, although dusty at the moment, were obviously washed regularly. Next doors' had bird droppings dried on it.

The houses had no front gardens, the pavement ran along the front of the houses. Davis and Green got out of the car and Davis knocked at the door. There was no answer and after a brief wait Davis knocked again, harder this time. There was still no reply but this time the front door at number two opened and an elderly woman stepped out onto the pavement.

'He's not at home, he never is these days.' She looked at the marked police car. 'You the police?' she asked somewhat unnecessarily.

'Yes,' Davis replied. 'Can you tell me where he is?'

The elderly woman pulled a face that Davis interpreted as trying to look as if she didn't care. 'I try not to get too involved with them, if you know what I mean, him and his friend.'

'Can you at least remember when you last saw Mr Wilde?'

The woman thought for a few moments. 'Well I'm not sure. It was a while ago.' She looked flustered, 'I can't think. Oh, yes I can,' she said. 'It was a Monday two weeks ago, I know because my Eric, that's my youngest, came to pick me up to go to the doctors.'

'Did he say anything to you, maybe suggest where he was going?'

She drew back a bit and her face had a look of disgust on it. 'I don't talk to him so much anymore. Not since he attacked that poor Mrs Blackstaff.'

Andrew's mother, Davis had heard about that from Constable Reed but he was prepared to hear this woman's version of it in case he learnt anything about Wilde.

'He attacked someone? What was that all about?' Davis asked her.

The woman looked up and down the street as if making sure what she said to Davis wouldn't fall on the wrong ears. 'It was dreadful, I couldn't believe it was happening here, this is a decent area, you know?'

'I can see that,' Davis said.

'Well, I should have known when those two moved in, it isn't right you know, I don't care what they say.' She lowered her voice. 'Two men together, you know,' she whispered now, 'co-habiting.' She said it as if the very word would cause offence.

Davis could see Green smiling at his side. If this elderly lady knew that one of the policemen she was talking to co-habited with another man she might be shocked into silence. Luckily she was unlikely to find out, although Green made no effort to hide his private life he didn't see the need to jump up and defend it every time somebody else was disparaging about homosexuals.

She continued. 'That bigger one, Andrew, he died, very sudden it was. Well, his mother came to get his stuff, it's only right you know? She was his mother, she was entitled.'

She looked at Davis for agreement. 'I'm sure she meant well. What happened?'

'That other one, used a girl's name, called himself Viv, came home and there was an almighty row. I thought he was going to kill her. I came rushing out to stop him.'

To watch the drama unfolding, Davis thought was more likely.

'Did you see what happened?'

'He threw her out of that door,' she said pointing to number four. 'She's not so young any more you know, he could have killed her.' She drew herself up a bit. 'I soon put him straight, told him to leave her alone.'

Davis wondered how brave she had been, he knew from Constable Reed that she had gone back indoors fairly quickly and phoned the police.

'After that I didn't want to keep an eye on the place no more.'

'You used to keep an eye on the place?' Davis asked.

The neighbour looked as if she thought she might have said too much, maybe got involved in something she knew nothing about.

'I only had the key for when they went away, they was worried about being burgled so I used to close the curtains at night and open them again in the morning, nothing else mind.'

Suddenly the elderly neighbour stopped herself and a look of curiosity crossed her face. Davis could guess what was coming and was surprised she hadn't asked earlier.

'What's he done? You're the second lot of police to be asking about him.' She put her hand to her mouth. 'No, he hasn't killed her, has he?'

Davis reassured her. 'Mrs Blackstaff is alive and well as far as I'm aware.' He made sure he didn't say why they were making enquiries; he doubted she had anything to add of any value, but she would enjoy sharing her news as quickly as possible.

There was nothing to be learned here now. He had arranged with the local force for a locksmith to attend to gain entry to Wilde's property and his driver had phoned the man to tell them they had arrived as soon as they'd got here. A small van pulled up and the sign writing on the side made it clear this was the man.

A cheerful man in his sixties got out. 'Hello, you must be the long arm of the law.' He had opened the back door of his van as he spoke to Davis.

Davis acknowledged who he was and asked how long it would take to get in.

'Well,' said the locksmith as he approached the door, 'I don't think it will take,' as he was speaking he had threaded a thin but stiff metal bar through the letter box, it was bent in a series of bends, 'long at all,' he said as he pushed the door open.

Davis was stunned. 'It's that easy?'

'When you know how,' the man laughed. 'To be serious, these old locks are next to useless. I know how to open it in seconds and you can be sure, so do most of the 'ne'er do wells'.'

He closed the door of his van. 'Still, your lot, the crime prevention chappies, make sure the people they visit know all about the risk.' He got back in his van and, with a cheery wave, drove away.

Vyvyan had loaded Tania's body into the boot of the Escort. He

189

had been looking forward to dumping her in the barn the other two girls had been left in. It would be a massive two-fingers up to the police. He was thinking that just as he sat in the driver's seat of the car. Suddenly a cold sweat came over him. How foolish could he be, how arrogant? The police might not have caught him yet but they weren't totally stupid. They may well have got the barn under surveillance now.

He sat without starting the engine for a few minutes. It could be difficult to spot anybody keeping an eye on the barn. If they were inside it and he went there, even if he didn't have the body with him, he would bring himself to the attention of the police and have to answer some very difficult questions.

He'd been thoroughly shocked by Mrs Trent's phone call. His next door neighbour in Ilfracombe had phoned him to say the police were in his cottage as she spoke. What she really wanted to know was why they were there. She had been useful in the past, looking after the place when he and Andrew had gone away. He'd forgotten that she had the number of his mobile phone. That was certainly a stroke of luck. Now he knew that the policeman in charge of the case was Detective Inspector Davis. It might be useful knowing that.

He'd have to find out more about this detective. Back to his immediate problem though, how to dispose of Tania.

He laughed to himself. Why not set light to the Escort and Tania's body where her father had died? He'd checked out the road this morning and the police had finished there. He'd drive there now, if there was nobody about he would do it.

190

Chapter Twentyseven

Davis walked through the front door of Wilde's house, there was no hallway and he glanced around the sitting room. It was neat and tidy, although there was a fine layer of dust suggesting that nobody had been here for a while. He went through to the kitchen; it was as neat as the living room. Davis was puzzled, he hadn't seen the stairs, he retraced his steps into the sitting room and saw a door set into the wall. He opened it and to his surprise the stairs were behind it. He climbed the narrow and steep stairs to find a very small landing. Two bedrooms led off it.

Davis looked into the smaller one first as its door was open. It had a desk in one corner with a computer and monitor set up on it. Above the desk were two bookshelves. Davis looked at the books, they were all related to computers and website designing. Davis wondered if these belonged to Wilde or his late partner. The computer would have to be examined by their technical staff.

He moved through to the bigger bedroom. There was a double bed in it and wardrobes fitted along the length of one wall. Davis opened each of the doors in turn but saw nothing of obvious interest.

Green had been searching downstairs and Davis went back down there to see if he'd had any luck.

Green was sitting at a small table in the corner of the kitchen reading a book.

'What's that?' Davis asked.

'It's Wilde's diary, of sorts.' He flicked back through a few pages and said, 'Well, it started as a diary, on some pages he's written down who he's seen or what he's done on a particular day.' He turned to a particular page. 'There's even a reminder about a dentist's appointment. But he has also recorded random stuff in here.'

'Anything we might want to see?'

'I'll say. There are bits and pieces, ramblings really, about people who have annoyed him.'

'Does that include our gang of four?'

'Not to start with.' Green turned to the front of the book. 'It starts off with somebody I think he must work with who keeps making jokes about gay people. It's just a rant really. There's other stuff as it goes along. But then, when his partner dies there a bit of a change, he makes threats to some of the doctors who he says should have realised Andrew

191

might have had another heart attack. Then the bit we want.'

He held open a page and pointed to a section. 'He's moaning here about the fact that he's always been picked on, even at school. He says not even his teachers or his parents ever tried to help him.' Green turned several pages. 'He's made his mind up to get revenge. He planned to kill the four men who he claims bullied him the most.'

'So far we know most of that,' Davis said.

'Yes, but he has written here that he wanted them to suffer for the rest of their lives as they have made him suffer. He says that instead of killing the men themselves he will target their children.'

'And yet he's killed one of the men now,' Davis said. 'I think Geoff Symonds realised it was Wilde and said so.'

Green flicked through the diary and stopped at one page and started reading it. 'He thinks he's going to get away with it.' He pointed to one paragraph. 'Look at this. "When it's all done and they are in agony I can get on with my life in peace, a peace they would never have allowed me. What you want you have to get for yourself. I will never let anyone else persecute me as they did.".

Green laid the diary down. 'I can't see how he thought he'd get away with it.'

'Arrogance,' Davis said. 'Most murderers, those whose crime is premeditated, think they are cleverer than the law, they'll evade detection. In reality there are so many ways for us to gather information that we are more than likely to catch them.'

Davis picked up the diary. 'Even without this we had the fact that Mr James remembered Wilde from school and put two and two together. Wilde couldn't have foreseen that the Beresfords would commit suicide and that he would murder Symonds. They too could have identified Wilde, as Symonds almost certainly did.'

He put the diary down. 'It's all well and good knowing that it's Wilde we're looking for; we need to find the man before he gets to the next child.' He looked around the kitchen. 'Where did you find this?'

Green pointed to a small bureau in the sitting room. 'In there.'

Davis walked over to the bureau and pulled the front down. There were various envelopes and other bits of paper sticking out from the sections inside the top of the bureau. Davis asked Green if he'd looked through them yet.

'No, not yet, I pulled the diary out first.'

Davis took a handful of the envelopes out and handed them to

Green then took the remainder himself. 'We need something that will tell us where he is staying now. He might have a rental agreement, a friend's address, even a telephone bill. If it's got a Chatteris number on it we might find it's a rental agency.'

He started on the bundle of bills and other correspondence Wilde had amassed.

After fifteen minutes of fruitless searching Davis said, 'There's nothing here. If he is renting a property, or has access to one somehow, he's not left anything for us to find here. Bag this lot up, everything and bring it back with us.'

Davis looked around, 'I haven't seen a bathroom, have you?'

Green pointed through the kitchen. 'It's through that door in the corner of the kitchen.'

Davis needed to use it before the journey home but he would have a quick look over it as well, Wilde might have concealed something in there.

Davis went through the kitchen and opened the door. The bathroom was clearly an extension built on the back of the house, which pre-dated the time when an indoor bathroom was considered essential. As Davis used the toilet he noticed a small picture frame on the wall. In it was a small paragraph of three lines on plain paper, probably printed on the printer upstairs.

It said,

"Vengeance is mine; I will repay, saith the Lord."
Romans 12:19.
"God helps those who help themselves."
Benjamin Franklin.
"Why rely on the Lord for revenge, when you can get it yourself?"
Vyvyan Wilde.

Obviously Wilde's homespun philosophy, maybe he put it there to encourage himself.

He took the frame from the wall, it may be useful to prove Wilde's intent if he could get the man in court.

He went back through to Green and said, 'We're not going to get anymore here.'

'I've found out where he works,' Green said.

'Really, where?'

'He's a postman.' Green held up a sheet of paper. 'His payslip.

193

There's a box of them here, but the last one is dated two months ago.'

'We passed a Royal Mail office on the way through the town; we'll go and see them.'

The car pulled up in a visitor's parking place and Davis and Green got out. A postman was cycling past and Davis called to him, 'Where can I find your manager?'

The man pointed. 'That door, Caller's Office,' and carried on.

Davis pushed the door open and walked in. A uniformed postwoman was standing behind a desk as he approached. 'How can I help you, sir?' she asked.

Davis showed his warrant card. 'I'd like to see your manager please.'

A few minutes later Davis and Green were sitting in a cramped office with a man who'd described himself as the Delivery Office Manager, Len Crane. Tall and slim he kept looking at the clock above the door even though they'd only just sat down.

'What can I do for you, you say you're from Cambridgeshire, how can we help?'

'Do you employ a Mr Vyvyan Wilde?' Davis asked.

Davis saw Crane's eyes narrow slightly as he asked, 'What has he done?'

'Why might you think he's done anything?'

Crane bounced a ruler on the edge of his desk a couple of times, giving himself time to think, then he said, 'We had to let him go, well, we asked him to resign.'

'Why was that?'

Crane seemed to be making a decision. 'I'm not sure how much I should say, but you wouldn't be here if it wasn't serious.'

Davis nodded his head in agreement.

'Vyv hated the constant banter about his name.' Crane put his hand up as if to hold back any unvoiced criticism, 'Don't get me wrong, we try to clamp down on any bullying, but you can't stop it.'

'Wilde was bullied because of his name?'

'Yes, almost from the moment he started here.'

'How long did he work here?'

Crane thought for a moment, 'Almost three years. He left some time after his partner died, that seemed to tip him over the edge.'

'What do you mean?'

'He had always resented the micky-taking, but after his partner died he started to get aggressive. I had to warn him once after he swung a punch at one of the blokes. Then, oh, let me see…' Crane looked up at a calendar, 'about two months ago one of our office comedians told a joke about tramps, only he used the American term 'bums'. One of the lads, Martin White, said, "Vyvyan's wild about bums." Of course everybody laughed.'

Crane gave a humourless laugh. 'To say Vyv went over the top doesn't cover it. He swung a mailbag he was carrying at Martin, which knocked him off balance. Before anybody could stop him Vyv had waded in with his boots flying. Two other postmen pulled him away and Martin wasn't seriously hurt.'

'Were the police called?' Davis asked.

'No. As I said, Martin wasn't hurt too much, and he knew he'd provoked Vyv.'

'Was that what led you to asking him to resign?'

'That was the incident as such, but it was his reaction when we got him in the office that made our minds up.'

'What happened?'

'He was ranting away for a bit, but you get used to that. We've got over fifty blokes here who all work very closely together for a couple of hours each day before they go out. Sometimes they get on each other's nerves and sometimes tempers flare. We might just tell them to calm down, other times we have to bring them in here and give them a stronger warning.'

'And that's what you did with Wilde?'

'We tried to. He came in and sat down just where you are sitting. I had our union rep in here with him, you know, a bit of support for him. I was going to read him the riot act, like, and then see what I could do to stop the blokes having a go at him. I mean, he wasn't a bad bloke in his own way. But as I said to him that we couldn't have him kicking our staff about he said, "If you can't stop them I'll fucking kill them."'. Crane wiped his hand across his brow. 'Well, I'll tell you, it wasn't exactly what he said that worried us, it was the way he said it. He meant it. He was deadly serious.' He shook his head at the memory. 'It was his eyes that disturbed me, totally cold, no emotion.'

'And you still didn't call the police?'

Crane looked uncomfortable. 'Well, it didn't seem like a police matter as such, more like a matter of keeping him out of harm's way.'

'How did you get him to resign?'

'After what he'd said I sent him home for the day. Then I called him in to see me after the morning shift had gone home the next day. I told him that it would be best if he transferred to another office. To be honest I wanted shot of him.'

'He didn't agree I take it?'

'No, he didn't. I'd found a vacancy in Exeter, but that would have meant him moving, and he didn't want to. I said he couldn't come back here and if he didn't go I'd sack him.'

'But you let him resign?'

'I gave him the option, it meant he'd be able to get another job, with a sacking on his record it might have been hard.'

He hesitated. 'There was one other problem that we were worried about.' Davis could see that Crane was uncomfortable. 'We suspected he was stealing mail.'

'What made you think that?'

'We had a complaint from a customer that several items of mail hadn't arrived.'

'What did you do about it?'

'We have a system in place where we send test letters, items that a dishonest postman might steal. We check whilst the postman is still out on delivery to see if the item was delivered as it should have been. If it isn't we investigate as soon as he returns from his round.'

'And that's what you did with Wilde?'

'We set the process in motion, but the assault happened the day before the test letter was due to go out.'

Davis thought this was hardly likely to have any bearing on his case. 'Do you know where he's moved to?' he asked.

'I didn't know he'd moved, we haven't seen him here since he left, but I'd have known if he'd redirected his mail.' Crane looked at the clock for about the tenth time in the five minutes they'd been in the office. 'Look, I've got to get going; I've got a meeting to get to. Give me a contact number, if he shows up I'll call you.'

Davis wrote his details on a card Crane gave him and got up. 'Thanks for your help. If Wilde does show up it's vital you get in touch immediately.'

It was the first time Vyvyan had disposed of one of the bodies in broad daylight. He had to make sure he allowed himself time to get well away from the vehicle before the fire became obvious.

He soaked two towels in petrol and placed them in thin plastic bags. These would go in each of the front footwells when he was ready. He drove the short distance to Horseley Fen Middle Drove and parked the car on the same spot Geoff had parked on.

He scattered a dozen or so tightly screwed up sheets of newspaper on the floor in the rear of the car and tossed a lighted match on them. The paper would burn for long enough for the upholstery to catch fire. Once it had the petrol soaked towels would burn fiercely. The car would burn out just as effectively as Geoff's had last night.

He walked back along the road without seeing a soul. Just before he got to the cottage he heard the explosion. From his back garden he could see the thick black smoke coming from the fire. Vyvyan was satisfied with his mornings work. He went indoors to have a shower; he had a couple of hours before he moved onto the next stage of the plan.

Chapter Twentyeight

Laura Reardon looked at the clock high up on the wall. It wasn't even three o'clock yet. Much as she enjoyed her job she couldn't wait for her shift to end today. This evening was going to be a special one. Gary Jackson had asked her out.

She'd had a crush on Gary for as long as she could remember, but she didn't think he'd ask her out. He was as shy as she was herself. How some girls asked boys out she'd never know. She was sixteen and had never been out on a date yet.

Her dad was very protective about her and said that most boys were only after one thing. But even he admitted Gary was different. He was seventeen and lived with his widowed mother. He worked hard in one of the factories on the new industrial estate. On most Sundays he went with his mother to the morning church service but wasn't too devout, just enough to be decent.

Gary had come into the supermarket three days ago and she had noticed he was taking his time choosing a magazine from the display. As soon as she was alone refilling the jam shelf he had approached her.

She had blushed as he'd asked her to go to the pictures with him, but had quickly accepted.

Now there were only hours remaining before she went out on her first date. The butterflies in her stomach would not settle.

Her manageress walked along the aisle. Laura had told the older woman about the date. Mrs Rose gave Laura's arm a gentle squeeze. 'Not long now, love. I bet you're excited.'

Laura blushed. 'I hope it goes all right. I told grandma I'd pop in tomorrow and tell her all about it.' She laughed, 'Gran told me about her first date with grandad. He worked on a farm and invited her up there. She said she spent the whole Sunday helping with the harvest.'

Mrs Rose smiled and said, 'Well at least you won't have to do that, still, it must have worked for your grandad, they were married a long time.'

Laura blushed again at the word married. Many, many times she had imagined what it would be like to be married. Not like her parents' marriage, her father was domineering and sometimes downright cruel to her mother. But just like her grandparents, her mum's parents, they had been married for over fifty years before her grandad died a few years ago. Grandad always treated Grandma properly, called her 'his treasure, the most precious thing in his life'.

Maybe one day Gary would say things like that about her.

Gillian Lewin scanned the list she had made of the properties whose rental agreements had started in the last six weeks. This was a far longer list than the one of commercial properties that the agencies had given them last week. There were just over seventy houses on the list, but she noticed that each agency had listed all the new rentals they had agreed in the last six weeks, not just those in the immediate area. Davis was sure that Wilde lived in or near Chatteris. Lewin worked her way down the list putting a line through all those who fell outside that area.

She was left with twenty-three properties. Each of these would have to be visited. If they were occupied by a lone man he would be asked to prove his identity. Lewin glanced at the clock, it was just after twelve, she'd see how Graham was getting on with tracking down Taylor, maybe they could grab a quick bite to eat before they carried on with their investigations.

She wasn't sure yet what she thought about Graham Peterson. They had worked together for some time now and got along as friends. Just recently however, after his split from his wife, they had seen a lot more of each other. It had started with fast-food dinners after work because neither could be bothered to cook and now it had progressed to planning to meet up occasionally for a meal or just for company. Nothing had happened to suggest they had a relationship rather than a friendship, but she had the feeling Graham might be moving that way. She thought to herself, if he does, I won't mind.

She went through to Davis's office. Peterson had been using it because he was telephoning every Taylor in the phone book and needed to get away from the noise of the printer running off Lewin's property list.

'Any luck?'

'No, I think the bloke's disappeared off the face of the earth. And before you say it, I've checked, he's not been registered dead.'

Lewin laughed. 'Do you fancy grabbing a burger in town?'

Peterson smiled, 'Why not. I'm not getting anywhere here, maybe the boss will have something to go on when he comes back.'

Lewin and Peterson sat in her car eating burger and chips. 'How many houses on your list now?' Peterson asked.

'Twenty-three,' she replied, trying not to splutter through a mouthful of chips.

'When are you going to start calling on them?'

'As soon as we've had this and I run you back.'

'I'll tell you what. We'll cover it together.'

Lewin felt a warm glow at the prospect of spending the afternoon with Graham. But that was ridiculous, she tried to tell herself, she had spent many a day working with him before now. Somehow, though, it seemed different.

They knocked at the first door on the list. They had left the car where they had parked for lunch. This house was on the High Street.

'It's not likely to be in town. I still think he needs somewhere remote,' Peterson said.

'We'd better check them all, we'll be slaughtered if he's on the list and we miss him,' Lewin responded.

The door was opened by a woman in her mid-fifties. The agencies had all refused to add names to the addresses citing data protection laws. Although the police could probably have got a court order to force this information from the agencies Lewin had decided that the addresses would be enough for now.

Lewin and Peterson both held their badges forward to identify themselves. 'Can I ask you who you are?' Lewin asked the woman.

'Mrs Williams, why?' the woman said defensively.

'We are checking the tenants of all recently rented properties. Do you have any means of identity we can check?'

Mrs Williams turned to a table just inside the door and opened her handbag. She handed her driving licence photo card to Lewin and asked, 'Will that do?'

Lewin glanced at it and smiled. 'Yes, thank you. Do you live alone or are there other occupants of the property?'

'My husband lives here. It's because of him we moved here, we're buying a house but needed to move here quickly, he works at that new research place.' She stopped for a moment. 'That's not why you're here is it? Nothing's happened has it? Those protesters are going to kill someone if they're not stopped'

'No, Mrs Williams, our enquiries are nothing to do with your husband's work. Thank you for your help,' Lewin said quickly.

Lewin and Peterson walked back to the car and Lewin crossed off the first address. 'Twenty-two to go,' she said with a groan.

Just after they left the fourth property Peterson got a call from Davis on his mobile phone.

'Sir, you found anything useful?'

'Not particularly, but that's not why I've called. The bastard's done it again.'

'Oh no, they've found Tania's body?'

'We're not sure of that yet. You won't believe it. The fire-brigade have called me about a car fire, it's on exactly the same spot as Geoff Symonds car last night. The car was still alight when I got the call so they haven't been able to examine it yet.'

'You want me to get up there?'

'Yes, I'm not going to get back much before eight tonight. There's been an accident on the motorway; I can't justify having the driver use his lights and tones, the traffic's too heavy.'

'Right, Phil, I'll ring you as soon as I find out anything.'

Peterson told Lewin about the fire and she turned the car round and headed out of town towards Horseley Fen Middle Drove.

By the time they got there the fire was out. Peterson approached the crew manager.

'Have you had a chance to search the vehicle yet?'

'No,' the fireman said, 'we've only just got the flames out. Don't tell me you're expecting another body?'

Peterson nodded grimly.

The fireman shook his head and called to one of his men. A quick inspection through the glassless windows revealed nothing. A crowbar was brought from the fire engine and the boot was prised open.

Peterson, Lewin and both firemen all swore at the same time. Lying on the floor of the Escort's boot was a body. Although it was burnt beyond recognition both detectives knew it was Tania. Vyvyan Wilde was dancing rings around them.

Peterson and Lewin decided to wait for the pathologist to arrive. As they waited Lewin looked over the fields and spotted Vyvyan Wilde's cottage.

'That's Middlefield Cottage, it's on our list of newly rented properties.'

'How do you know that's it?'

Lewin laughed. 'Not long after I joined the service I had to go there and help round up a herd of cows that had escaped onto the road.'

'That can't have been much of a problem; I bet there's hardly many cars use the road.'

'That's why they sent me out probably.'

'I tell you what, you wait here, I'll drive down there and check it out,' Peterson said.

Vyvyan heard the knock on the door as he was doing his ironing. He liked to maintain a neat and tidy appearance. He was immediately alert. Nobody he knew would know he was here. He'd used a false name to rent the property, one of the advantages of his last job as a postman had been the chance to steal enough documentation to back up a false identity.

He opened the front door.

'Afternoon, sir,' Peterson said. 'We're investigating a series of crimes and are checking out recently rented properties, can you tell me your name?'

'Mr Innes, Colin Innes.'

Peterson wrote the name down in his notebook. 'Do you have any identification you can show me, sir?'

Vyvyan put his hand in his pocket and pulled out his wallet. He had managed to steal a driving licence photo card, one bankcard and a National Trust membership card in the name of Innes. He had also joined the Chatteris library and obtained a DVD rental card from a newsagent all in the Innes name. He couldn't show this policeman the driving licence as it had a Devon address on it.

He pulled out the library card and the national trust card. 'What about these, just don't ask if I've got any overdue books,' he laughed. He handed the cards over. 'If you need something with an address on I have the rental agreement or an electric bill, I haven't been here long enough to get much else.'

Peterson examined the cards and handed them back. 'That's okay, sir.' He turned away and gave a small wave. 'Sorry to have troubled you.'

Vyvyan shut the door and quickly ran into the toilet to be sick. Although he had managed to look cool and unflustered his insides had been churning whilst the policeman was there.

Peterson returned to the burnt out Escort just as Dr Watson arrived.

'This is getting a bit tedious,' the pathologist said. 'Where's Phil?'

'On his way back from Devon.'

The pathologist looked bemused. 'Not a day out I take it?'

Peterson nodded towards the car, 'He's gone to the home of the man we think is responsible for all this.'

'You know who it is?' Watson asked, surprised.

'We think we do, one of the fathers named him and there's certainly enough to point us his way.' Peterson looked frustrated, 'We just can't find the bastard.'

Watson had a quick look at the body and said, 'There's not going to be much I can tell you for a while. The body's too hot to touch at the moment.' He glanced at his watch. 'I'll get on with the post mortem this evening.'

Peterson and Lewin nodded and walked back to Lewin's car, there was nothing left here for them to do at the moment.

As they drove off Lewin asked, 'Anybody home at Middlefield Cottage?'

'Yes, not our man I'm afraid.' He tapped his notebook, 'A Mr Innes, got it noted, we'll add him to the list of checked properties when we get back to the office.'

Vyvyan had washed his face and had a cup of tea after the visit from the policeman had upset him so much. He had to carry on with his plan, but for the first time he was nervous.

He was confident they hadn't realised he was the man they were looking for but it had still shaken him to have the police on the doorstep. It made him realise how easy it would be to make a mistake.

His planning had been meticulous. He had used the stolen identity for what he needed up here at Chatteris. But he made sure that he only did what he had to do with it. Registering with the library and newsagent had been very low-risk but had given him extra pieces of ID, useful, as he'd proved today.

The master-stroke though had been in not registering Andrew's death. That had been left for him to do by Andrew's mother. She had decided that after Andrew had so publicly shamed her, by not only declaring to the world that he was homosexual, but also actually preferring his perverted boyfriend's company rather than hers, that she would wash her hands of him.

In addition to not registering the death he hadn't cancelled

Andrew's bank account, driving licence or any other official means of identification.

When he had completed his plans in Chatteris he intended to move to Scotland. He had bought a small cottage on the outskirts of Aviemore having cashed in Andrew's extensive shares portfolio. There nobody would be any the wiser that he was not Andrew Blackstaff. Vyvyan Wilde would cease to exist.

He must make it a priority to find out more about this Davis, the policeman. Nobody must be allowed to stop him now. He would have to find a way of evading capture or, better still, neutralising the threat.

Chapter Twentynine

He had one final part of the plan to put in to action. This one was going to give him a great deal of pleasure. Wart Taylor had been a sadistic schoolboy who enjoyed committing minor acts of vandalism and then bullying his fellow pupils into confessing that they were the guilty party. Geoff Symonds, Alan Beresford and Bob James had never been victims of this as part of his inner circle of friends, but although Vyvyan had been part of that group his place had been at the cost of accepting the bullying of the other four.

One of the worst incidences had been when Vyvyan had agreed to look after his neighbour's pet rabbit whilst they were away. The father worked on the farm for Vyvyan's father and lived in the cottage just off the road. Wart had strangled the rabbit on the first day the neighbours were away, just to see how it died. He had immediately told Vyvyan that he would have to claim responsibility for the cruel act. The other three had backed him up and Vyvyan had spent the week waiting for the return of the rabbit owners in a haze of fear.

He knew this was more than just embarrassing; he would be regarded as a freak, disgusting, a killer of a loved family pet.

Every day for that week the three boys had tormented him but Wart was the worst. He kept describing to Vyvyan how it had felt to grip the rabbit's throat and squeeze. How the rabbit had struggled. Vyvyan had felt sick hearing it and dreaded what was going to happen to him. He had been made aware that if he failed to confess his guilt he would face a far worse punishment from the three of them than anything his parents would impose on him.

The Saturday the neighbours were due to return Wart had called round to see Vyvyan and made sure that Vyvyan knew what was expected of him.

'You tell them you did it just because you wanted to, okay,' Wart had said. 'Don't make any excuses, you just did it.' He'd given him a hard dig in the ribs and said, 'If anybody finds out it wasn't you who did it we'll board you up in Tucker's Hole.'

Tucker's Hole was the local name for a derelict barn just outside Chatteris that was full of rats and spiders, Vyvyan's two biggest fears. Wart, who claimed to be afraid of nothing, had gone in there one time and set off a smoke bomb, usually used in molehills. He had run out fairly quickly followed by more rats than the boys could count. Much to

205

the amusement of the other four he also had two huge spiders on his jacket after running through their webs. Although he had had the better laugh, he had picked them off and chased all three boys with them, eventually squashing one on Bob James's head and the other on Vyvyan's arm.

Vyvyan had been indoors when the neighbours arrived home. He had almost been sick with worry and as their car pulled up on their drive he felt tears pricking at his eyes. Within minutes there was a scream of anguish from the daughter of the family. Three minutes later her father was knocking on the Wilde's front door. Vyvyan's father was out working on the farm and it was his mother who answered the door.

Vyvyan heard the angry voice of the neighbour and his mother's apologetic tones. Then she called to him to come to the door.

As soon as the neighbour saw Vyvyan he shouted, 'What the hell happened here?'

Vyvyan's throat was so dry he didn't think he'd be able to speak. He almost started to mutter an apology then remembered Wart's warning. Dreading what was to come he squared his shoulders and said, 'I did it.'

'And that's it,' the angry neighbour said, 'you just did it. What the hell for? My Sarah's distraught; you've ruined our holiday. There's something wrong with you.'

Vyvyan's mother was in tears. 'Why did you do it, son?' she asked.

Vyvyan wanted to cry, he wanted to shout that he didn't do it. That the only thing wrong with him was that his parents had saddled him with a stupid name that made him a victim of merciless bullying. But he knew the bullying would get worse if he said any of that. There was nothing his parents could do to save him from any of it.

Vyvyan shrugged at his mother's question, 'Because I wanted to.'

Suddenly she was as angry as the neighbour. 'You're evil. I'm ashamed to call you my son. Get to your room, your father will deal with you when he gets home.'

Vyvyan knew what that meant, the strap. A thick leather strap wielded by his father. A half dozen of those across his buttocks and not even the thickest of trousers could protect him. He had endured several of these punishments over the years and lived in fear of the next one. He knew it was coming now.

It was Monday before Vyvyan left the house. He normally cycled to school in Chatteris, a distance of almost four miles. He could hardly put his backside on the saddle this time. He wrapped a towel over the saddle and put a sponge from the bathroom down his trousers to give more protection to his bruised bottom.

When he got to school the lads were waiting for him. The news had travelled about his killing the rabbit and as he parked his bicycle in the bike racks an older girl called out to him, 'You sad little murderer, we all hate you.'

Wart and the others led him into the school gym, which was deserted at this time of morning.

'Well, did you say it was you?' asked Wart.

For once, driven by the pain he felt in his bottom after four long miles in the saddle Vyvyan tried to fight back. 'Yes I did, but I've half a mind to tell the truth, my dad leathered me, you bastards.' There were tears in his eyes as he shouted his response and he didn't see Wart's fist aiming for his stomach. The air rushed from his lungs and he fell to his knees.

'If you ever tell anybody that I did it you'll be begging me to put you in Tucker's Hole by the time I've finished with you.'

Geoff Symonds said, 'Did your dad really belt you?'

Between gasps for breath and tears Vyvyan said, 'Yes he did, I got six goes of the strap.'

Bob James said, 'I bet his arse looks like raw meat.'

'Show us,' Wart demanded.

'No way,' Vyvyan responded hotly. He wasn't going to bare his backside to anybody, least of all these four.

Wart grabbed hold of him. 'You either show us or we'll tear your trousers off and boot your arse all round this gym.' He pushed him away and said, 'Which is it to be?'

Vyvyan looked at the four of them, their faces showed savage excitement. He knew they would kick him and he couldn't face any more pain. Even the humiliation of dropping his trousers would be easier to take.

He turned round and undid his belt and trousers. He lowered his trousers to his knees and gently pulled his underpants in towards the middle, there was no way he was dropping them.

There were howls of laughter from the four lads. Wart said, 'Bloody hell! Your old man really went to town on you, didn't he?'

Alan Beresford said, 'If my arse looked like that I wouldn't have biked in.'

Just as Vyvyan was about to straighten up a stinging jolt of pain hit his buttocks. He yelled out in pain, Wart had kicked him as hard as he could on the biggest of several bruises spread over his backside. Before he could get away all four lads were kicking at him. Boots were flying in and he fell over.

Wart stood over him and placed one of his heavy Doc Martins on Vyvyan's backside. 'We always said you were a gayboy,' he said, 'now you've got your arse out for us.' He ground his boot into Vyvyan's backside as hard as he could, twisting it as he did so. The pain was excruciating and Vyvyan cried out in agony.

Wart, Geoff, Alan and Bob all aimed one last kick at him as he laid on the ground, then left the gym laughing at what they'd done.

Eventually Vyvyan was able to stand up and pull his trousers up. The slightest movement was agony but he couldn't face the extra humiliation of going to the school nurse. He would have to suffer in silence.

There was no way he could sit properly in lessons. He sat at the back of the class and tried to perch on the chair, keeping his bottom just off the seat by bracing his back and letting his thighs take his weight. At the end of the day he had to walk home pushing his bike, even trying to ride standing on the pedals was too painful.

From that day on Vyvyan had nothing more to do with the others. He avoided the places they used to meet and hid out in the school library during breaks.

He dreamed that one day he'd be able to get his revenge on them. One day he would make their lives as agonising as they had made his.

Laura looked in the mirror. She didn't wear make-up but she had spent ages on her long, dark hair. She'd washed and conditioned it as soon as she'd got home from work. It had taken ages to blow-dry, as it was so thick. Mrs Rose had driven her home to give her more time to get ready. Her mum had helped her brush it and after much worrying she had decided to put it in a ponytail. It hung long and shiny down her back.

Her mum was always telling her how pretty she was but, like most young girls, Laura wasn't so sure. As she saw her reflection in the mirror this evening she did have to admit that she looked good. She immediately felt embarrassed at being so conceited, 'self praise is no praise' her gran was always saying.

Laura wondered whether to put a coat on, there was still a chill in the spring air. She decided against it. She had a red knee-length skirt on and a white blouse. Over that she had a thin cotton jacket. As she gave yet another twirl to see the skirt flare there was a knock at the door. She almost let out a yelp of excitement.

Her mum opened it. She heard Gary. 'Hello, Mrs Reardon, I've called for Laura.'

Mrs Reardon stood aside as Laura came to the door. 'Hello,' she said shyly.

Gary's eyes widened, 'Wow, you look lovely.'

'Now then, Gary Jackson,' Laura's mum laughed, 'you behave yourself with my daughter.'

Gary blushed as deeply as Laura ever could. 'Sorry, Mrs Reardon...' he stammered.

'I'm only joking, I know your mum, you're a good lad, I'm pleased you've asked Laura out.'

'Mum!' squealed Laura.

Mrs Reardon laughed again and kissed Laura on the cheek. 'You two have a good time. Have you got your phone on you?'

'Yes, Mum.' She stepped out the door. 'I'll see you later.'

Vyvyan had been waiting for Laura and she hadn't come past the place he had planned to snatch her. He couldn't understand it; he'd seen her at the supermarket today. Maybe the police had got wise to him. Maybe they'd warned Wart to take care of his family.

But he doubted they would have been able to find him. They probably didn't know, as Vyvyan had found out, that Wart had changed his surname.

Several years after they had left school Wart's father had knocked down and badly injured an eleven-year old boy. Instead of summoning help he had hidden the boy in a ditch and driven off.

When he'd taken his car to a garage to be repaired, claiming he hit a dog, the mechanics had discovered human hair in the dented bodywork. By the time the police had interviewed Travers Taylor and he had revealed the boy's whereabouts the lad was dead.

The media coverage was extensive and savage towards Taylor. He received a lengthy jail sentence.

For Wart, William Robert Taylor, there was a consequence too. He was due to marry Lisa Reardon in three months time. The day after his father was jailed he went to see Lisa as usual. Her mother opened the door to his knock.

'You'd better come in,' she said.

That struck William as an odd greeting, even during the families darkest hours of the trial Lisa's family had been welcoming to him. He followed Mrs Reardon through to the lounge. Her husband was sitting in his usual seat in front of the television, Lisa was sitting on the sofa and had obviously been crying. As he went to sit beside her Mr Reardon turned the television off, an unheard of thing in the Reardon house. William realised something was wrong.

Mr Reardon faced him, he was a thin man whose skin looked as if it was so tight on his face it might split open. 'William, as you know we are looking forward to you marrying our Lisa, but…'

As he said 'but' Lisa stifled a new cry and ran from the room. William didn't know what to do, follow her or hear what her father had to say. He looked back at Mr Reardon, he didn't look happy, William decided to stay and listen to him.

'As I was saying, we are worried. You've seen how much trouble what your dad did has caused.'

Mr Reardon put up a bony hand to stall William's protest. 'Now, lad, don't worry, we don't want to stop you two marrying. Our Lisa's old enough to go ahead without our say-so if she wanted.'

William wondered what the problem was in that case; maybe they wanted the wedding postponed.

Mr Reardon glanced at his wife as if looking for support. 'We don't want Lisa having the Taylor name.'

William was stunned, he said he didn't want to stop them getting married, but now he was suggesting they live together. Well he wouldn't have it, him and Lisa had set their hearts on a wedding and that's what they would have. Before he could say this Mr Reardon carried on.

'We want you to change your name rather than Lisa change hers.'

William wasn't sure he'd heard right. 'You want what?' he asked.

Lisa's father laid his cold hand on William's arm, 'When you marry we want you to take the Reardon name. It will avoid all the nastiness in the papers.'

William held the slightly mournful gaze of his soon-to-be father-in-law. 'Are you serious?' he asked.

'Absolutely,' Mr Reardon said.

'It's for the best,' his wife added, in what she thought was an encouraging tone.

William couldn't think straight. He had all the worry of his father's trial. His mother was almost suicidal with depression, torn between a very stretched loyalty to her husband and heartfelt sympathy for the young boy's family. He, William, had been planning the wedding with Lisa for some time. His brain felt like it couldn't cope with any more.

The Reardons took his silence as a sign of his refusal to agree. 'We will try to persuade Lisa to delay the wedding if you won't do as we asked,' Mr Reardon said.

'What does she say to this idea?' William asked.

'She thinks it's a good idea,' Mrs Reardon answered, 'but she doesn't think you'll go along with it.'

Before William could respond Lisa came back in the room and sat next to him. She kissed him and he felt the wetness of her tear-stained face on his own.

'I love you and we're getting married on the day we set, no matter what.' As she said that she looked at her father defiantly. 'But, William, they are right. There isn't a person in Chatteris who doesn't know the Taylor name now, and hate it.' She held his hand tightly in her own. 'Please, I know it's unusual, but there's no legal reason to stop you taking my name instead of me taking yours.'

William looked into the eyes of the girl he loved. He had no idea what the future held for him but he knew that he wanted to face it with Lisa. He wanted that, he wanted her, more than anything in the world.

'I'll do it,' he said. Before he could say any more Lisa had thrown her arms around his neck and was crying again, tears of relief this time.

The name change had only been a partial success. Too many people knew William to forget who his father was. As the years went by the hatred for the Taylor name persisted but most people decided it was unfair to burden William with his father's sins.

William had plenty of his own sins though. He had been a bully as a schoolboy and, after a few years, became a bully of a husband. Lisa buried herself in her life as a mother of their two children, of which Laura was the younger child.

Chapter Thirty

Vyvyan remembered that Laura occasionally finished work at different times. He decide to drive to the street Laura lived on, if the police were there he might be able to spot them. It was a slight risk, both because they might be looking for him and because he hadn't changed the number plates on the car he'd stolen just after that visit from the police this afternoon. The usual technique had worked again. He'd taken the bus to Ely and sat on a bench outside the main post office. He'd been there only two minutes when a harassed looking woman had jumped out of a four-year-old Renault people carrier. She'd left the engine running and the driver's door open. As she passed Vyvyan he calmly got off the bench and walked to the car. She was still facing the post office as she saw the reflection of her car as it was driven away.

Vyvyan had driven through the estate Laura lived on once and had then waited out of sight near the supermarket. After a while he decided to try the estate again. He was just driving through Enderby Street, the road that led to Greengage Road, where Laura lived, when he saw her walking along arm in arm with a boy of her own age.

Damn! He thought. He couldn't afford any delays. The police weren't totally stupid, they might work out what was behind the death of these girls and eventually they'd find Wart's new name and then his address.

He carried on driving and decided that they were probably going to walk into town. He realised that they would end up walking along the same alleyway that he had chosen as the abduction point for Laura as she walked home from work.

He quickly drove to the far end of the alley. There were no houses on this road, just the now closed down furniture store. He had his pads and bottle of chloroform in the car with him. He quickly made up two pads. The first time he had checked this position as a possible abduction point he had noticed that he could see a reflection of the alley in the furniture store window.

Laura and Gary were just over half way along it now. He knew what he was going to do. He had the engine running and just as the young couple reached the end of the alley he roared forward blocking the opening.

As he threw the door open both youngsters came to a sudden halt.

Without delay Vyvyan swung a punch at Gary's jaw that knocked him to the floor stunned. Before Laura could think of screaming he had the first pad pressed on her face. She quickly slumped in his arms and he dragged her into the car.

As he put his hand on the door to get back in he had a quick thought. He took the second pad from the plastic bag and covered Gary's face with it. Once he was sure Gary was out cold he lifted him into the car as well.

He got back in the car and drove calmly back to Middlefield Cottage.

Vyvyan pulled up in front of the barn. He quickly got the doors open and drove the Renault inside. Neither of the youngsters was stirring yet. He lifted Laura out first and placed her on the bench. He looked around the barn; he had never anticipated having two captives at the same time. He decided that he would have to tie the boy to one of the solid wooden upright supports in the middle of the barn.

He half dragged half carried the boy to the support. He sat him on the floor and tied his arms behind him, one either side of the support. Later he would make him stand up and tie him more securely.

He gagged the boy and then turned his attention to Laura. He liked to get them undressed while they were still unconscious, that way they didn't start panicking thinking they were going to be raped.

He used the sharp knife to cut through her clothes, she wouldn't be wearing them again. Now she was naked he positioned her so that he could bind her to the bench.

He wound the tape tightly over her ankles and wrists, Laura wasn't as strong as Tania had been, he needn't worry about her breaking free. He turned her head so that she faced the roof and taped it to the bench across her forehead. He liked the fact that the girls couldn't move their heads. They couldn't see anything out of the very narrow field of vision it allowed them. It left them feeling more vulnerable, more scared.

He gazed at her lying on the bench. The sight of her naked body didn't arouse him, none of the girls did. But it did make him feel powerful; he had a weapon he could use. It was more powerful than any of those the bullies had had at their disposal. He could use the love they had for their child.

Vyvyan checked the time, he had one more job to do this evening. He'd found out where the police detective lived and he knew there was

213

no time to lose if he was going to stop Davis interfering.

Vyvyan backed the Renault out of the barn and drove to the new Poppyfields housing estate. It was so easy to find out where somebody lived if you had a name and the internet.

Vyvyan had just turned into Harrison Drive and worked out which house was Davis's when the door opened and a young man came out. Vyvyan tried to appear uninterested in the lad and drove to the end of the road. He turned into the next road and pulled up. Within a minute the lad had passed Vyvyan and he decided to take the risk that the lad was heading to the shop in the next street.

Vyvyan didn't want to pass him in the car too often so he turned round and quickly drove the long way round to the mini-supermarket.

He parked outside and had just switched off when the lad came round the corner. Vyvyan wasn't sure how to grab him, try to persuade him to get in the car or force him. He might as well follow the lad into the shop and see if anything occurred to him.

Vyvyan saw the newspaper rack just inside the door and went over and picked up a copy of the Daily Mail. He pretended to read the back page whilst watching the policeman's son. The lad went round picking up a few small items and made his way to the till. Vyvyan went to the counter with the paper and queued behind him.

The young assistant obviously knew the lad.

'Hello, Adam, are you going to the game on Saturday?'

'We're hoping to, I've promised to help out at the station car wash weekend, but dad says if he can finish on time we'll be there.'

'Great, I'll text you when we get there, if you make it we'll meet up.'

Adam paid for his shopping and left.

Vyvyan had the right money for his paper and was outside the shop seconds after Adam.

'Excuse me, it's Adam Davis isn't it?' Vyvyan said to him.

Adam looked at Vyvyan with no hint of recognition on his face. 'Yes, I'm sorry, I don't know you.'

Vyvyan said, 'Sorry, Detective Sergeant Worth. I've just been assigned to your dad's team from the Ely CID until this latest case is over.'

'Oh, right.' Adam said, not sure what else there was to say.

'I'm on my way to see your dad, I haven't got my sat-nav with me so I was expecting to have trouble finding your house. Can I give you a lift and that'll solve that problem?'

Adam wasn't sure but he knew his father's investigation was under pressure so it was likely he'd get reinforcements. It seemed a bit cheeky to ask to see his id. He opened the passenger door and got in the car.

'Which way?' Vyvyan asked.

Adam pointed and said, 'Go that way and then turn left.' Just as he finished saying that the vehicle came to a sudden halt as the man jammed the brakes on. Adam hadn't had time to put his seatbelt on and was thrown forward off the seat.

'So sorry, I thought that little girl was going to run out in front of us.'

Adam was just thinking he didn't remember seeing a child on the pavement when the man leant down to help him up. Adam was surprised to see a white pad in his hand. He was about to ask what it was when it was clamped to his face and Adam lost consciousness.

Peterson and Lewin called on every one of the recently rented properties on their list. It had taken until just before eight o'clock. At six of the properties nobody had been at home and Lewin would call back at different times on the following days until she found somebody. At the others she and Peterson had examined various documents to establish the identity of the residents.

As they got back in the car after the last tenant had shown them a driving licence proving he wasn't Vyvyan Wilde, Peterson said, 'Pizza or McDonalds?'

'I can't be bothered to drive to either and queue,' Lewin said. 'I've got a Tesco's take-away for two in the fridge, come back and I'll do that up.'

Peterson grunted agreement.

As they drove the ten-minute journey to her home Gillian wondered whether Graham was asking himself the same question she was asking herself; would either of them want him to go home after they'd eaten.

Vyvyan had decided to tie Adam Davis up facing Laura, let him see how useless his father was going to be in saving this young girl. He came round and slowly took in his surroundings. Adam was an intelligent lad and realised immediately who had grabbed him. He held Vyvyan's gaze.

215

'What do you want with me?' he asked.

'Time, that's what you can buy me, time. I don't want your dad getting too close to me yet.' He laughed, a short, humourless laugh. 'Well, ever really.'

Adam said nothing, he was scared, more scared than he'd ever been before. He knew from what his father had said that this man had killed at least two other people. He didn't want to be added to that list.

Gillian Lewin had finished loading the dishwasher. There wasn't much in it, but she couldn't be bothered to wash up by hand. She had offered Graham a beer and he'd gratefully accepted. He was now slumped in front of the telly looking as drained as she felt. She wasn't sure if he wanted to stay or just couldn't be bothered to go.

She saw the clock on the microwave, just gone nine. She wanted to go to bed, if Graham stayed was he expecting sex? She wasn't sure if that's what she wanted yet. She threw the tea towel on the side, she wasn't sure of anything really.

She hadn't had a partner for sometime now. The last one was a regular nine to five man and he hated her irregular hours. He had to go when he told her that she should give up the job. She'd vowed then to give men a wide berth, but at least Graham would understand the demands of the job, and she did quite like him. It had sort of crept up on her recently, that slight tug in the stomach when she saw him. The extra enjoyment of being in the same room. The things that after a few years of a relationship went unnoticed, but at the beginning, before it was even a relationship, made life sharper, more real, more intense.

She went back into the front room, Graham was all but asleep. 'Come on you,' she said, gently pushing his shoulder, 'wakey, wakey.'

Graham groaned, 'Oh, God. I feel knackered.' He got slowly to his feet.

Gillian made an instant decision. 'Stay, don't bother going home.'

Graham nodded, 'Okay.'

Gillian thought he must be tired, he hadn't quite registered the implications of staying. She went back to the kitchen and locked the back door. As she came back into the lounge Graham was going upstairs. This wasn't the first time he'd been in Gillian's house. At some stage each of the team had had the others round for a meal. Graham knew where the spare room was but seemed to hesitate as he got to the top of the stairs.

Gillian was right behind him. 'It's up to you.' She pointed to the spare room and her room. Graham smiled slightly, sleepily, and she felt a tremor of excitement as she waited the few seconds for his answer.

He moved towards her room, 'I wondered if you thought the same.'

She reddened slightly and said, 'I'll just use the bathroom.'

Five minutes later as she walked into the bedroom after a quick shower with the towel loosely wrapped around her she saw Graham fast asleep on the bed.

Vyvyan hadn't had time to examine Laura's phone when he'd brought her back to the barn. He'd just waited for her to regain consciousness. He picked up the phone now and looked at it. Like all kids these days it was a newish one. He flicked through the menu; good, it would do video. Let Wart see the terror on his precious daughter's face.

He heard Laura crying and turned to face her although he was standing outside her range of vision. He saw her trying to move her head and then the jerking of her arms and legs as she tried to get up.

The young lad had heard her moving about. He was tied facing her and tried to call to her through the gag. The muffled voice frightened her, 'Who's that? What's happening?'

Vyvyan waited for a few seconds to let her fear build up. Then he approached the bench. It was clear from the look on her face that she recognised him from the alley.

Her eyes widened with fear. 'Who are you? What do you want?' The last words were almost a scream.

Vyvyan said, 'I have some unfinished business with your dad, I wanted to get his attention.'

'What's my dad done to you?' she said through her tears.

'That's nothing to do with you, your job is to ensure he does as he's told,' Vyvyan snarled. He picked up the phone again and walked over to the ledge where the knife was. He hid that behind his back and as he moved back towards Laura he dialled her father's number.

'What's up?'

'That's no way to greet your daughter, is it?'

'Who the fuck is this?'

'Still a charmer, I see.'

There was a silence that seemed to stretch into minutes but was only seconds. Then Vyvyan heard, 'Oh my God. It's you.'

Chapter Thirtyone

Davis arrived home at a quarter to nine. The first thing Anita said was, 'Adam's gone out and I can't get him on his mobile.

Davis was starving and was more interested in what Anita might have ready for his dinner. 'When did he go out?' he asked.

'A couple of hours ago, he said he was going to Fazel's and then probably to Alex Jardine's about Saturday's car washing.'

Davis saw lasagne on a plate in the microwave, well, that had to be better than a salad again.

'Did he take his mobile with him?' he asked as he pushed the buttons on the microwave to reheat his dinner.

'He never goes out without it,' she snapped.

Davis could hear the worry in her voice and took his own mobile out of his pocket. Adam might have ignored his mother's calls if he thought she was going to ask him to call in at the shop again on the way home, but he knew better than to ignore his father's call.

Davis let the phone ring until the voicemail function kicked in. He left a message that Adam should ring home immediately and hung up. This was unlike Adam, Anita was right, he was never far from his phone.

He stopped the microwave and went into the front room to find the phone book, let's hope the Jardines weren't ex-directory he thought. A few seconds of checking later he found the number.

Mrs Jardine answered the phone.

'Hello, it's Phil Davis. Is Adam there?'

'No.' Mrs Jardine said. Davis had only met her a few times and each time he thought she was a bit of a cold woman. 'Alex was expecting him but he didn't arrive.'

'Has Alex heard from him tonight?'

'Not at all.' She obviously wasn't interested in whether Davis was worried about his son's whereabouts.

Davis thanked her and ended the call. Now he was beginning to feel a niggle of worry. Adam was old enough that he often went out in the evening on his own. But his mother usually knew where he'd gone and he always had his phone on him.

What should he do? He knew from his work that there was a period of time when a child had disappeared that the parents weren't sure what to do. They hoped nothing unpleasant had happened to their child but

218

feared that calling the police would confirm it had. They hoped their child would walk through the door blissfully unaware of the anguish of their parents. Or maybe they were with a friend and had forgotten the time.

But as a policeman Davis knew that the first hours were vital if a child really had gone missing.

Anita had been waiting in the doorway whilst he made the call to the Jardines. She voiced the fear he was beginning to feel.

'That man hasn't got him, has he?'

Davis tried to reassure her. 'It's unlikely he knows we're on to him. He certainly won't know I'm leading the investigation.' As Davis said that he hoped to God he was right. Wilde had been one step ahead of them all the time, maybe he was again.

Vyvyan realised that Wart recognised him. He'd killed Geoff Symonds because of that but now he realised it was inevitable that the victims would eventually work out who was behind the reign of terror.

Maybe it was better that they knew, it would add to their anguish for them to know that their past, something they couldn't take back, had caused their present hell. He planned to disappear anyway after he'd finished with Laura.

'Hello, Wart. I bet you didn't think you'd here from me again.'

'What the hell are you doing with my daughter's phone, where is she?'

'She's a little tied up at the moment.' Vyvyan couldn't help laughing at his own joke. 'But it doesn't matter, we're going to play a little game.'

'I'm not playing games with you, I'll call the police.'

'You can if you want, I suspect they're already looking for me. But do you want to risk me finishing my little game before they find me?'

Wart's voice had lost some of its bluster now. 'What do you want?'

'I want you to carry out some tasks for me. You might have to tell your family that I've got Laura, because this is going to take a couple of days, but none of you must tell anybody else.'

'Why can't you let her go?' Wart was pleading, his voice betrayed the fear Vyvyan wanted to hear. 'I'll come to you, this is because of what I did before Laura was born, let her go.'

'Now that might be fun, but I'm sure you'll appreciate that I want to do more than getting my own back on you?'

'What do you mean,' Wart asked.

'I want to destroy you.' Vyvyan shouted angrily.

'No, no, please don't hurt her. I'll do anything you want. I'm not asking, I'm grovelling. Please Vyvyan, please, let Laura go, she's my daughter, it's me you want, not my child.'

'I was somebody's child,' Vyvyan screamed in fury, 'or didn't that matter to you?' He calmed down. 'You love your daughter, don't you?' he asked deviously.

'Of course I do,' Wart said desperately. 'She's my little baby, please Vyvyan, she's only sixteen, she's never done any harm.'

'No, but you have. You harmed me. I've had to live with your torment all my life.' Vyvyan started to get angry again, years of suppressed fury bubbling to the surface. 'I've had to live with your vicious hate, your destroying of my life, your fucking torture of me.'

With the last words he slammed the knife blade deep into Laura's hand. Wart heard the howl of pain and desperately called his daughter's name.

'Laura, Laura, please God.' He was sobbing with fear now.

Vyvyan heard a voice on the other end of the phone. 'Who's that?'

'It's my wife.'

'What's her name?'

'Lisa, she's worried sick, she's heard me calling for Laura.'

'Put her on the phone.'

'No, please, don't tell her yet.'

'If you don't put her on I'll stab Laura again.'

Vyvyan heard a whispered few words and then a woman's voice, 'Who is this?'

'I'm the man your husband persecuted. I'm the man your husband bullied and tormented without mercy.'

A scared voice asked, 'What are you doing with my Laura?'

'I'm using her. Because your husband loves his daughter he'll do as I want.'

Laura's mother was as desperate as her husband. 'He loves me as well, take me instead, he'll do as you want,' she begged in a cracking voice.

Vyvyan laughed, 'I don't think so. Put William back on the phone.'

He heard the phone being passed over and William said, 'What do you want me to do?'

'Where do you work, William?'

220

The question threw William for a moment, 'Where do I what?'

'Work, I take it you have a job?'

'Yes, yes I do, I work at Bennett's the engineers. I work in the admin office.'

'I want you to go to work tomorrow as normal.'

'I can't, for God's sake, how can I go to work?'

'You will,' shouted Vyvyan. 'Do you know what torture it was waiting for a week for my neighbours to come home after you killed their rabbit?'

'Is that what this is all about, because I killed a rabbit and you got in trouble?'

'Got in trouble,' Vyvyan felt a fury as if the injustice had happened just yesterday. 'I got thrashed, you bastards attacked me and my parents never let me forget what happened. Well I'm going to make sure there's never a day in your life you don't remember this.'

'I'm sorry, how could I have known what would happen? I wouldn't have done it if I'd known.' Vyvyan could hear the panic in William's voice and loved it.

'So you didn't think there'd be any trouble if I confessed to killing some child's pet rabbit? They'd just come home and say, "That's okay, we didn't like the thing anyway." Is that what you thought when you made me say I'd done it?'

'Vyvyan, we were just kids,'

'That's no excuse, you and your buddies made my life hell. Well, welcome to hell yourself. You go to work as usual and I'll phone you to make sure you're there. I'll phone the reception and ask for you. You mustn't tell anybody about Laura, nor must your wife. Tell your son that she has gone to stay with a friend.' Vyvyan stopped for a moment. 'Where does your wife work?' he asked.

'She's a nurse, a nurse...' William could hardly complete a sentence he was so distressed. 'She works at Hinchingbrooke... in the high dependency ward.'

'Really, that is interesting. Did you know Mr Fennell is in there right now?'

'Yes, he's one of Lisa's patients.'

'Really, he was your favourite teacher, wasn't he?'

'I don't know about that.'

'He's certainly come up in the world.'

Their old teacher had become the local MP, a position he'd held until the last election when ill health had caused him to stand down. It was widely expected that when he recovered he would be given a peerage so that he could continue his work of education reform from the House of Lords.

'He never minded you bullying me, did he?' He always stuck up for you.'

'I'm sure he meant no harm'

Vyvyan's anger flared again. 'Are you,' he shouted, 'or is it just convenient to remember it that way because I have your daughter at my mercy?'

'No, I didn't mean...'

'I don't care what you meant,' he snapped. 'I'm going to send you a couple of pictures, just to encourage you to do as I say tomorrow.'

Vyvyan hung up and turned to Laura. He took a picture showing her taped to the bench and then took a close up of the wound on her hand. He sent them both to William's phone and then switched Laura's off.

Davis decided to try Adam's phone one more time before he reported him as missing. He dialled the number and to his relief the call was answered.

'Adam, where are you? Your mother's been worried about you.'

'If I were you I'd be very worried.' Vyvyan said chillingly.

Davis felt like his stomach had risen to his throat. He'd never heard this man's voice but he knew who he was instantly. However it had happened this investigation had taken a disastrous turn. He had been frustrated enough at their lack of progress, but now his own son was now in danger, what the hell was he going to do.

Anita had initially looked relieved when the call had been answered but as she saw Davis's face cloud over she began to worry again.

'What's the matter? Is he all right?'

Davis held a hand up to silence her and said to Vyvyan, 'What do you want of me?'

'I like that, you're the first parent to grasp straight away that this is my game, I'm in charge.'

'You've proved how far you're prepared to go, I'm listening.' As Davis spoke he was trying to keep a level head. He knew from what the other parents had said that Wilde had a short fuse and was likely to injure his captives if their parents annoyed him.

All the same his brain was racing with a jumble of thoughts. Uppermost of those was how he was going to get his son back. He kept getting flashes of the image of Alice lying on the floor of the barn but with Grace's face instead of Alice's. He couldn't let Adam die, like the parents of the girls he would have to do whatever Wilde asked of him.

Anita had worked out what had happened and sat down heavily on the sofa with tears running down her face. Her son was in the hands of a murderer, she couldn't lose another child, please, God, no.

'What I want is simple. You must stop this investigation into me.'

'That would be impossible.'

'You know I mean business, do you want me to prove it?' Vyvyan raged.

Davis had to think quickly if he was to save Adam from harm. 'If I stop the investigation my superior will take me off the case and put another officer in charge. What I can and will do is change the direction of the investigation.'

'How will you do that?'

'That depends on how much time you need.'

'I'll be finished by Sunday. You can get me three clear days I hope?'

'Yes, I'll make sure my officers are working on dead-ends until then.'

'Good. If you do that your son will live, after all, my gripe isn't with you.'

Davis wanted to ask if there was anyway of stopping this violence, ask whether Wilde had already snatched another child but the phone was dead.

Adam wanted to shout out to his father not to listen to this freak, carry on and find him, he, Adam, would take the risk. But the words would not come. His throat felt tight with fear, his mouth dry. He wanted to believe he was a man, ready to take on the world. But right now he wanted his dad to do what his dad had always done; put things right.

As soon as the phone call ended Davis picked up the house phone. Before he could dial Anita was screaming at him.

'He's got him, hasn't he?' She jumped up from the sofa and slapped his face, 'It's your bloody fault, you always put your job first.

Now look what's happened.'

She was almost hysterical and Davis had to admit to himself that panic wasn't far away in him.

'I'm going to get him back,' he said, as much to reassure himself as Anita.

'You haven't rescued any of the others, have you?' she shouted, 'why the hell should I think you're going to save my son?'

Davis felt the fury of all those frustrated years rising in him. 'He's my bloody son as well. Do you not think that I love him?' He wiped away a tear that stung the corner of his eye. 'I loved Grace and there's not a day goes by that I don't wish she was with us and yet you have always treated her death as your tragedy, not ours.'

He moved to Anita's side and tried to take her hand. She pulled it away and wouldn't meet his gaze. There was no softening of her attitude.

'I'll do everything I can to get our son back,' he promised.

'You'd better,' she said with a harsh, desperate edge to her voice.

Chapter Thirtytwo

Vyvyan looked around him. He had never imagined that he would have three children at his mercy at the same time. He hoped he hadn't over-stretched himself. It was a risk taking the policeman's son, but at least Davis knew what would happen if he crossed Vyvyan.

Davis picked the phone up again after Anita had stormed into the kitchen, slamming the door behind her. He called Peterson's phone, it rang several times before it was answered. A sleepy voice said, 'Hello.'

'Graham, he's got Adam.'

Peterson's voice was suddenly alert, 'He's what? How?'

Davis's voice had lost some of its usual assertiveness.' I don't know, he answered Adam's phone when I rang him.'

'What did he want?'

'He wants me to back off. I told him I'd tell my team to investigate dead ends.'

'And what are we going to do?'

'We've got to get him, Wilde I mean.'

Anita rushed back from the kitchen. 'You bastard, you told that man you'd leave him alone. He said he'd let Adam go if you did. If my son gets hurt because of you I'll never forgive you.' The words came out in a rush. Tears were streaming down her face.

Davis said to Peterson, 'Meet me at the office, phone the others, I want Bellamy in as well, his son will be all right, mine might not be.'

Peterson hung up and Davis turned to Anita who had collapsed on the sofa. He knelt on the floor beside her. 'I'm as scared as you, I love my son as much as you do, but I can't hide from the truth, this man kills the children he snatches, even if their parents do as he wants.'

'And you're going to get our son killed,' she shrieked.

Davis didn't have time to argue with her. 'I'm going to get our son back in one piece,' he said more determinedly than he felt. He looked down at her. 'Do you want to come with me?'

'Don't be stupid,' she spat at him. 'If that man rings someone needs to be here.'

Not for the first time Davis didn't know what to say to his wife. He put his jacket back on and pocketed his mobile phone. He turned to Anita but whatever he might have said was stalled by the look of hatred in her eyes.

Davis's team met in the CID office. Davis had phoned Malloy on the way in and he arrived just after the others. As he walked into the office he gestured Davis to come into Davis's own office.

'Phil, I don't know how this man has got to your family this easily, but I'll do all I can to get your lad out of this safely.'

Davis couldn't speak for a few seconds, the fear for his son's life and the words of his friend brought a lump to his throat.

Malloy understanding immediately said, 'If you feel you can't deal with leading this investigation under the circumstances I'll take charge of it personally, it's up to you.'

Davis shook his head. 'No, I want to get this bastard myself.' He tried to smile, 'Besides, I'd never leave you alone, I'd be driving you mad looking over your shoulder all the time.' He opened the office door, 'I've got to do this.'

Malloy nodded. 'Let me know if you need extra men, the Chief Constable will have to take the flak if the Home Secretary's visit to the research centre gets overrun with protesters, this takes priority now.'

'For now we'll keep the team as it is, I don't want to spook Wilde.'

Both men went into the main office and faced the rest of the team.

'I expect Graham has told you all about Adam,' he said. 'He was taken earlier this evening and I've assured Wilde that we'll look the other way while he finishes his campaign in return for Adam's safe return.'

He stopped for a moment trying to keep his voice from cracking.

'We know, however, that he isn't likely to let him go no matter what I do.' He hesitated for a moment. 'I can't in all conscience do that anyway and condemn someone else's child to death.'

Peterson said, 'What do you want us to do, Phil?'

Davis wasn't sure what to say, his mind felt fogged with worry for his son. He had to do something, had to provide some direction or Malloy would take over. Davis didn't want that, he wanted to be the one who rescued his son.

'We have been trying hard enough to track him. It's difficult but I still think our best shot is finding Taylor. Gillian, how did your search for him go?'

'We can't find Taylor anywhere, we might have to consider he's moved away some time ago,' she said.

'Right,' said Davis, 'I want to know about every crime or public

226

disorder that's phoned in.'

He turned to Malloy, 'We know he gets the parents to do something that draws attention to themselves, we need to react quickly this time.'

'I'll make sure everything even remotely likely is referred to you immediately,' Malloy said.

Davis glanced up to see Peterson's rub his eyes, he looked up at the clock. It was almost midnight, the team had been on the go all day.

'I think it would be best to start afresh in the morning. I believe Wilde won't harm Adam until he's finished what he wants to do. We don't know if he's snatched anybody else yet, but if he has he hasn't had much chance to do anything.'

Peterson and Lewin started to protest immediately. 'We can carry on, Phil.' Peterson said.

Davis held up a hand to stall them. 'We have no more to go on now Adam's been taken than we did before, we're still dependent on Wilde making a move and I don't think that'll happen overnight.'

He turned to Malloy, 'Make sure the duty officer knows to get in touch with me if anything comes in.' Malloy nodded.

Davis turned to the rest of them. 'Go home, get some sleep. Be back here at six.' With that he walked out towards his own office.

Peterson caught up with him. 'What are you going to do, Phil?'

Davis looked grim, 'I'm going to take the files home and go through everything we've got.' He looked at Peterson, 'I'm also going to try to comfort my wife, but I don't think I'll be able to.'

Friday

William and Lisa Reardon had not slept a wink. Lisa was at first furious beyond words with her husband. Eventually she had started to cry again and said, 'We're never going to see Laura again, are we? What the hell did you do to this man?'

'It was years ago, when we were at school. He was just a kid, we all were.' He took his wife's hands in his own. 'He's got to let her go, we'll do what ever he asks, there'll be no reason to keep her.'

'There's no reason for him to have taken her now,' she sobbed. 'For God's sake, how many years has this weirdo had to brood on this, he's mad.'

'Well over twenty years, I haven't seen him since we left school.'

Lisa dried her eyes and said to William, 'I want to know exactly

227

what you did to him, I want to know what he might have in mind for Laura or us.'

'It's not worth going over, it's history.'

'Not to him it isn't,' Lisa said hotly, 'he's kidnapped my daughter; you tell me now what you did to him.'

There was a harder edge to her voice than William was used to and he decided he'd better do as she asked. During the sleepless early hours of Friday morning he told Lisa all that he and his friends had done to Vyvyan.

Davis got into the office and put the kettle on just in time to see Gillian and Graham get out of her car. He had seen Graham's Ford in the car park and assumed he was already in. So he had been right in thinking there was something going on between them.

He wouldn't mention it, they were both adults, as long as it didn't affect their work he wasn't bothered by their relationship. Mind you, it wouldn't take long to get all round the station.

He made a coffee and sat down to look at the reports that had come in yesterday whilst he was away. If there'd been anything urgent one of his team would have told him so he quickly skimmed over them. A couple of minutes later both detectives came through the door.

Peterson said, 'Morning, sir, any news?'

Davis shook his head.

'I've just picked a report up as it came in.' Peterson continued. 'A young lad, seventeen, his mum says he didn't come home last night.'

Davis groaned, had Vyvyan beaten them to it again?

'What's his name?'

Peterson looked at the copy of the report, 'Gary Jackson.'

'So it's not our man Taylor's son then.' Davis was thoughtful for a minute. 'Not unless he did change his name.'

'What reason would he have to do that?' Lewin asked.

'I don't know,' Davis replied. 'But it might explain why we can't find him.' He turned back to Peterson, 'It's not likely though. What do we know about this lad?'

Peterson read from the top. 'Gary Jackson, seventeen, lives at twenty-nine Flanders Road with his mother. Works at Speedmasters round the corner. Mother said he went out on a date last night and hasn't come back.'

'Any mention of a father?' Davis asked as Bellamy and Green arrived.

'Not on the report.'

Davis pondered for a moment then said, 'I can't see a connection with our current case, but we'd better check it out.' He drained his coffee in one more gulp and said, 'Gillian, you come with me. Did you have any luck checking out all the new rentals yesterday?' he asked her.

'We've called on the new rentals, not all of them were in.' Lewin said. 'I'll call on those until somebody is.'

'Give the list to Bellamy.' He turned to Bellamy, 'Visit each address, if nobody answers try the neighbours. Find out where they work and go there. I want that list checked out by lunch time.'

Davis got up to go and see Mrs Jackson. 'We have got to face the fact that Vyvyan Wilde is almost certainly going to snatch another child,' he said grimly, 'the last week has shown that there won't be much time between the death of one and the snatching of the next one. If he's had more luck tracing Taylor than we have then Taylor's child could already be in trouble.'

He looked at them both and they could see the pain in his eyes. 'The nearer he is to achieving his goal the more danger Adam is in.'

There was nothing for the others to say, they knew Davis was right.

Vyvyan had slept well. He always did when he was happy. At the moment, with his revenge almost complete, he was very happy. He had expected one or two hiccups along the way and so far there hadn't been any that he hadn't been able to solve immediately. He congratulated himself on the masterstroke of kidnapping the policeman's son. It should buy him the time he needed to finish his campaign of revenge. The boy would have to die; he wasn't going to risk leaving him alive to give his father too much information that might allow the police to track him down.

He cooked himself a full breakfast and took his time eating it. He'd forgotten to ask William what time he started work but it was just past nine now so he expected that the admin staff should be at work.

He found the number for Bennett's in the Yellow Pages and called them. A minute later he had been put through to William.

'Hello, William, how are you?'

'How's Laura, is she okay?'

'Very commendable, asking about your daughter, but I want to know how you are. Are you enjoying work?'

William was shocked, 'Enjoying it? I can barely think what I'm

229

doing. Please, let Laura go, I'll do anything you want.'

'There's plenty of time yet. Talk to you later.' Vyvyan hung up.

Gary Jackson had no idea what was going on. He had been trying for some time to pluck up the courage to ask Laura Reardon out on a date. He'd known her at school and seen her regularly at the supermarket. As far as he was aware she'd never had a boyfriend, something he couldn't understand as she was, in his opinion, very pretty. She was shy and didn't go out much, but then the same could be said for himself.

He had finally taken the plunge and asked her to come to the pictures with him.

God knows what had gone wrong. This man who had abducted them both had seemed to know they were going to be at the end of the alley. He was fairly certain that Laura hadn't known him, but the man appeared to have a grudge against her father.

So far he hadn't been hurt himself, but he had seen the man stab Laura's hand and had almost thrown up. That had made him hate the man with a violence that he didn't think he had in his body. Although he went to church he wasn't a particularly pious person, but he did know that you shouldn't hate your fellow man. How could he not though?

Laura had done no wrong to anybody, and he suspected that he loved her. Even though he was only seventeen he knew well enough that love was something that grew over time, but he had known her some time, just not well.

He also despised the man for stripping her naked. Not only for the embarrassment it obviously caused her but also because he didn't want the memory of the first time he saw her body to be tainted in this vile way.

He'd felt worse when the other boy was brought in by their captor. He heard the conversation with the boy's father and had worked out what was going on there. The father was the policeman in charge of the case. He had agreed to give the man some space to finish his crimes. Gary knew Laura's rescue was in his hands. He couldn't see the other boy, one of the higher partitions was in the way, and his gag stopped him calling out, but he hoped the lad would help him if he could.

Gary didn't know how he was going to be able to help Laura but he was going to try. The man had tied him loosely at first. Then after securing Laura to the bench he had made Gary stand up and had tied his hands behind his back whilst he leant against an upright wooden beam. He had then tied his legs together as well. By the time that had happened Gary's head had cleared from the effects of that stuff on the pad. When the man had tied him up he had flexed his muscles as much as he could, as a consequence the ropes weren't as tight as they might have been.

He still couldn't get out but during a night in which he couldn't sleep he had managed to make them feel slightly looser. The rope looked new, which meant it hadn't been stretched yet. If Gary tried hard enough he might get enough slack to slip his hands out.

If he did he would rescue Laura, surely she would love him then?

Chapter Thirtythree

Davis was only half way up the path when the front door was opened. The garden was neat and well stocked with spring flowers. Mrs Jackson was standing on the doorstep almost urging him to move faster. Without waiting to confirm their identification she showed them into the front room. The inside of the house was a neat as the outside. There were several china dolls on a sideboard against one wall and a series of photos on a cabinet under the main window. Some were of a man in his thirties and the others of a young boy as he grew up.

Mrs Jackson was desperate to tell the police about her son but her innate politeness saw her offer them a hot drink first.

'No thank you, Mrs Jackson,' Lewin replied. She picked up one of the photos of the young man and asked, 'Is this your son, is this Gary?'

'Yes, he's my only son.' It was clear she was having difficulty controlling the tears that must have flowed earlier. What must have been this morning's fresh make up had run slightly and smudged where she had wiped it.

Lewin replaced the picture and pointed to the picture of the man. 'And that's your husband?' she asked.

'My late husband, he was killed driving home from work one day.' She dabbed at her eyes again and said, 'It's why I worry so much about Gary. His father was a careful man, he was a lovely husband and he adored our son.' She brushed the frame of the photo as she looked at it.

'The other driver was drunk, it wasn't even six o'clock but he was drunk. He drove straight through a red light and hit my Shaun. He died instantly.'

She picked the photo up and held it tightly to her as if it could provide some comfort. 'Gary was only nine, he took it very badly. He didn't say a word to anybody for days afterwards. He wouldn't let my father near him. He'd always been close to his grandad, but seemed to think it would be disloyal to his father to allow another man to help him.'

She put the picture back on the cabinet and turned to the detectives. 'Please find my son, I don't have anybody else left.' She sat down on the sofa and cried quietly into a wad of tissues.

'When did he leave home?' Davis asked.

'Last night, just after tea. He was taking a girl out, the first time it was. I don't know who she was, but he'd said she was a very nice girl.'

'Do you know anything about her?' Lewin asked.

Mrs Jackson shook her head. 'Gary's always been the sort to play things close to his chest. He rarely tells me anything about his work or his friends. Don't get me wrong,' she said, 'he's a lovely son. He's always ready to help me out, he just tries to make sure I don't worry.'

She stopped for a moment and asked, 'Do you have children?' to both of them.

Davis felt a spear of pain in his heart, his son too was missing and he knew the danger Adam was in. He wasn't going to tell her his own son had been kidnapped, there might be no connection at all, maybe this lad had just spent the night with the girl. They'd have to find out more about him. He said, 'I have a son, almost the same age as your Gary.'

Lewin tried to get the enquiry back on track. 'Where was he taking her?'

'He was going to take her to the pictures. I don't know what was on but he seemed to think she'd like it.'

'How was he getting there, does he drive?'

'No, he's going to start taking lessons soon, he sent off for his licence last week. He walked last night.'

Davis turned to Lewin, 'That means the girl must be local, we'll make enquiries at his workplace later.' He turned to Mrs Jackson. 'Can I ask what your maiden name was, please?'

Mrs Jackson looked surprised.

'It's just part of a routine for missing people,' Davis said, not wanting to worry her more than she already was.

He really wanted to know if there could be any possible connection with the Vyvyan Wilde case. For all they knew Wilde had discovered Taylor had no children and had gone after a nephew.

'My maiden name was Banks.'

Davis nodded, it didn't seem likely there was a connection. In a way it was a relief, but that meant there was another missing child out there somewhere. Gary Jackson might not consider himself a child at seventeen and working, but he wasn't very worldly wise by the sound of things, Davis's team was going to be hard pressed to spend much time on this whilst Wilde was on the loose.

'He works at Speedmasters I understand. We'll go straight there, maybe he's told a friend where this girl lives.'

Mrs Jackson said, 'He might have done but most of the men are older than him, he hasn't made many friends there yet.'

'Okay, Mrs Jackson. We'll make enquiries and either myself or my colleague will come back to see you later. Do you have anybody who can wait with you?'

She shook her head.

'Please try not to worry, I know that's easy to say, but teenagers can be very inconsiderate at times. Maybe he's stayed with a friend and not rung you.'

'He hasn't, he wouldn't, he'd ring.'

There was nothing else for Davis and Lewin to say and they left.

Vyvyan decided to ring William again. It was almost lunchtime. This time he dialled William's mobile phone. William answered almost before the first ring had finished.

'You are eager.' Vyvyan taunted.

'Please, I can't cope with much more of this, how's Laura?' William did sound desperate. Vyvyan felt a surge of excitement at the power he had over him.

'At the moment she's okay, but I'd like to remind you that whether she stays that way is entirely up to me. All you can do is pray you don't annoy me.'

'I've told you, I'll do what ever you ask, whatever.'

'For now I want you to carry on at work. What time do you finish?'

'Five o'clock,' William answered.

'I'll ring you at home at half-past. I think I have a little job for your wife in mind.' Vyvyan hung up before William could ask what the job was.

He went outside to the barn and unlocked the door. As light flooded the room he saw the young lad's head snap upright, obviously he had fallen asleep. The policeman's son looked at him coolly, he was scared, Vyvyan could tell, but he wasn't terrified. Not yet, anyway.

Laura couldn't turn her head but he could see her body tense on the bench as he approached.

He stood beside her and looked down at the frightened face. He doubted she'd slept much. She had been an attractive girl when he'd been watching her as he had planned where to snatch her. Now her eyes appeared sunken and fear had etched lines on her face, a face that should have been too young for such lines.

Vyvyan had little sympathy for her. Her father had caused him so much worry and pain. Remembering that made him angry and he pressed on the wound on her palm.

She cried out in pain. Gary Jackson shouted at him, 'Leave her alone, you bastard.' He was shocked at himself using that kind of language but he was terrified for Laura's sake. The gag muffled his words but enough could be made out so that they were understood.

Vyvyan turned to him and said coldly, 'At the moment this is nothing to do with you. If you want to survive I'd keep your stupid mouth shut.' He picked the knife up and held it close to Gary's face. 'If you can't keep quiet I might cut your tongue out.'

What frightened Gary more than the knife was the complete lack of emotion in this man's eyes. He truly was evil. Gary would have to do something, because if he didn't Laura was going to die. Of that he was sure.

Davis and Lewin had visited Gary's workplace and had found he was as secretive there as he was at home. His boss, a Mr Brown, said, 'Didn't even know he had a date. Good lad he is. Works hard. Gets on with the job. I'll show you where he works.'

He led them into a small workshop and with a greasy finger pointed to a bench. 'He works over there at the moment. Learning the trade, he is. Strips down engines. When he knows how they come apart we'll show him how to put them back together.' He gave a little smile at what he considered a joke. He pulled a rag out of the pocket on his blue overalls and wiped his hands. They looked just as greasy when he'd finished.

'Does he have any particular friends here?' Davis asked.

Brown shook his head, the light from the overhead strip lights reflecting on his glasses as he did so. 'Not as you'd say, no. Don't get me wrong. He's popular. Gets on with people. But not over much with anyone in particular.' Brown pointed back through the doors to the main workshop. 'Most of the lads are older. He's the first youngster we've taken on for a while. Knew his dad. Poor bloke. Thought I'd help the boy.'

There was nothing to find out here. Davis gave Brown a card with his number on it. 'If he gets in touch ring me please, his mum's worried sick.'

Mr Brown nodded. 'Will do. Bloody kids.' With that he turned back to the office and left Davis and Lewin to find their own way out.

As soon as they left the workshop Davis phoned Malloy. Whilst Davis was out of the office, Malloy was coordinating any information that might relate to Adam's disappearance. 'Any news yet?'

'Sorry, Phil, nothing.'

Davis hung up and drove back to the station. Whilst they had been out Peterson had checked with the local hospitals to see if Gary Jackson had been admitted. He hadn't.

Davis took the cup of coffee Green offered him and said, 'I've got a bad feeling about this. We're expecting a person of that age to go missing and one has.'

'But there's no connection with Wilde,' Peterson said.

'There's none we can see,' Davis countered. 'Okay, I know there might not be a connection at all, but I'm not sure.'

'I still think our best chance is to find Taylor,' Peterson said.

'But we haven't had any luck there, have we?' Davis said, frustrated.

'What about that idea that he'd changed his name?' Lewin asked.

'If he has we won't know where to start looking. He could be right under our nose and we'd never know. Anyway,' Davis continued, 'why would a man change his surname? A woman usually does on marriage but in all my time I've never known a man change his name unless it was part of a witness protection programme.'

Davis wasn't used to being this empty-handed when he was searching for a suspect or witness. Usually they had something to go on, but this time two men, Wilde and Taylor, seemed to have disappeared into thin air.

'Has Bellamy been in touch?' Davis asked.

'He rang about half hour ago, he still had four more to do. He's checking the neighbours of those still out as you asked.'

Vyvyan deliberately waited until just after six before ringing William. He wanted him to suffer as much as possible while he held Laura but he was aware that he didn't have unlimited time. The kidnap of six young people and the murder of three of them and of one of their parents was a major crime. Now he had taken the son of the investigating officer the police would throw as many resources as they could muster in to tracking him down. He had been shocked when that policeman had knocked on his door but for that to have been the only brush with the law through this campaign was something to be both surprised and grateful about.

William answered immediately again and Vyvyan didn't give him time to say anything before he demanded to talk to Lisa. 'What do you want with my wife?' William demanded.

'William, I'm not sure you grasp the situation. We're not at school now.' Vyvyan's voice was cold and William was about to apologise but was scared to interrupt. 'You're not calling the shots anymore. If you challenge me again Laura will pay the price.'

'I'm sorry, Vyvyan. It's just she's as frightened as I am.'

'Put her on the phone now.'

Lisa's voice betrayed her mental state, she was either crying as she spoke or had been very recently.

'Hello, what do you want me for? Please tell me if Laura's okay.'

'I want you to do something for me. If you do it Laura won't get hurt again, if you don't I'll tell her that what happens to her is happening because her mum doesn't love her enough.'

'No, please… that's not true. Please don't say that to her. I'll do what ever you want.'

'William tells me that you work on the high dependency ward.'

'Yes,' she replied hurriedly.

'You have a patient called Fennell?'

'Yes, I do.'

'Is he expected to live long?'

'He's had surgery for stomach cancer but he's expected to be okay, in fact he won't be on my ward much longer.' Lisa couldn't make out what this had to do with Laura but was too frightened to ask.

'He won't be anywhere much longer. I want you to kill him.'

'You want what,' Lisa screeched. 'I can't kill him.' She was gabbling now. 'I'm a nurse, I can't kill anybody.'

'It's up to you, but I'm sure Laura would want you to.'

'Please, you can't ask me to do that.'

'But I just have. I'll give you two minutes to think about it.' Vyvyan hung up.

He walked outside to the barn and after unlocking walked straight up to Laura. 'It's time your parents heard from you, just to let them know how you are.'

She met his gaze and he could see the terror in her eyes. She knew he wasn't going to be offering her a cosy chat with her mum and dad.

'Don't hurt me again, I've never hurt you. Please, can't we talk?

I'm sure we can work something out if we talk about it.'

'What do you think you could do for me? Your only use to me is as a weapon.' He held the knife just in front of her face and said, 'This knife can cause your parents so much distress they'll do just about anything for me.'

Vyvyan bounced the flat edge on her forehead, 'Don't worry though, I'm sure mummy will do as she's told.'

Vyvyan dialled the Reardon's number again and Lisa answered, she began speaking as soon as the connection was made. 'Please, I beg you. I can't kill a man.'

'Oh dear, I think Laura wants you to.' he put the point of the knife blade on her uninjured palm and pressed lightly.

Laura gave a small cry of pain and Lisa said, 'No, wait, I'll do anything else.'

Before she could say anymore Vyvyan pressed harder on the knife and a crimson puddle of blood formed in the middle of Laura's palm. She started to scream and Vyvyan eased the pressure a little.

'Maybe you've had a rethink?' he asked Lisa.

Lisa was crying now, calling Laura's name. 'Laura, oh, my baby, Laura, please, please don't hurt her anymore.'

'So you agree to do as I've asked?'

'Why do you want me to kill him? Surely that can't do you any good?'

Vyvyan was angry, why was she messing him about? He forced the knife straight through Laura's hand and wrenched it back and forth. She screamed and her body thrashed around as much as it could whilst it was taped down.

Gary Jackson, who until now had remained quiet, shouted out to him, 'Leave her alone you bastard, I'll kill you if I can.'

Vyvyan pulled the knife from Laura's hand and swung round to face Gary. 'But you can't can you? You're just a pathetic little boy.'

He jabbed the knife under Gary's chin once or twice, each time piercing the skin but not doing much damage. Gary tried to pull his head higher. Vyvyan slowly pushed the knife under his chin and then pushed slightly harder. The tip of the blade slid into the fleshy part of Gary's chin making him wince, but he didn't utter a sound as he began to bleed.

Vyvyan pulled the blade out and turned back to Laura. He said to Lisa, 'Her boyfriend seems to want to help her more than you do.'

Lisa was shocked, 'You've got Gary as well?'

'Is that his name? He won't be going anywhere for a while, but he needs to understand just how vulnerable he is.'

Vyvyan held his thumb over Laura's newly injured hand without touching it. 'Are you ready to do as I've asked?'

'Yes,' Lisa said with despair in her voice.

'You will? Good. I'm sure Laura appreciates that, I'd pass the phone to her but she might not be able to hold it.' Vyvyan laughed loudly and said 'I wonder what I'd have done to her next. You've seen the photos I sent William have you? I have plenty of young flesh to use my knife on.'

'I'll do it, I said I'll do it, you don't need to hurt her anymore.' Lisa was begging Vyvyan and he loved the power he felt.

'When is your next shift?'

'Tonight, I should have gone in last night but I said I had a family problem.'

'You didn't tell them what it was, did you?' Vyvyan asked menacingly.

'No,' Lisa said panicking, 'I just said a family problem.'

'Right, go back tonight; I want you to do it tonight.'

'How am I supposed to do it?'

'That's up to you, you're the nurse,' he said callously. 'What time do you get home?'

'I've got a long shift tonight. I finish at eleven o'clock, I'll be home just before midday.'

'I'll phone you after mid-day. If you haven't done it, Laura will pay the price.' Again he hung up without warning.

Chapter Thirtyfour

Saturday

Friday had petered out into another day of dead-ends for Davis and his team. They had not found Taylor, not found Gary Jackson, not found Wilde and, as a consequence, not found Adam.

He was acutely aware that Adam had been in Wilde's clutches for twenty-four hours. Every hour was increasing the risk of Wilde harming him.

He was convinced that Vyvyan Wilde would have snatched another child by now. If his suspicions were right Wilde's campaign was in its final few hours, he needed a break, he needed Wilde to slip up in some way.

As he sat at his desk thinking about this he realised that today was the day he had promised to take Adam to the football match. He wished with all his heart that he could go to that match with his son. To stand side-by-side cheering on their local team. To enjoy the simple pleasure of his son's company. He thought of all the times he'd let his son down because he had a case that needed his attention. Today it was Adam that was the case, he needed his father's attention like he never needed it before.

Anita was still distraught and had refused offers of having a policewoman with her. She had made two brief phone calls but not told Davis whom she had been talking to. When he had come home she had looked at him with a momentary flash of hope, but at the shake of his head the look of disdain, even hatred, had returned.

He got in the office just before six this morning determined to do something different, something, anything, that they had overlooked.

As he sat in the office alone he started to wonder how Wilde had known where or when to grab his victims. They weren't sure yet how he had found them, but once he had Wilde would have needed to spend an amount of time watching them.

Bellamy had two more rented houses to try today. He and Green could do one each and then both of them and four uniformed constables he's got from Malloy could do house to house enquiries in the roads where each victim lived. Maybe somebody had seen Wilde. Maybe, maybe, it was all maybes at the moment.

Green came in followed a few minutes later by Bellamy. Peterson and Lewin came in together again just before six-thirty.

Bellamy switched the kettle on and said to the group, 'I'm going to get something from the canteen, does anybody else want anything?'

Green, Peterson and Lewin quickly gave orders for filled rolls and coffees. Davis was hesitating. 'Sir?' Bellamy asked.

'Sod the diet; get me two bacon and egg rolls.' As Lewin started to say something he held a hand up to stop her. 'One little reminder from anybody about me losing weight and I'll have you all on an exchange posting to Siberia.'

There was much laughter but nobody joked about his weight.

Vyvyan decided to go in to town. If he waited around all day he'd go mad. He had lain awake for several hours last night, he was sure that it was waiting to find out if Lisa had killed Fennell. This remote control murder, as he thought of it, was almost as exciting as doing it himself.

He needed to do some shopping and the fresh air would do him good. He tidied up the breakfast things then made sure the barn was locked up properly. He got into the little Fiesta and drove into the centre of Chatteris. He'd bought this car privately and hadn't registered it at all.

He was going to get a few bits in the supermarket where Laura worked. He parked in their car park round the back and walked up the alley beside the shop into the High Street. The first place to go was the paper shop. He liked to get a paper most days. He lived too far out of town for a delivery and in any case he couldn't risk having one of his captives shouting out if they heard anybody coming up the track.

That was the reason he'd asked for his mail to be held at the local delivery office. He'd claimed he had a dog that he couldn't control properly. There wasn't much mail; after all he hadn't advertised his being at the cottage. There was always some though in any week, utility bills, advertising, junk really. He collected that after he bought his paper.

He was strolling through the High Street on his way back to the supermarket enjoying the strengthening sun when he heard his name called out.

'Vyvyan Wilde, there. Stop!'

Vyvyan had the presence of mind not to panic. He calmly looked round, ironically, considering all this current activity was caused by his name, his fellow shoppers were looking for a woman. But, damn, there

241

was Bob James, about a hundred yards behind him pointing his way and beginning to run towards him. He casually carried on walking just picking his pace up a little bit. He crossed the road and was only a few yards from the alleyway leading to the car park.

He heard Bob shout, 'He's a killer, stop him.' Luckily for Vyvyan nobody seemed to think Bob was shouting about him. As soon as he was out of sight in the alleyway he ran as fast as he could to his car. He used the remote unlock fob as he approached the car and was inside and had the engine running before he saw Bob appear at the top of the alley. He swung the car out of the car park and instead of heading for the main road drove as quickly as he dared through the back streets of the housing estate. After several turns he came out near the far end of town. He turned right and headed out of town on the Ely road.

He seriously thought about running away now, but that wasn't practical. He had at least to go back to the cottage and collect his personal things. He knew he could never go back to Devon and had taken what he needed from there before he left. He had enough of Andrew's paperwork to assume his identity and that was all in a folder at the cottage. He also had a little Peugeot tucked under a cover in the barn that he had registered in Andrew's name. When he finally fled it would be in that car. Nothing associated with Vyvyan Wilde could come with him to Scotland.

He turned back into Chatteris further down the road and carefully drove back to the cottage. He had to make sure the car was hidden now; Bob had probably noted the number plate.

He would have to accelerate his plans, he felt under pressure for the first time.

Davis felt a surge of excitement. He'd just had a phone call from an out of breath Bob James. Bob had seen Wilde and tried to chase him, but Wilde had escaped. Bob had been quick witted enough to note the make and number of the car Wilde was driving. Those details had been circulated to all police vehicles on the road. Davis had asked for the force helicopter to sweep the area as well. It was a long shot that they might find him but it was worth it.

He called the rest of the team together. The five of them sat around one of the desks with fresh cups of coffee.

'Our man has been seen in town, apparently going about his shopping as if nothing were amiss.'

'Maybe that means he hasn't got another victim yet,' Lewin said.

'Remember he was in Peterborough when he made Bob James walk around dressed in his wife's clothes. At that time he had Abigail in his clutches,' Peterson said.

'I think we have to assume he has Taylor's child,' Davis said. 'He's been following his own plan so far. We've got to accept that he's had more luck tracing Taylor than we have.'

Davis picked up a report from his desk. 'I'm still not happy about this young lad going missing. We've checked that his family have no connection with Taylor, but what about his girlfriend? What if she's Taylor's daughter? Gary Jackson may have been snatched because he was with her.'

'At the moment we have no idea who she is,' Lewin said. 'Neither his mum nor his boss knew who he was taking out.'

'But Wilde has never kidnapped two people at once,' Green pointed out. 'What if they've just run away together?'

Davis said, 'Whilst we don't know what the girlfriend is like we do know something of Gary Jackson, I'd say there's little chance of him doing a bunk.'

He pointed to the wipe clean boards that held the information they had gathered since Alice's murder. 'Each parent has had to do something that they wouldn't want to do. In each case that has brought them to our attention. I want to know about every single crime committed until we find Wilde. The usual crap we'll be able to rule out, but anything that seems out of the ordinary, we investigate.'

Gary Jackson was trying hard to be courageous. When he had first been tied up he had decided that he would have to be Laura's hero, that he would have to break free and rescue her. But he had been reminded, painfully, that this man held the upper hand. He had continued with the attempts to stretch his bonds enough to escape them, but he was still someway from achieving that yet.

What he would do if he escaped he wasn't sure. Freeing Laura would be one thing, but he didn't know if they'd be able to get out of the barn. He shuffled around as much as he could to see what options there were. Would the other boy be able to help? He'd heard nothing from him, maybe he was gagged like himself. He tried hard to push the gag from his mouth but it was too tight.

The barn seemed to be divided into sections by a combination of low walls and wooden partitions. One section held two cars, there was a small one under a cover and the Renault the man had used when he snatched the two of them. The main section, the one they were in had low wooden walls along one side giving what Gary assumed must have been pens for animals. Some of these had been altered to make the bench that Laura was currently bound to.

The barn had two small windows in the section they were in, both had bars on them. The only door he had seen was the one behind him, but he knew there must be a bigger one in the section the cars were in, as they couldn't have got through the gap between the sections.

There was nothing he could use as a weapon other than the knife. Obviously the man didn't think they would be able to escape their bonds as he'd left the knife on one of the window ledges.

Gary had serious doubts about whether he could stab a man, even to defend Laura. It was such a brutal thing to do, so final an act of violence. It would be best if they could just run away.

He redoubled his efforts to slip out of the rope, ignoring the pain it brought to his wrists.

Green called to Davis, 'Sir, Crawford's just reported a man in March Broad Street. He's walking up and down with a board proclaiming the end of the world and shouting that everyone's going to hell.'

Davis didn't know whether to laugh or not. He had to be alert to the fact that this could be Taylor, it sounded just the sort of thing Wilde would order a desperate father to do; pointless and humiliating.

'Right, you stay here,' he said to Green. 'If any other reports come in I want to know. Graham, you come with me.'

He turned to Gillian, 'Go back to Gary Jackson's mother. Ask her if you can search his bedroom. I've been thinking about that diary Wilde had in his house. Some times people write down what they could never say to another person. If Gary's written his thoughts down about this girlfriend we might be able to trace her.' He turned to Bellamy, 'You go and see Bob James, I want to know everything he saw Wilde do, what he was wearing, how he looked, what direction he drove of in, what he was carrying.'

Davis and Peterson set off for March, some seven miles away. Peterson was driving and they had Motorhead on the stereo again.

244

Although he wasn't listening to the row they made he saw the display on the radio/cd player. The current track was called 'Sweet Revenge'.

He swore and slammed his hands together in a loud clap.

'We've missed a trick here, we need to know what Taylor did to Vyvyan Wilde.'

'What do you mean?' Peterson asked.

'So far he's had the other three do something that related to what they made him do. Beresford made him steal sweets from the shop his mother worked in, so he had to rob a shop. Bob James made him walk home in a pink skirt, so he had to wear women's clothing in public. Geoff Symonds made him pierce his own ears and had to cut off one of his own.'

'So if we find out what Taylor did to Wilde we'll have an idea what Wilde will want Taylor to do?'

'Exactly. And knowing that might lead us to him more quickly than running around chasing every clown on the streets.'

Davis picked up his phone and dialled Bellamy's mobile phone. 'Bellamy, the first thing I want you to ask Bob James is what Taylor did to Wilde. When you find out, call me.'

Bellamy acknowledged the instruction and Davis ended the call. Peterson was driving as fast as he could and they were just on the outskirts of March, where the Saturday traffic was making fast driving difficult. Peterson turned right at the roundabout and accelerated hard. He overtook two cars and reached sixty just as they entered the forty limit.

Davis reached over to the back floor where Peterson kept a magnetic blue light. 'I think we'd better have this on now we're getting into town.'

Peterson overtook a van as they passed a safety camera, causing the light to flash twice at him.

Davis braced himself as Peterson braked heavily as they approached a set of traffic lights on red with a small queue of cars waiting to go through. 'If this is just some nutter having a rant I'm going to run him in for something,' Davis said, 'just for the grief he's caused us.'

Peterson couldn't risk going through the lights in an unmarked car and had to wait a few seconds but as soon as the lights changed and traffic from the side junction stopped he sounded a warning on his horn and pulled out past the waiting cars.

As they sped the High Street Peterson had to weave in and out of the traffic. As they got onto Broad Street Davis shouted, 'There he is, let me out here and go round.'

The man was walking down the opposite side of Broad Street. The road was split down the middle by a row of parking bays. Davis leapt out of the car as Peterson came to a halt. As he slammed the door Peterson gunned the engine and carried on to drive round to the other side.

Davis ran through the parked cars and chased after the man with the board strapped to his front. He had to remember that if this was their man he hadn't committed a crime himself, he was a desperate man trying to save his daughter.

The man was less than fifty yards ahead now. He was walking surprisingly quickly and shouting loudly as he did so.

'Repent, repent. All sinners will go to the fires of hell. Those who repent will sit by the side of the Lord.'

Chapter Thirtyfive

Lisa Reardon was driving home. Her legs felt like jelly on the pedals and she was shaking so much she was surprised the car wasn't swerving all over the road. She had deliberately killed a man.

She had been worried sick all night. She had no doubt in her mind that the man holding her precious Laura would kill her if Lisa didn't do as he'd ordered. But she hadn't wanted to do it. That was probably too mild a way of stating it, she was totally opposed to taking a life. She was a nurse, a nurse in the high dependency ward. Her whole life was geared to preventing people from dying.

This time though she'd only had the prevention of one death on her mind; her daughter's.

She had wondered how she would kill her patient once she had decided that she would do it. Although, if it came to it, she would do it in a way that would mark her out as the guilty party, she wanted to watch her children grow up. If she could kill Fennell without being found out, she would.

The shift had almost been over before both the means and the opportunity had presented themselves to her. It was known before Fennell's surgery that he had a weak heart. She had thought that an induced, fatal heart attack would be the best way of despatching him.

When she was in the dispensary she had seen some vials of epinephrine. This was a substitute for adrenaline and was used to help patients with anaphylactic shock. If the patient received an overdose of it and already had a weak heart, death was almost certain.

There was little chance that it would be detected. Although there were tests that would show the presence of the drug it was unlikely an autopsy would reveal it had killed Fennell.

She had pocketed two of the vials without being seen. There were two nurses in the high dependency ward. Unusually Fennell was the only patient on the ward at the moment. That meant that both Lisa and her colleague took turns in watching him and in attending to other duties away from the ward.

On the last occasion her colleague was away, this time on a tea break, Lisa used an already used hypodermic syringe to inject the epinephrine into the intravenous line supplying Fennell's saline solution.

She had timed her move to perfection; she had disposed of the syringe and settled herself back behind her desk as her colleague returned to the ward.

As nurse Hodgin put a polystyrene cup of coffee on the desk for Lisa she asked, 'Any change?'

Lisa was nervous, no, terrified, but tried to keep her voice even. 'No, still out of it.'

Just as she said that Fennell started the spasms that the drug induced, indicating his heart was giving out.

Both nurses rushed to his side. Only one of them knew straight away that there was nothing they could do to save him.

Davis puffed as he caught up with the man, if only he'd stuck to his diet, he thought, the occasional chase like this wouldn't be so hard. Maybe those rolls this morning weren't a good idea, tasty as they were.

He put his hand on the man's shoulder to bring him to a halt. 'Hold on a minute, I'd like a word with you.' He held up his identity card, more to give him time to catch his breath than to prove who he was.

'Can I ask what you're doing?'

The man looked at him with wide-staring eyes. As he faced Davis a powerful waft of alcoholic breath came from him. He swayed a bit and tried to support himself on Davis.

'I'm saving the world, good sir. I'm... I'm a messenger... messenger of,' the man stopped and belched softly. Davis turned his head away, nauseated by the smell. 'I'm a messenger of the Lord.' The man raised his fist in the air. 'He will smite the unrighteous,' he shouted. 'They will burn in the fires of hell.'

Peterson had pulled up beside them and was standing by the car grinning broadly at Davis's plight. There was little chance that this was their man. His clothes spoke of many weeks of unwashed wearing and his drunkenness was clearly genuine. This wasn't a man pretending to be something he wasn't to save his child's life.

Davis looked at the wooden board that hung on the man's chest. 'The Lord loves those who repent,' was painted on one side in bright red gloss. On the other side it said 'Repent or die.' Despite Davis's assertion to Peterson that he would run the man in for something he couldn't for the life of him think of a suitable and fair charge. The man wasn't causing a nuisance or a breach of the peace, although either of those charges could have been used to get him off the street if Davis could be bothered enough.

Davis's eye was caught by a burger van further down the street. The man, who Davis guessed was in his sixties, was thin and his clothes hung on him suggesting he had lost a lot of weight. Gently taking hold of the man's elbow he said, 'Come with me.'

He led the man to the burger bar and took a ten-pound note from his wallet. Handing it to the man on the burger bar he said, 'Give him burger and chips and hot drinks to the value of that.' Mindful of the man's drink problem he said, 'Don't give him any change, I don't want him buying booze, he spends it all here.' Davis had held up his identity card as he spoke to show the burger seller he was a policeman.

'Will do,' the man replied, flipping a burger.

Maybe doing a good deed towards this self-appointed messenger for the Lord would bring its own reward for Davis, if there were a God.

Davis returned to the car to find a grinning Peterson waiting for him. 'Don't say a bloody word,' he warned Peterson.

'Okay, Mother Teresa,' Peterson replied.

Vyvyan glanced at the clock again. He had told Lisa that he would phone just after mid-day. It was now almost one o'clock. That ought to be enough extra time to have her and William sweating.

He switched Laura's phone on and called their home number. Lisa answered. Vyvyan wasted no time. 'Have you done it?'

He had already checked the national and local news on the television and radio but had seen no mention of Fennell's death. As a former MP he would have thought it would have merited at least a passing comment.

'Yes,' Lisa replied, her voice betraying the pressure she was under. 'Is Laura okay?'

Vyvyan ignored the question. 'Why have I not seen his death on the news?'

Lisa wanted to make him answer her question, she was desperate to know her daughter was safe. But she knew not to push him. 'They'll wait until the family's been told and let his office put a statement out. It will probably be released just in time for the six o'clock news.'

Vyvyan realized she was almost certainly right. He may as well move onto the next part of his plan, the final part. Well, almost the final part. After he had made William suffer for a while longer he would kill Laura and that unfortunate boyfriend of hers. The policeman's son would have to die as well.

'Has William gone in to work today?'

'No,' Lisa said, 'he doesn't work weekends. Please, is Laura okay? I did as you asked, you promised.'

Vyvyan ignored her desperate pleading. 'I want to talk to William.'

Vyvyan heard a few words whispered and then William came on the phone.

'William, I presume you want your daughter to live?'

'Of course I do, Vyvyan, please, Vyvyan... don't hurt her.'

'That's up to you, William'

'I'll do anything, you don't have to hurt her.'

'Then listen closely because Laura's life depends on you.'

Davis and Peterson were back at the police station. Peterson had told Lewin and Green about Davis's encounter with the drunk, to much laughter. Davis said to him, 'For that you can make the coffees.'

Peterson saluted, 'Yes, sir.'

'Did you get anywhere at Jackson's, Gillian?'

'No, sir. There was nothing there giving any clue as to who his friends were, or anything else personal come to that. He seems a very neat and tidy lad.'

Davis looked pensive for a minute, then said, 'There's been something nagging at me since we went to Devon and I've just realized what it is.' He turned to Green, who, along with Bellamy, had come back from the final checks on the rented properties empty handed and asked, 'Did we get the name of the person whose identity Vyvyan Wilde stole?'

Green thought for a moment and said, 'No, the manager didn't mention it.'

Davis picked the phone up and dialled a directory enquiries number. Having obtained the phone number for the Ilfracombe delivery office Davis asked to speak to the manager.

'I'm sorry, sir, he's finished for the day. Can I take a message?'

Davis explained who he was and said, 'I need to know the name of the customer who complained that his mail was going missing on a delivery covered by Vyvyan Wilde. I need that information as soon as possible though, it's urgent.'

The postman acknowledged Davis's request and took his number. 'I'll send somebody out to find the postman who's on that delivery; as soon as he finds out what you want he'll ring you.'

Davis thanked the man for his help and hoped he wouldn't have to wait too long.

William was aghast, 'You want me to do what?'

'I would have thought what I asked was clear enough.' Vyvyan said savagely. 'You must convince the police that you killed those girls.'

William was struggling to take all this in. He didn't really follow the news and hadn't heard about the previous deaths. To know that Vyvyan had killed them filled him with dread. Why should he believe that Vyvyan would release Laura? He asked Vyvyan this.

'What choice do you have?' Vyvyan responded with a sneer in his voice. 'I'll have achieved what I set out to do once you're charged with murder. There'll be no need to kill your daughter. I couldn't afford to have the other girls spoil my plans.'

William had grave doubts about the truthfulness of that, but there was nothing he could do but pray that Vyvyan wasn't lying.

Vyvyan wanted William to have some incriminating evidence; he also had to get rid of the Renault. He planned to burn the barn down with all three of his victims in it.

'I want you to collect a car soon. It will have in it various items that you will leave in the car. You'll drive straight to the police station and admit to being the killer of Alice Beresford, Abigail James, Tania Symonds and her father Geoff. Amongst the items in the car will be the knife that killed two of the girls.'

'Where do I collect it from?' William asked, resigned to his fate.

'I'll phone you and tell you later,' Vyvyan shouted, his patience rapidly running out as he felt that he was having to rush some of his plans.

He ended the call to William and went out to the barn. He carried a small plastic bag with him and put into it the duct tape he'd used to bind the girls, some of the old chloroform soaked pads and the knife that he'd used on the girls. He opened the big doors and reversed the Renault out of the barn. He put his bicycle in the back of the car and secured the barn.

Vyvyan wasn't sure where to leave the Renault, he wanted to make sure he wasn't caught on cctv, the police were probably monitoring them, looking for him. Eventually he settled for the playing field on the outskirts of Chatteris.

He locked the car carefully after getting his bicycle out. He had removed the car key from the bunch it had been held on and after making sure nobody was looking he slipped the key on the ground behind one of the front wheels. He was as certain as he could be that he'd left no traces of himself in the car. He'd used gloves when he drove it and always wore a wooly hat when driving the stolen cars so as not to leave hairs behind.

The ride home took him less than fifteen minutes and as soon as he got back in the barn he phoned William and told him where the car was.

William said, 'I want to know Laura is still alive before I do this.'

'I'm making the rules here, William, not you.'

William was defiant. 'Let me hear her voice, if you've already killed her you've got no hold over me.'

Vyvyan was annoyed that he had to give into William but it didn't matter. He held the phone behind his back and said to Laura, 'All you say is, "hello daddy," okay?'

She tried to nod to say she understood but the tape round her head stopped her.

Vyvyan said to William, 'You can say hello to Laura, if you try to say anything else she'll be hurt.' With that he held the phone to Laura's ear and said, 'Say hello to him.'

Vyvyan hadn't given his captives anything to eat or drink since he'd snatched them. Laura's throat was dry and she was scared, her voice came out as barely a croak.

Her father knew it was her though. 'I love you, Laura.'

Vyvyan took the phone away from her quickly and said, 'Now you know your precious daughter is alive get on with what you've been told to do. I'll release Laura when I hear on the news that you've been charged with the death of the girls.' Vyvyan ended the call and switched the phone off.

He went back into the house to make sure it was ready for him to leave. He had originally intended just to burn down the barn and claim it was a little accident. That was before he knew he was going to leave three bodies in it. Now it was best to burn everything. He collected together all the items he'd need to take with him. That didn't amount to much, the paperwork in Andrew's name and some of his own personal things. He had a small suitcase of clothes and other essentials. The little Peugeot had a full tank of petrol and that would take him well over the border into Scotland before he had to refill.

Chapter Thirtysix

Two of the phones in the CID office started ringing within seconds of each other. Davis picked up one of them, it was the postman from Devon.

Peterson got the other one. The duty officer said, 'I think you'd better come down here, sarge, we have someone I think you should see.'

Peterson was used to the evasive nature of Sergeant Bull's calls, he always tried to make sure he didn't say anything too specific. That way, if a senior officer thought his time had been wasted, Bull could say his call had been misunderstood.

Peterson knew better than to press his colleague for any more information; it was quicker to go downstairs.

Davis wrote down the name the postman gave him and was just about to follow Peterson downstairs when he remembered he'd heard that name in the last few days.

'Gillian, the name of the man renting that cottage on the Somersham road, what was it?'

She thought for a few seconds and said, 'Graham wrote it in on the list when we got back to the office.'

She picked the list off the desk and before she could read the name Davis said, 'It's Innes, isn't it?'

She looked up at him surprised, 'Yes, why?'

'It's our bloody man, it's Vyvyan Wilde.'

He jumped up from his seat. 'Follow me,' he shouted urgently to Lewin and Green.

A surge of excitement ran through Davis, maybe they would be in time to rescue Adam, he had to believe they would be. The alternative was too dreadful to contemplate.

Davis ran down the stairs followed by the other two. They caught Peterson as he entered the reception area.

'Graham, we've got him.'

'Peterson looked grim, 'I know, that's him,' he said pointing to a man sitting in a seat with Sergeant Bull standing guard over him.

Davis looked at the man. 'That's not Wilde.'

Peterson was quick on the uptake. He turned to the man. 'Are you William Robert Taylor?'

The man looked flustered, 'No, I'm...'

Davis knew there was little time to loose. 'We're searching for

Vyvyan Wilde in relation to several murders; does he have your child?'

William broke down in tears.

Davis said to Peterson, 'I know where he is, let's go.' He shouted to Bull, 'That man isn't our murderer but don't let him go.' The last thing they needed was for him to warn Vyvyan in an attempt to save his child's life and giving Vyvyan the chance to kill his captives and escape.

Gary Jackson had been working on his bonds as much as possible. When the man had gone out in the Renault he had worked at the rope, stretching it by twisting his arms as far as he could and then trying to pull them apart. At last he had been able to slip one bloodied wrist out of the ropes.

The first thing he did was to pull the gag from his mouth and call out to the other boy tied up round the corner. 'I've got my hands free. If I can get out of these ropes will you help us?'

The boy was gagged as well, that was clear. But Gary could understand the muffled words enough to know he had an ally.

With his arms free he bent down to try to untie the rope around his legs.

The sudden movement in his arms brought him a shock of pins and needles. As he was rubbing his arms to try to get some feeling into them he heard a noise outside, it was the man coming back! He quickly put his arms behind him again and loosely held the rope to make it look like he was still bound.

The man came back in and Gary heard him call Laura's dad. He knew from what the man was saying that whatever this bizarre situation he was in was all about, it was coming to an end. He also knew that there was very little chance the man was going to let them live. He had killed the other girls and had made no attempt to cover his face at all.

Gary was desperately trying to think of a way of stopping the man. Just another couple of minutes would have been enough to untie his legs and then he might have been able to help Laura.

He was surprised when after the call the man had left the barn. He quickly bent down and it was the work of a few moments to free his legs. He moved unsteadily over to Laura.

He leant in towards her and said, 'Laura, I'm going to get you out of here. You must be quiet.'

The man had taken the knife away but he'd noticed a piece of broken glass on the floor in the corner and picked it up. In less than a minute Laura was released from the bench. Gary helped her stand on the ground. The man had burnt her clothes so Gary took off the jumper he was wearing and slipped it over her head, she carefully fed her damaged hands through the sleeves.

'We might need to run away. You'd better move about a bit to get your muscles working.'

Laura was still numb with fear and just nodded in response, but Gary was pleased to see she started to walk up and down the barn moving her arms from side to side.

He quickly freed the other boy and said, 'We need to find a way out or a weapon.'

The boy nodded and after rubbing his arms and legs for a few seconds went to the door and tested it. It was locked, he tried the bigger doors the car had gone through, they were locked as well. Gary spotted an old spade standing against the wall, it was just about the only thing he could see that he might use as a weapon. The locks were on the outside so there was no chance of using it to break out.

He called quietly to the boy, 'What's your name?'

'Adam, Adam Davis.'

'I'm Gary, that's Laura. We're going to have to attack this man.'

'Vyvyan Wilde, that's his name. My dad's a policeman, he's been trying to catch him.'

'I know,' Gary said. 'I've heard him on the phone.'

Gary decided the best thing to do was to hide Laura and then he and Adam would lay in wait for the man to come back. He pulled up the cover that was on the small car and tried the door, it was open. He called softly to Laura, 'Get in here, keep down and wait till I call you, then we run.'

'Can't you drive this car out of here?' she asked him in a shaky voice.

Gary hadn't started taking driving lessons yet but that wouldn't have stopped him taking the car to escape if he could, the boss had let him drive a car around the yard a few times, so he knew he could do it.

'There are no keys in it, I checked.'

Davis was driving with the other three members of the team in the car. He had called for uniformed back-up to follow them to Middlefield Cottage.

'He gave me his name and showed me a couple of bits of identification,' Peterson said. 'The cottage overlooks the road where he set fire to the cars with the Symonds in.' He was livid with himself. Although Wilde had provided proof of his assumed identity, Peterson knew Adam Davis and probably the other two wouldn't be in trouble if he'd seen through Wilde's trickery.

'It explains why we couldn't find him after he torched the other cars, he was only minutes away from home,' Davis said. He looked briefly at Peterson sitting beside him and guessed at what he was thinking.

'Graham, I'd have accepted his id as well, we all would.'

Peterson was grateful for the reassurance, but would Davis feel the same if they were too late?

Middlefield Cottage was less than a mile away now. Davis had the blue light on the car and was driving as fast as he could. Previously Wilde had killed his victims whilst their fathers were carrying out the task he had given them. He knew they had no time to spare. As they rounded the bend at the top of Ferry Hill they could see Middlefield Cottage in the distance.

Vyvyan had poured petrol on the bed and down the stairs, he poured some in the front room and dropped the can. He'd had enough experience of burning things now that he knew not to pour any in the kitchen. It was from there he intended to make his escape. He put the suitcase by the back door. He checked that he had got none of the petrol on himself and washed his hands, he didn't want to smell of petrol.

He struck a match in the safety of the kitchen and lit the roll of twisted newspaper. He opened the serving hatch and threw the burning paper through the gap, there was an immediate explosion and he felt the hot air rush through the opening.

He didn't wait any longer; he picked up the suitcase and fled out the door.

'It's on fire,' Davis shouted, seeing the orange glow through the windows. He accelerated even harder as he came out of the bend. The car rocked as it sped over the bumpy roads with the suspension bottoming as they hit a particularly deep bump.

Just then Peterson pointed, 'Look, there's someone coming out.'

All three captives in the barn heard a loud bang and saw a fierce orange glow through the small windows, the cottage was on fire. Gary knew that the man would be coming quickly. Setting fire to the house was obviously part of a plan to cover his tracks. He positioned himself to one side of one of the large doors. It was the door the man had used when he'd taken the Renault out. He held the spade ready to strike the man as he came through the door.

Adam stood the other side with a length of the rope ready to tie the man's hands together.

Davis braked hard as they approached the drive Middlefield Cottage was on. This was more of a dirt track than a proper road and the car skidded sideways as he turned onto it. He let the throttle up for a second and the wheels found some grip, he floored the throttle again, desperate to get to his son. He could see Wilde unlocking the barn that stood beside the cottage. He had to get there before Vyvyan got inside the barn, he couldn't let him get near his son.

Vyvyan didn't hear the sound of the approaching car as he undid the lock on the barn, the roar of the flames was too loud. He pulled open the door and rushed into the barn. He needed to get the Peugeot out in to the open and then set fire to the barn; he had another can of petrol ready for that. As he put his suitcase on the floor behind the car he glanced over to the bench.

His heart lurched as he saw the bench was empty, Laura had gone!

Gary had heard Wilde unlock the barn door. He lifted the spade high in the air. He could barely breathe as the seconds it took for the door to open stretched out. His mouth was dry and he was sure Wilde would hear the pounding of his heart. Wilde stepped into the barn and looked over to the now empty bench. For a second Gary couldn't make his arms move then, as Wilde noticed him, Gary brought the spade down on Wilde's head with all the force he could muster. The spade's edge hit Wilde right on the top of his head and split it open. There was no need for Adam to tie his hands. Vyvyan Wilde was no threat to any of them now.

Davis braked to a halt and threw the car door open. Despite his bulk he leapt out of the car before the others could. He ran to the open barn door, not knowing whether he was in time to save his son.

Just as Peterson came running in followed by the other two Davis saw Vyvyan Wilde lying on the floor, his head a bloody mess. To his amazement Adam was standing to one side with a rope in his hands. Davis rushed to him and held him tight. He had never felt such a surge of relief in his life.

Davis looked down at Wilde. There was no doubt he was dead. Davis was struck by the irony of the situation. Wilde had waged this campaign because of what had happened to him as a child. He had targeted children. And, finally, he had been killed by one of those children.

Davis pulled his phone from his pocket and dialled his home number to tell Anita her son was safe.

Unbroken
The first novel by Michael Gasson.

Dan Edwards wins the lottery. It's not the jackpot everyone dreams of and he decides to set up his own business. Rivals harass him, attack him and kill his fiancée.

Vowing to bring the killer to justice he fights back.
He discovers someone, a colleague, a friend, is betraying him. Can he find the traitor before time runs out and he's killed?
Slowly he becomes attracted to the beautiful policewoman investigating the attacks, plunging him into emotional turmoil.
With his own life and that of his son in danger he must confront his rivals head on if he is to remain unbroken.

To read Unbroken order your copy via:
www.chestnutpublishing.co.uk